The Demon's Wife

A Novel of the Supernatural and Attempted Redemption

By
Rick Hautala

JournalStone
San Francisco

JOURNALSTONE
YOUR LINK TO ARTISTIC TALENT

JournalStone books may be ordered through booksellers or by contacting:

JournalStone
www.journalstone.com
www.journal-store.com

ISBN: 978-1-936564-95-8   (sc)
ISBN: 978-1-936564-98-9   (ebook)
JournalStone rev. date: September 13, 2013

ISBN: 978-1-936564-97-2   (hc)
JournalStone rev. date: August 16, 2013

Library of Congress Control Number: 2013941615

Printed in the United States of America

Cover Design: Denise Daniel
Cover Art: M. Wayne Miller

Edited by: Norman Rubenstein

Dedication

This book has got to be dedicated to Holly, who edited this

book—and lives with me—with love, patience, and

understanding.

I don't know how you do it.

Also, a special shout out to Hank Schwaeble who helped me out

of a legal jam …

Thank God it was a fictional one.

Endorsements

"The Demon's Wife asks the question *What do you expect when you marry a demon*? Rick Hautala answers that question with harrowing suspense, dark mystery, and masterful plotting. Not many women can say they're in love--or lust--with a man who has a tail, but Claire McMullen can. This DEMON has style, sensuality and soul." — **Robert McCammon**

"*The Demon's Wife* is wonderfully entertaining and entirely compelling, a horrifying and heartfelt urban fantasy sure to appeal to fans of Charlaine Harris and Kelley Armstrong. Cloaked inside this dark, frightening tale is horror legend Rick Hautala's surprising treatise on the purifying, redemptive power of love." — **Christopher Golden**, New York Times best-selling co-author of *Joe Golem and the Drowning City* and *Father Gaetano's Puppet Catechism*

"Rich in detail, and with a unique and devilishly good premise, Rick Hautala's *The Demon's Wife* is a completely compelling journey into a most-unusual marriage of the supernatural and earthly. A master of horror, Hautala conjures up twists and turns that will keep readers guessing what will happen next to the demon's wife, Claire, and her very different husband, as the pages go flying by." — **Matthew Costello**, Author of *Vacation* and *Home*

"*The Demon's Wife* is a sly examination of the strangest marriage you will ever see. It's a fast-paced, mordant examination of contemporary relationships, full of clever twists and irreverent reversals that turn the ideas of love and standard theology inside-out. Echoes of Wodehouse and Sheckley resonate through the pages. A fitting capstone to a magical career." — **Thomas F. Monteleone,** 4-time Bram Stoker Award winner

Chapter

1

————Enter Samael

Now, Claire McMullen says she might never have married Samael if she had known that he was a demon. Then again, his demonic nature might be what attracted her to him in the first place. He certainly had "devilishly" good looks—impeccably dressed with long, dark hair, even darker eyes, a terrific build, and a smile that captivated both women and men, in various ways. She didn't find out about the tail until later.

Of course, it's easy for her to say that now but at the beginning, back when neither she nor anyone else knew how things would eventually turn out, it was quite another story.

Picture this, because it's all too easy:

Claire was in her early thirties. She was tall and lanky—not skinny—with pale, freckled skin and round blue eyes. The only thing she liked about herself was her hair—a long, thick mass of curly tangles so bright red people often thought it wasn't her natural color. Her hair was the first thing about her that Samael noticed.

She also had a job she hated, a roommate she...tolerated. She also had a mountain of debt—mostly from college loans—that she had concluded was never going to be paid off. She also had, of course, the usual expenses for room and board, electricity, heat, cell phone, Internet, and weekend nights bar-hopping around Portland, always on the prowl for Mr. Right...or at least Mr. Right Now.

Let's consider her job for a moment.

For the past seven years, she had worked as a purchasing agent for Montressor, a chemical company in South Portland, Maine. What this had to do with her degree in Communications from Ithaca College, in upstate New York, she had no idea. Then again, most of the friends she was still in touch with from college had jobs that had absolutely nothing to do with their majors. The best writer in her class—Ally Dixon—was working as a nanny for a doctor in Austin, Texas. At least Claire hadn't studied the bottom of beer and booze bottles, like many of her college friends. With the background she'd had growing up in Aroostook County, Maine, and wanting so desperately to escape, she studied harder than most students. To offset the need for student loans, she had worked part-time in a donut shop—Tony's Donuts—in downtown Ithaca for three years, summers included. To this day, the smell of fresh-baked donuts never failed to nauseate her.

So five days a week, from seven o'clock in the morning until four o'clock in the afternoon, she sat in an office not much bigger than a broom closet. There were no windows, and her only lifelines to the "real world" were cruising Facebook and listening to WXPN, a radio station from Philly that she streamed over the computer, no matter how many times Marty, her boss, told her not to because she was taking up too much of the company's bandwidth.

After another seemingly endless day in a seemingly endless parade of days in what amounted to little more than an experiment in sensory deprivation, she would come home to the small apartment on Congress Street that she shared with Sally Lewis.

Sally was, as they say, "a piece of work." She had grown up in a rich family in Cape Elizabeth, and never seemed to lack money even though her current job as a bookstore manager didn't pay all that well, considering how hard she worked.

Claire hadn't always felt this distance with Sally. In fact, they had been close friends for several years, back when Claire had first moved to Portland to be closer to Billy Carroll, her boyfriend at the time. That hadn't turned out as well as she had hoped. Most relationships don't, right? But once she was back in Maine— something she had vowed to avoid—a kind of inertia set in, and she…well, she simply stayed here now that she was familiar with the city. At least she hadn't moved back home to the "County."

Claire met Sally when she had worked part-time over Christmas at the local Borders bookstore. Sally was a manager there, although year after year, her job looked increasingly shaky, what with the economy and people not buying books like they used to. She kept threatening to pack up and move—maybe to Florida or some Caribbean island. More and more, Claire wished Sally would do exactly that, even though she had no idea how she'd make the rent without a roommate. She didn't have many friends locally, and she didn't like the idea of searching for a new roomie on Craigslist or whatever—

And she hadn't forgotten about the "Craigslist Killer either."

In spite of her bluster and job insecurity, Sally stayed where she was—in the apartment and at Borders—and Claire stayed where she was.

On weekends, like I said, they went out. Sometimes they went with friends of Sally's from the bookstore. Sometimes it was just the two of them. On the night she met Samael, it was just the two of them.

It was Sally, in fact, who first noticed him that night at Margarita's Grille. They had tickets to see "The Economy," a local band that had made it nationally and was playing a "coming home" gig at the Civic Center. Before the show, they decided to grab a quick bite to eat and have something to drink.

That's when they wandered into the bar.

At the time they met him, neither one of them knew that he spelled his name "Samael." That might have given her a hint of his demonic nature, too, but how could she have known? They could have Googled the name, perhaps, but no one expects to meet an actual demon, face to face…not in a city like Portland, Maine. New York City? Sure. No problem. Both of them assumed he spelled his name the usual way: "Samuel," even though he pronounced it without the "U."

Sam-a-el.

On the night they met, Sally tried calling him "Sam" a few times. It irked Claire, but as the drinks flowed, Sally even tried "Sammy" once or twice. To Claire, it didn't "sound" at all right. He was definitely not a Sam much less a Sammy. He appeared not to appreciate being called that, either. After Sally used the nickname a few more times, Samael politely—but firmly—corrected her—once—and asked that she please use his full name, "Samael," and to pronounce it correctly. He even wrote it down on a bar napkin…along with his telephone number, which he slid over to Claire.

Claire experienced a thrill when he scooted his chair closer to her.

"So what do you do?" he asked. His dark eyes were focused on her…a little too intently, maybe?

"Not much."

"I manage the Borders," Sally chimed in. "Believe me. I could tell you stories."

"Go on, Claire," Samael said, still staring at her like she was the only woman in the bar.

Claire sighed. "I work as a purchasing agent for a local chemical company. I order the stuff they put into your drinking water and the salt they spread on the roads in winter. It's a soul-sucking job."

Samael chuckled, and Claire was concerned she had said something wrong.

"Interesting choice of words," he said as if to allay her embarrassment. "'Soul-sucking.' Nice turn of phrase. I like it."

"Talk about 'soul-sucking, '" Sally went on, all but wedging herself between Claire and Samael. "I should tell you about this one guy last week." As she launched into a detailed rendition of one of the barely literate idiots who worked for her, much less patronized the store, Claire noticed that Samael barely listened to her. His dark eyes—which, in this lighting, now appeared to be flecked with gold—never left hers. She should have felt uncomfortable, but she didn't.

While they were both trying their best to ignore Sally, Claire felt a subtle tug on her hair and glanced over at her shoulder to see that Samael had curled a lock of her red hair around his forefinger and was twirling it like spaghetti on a fork. She shot him a 'What the fuck?' look, but he simply smiled at her.

And the truth was, she didn't mind in the least.

Claire wasn't the kind of girl who took a man home on the first date, no matter what...and this wasn't even a date. She and Sally had first noticed Samael sitting in the bar with either a friend or business colleague, and they had made a point of sitting where he couldn't help but notice them.

And it worked.

His business partner or friend left, and Samael came over to their table and introduced himself. He took a seat at their table as if he owned the place, and his lines were the smoothest Claire had ever heard...and she had heard plenty. It was obvious from the get-go that he had money and wasn't simply pretending to have it. Having grown up poorer than poor, Claire could always tell the real money from the fake.

Claire caught the signals from Sally that she wanted to sink her hooks into this guy. She was the kind of girl who would take a man home on the first night, date or no date. But Samael made it clear that he was much more interested in Claire. After he excused himself and left, saying he had to go home but hoped to see them again—both women watching him go and admiring his broad shoulders and slim hips, Sally turned to Claire.

"I dunno...I mean, he looks good...tasty, but...I'd say he's kind of a dickhead."

Claire was still staring at the door he had used to exit the bar. She had the weirdest sensation that he hadn't walked out into the night, but that he had vanished...like a magician in a puff of smoke. His face—that smile...*and those eyes!*—were seared into her memory. She barely paid attention to what her friend was saying.

"Claire? ... Are you listening to me?"

Claire shook her head, feeling like she was just waking up, and everything was hazy. She looked at Sally.

"Huh?"

"I said..." Sally leaned close and looked around as if suspicious that Samael was lingering nearby and would overhear her. "I think he's kind of a dickhead."

"I don't think so," Claire said. She took a slow sip of her mojito and looked longingly at the door as if expecting—wishing he would reappear in the doorway, walk over to her table, and sweep her off into the night. The napkin with his name and phone number on it was a wrinkled wad in her sweaty palm.

"I don't know," was all she said as she looked down and flattened out the napkin, relieved to see that the name and number were still legible. She suspected Sally was reading a lot more into what she said and did, but she didn't care.

"I mean," Sally went on, "come on. The clothes, the haircut, the tan...in the middle of March? In Maine?" She snorted. "All too perfect. Who's he think he's kidding?"

Claire felt an urge to rise to Samael's defense, but she let Sally's snarky comments lie where they fell.

Go ahead and talk yourself right out of any interest in him. That leaves the field wide-open for me.

Sally took out her cell phone and glanced at the time.

"Think we should get going?"

Claire considered, took another sip of her drink, emptying her glass, and then nodded. She could sit here all night, and that wasn't going to bring Samael back into the bar...Not tonight. But she had his phone number, and she damned well intended to call him. Not tonight. Maybe not even tomorrow. There was no point in looking desperate. That'd scare him away. Definitely, she'd call him soon. She was smiling as she slipped the napkin into her coat pocket. Then she slung her purse over her shoulder.

Both women kicked back their chairs and stood up. Claire started walking toward the door, thinking how foolish it was to get excited, thinking that she'd soon be touching the same door latch Samael had just touched. No one else had left the bar since he had left, so she'd have direct contact with something he had touched.

What are you, crazy, thinking like this?

"I gotta use the little girls' room," Sally said.

"I'll meet you outside," Claire said, not wanting anyone else to touch the door before she did. She looked straight ahead as she walked to the door and, feeling a curious tingling thrill inside, put her hand on the latch and pressed it down. The lock clicked, the door opened, and a cool, damp breeze blew into her face, raising goosebumps on her arms as she stepped outside.

The parking lot was empty except for three cars. Not a rocking night tonight. The surrounding streetlights cast a cold, eerie blue glow onto the pavement and the remnants of the last snowfall. *Hopefully, that had been the last storm of the winter,* Claire thought, *but knowing Maine, there could be a blizzard in May.* At the far end of the parking lot, she noticed a black Mercedes, and the foolish hope— conviction?—that this was Samael's car and that he was waiting for her to come outside filled her. It certainly looked as though someone was sitting in the driver's seat, but at this distance and in the darkness, it was impossible to be sure.

Claire felt suddenly isolated and vulnerable as she looked around, certain, now, that if not Samael, then someone was watching her from the shadows. The street was unusually quiet, but on a cold night like this, what would you expect? The distant sound of traffic passing by on I-295 sounded like tearing paper. Claire sidled over to the side of the restaurant and looked around, avoiding the bright lights because it made her feel like she stood out all the more. If she smoked, this is when she would have lit up. A peculiar emptiness…a sense of disappointment or of something irretrievably lost filled her, making her feel hollow inside.

She glanced at the door, then at her wristwatch, then at the door again, expecting Sally to come out of the restaurant any second now, but there was no sign of her.

What's taking her so damned long?

Claire had the disquieting feeling that, for whatever reason, Sally had ditched her. She started walking, pacing back and forth under the awning as icy tension wound up inside her. She thought maybe she should go back inside and use the restroom, too.

No…I can wait.

Instead of going back inside, she increased her pacing, fighting the feeling that somewhere…out there…in the darkness…someone was watching every step she took. The rhythm to the oldies song by The Police began to play in her head.

"Every move you make…"

"Stop it," she whispered to herself, her breath coming out a mist.

But no matter where she looked or what she thought about, the unsettling feelings only got worse.

Finally, the restaurant door opened. Claire jumped and turned to look, expecting to see Sally, but she stepped to one side, disappointed, when a couple exited instead. Her back was to the wall, but she didn't realize she was standing at the corner of the building, almost in the darkness—when a rough hand clapped over her mouth, and a strong arm wrapped around her stomach, tightening so hard it forced the wind from her lungs.

"Make a sound, and you're dead," a man's voice whispered.

~ * ~

One of her shoes flipped off her foot as the man dragged her backwards, into the darkness beside the building. She had a brief sensation of vertigo, like she was falling backwards, spinning down into darkness. The most vivid detail she remembered later was the stench of the man's breath, which smelled like rotten onions and was as hot as a furnace on the side of her face. Because his hand was covering her mouth, any sounds she was making were smothered. Snot blew from her nose. Later, she thought she remembered hearing the sharp, pained whimpering of a dog that might have been hit by a car or something. She never could believe that such a sound had come from her.

She clawed at his hand, trying to pull it off so she could scream. She kicked his shins as hard as she could but couldn't get enough oomph behind it. She wiggled and thrashed from side to side, but he seemed to be supernaturally strong. It was like struggling to lift a gigantic rock.

Claire wasn't a weakling. She worked out...irregularly, but she had never felt so overwhelmed and helpless in her life. Fury and fear rose up inside her as she squirmed and fought and gasped for air...all to no avail.

The man's other hand was all over her. Touching, rubbing, squeezing painfully. By the time he took his meaty paw off her mouth, she was too exhausted to cry out. He zipped the front of her coat down and reached inside, squeezing her breasts again, so hard the pain brought tears to her eyes. He grabbed the front of her blouse and ripped it down with a quick, savage movement. Buttons flew in all directions. She heard them clatter on the pavement like tumbling dice.

This is it...He's gonna kill me, was her only clear thought as tears of frustration burned her eyes.

But then something extraordinary happened.

Her assailant went suddenly limp. The bear hug he had on her relaxed, and he slumped forward. His chin dug painfully into her neck, and the stench of his breath was suddenly whisked away by cold, fresh air. Claire lurched to one side, shaking herself free of the man's arms. Even in the darkness, she could see that his eyes were rolled back in his head. They glistened like soft-boiled eggs, bulging from their sockets. His mouth dropped to one side, and he looked for all the world like he was having a stroke.

"Where am...What?...I didn't..."

He stared at his hands as though amazed that they were part of him.

"I...I never..."

Then he sank slowly to his knees like a collapsing accordion. When his knees hit the pavement, he rolled his head to the side and stared up at Claire.

"I'm...so...sorry," was all he said before pitching forward. "I...didn't do it... It wasn't me..."

His face and chest hit the pavement at the same instant, making a loud thwacking sound that, Claire later found out when she testified against him in court, broke two of his front teeth.

While Claire was still trying to process what was happening, another figure—in the darkness, she had no idea who—rushed around the side of the building and grabbed her by both arms.

"Are you all right? Did he hurt you?"

Claire shook her head, still having trouble focusing, but how could she forget that voice?

"Samael?" she said. "Where did you—"

And that was all.

She collapsed into his arms, and he held her, trembling as adrenalin washed through her system. He made soft cooing noises into her ear as he stroked her back and shoulders. She buried her face into the crook of his neck, only distantly aware of the faint smoky smell that clung to him.

He must be a smoker, she remembered thinking crazily, and she imagined he was a fire blazing in a fireplace—warm...comforting...

After a while—she had no idea how long—she got a grip and began to calm down...enough, at least, so she could pull back and look up at him. Even in the dimly lit alley beside the restaurant, she was entranced by the sculpted perfection of his face.

And his eyes!

Good Lord, they glowed in the darkness with a golden light that she found more intoxicating than the three mojitos she'd consumed. His arms tightened around her, and he smiled.

"Oh my God!…Oh my God!"

Sally's voice pierced the night at the same time as a police siren started wailing in the distance.

"What happened?…Are you all right?"

As painful as it was to break off the embrace, she turned to see her roommate running toward her with something other than her purse in her hand. Only much later did she realize it was the shoe that had flipped off her foot when the man first grabbed her. She had cut her left foot on something—probably broken glass—behind the restaurant.

Speaking of the man who had assailed her, he was still down for the count, lying with his head cocked to one side and looking like he was deep asleep. A pool of dark liquid spread from his nose onto the pavement, looking like spilled India ink.

Samael still had his hand on Claire's shoulder as she turned to Sally and nodded. The most she could do was grunt and nod. When Sally moved closer, though, something peculiar happened. Claire felt a sudden surge of protectiveness, as if she had to keep her away from Samael.

"Did he…? Oh, my God, Claire!"

Sally appeared to be more upset than Claire, but then again, that was Sally's MO, and Claire was no doubt still in shock. The full impact of what had just happened—and what could have happened—wouldn't hit her until much later that night, when she was trying to fall asleep.

"I—I'm fine…" Claire said, panting and shaking her head up and down. "I just… He…He came out of nowhere, and—No, Samael didn't try to hurt me."

She was amazed to hear how distant and fragile her voice sounded. It was like listening to someone else talking. Even the sound of her breathing and the rapid expansion and contraction of her chest seemed oddly foreign. No doubt, she was just beginning to realize how close she had come to experiencing some genuine horrors she didn't even want to try to comprehend.

As she was speaking, and as Sally fussed about what had just happened, Claire clutched her blouse, pulling it closed to cover herself. The night air was cold on her face, and her teeth chattered as she shivered. The skin on her shoulders and back burned from her assailant trying to yank off her bra. Her stomach dropped when the police cruiser pulled into the parking lot, its siren wailing and its emergency lights flashing bright blue.

The man on the ground made a watery moaning sound and then stirred, sliding his hands under himself as if preparing to get up. Samael casually placed the toe of his shoe on the man's back and pressed him down hard enough so the man's face slammed against the pavement with a thud that sounded like a watermelon hitting the ground.

"You're not going anywhere—except to jail," Samael said. His voice was low and casual. Claire couldn't help but be impressed by his command of the situation. Even after the patrolmen got out of the cruiser and hurried over, Samael seemed to be the one in control. Claire watched in stunned silence, all too aware of Samael's arm resting lightly around her waist as the cops cuffed the assailant and loaded him into the back of the cruiser.

One thing that struck Claire as odd was her assailant's total compliance. Once he was on his feet, he gawked around as if looking for a clue as to what the hubbub was all about. What was happening? His nose was spewing blood, and his broken teeth and lips were covered with blood, but he made no move to wipe it away. He looked completely dazed, and who would blame him, after getting his face smacked so hard against the pavement?

Claire was left wondering why the man had let her go so suddenly.

Had he had a sudden jolt of guilt or remorse about what he was doing?

Is that why he'd said, "It wasn't me?"

Or had Samael come around the corner at that point, and the man, realizing he'd been caught in the act, had given up?

But why hadn't he tried to get away?

And how had Samael known what was going on behind the restaurant?

How had he appeared so fast? Hadn't he already left to go home…unless he had been waiting out in the parking lot for her to leave?

The exact sequence of events was a blur, and her stomach sank when one of the patrolmen—his badge read "Officer Tompkins"—came up to her and asked, "You all right?"

He shined a flashlight into her face. It was so bright Claire had to squint and shield her eyes. She nodded and made a funny little gasping sound, but anything she might have wanted to say was stuck somewhere deep down in her throat.

Samael was still standing beside her, holding her close to him. His body heat was amazing. When he shifted from one foot to the other as if to break contact with her, she was suddenly fearful that she would fall down without his support. Her left foot had a hot, dull pain. Glancing at Samael, Claire once again was struck by the intense brightness of his eyes in the darkened alleyway. She felt a wave of shame when she wondered what his eyes would look like in her bedroom…with a single candle burning…after they had made love.

Stop it!…Jesus, don't think such crazy thoughts…Keep focused here.

But there was no way she could sort it out and make sense of what had just happened. Her last clear memory was of Sally, telling her she had to use the restroom and then waiting in the parking lot, feeling creeped out. After that, everything got jumbled up. It was like she was drunk and spinning around wildly on a merry-go-round. Fragments and images flashed across her mind with the speed of lightning that blended together and dissolved before she could register any of them.

Then…Samael.

"An ambulance is on the way," Officer Tompkins said, angling his light away from her eyes. Claire let out a moan and started shaking her head.

"No, I—I'm all right…I don't need to go to—"

She didn't finish her sentence because, when she took a step back, she finally felt the full pain of the gash on her left foot. She would have fallen down if Samael hadn't been there to hold her up.

"And you're the boyfriend?" Officer Tompkins asked as he directed his beam of light into Samael's face.

Samael didn't even blink as he shot a quick glance at Claire that made her wish he would say yes. But he turned back to the cop and said, "No, I was just leaving—going to my car after having a few drinks with a friend, when I saw what was happening."

Claire felt deflated.

The cop looked over his shoulder toward the parking lot. She didn't need to look to see what he was checking out. It was an obvious question: *How could Samael have seen what was going on when there was no direct view from the parking lot to here?*

Before the cop could frame the question, though, Samael volunteered an answer.

"The guy grabbed her out in front of the restaurant and dragged her back here." He made a gesture toward the ground. "You can see where her feet—one shoe was already off—scuffed the ground."

The cop shined his flashlight beam down onto the pavement. Even Claire could see the trail her feet had made through the debris on the ground. At a certain point, blood from her cut foot stained the ground. She winced as the cut began to throb.

"Is that what happened?" the cop asked Claire.

She gritted her teeth and shook her head.

"Yes. I think so. I don't know for sure...It all happened so...fast."

The wailing sound of the ambulance's siren drew closer, and then its flashing red emergency lights split the night.

"Let's get you to the hospital and have you checked out first," Officer Tompkins said. "Then you can make a statement."

She caught the shifty glance he shot at Samael as if to say: *I know you were involved in this, too...Maybe I should haul your ass in.* For whatever reason, the cop certainly looked as though he'd taken an instant dislike to Samael.

"I'll go with you," Samael said just as Claire started to turn to him to ask if he'd come along. She couldn't miss the look Sally gave at Samael as she stepped forward and said rather loudly, "No, I'll go with her. She's my roomie."

"You don't have to come, Sal," she said. "I'm fine, and besides..."

She twitched her head toward Samael to indicate that she'd much prefer having him come with her, but Sally's expression hardened, and she shook her head decisively.

"I'm coming, and that's final," Sally said, sounding a lot like Claire's mother.

"But you'll miss the concert. You've been waiting—"

"Fuck the concert!"

Claire noticed that Samael had the good sense to step back and stay out of this. That made her feel all the more confident in her opinion.

"Seriously. I'll be fine," she said, all but glaring at Sally wishing she'd back off. "Give Alice a call. She can use my ticket. I know she wanted to go, too."

Sally started to protest again, but Claire cut her off with a sharp glance.

By now, the ambulance had come to a wailing stop in the restaurant parking lot. The entrance to the restaurant and the sidewalk were filled with rubberneckers. Claire felt like a bug under a magnifying glass as she limped over to the back of the ambulance. The EMTs were getting out a stretcher, but she waved them off, saying, "I'm all right...I'm all right."

Before she climbed into the back of the ambulance, she glanced at Samael, who was standing at the edge of the crowd, looking like he was trying to fade away. The eye contact between them was intense, but it was impossible to read his thoughts. He looked intrigued, angry, detached, and passionately in love, all at the same time. Claire's heart was racing as she stared back at him, wondering if he was going to turn and walk away now that she had all the assistance she could need.

But that's not what he did, and that may have been the first step along the path to his own destruction. Because, instead of walking away and figuring out another way to get to Claire and possess her soul—if she was the person he was determined to corrupt—he shouted to her loud enough to be heard above the noise of the crowd: "I'll follow in my car."

Through her pain and turmoil, Claire was nearly bursting with happiness when she called back to him: "See you there."

Chapter

2

————Double Ditch

The rest of the night—the ambulance ride to the hospital, the waiting in the ER, the statement to the police, the hospital checkout at three A.M., including a brief talk with a rape crisis counselor—all went by in a blur. The only stable thing, it seemed, was Samael's smiling face, glimpsed several times in passing as she was wheeled from one examination room to another, to be prodded and poked and have blood samples drawn and blood pressure and temperature taken and have the cut on her foot swabbed with disinfectant, stitched up, and bandaged.

The absolute worst time—the only time emotions welled up so much she actually broke down and cried—was when she spoke with Louise Allen, the rape crisis counselor. Only then did the stark reality hit her of what had happened—and what might have…what would have happened—if Samael hadn't shown up when he did.

Through her stay at the hospital, her cell phone rang repeatedly. Each call was from Sally, and every time she was able, Claire answered the phone and assured her roomie that she was fine. Because the cut was on the outside edge of her left foot, she would probably limp for a week or so. Other than that, after around three in the morning, she was anxious to get the hell out of there and go home.

Nearer to four o'clock—after how many final checkups, questions, and forms to sign—she was dressed and ready to go back to the apartment. Still, the hospital personnel kept her in a private room, sitting on another examination table and waiting. After a while, a knock sounded on the door. The door opened only after Claire called out, "Come in."

Another doctor—one she was certain she hadn't already spoken with yet—entered with her file in hand. He took a few seconds to scan the charts, flipping pages and nodding as he read. Claire was amazed that they could have generated so much information about her in such a short time, and she was anxious, now, to be on her way.

"Looks like you're all set to be released, then, Ms. McMullen." He took a small pad from his jacket pocket and started scribbling on it. "I want to give you a couple of prescriptions." He kept talking as he wrote. "One's so your foot won't get infected. The other's a pain killer."

Claire nodded, determined not to use the meds if she didn't have to.

When the doctor was done, he tore off the prescription sheets and handed them to her. She clutched them tightly in her hand and, at that instant, recalled the name and phone number Samael had scribbled on a napkin for her...

Had it really been earlier this evening...or last night, by now...?

God, it seems like days ago!

She wondered if she still had that napkin in her purse, but she doubted she would need it. She was positive Samael would be waiting for her when she got out. Her major concern was how much of a wreck she must look. Her hair was disheveled, and her makeup needed a serious touch up. Maybe she'd get a chance to fix herself up before she left the examination room. Already, she was anticipating how she would react when she saw his handsome, smiling face again. She couldn't help but wonder if this incident had brought them close enough together so they might venture a hug and maybe even a little kiss.

Her legs were so rubbery they felt unhinged when she hopped down from the examination table and stood up for the first time in what seemed like a very long time. The sudden blood rush from her head made her dizzy, and she had to place one hand on the edge of the table to help her keep her balance.

The doctor—the name tag on his jacket read Dr. Levine—didn't miss her momentary relapse, and he said, "You're bound to feel a little woozy from the pain meds we gave you earlier, before we stitched the wound."

Claire didn't remember being given any pain meds, and she had only a vague memory of them stitching the cut on her foot, but she grunted and nodded.

She limped horribly as she walked over to the door.

"Thank you...for everything," she said, all too aware of how lame she sounded. Doctor Levine smiled and indicated the wheelchair by the door.

"Sorry," he said. "You'll have to sit back and enjoy the ride."

Begrudgingly, Claire sat down in it.

As Dr. Levine pushed her out of the room and down the corridor to the waiting room, anticipation built about what she would say or do when she saw Samael. She was frightfully aware of the ambient sounds of the hospital—the hushed voices, the beeping of medical equipment, the squeaking of a wheel on a passing gurney.

She ran her fingers through her hair, trying to compose herself as best she could for how she—and he—would react.

When the doors to the waiting room swung open with a whoosh, Claire quickly scanned the people, assured she would notice Samael in a flash. Hell, she hardly knew him, so why was she feeling so attached to him already?

Her pulse was racing as she sat there, looking around. Then her stomach dropped with a cold, nauseating rush when she realized—

No!...This can't be!

—that he wasn't there.

"Do you have a ride home, Ms. McMullen?"

Doctor Levine's voice sounded like it was coming from miles away. When she looked up at him, it was like looking through the wrong end of the telescope. He appeared to be impossibly far away. A loud rushing sound filled her head as another, stronger wave of dizziness swept through her.

She nodded and said, "I'm all set," but her voice sounded like someone else's.

Maybe he stepped out for coffee...or went to the restroom...or went outside to bring the car around.

She wanted to—she had to believe there was a reasonable explanation for why he wasn't there. Her expectation that they would lock eyes and rush to each other in a passionate embrace now seemed so naïve...so foolish. After sitting there gaping at the assortment of people seated and pacing back and forth in the emergency room, she had to face the cold, hard fact.

He had ditched her.

"Fuckin' men," she muttered.

"What's that?" Doctor Levine asked, turning to her.

The momentary rush of disappointment quickly passed. This was so typical.

"Oh, no...nothing at all," she said. "Thanks again for all your help."

"That's what we're here for," Doctor Levine said.

Claire forced a smile as she looked. He seemed nice enough. Good looking in a plain sort of way. And a doctor, so he's obviously doing well. Exactly the kind of prospect her mother would want her to bring home.

Safe...Sane...Ordinary...And oh, so boring...

"Don't forget to make a follow-up appointment with your physician to have those stitches taken out in about a week."

"Will do," Claire said, thinking how much he sounded like her mother.

"Well then," Dr. Levine said, and without another word, an orderly came up to them and started pushing the wheelchair toward the exit door. The doors automatically whooshed open when they got to them. A cold, damp breeze blew into her face, chilling her as she rose shakily from the wheelchair. Her left foot was pounding with pain.

"Thanks," she said to the orderly, who spun the wheelchair around like he'd done this thousands of times and darted back into the hospital.

"Great," Claire muttered when she realized it was drizzling. She was positive it would start raining before she got back to her apartment. The early morning air had that feeling to it. Across the parking lot, the streetlights that surrounded the perimeter glowed like huge, purple dandelion puffs against the gradually lightening sky.

While still inside the shelter of the entryway, Claire fished her cell phone from her purse and hit the speed dial for Sally's number. After four rings, the phone went to message.

"Fuck!"

She ended the call and dialed again. This time—on the third ring—Sally picked up. She said something Claire found impossible to hear.

"Hey, Sal…You hear me?"

"Claire…?" Sally mumbled.

"Can you—?" Claire started to ask, but then she said, "Never mind," and she cut the call.

"Screw it," she said as she slipped her phone back into her purse. After considering calling for a cab, she decided to hell with that, too. Her apartment was halfamile away. She could make it, even with her injured foot. So what if it started to rain? She wouldn't get all that wet before she got home. After pulling her jacket collar tight around her neck, she stuck her hands into her jacket pockets.

That's when she felt the crumpled-up bar napkin.

A thrill went through her as she withdrew her hand from her pocket, clutching the note. That thrill, however, quickly shifted into irritation when she thought about how Samael had dumped her.

"Fuckin' asshole," she whispered. She was tempted to throw the napkin to the wet sidewalk where it would dissolve into pulp, but then she stuffed it back into her jacket pocket…

Why don't you get rid of it, she asked herself.

She didn't have a good answer, so she started walking.

Her progress was slow because of her limp. Every other step sent a hot, tingly jab of pain up through her ankle to her knee. A few late-night walkers or early risers passed by, hurrying to get wherever they were going before it started to rain, but they ignored her.

That's a good thing, she thought.

She didn't want some street creep to see her vulnerable like this.

Shoulders hunched and trying her best to ignore the sharp pain, she was about a hundred yards away from the hospital when the rain did, indeed, start falling. It was a cold, late March rain that bordered on snow, and with the wind blowing in off the ocean, it had—as they say—"teeth." The pain in her foot radiated in painful throbs up her leg. Within minutes, her hair was a tangled mess of wet curls that clung to her face like slugs. The rain was coming down so hard it all but obscured the streetlights around her. A few cars passed by, their tires hissing like a nest of snakes on the wet asphalt. Their lights barely pierced the downpour, and a dense mist began to rise as the cool rain hit the warmer asphalt.

"Jesus...Christ...Just...Fucking...Great," Claire mumbled as she walked as fast as she could.

She walked with her head down, heading toward Longfellow Square. The runoff from the sudden downpour was streaming down the sidewalk in dark, shimmering sheets. She was concerned that the bandage on her foot would get soaked through. That sure wouldn't help with the healing. But the doctor had given her extra pads and a roll of medical tape, so she could replace it when she got home.

If I ever get home.

She was used to walking around Portland—even late at night...or early in the morning—but her apartment building had never seemed so far away as it did right then. The chill bit through her jacket and jeans, and her teeth were chattering wildly. She didn't notice the car that had pulled up quietly a few feet behind her. She jumped when the horn tooted three times.

At first, she ignored it, thinking some yo-yo wanted to give her a hard time.

Eyes straight ahead, she kept walking.

The car didn't speed up and pass her by. It kept pace with her, like a hungry animal stalking wounded prey. Claire slipped her hand into her purse and gripped her cell phone, ready to call 911 if things got bad.

The driver honked his horn again, so Claire—still without looking—raised her middle finger and shouted, "Fuck off." She wasn't sure if the driver heard her or not. She didn't care. All she wanted to do was get home.

But then, still keeping pace with her, he hit the horn again—longer—and she was finally forced to stop and confront this asshole before it went any further. She turned and faced the car. In the rain, all she could tell was that it was dark and kind of fancy. In the downpour, she couldn't tell the make or model.

As she stood there with rain beating down on her, the tinted window slid down like a thin sheet of dark ice, shifting aside to reveal the darker depths below. All she could see of the driver was a dark silhouette that looked like it had been scissored out of the night.

"You look like you could use a ride."

She hadn't heard him speak many words since they first met last evening at Margarita's, but the shock of recognition hit Claire hard. She had to catch her breath. After a moment, she leaned closer to the car and now saw that it was, indeed, a sleek, dark Mercedes.

It was the same one she'd noticed in the restaurant's parking lot.

The window on the passenger's side slid all the way down now, and by the pale green glow of the dashboard lights, she could easily make out Samael's features. When he looked at her and smiled, his teeth caught the light just right and gleamed with a faint iridescent glow.

It was definitely Samael.

Her first impulse was to ignore him…not say a word and walk away. He'd already ditched her once tonight. She wasn't about to be humiliated again.

Her second impulse was to turn to him, let him see what a sodden, disheveled mess she was, and tell him to go fuck himself.

But her third impulse—the one that gripped her with undeniable power and overwhelmed the first two—was to smile back at him, laugh as if this was just the silliest thing that ever happened to her, and get into the car.

Which is exactly what she did.

~ * ~

"I'll get your car seat wet."

"It's seen worse."

Claire wasn't sure what he meant by that as she settled herself in the seat and then clicked the seatbelt around her waist and chest. It struck her as silly to belt up with less than a quarter mile to go, but so be it. The thought crossed her mind, though, that she was restraining herself, and Samael could take advantage of her if he had any bad intentions…like that man in the alley.

"So—umm, where'd you disappear to?" she asked.

She figured it was best to get it all out in the open instead of letting it fester. She told herself that this didn't change a damned thing. It had been unreasonable of her to expect him to wait for her all night at the hospital, but that's exactly what she had done. He had to know that even though they barely knew each other, he had let her down. Otherwise, it wasn't a promising way to start a relationship…

She chided herself for thinking so much ahead of things.

He had been at the hospital…and now he was driving her home…a little late, maybe, but what the heck?

That's all, though.

There's no "relationship" here.

"I got a call I had to take," Samael said.

He kept his eyes focused straight ahead on the road. The windshield wipers slapped back and forth, scooping fans of water to the sides of the car. Claire had the momentary sensation that they were underwater, somehow totally isolated from the rest of the world. She noted how this wasn't the first time Samael had created the illusion that when she was with him, the rest of the world could slide into the background without notice.

"I figured you'd be in there a lot longer. You know how hospitals are. So I thought I could slip out for a few minutes."

Claire made a harrumphing sound and told herself she was a fool for believing anything he said or for allowing herself to think there was anything special happening here. What would a guy like Samael, obviously rich and successful, be doing with a woman like her, anyway? No doubt, he had his pick of any number of gorgeous, wealthy, stylish women to function as adornments to his lavish lifestyle. While she acknowledged that she wasn't particularly unattractive, she was also realistic enough to know she was no raving beauty, either.

Except for her blazing red hair, so maybe he had a thing for redheads.

"You didn't have any obligation to stick around," she finally said, once she was sure she could control the pitch of her voice. She intended to sound casual, but it came off as sounding a little desperate…especially looking like she did right now.

He drove for a while in silence, but not far because he pulled up to the curb directly in front of Claire's apartment building. She looked at him with a mixture of suspicion and amusement.

"Wanna tell me how you know?" she asked.

He sat there with his hands draped over the steering wheel, his long fingers hanging loosely. The engine was purring, the wiper blades slapping back and forth. He stared straight ahead as if he was still driving. The reflected lights of the city played across his face, creating the illusion that his features were shifting…changing shape even as she watched him. It was both unnerving and intriguing.

"How did I know what?" he asked, turning to her. His eyes glowed like chips of ice in the darkness. He was smiling, but there was a ravenous look about his smile that for some reason made Claire think of the "Big Bad Wolf."

Claire nodded to indicate the building they were parked in front of.

"Where I live. This is my place."

"It is?"

He sounded surprised, but a mocking note colored his voice.

"Uh-huh."

"I pulled over where I saw an empty parking space. I figured you couldn't live far from here because you were walking in the rain. If you lived on the far side of town, you would have called a friend…or a cab."

Claire nodded, still suspicious. It sounded reasonable enough, but still—she wasn't sure. She had the sudden paranoid thought that maybe this guy had noticed her at some point and had been stalking her for…

Who knew how long?

Maybe running into her at the restaurant and then following her to the hospital had all been planned, somehow.

Not likely, she decided…*I'd have noticed a guy like this right away.*

"Well…thanks for the ride, such as it was," she said with a laugh.

"The doctor must have given you a prescription. Do you want me to drive you to the Rite-Aid in the morning to fill it?"

Claire shook her head.

"I have a couple of pills to get me through until I can fill it. My roommate will run down to the pharmacy for me."

"Ahh, yes. Sally," he said, nodding.

Claire glanced at him, then looked over her shoulder at her building, and then back at him.

"Thanks for the ride, then," she said.

The door latch clicked, and the car door swung open. The air had a chill, and the rain came down hard. Fitful gusts blew needle-sharp spray into her face.

I can't look any worse than I already do, she thought bitterly.

Shivering, she cringed inside her coat, pulling the collar up around her neck as she prepared to make a dash to the front door.

But then—somehow—Samael was out of the car and standing beside her on the pavement. She hadn't even noticed him getting out and running around the car, but—somehow—he had produced an umbrella as he extended a hand to help her out of the car. The umbrella expanded, and she felt safe under its shelter. She glanced at Samael and smiled.

"Thanks," she said, but that didn't begin to express the amazement she was feeling, considering how fast and smooth he had moved.

"It's the least a gentleman can do," he said. "Is this your door?"

As if you have to ask, Claire thought wryly but didn't say.

Side by side, with rain beating a wild rhythm on the umbrella, they walked under the sheltered alcove at the front of the building. Samael collapsed the umbrella and shook it, and they stood there, looking at each other in awkward silence for a long moment. Cars passing by on the street seemed to recede into nothing. The night and everything around them seemed so distant, but Claire tensed when a low grumble of thunder sounded above the sounds of the passing traffic.

"That's weird," she said, leaning forward and scanning the sky.

"What is?" Samael glanced up and down the street as though expecting to see something unusual.

"You usually don't hear thunder in March, is all."

As soon as she said that, a faint blue glow flickered in the dark sky above the city. Seconds later, another low roll of thunder sounded above the steady downpour of the rain.

"Global climate change," Samael said, smiling at her.

Once again, she was struck by the faint bluish glow of his teeth, like they were reflecting the flickering lightning.

Claire was tossing back and forth in her mind, wondering if she should invite him up to her place—to dry off, at least. She knew—and she knew that he knew—exactly what that would mean, and making a move like this was so uncharacteristic of her. It was something Sally did all the time. Claire couldn't count how many times she had suggested to Sally that being so easy might be exactly why she was having so much trouble establishing a long-term, committed relationship with anyone…if that's what she was looking for.

But then…look where it had gotten her…

"So…you—umm, wanna come up for some coffee or something?"

The words were barely out of her mouth before she could consider them. She was instantly irritated at herself for resorting to so obvious a cliché.

"'Coffee,' huh?" Samael's voice had a husky echo in the dark confines of the alcove. The sidewalk behind him danced with falling rain.

Claire couldn't dispel the feeling that the two of them had somehow entered a magical bubble where the rest of the world passing by them wasn't at all real and didn't matter in the least. She was staring at him—the planes of his face, the glow in his eyes—and she was thinking with every passing second that, yes, she damned well wanted him to come up to her place for coffee or anything else he might have in mind.

"Or a nightcap, if you'd like," Claire added, thinking immediately how foolish that sounded, so early in the morning.

What time is it, anyway? She wondered. If she stepped out onto the sidewalk, she knew she'd be able to look up and see the time and temperature display on One Canal Plaza, but she didn't want to know the time. It might burst the illusion she was constructing here.

"Another time, maybe," Samael said even though he didn't turn to leave. He simply stood there, staring at her like he was waiting for her to say or do the right thing.

What the fuck? Claire thought, immediately stung by his refusal. For a moment or two, she wanted to believe she hadn't heard him correctly.

Is he ditching me again?

She studied Samael with surprise and relief warring inside her. It wasn't at all like her to be so forward with a man, any man,…even one who seemed to have it all.

Except he doesn't seem all that interested in me, Claire thought. And *why should he? I'm so far out of his class, and we both know it.*

"Well, then…umm…thanks again for the ride."

"My pleasure," Samael said.

This is your chance, Claire thought. The least you could do is give me a little hug and maybe…just maybe a kiss on the cheek.

But…no.

Samael bowed his head and then turned. The umbrella magically sprouted again, looking like spreading bat wings that shielded him from the rain as he walked around his car to the driver's side, opened the door, and got inside. Claire couldn't see him through the tinted glass, but she could feel—or, at least, she wanted to hope—that he was watching her and maybe…just a little…regretting that he hadn't accepted her invitation to come upstairs for that cup of coffee.

"You'll never know what you missed," she whispered as Samael's car started up and pulled out onto the street. It didn't take long for his car to be lost in the rain-slick darkness, and once it was gone, Claire had the unique sensation that it had never been there in the first place—that she had imagined the ride home and everything else.

And all she was left with was a lonely, aching feeling that she was the one who had missed out.

"Screw it," she muttered, still staring down the street. She reached into her coat pocket, took out the napkin with his name and phone number, and crumpled it up and tossed it onto the sidewalk, where it instantly turned into soggy mush. She was tempted to step out into the rain and grind it underfoot like she was crushing out a cigarette, but enough was enough.

As she keyed the door open, she told herself she'd be a fool to think about this Samael guy ever again, but then, the next morning—Saturday—bright and early, a huge bouquet of flowers arrived with a handwritten Get Well card from Samael, saying:

"I hope you're feeling better and I hope to see you soon."

"You slick devil," she whispered, not knowing how true that was.

Chapter

3

——— Burning Boat

Things happened fast after that.

It was, as they say, a "whirlwind courtship." After she received the flowers on Saturday morning, Samael called and asked—if she was feeling all right—if he could take her out for lunch, maybe to Dominick's, the "floating" restaurant on a huge barge on Casco Bay, beside Chandler's Wharf. Although she wasn't a huge fan of seafood, Claire didn't hesitate. She had always wanted to eat there, but felt she couldn't afford it. So she spent the next hour fussing about what to wear and how she should do her hair.

Sally got up late, as was usual for her on weekends. Around noon, while Claire was touching up her fingernails in the kitchen, her roommate hovered around, clattering dishes and banging pots and pans as if that was the best way to demonstrate to Claire that she was irritated and/or couldn't care less where she was going or what she was doing. Sally's cat, Mittens, stuck her tail into the air and left the room; and when Claire couldn't take it any longer, she decided to say something. Not wanting to start an argument, Claire chose to take a gentle approach.

"So…how was the concert last night?"

"Huh? Oh, great...except I kept getting these text messages from someone."

"Really?...Who?"

"Oh, sure. Go ahead 'n play all innocent now."

"What are you talking about?"

So much for nonconfrontational.

"Who do you think?"

"I don't have a clue."

Claire's first thought was: What if it was Samael?...What if somehow he had gotten Sally's cell number and had been texting her?

"You, you moron. You only sent me, like, fifteen or twenty messages."

"The hell I did. I called you once, early this morning, but you were too groggy to talk, and then I...walked home."

"I don't remember you calling this morning."

"Well, I did."

"You want me to show you the texts?" Sally said.

Sally's face was pale, her expression pinched with eyes narrowed to two dark, glassy beads that looked like they would shatter if she opened them too wide. Before Claire could respond, Sally grabbed her purse from the counter where she usually tossed it after a night out. Huffing under her breath and frowning, she dug until she found her cell.

"Hold on," she said as she pressed a few buttons to call up the record of messages received. Smirking, she held the phone out so Claire could see.

"See?...Satisfied?"

Sure enough, there was a string of messages, all listed with the times they had been sent. Claire cocked her head to one side and studied the screen. She didn't try to count them all. She guessed more than twelve. But all of the texts had originated from her phone.

"That's...really weird," she said, genuinely perplexed.

"Irritating's more like it."

"Honest to God. I didn't text you last night."

Sally's smirk said it all, before she turned her phone off and tossed it onto the counter. Then she leaned back, folded her arms across her chest, and scowled as she looked at Claire. "It was really irritating."

"Talk about irritating." Claire waved her hand in front of her nose. "I wish you'd change the cat litter sometime soon."

"I can't smell anything," Sally said.

Claire sniffed and said, "The smell's so bad Mittens has stopped using her litter box," but she didn't want to get off on a tangent, complaining about Sally's cat. She couldn't stop wondering about those texts last night.

"Maybe I, like, butt-dialed all of them or something?"

Even she knew how ridiculous that sounded.

"They were all different...and perfectly coherent."

"Wait, you're saying I sent a different text each time? And they made sense? Like no spelling or grammatical errors?"

Claire was flummoxed, for sure. Even with Auto-Correct, her friends complained that her texts often bordered on gibberish, making little to no sense. There was no way she could explain any texts from last night...unless she had sent them while semiconscious or unconscious. Maybe the meds the doctors had given her at the hospital had really walloped her.

"And none of them were, like, all garbled and full of misspellings and stuff?"

That gave her pause. She always explained that her thumbs weren't coordinated enough for texting, and that she preferred talking to a real person on the phone...the way you're supposed to.

"Can I read a couple?"

"Why bother? You irritated the living shit out of me enough last night. I was trying to enjoy the show."

"I'm sorry. I really am, but I...I never—" Claire held out her hand, shaking it impatiently. She hoped the new layer of fingernail polish was dry enough and wouldn't smudge. Samael was going to be here in half an hour.

"Come on. Just lemme take a look."

Reluctantly, Sally picked up her phone and opened up the list. She was still scowling when she handed the phone to Claire.

"Hmmm," she kept saying as she read the messages in order. For one thing, Sally was right. There were no spelling or grammatical errors. Each message was clear and precise with absolutely no "text-speak." The other thing that struck Claire was that none of the texts "sounded" like her. The first few were chatty—

"Hey! How are you doing? Are you enjoying the concert?"

"Don't worry about me. I'm doing fine."

—and could have been from anyone, asking what her friend was up to. But the tone quickly changed, and the last few came across as accusatory and more than a little self-pitying.

"I don't mind being here all alone. Seriously. I'm fine. Don't you worry about me. I'll be fine. Enjoy yourself!"

The last one was—"Thanks for nothing. You call yourself a friend? Deserting me when I needed help the most! I was almost raped, and you weren't there for me!"—downright combative.

"I swear to God I never sent these," Claire said.

"See if I help you out the next time you need it."

"You didn't help me out this time!"

"You want to, you can delete me from your phone and your friends list."

Claire was astonished. When she had finished scanning the texts—as it turned out, there were eighteen of them—she stood there shaking her head from side to side, her mind a roaring blank as she handed Sally's cell phone back to her.

"I guess I'm sorry," was all she could say, "but I didn't do it."

"They came from your number. That's all I've got to say."

"But I didn't write them or send any—"

This was getting ridiculous. Sally was primed to fight for fighting's sake. A sudden crushing sensation filled her chest as she looked at her roommate. Sure, she may not be her best or closest friend, but they had been through a lot together over the last few years—including Sally's unplanned pregnancy and abortion—and there was no way, no way, even on the deepest subconscious level, that she would ever say anything hurtful or spiteful to Sally.

"I have no idea how it happened," Claire finally said, hoping to finish it with a shrug.

Sally gave her one last withering look and then, without another word, stormed out of the kitchen and into the living room with a bowl of Rice Krispies in hand. Claire didn't feel comfortable letting it hang like this, and she was about to follow after her, but before she moved, the buzzer sounded.

"Oh, shit!"

She rushed over to the intercom and hit the TALK button.

"Hey. You're kinda early."

"I'm right on time."

His voice sounded flat over the speaker, but Claire barely noticed because Mittens let out a rising howl the instant Samael spoke. Then she darted from the living room like her tail was on fire. Claire watched her go, confused, and then glanced at the wall clock next to the stove.

It was a quarter to twelve.

He was fifteen minutes early, but she wasn't about to dispute it.

"I'll be down in a few," she said, and then clicked off.

She was still wondering what had set Mittens off, but she was more intent on looking terrific for Samael as she went to her bedroom to finish getting dressed. If he was going to be early, she made sure she took all the time she wanted.

She'd teach him.

Twenty minutes later, she grabbed her purse and coat from the rack next to the door. Without another word to Sally and with no sign of Mittens anywhere, she headed out the door.

But as she was swinging the door shut behind her, she glanced back and saw Sally in the living room doorway, watching her with a dark scowl. For the rest of the day, Claire was puzzled—you might say haunted, even, by the expression on her roommate's face.

~ * ~

"So. I never got to ask you at the bar…what do you do for work?"

Claire felt a little bit foolish asking such a basic question. She was so comfortable being around Samael, she felt she had known him for years. She would have assumed they were well past such "getting to know you" questions. The truth was, there was so much about him—everything—she had yet to discover, and she thrilled at the prospect.

"Sales and service," he said, his voice a touch distant, as if the subject bored him as much as he expected it would bore her. "Buying and selling and, maybe, a bit of trading now and then."

"Really," Claire said, and then she fell silent and took a moment to look around.

Dominick's wasn't the kind of restaurant she and people she knew usually went to for lunch, dinner, or anything else…not on her salary. It was a gorgeous day, after the rain last night, and they had a window seat—one of the best tables in the place—looking out over Portland Harbor. The water sparkled in the sunlight, and huge, tumbling fair-weather clouds rolled over the South Portland skyline. Lobster boats and pleasure craft dotted the water, bobbing up and down on the gentle swells. The day had a bright, almost surreal intensity.

Claire was convinced it was being with Samael that made everything appear so…different.

One thing she did notice…something that struck her as peculiar, was the way, even with brilliant sunlight pouring in through the window, Samael's face appeared to be cast in shadow and deeply lined. His eyes remained bright, darting back and forth as he watched the activity going on around them. He looked distracted and aloof. He reminded Claire of a caged beast, one that wasn't at all comfortable being confined but was a master of appearing at ease in such a situation.

Finally, when she became slightly annoyed by him looking around, she asked, "Are you expecting to see someone or something?"

Samael shifted his intense gaze to her and, after a moment, his top teeth dimpling his lower lip, shook his head.

"No…Why?"

"I dunno. Just the way you seem to…" She shifted uncomfortably in her seat and cast a wary glance of her own around the dining room. "Distracted, I guess. You're not married and looking out for anyone who might know you and get word back to your wife, are you?" She arched an eyebrow.

"Don't be ridiculous. Of course I'm not married."

Samael slid his hand across the table and patted the back of her hand, like he was reassuring a child. Something within her didn't approve of the gesture—it seemed a little too patronizing, but she had to admit that his touch sent a tingle up her arm.

"It's just there are some…some clients of mine here, and I'd prefer them not to see me."

Claire bristled at that, wondering if, for some reason, he might be embarrassed to be seen in public with her. Apparently reading her mind, he tightened his grip on her hand and said, "I prefer not to discuss my business when I'm trying to relax…with a beautiful woman, I might add."

Claire kept looking away, scanning the patrons in the restaurant and wondering how any of them might be connected with Samael. Most of them—the ones she could see clearly, anyway—seemed not to be enjoying either their lunches or their environment. Their expressions struck her as superficial…plastered on while in public to be removed—like masks—when they were alone. She attributed the curious deadness in many of the people's faces as "symptoms" of their empty, pointless lives. She, on the other hand, had never felt more alive.

They engaged in small talk throughout their meal, and Claire found herself swept away simply listening to Samael speak…and looking at him, watching him was divine. She felt giddy and found herself laughing at the most mundane things. She had to keep reminding herself to play it a little cooler. No sense looking like a yokel from the "County" on their first real date.

After a while, before dessert, Samael excused himself and went to the restroom, so Claire sat there staring off across the harbor while trying to rein in her racing thoughts.

This is all going too fast…

She couldn't deny that Samael was special…unique, and she was determined to take this as far as it would go, not to let him get away if she could help it, but she kept warning herself not to go too far too fast.

Let whatever is happening here evolve on its own time…

Que sera, sera…

If it's meant to be, it's meant to be, and dozens of other meaningless platitudes rolled through her mind, but something inside her wanted to dismiss them and say, "To Hell with all of it…I'm gonna jump!"

After a while—How long?… It could only have been a few minutes—she realized Samael had been gone longer than seemed necessary. The panicked thought that he had ditched her again sent tingling chills through her.

She shifted in her chair and kept glancing in the direction of the restrooms, wishing…hoping…praying he would return soon. An almost childish desperation of wanting never to let him out of her sight filled her with longing. At the same time, the feeling struck her as amusing.

What the hell's the matter with me? She kept asking herself as she stared out over the water, tracking a lobster boat as it slid slowly toward one of the commercial wharves. The wake cut a foam-ridged 'V' in the blue water. Seagulls swooped and darted around the stern of the boat, looking to steal any bait from the bait barrel or that might fall into the water.

You're infatuated…that's what…with his kindness…his essence.

"Hey, there."

Samael's voice, coming so suddenly from behind, startled her and made her jump, almost spilling her coffee.

"Don't ever sneak up on me like that again," she said, laughing.

"What? Jumpy?"

Claire scowled.

"Sorry," he said as he pulled his chair away from the table and sat down. A mischievous smile curled his mouth. "So." He clapped his hands together. "You want dessert?"

Ah, the eternal question, Claire thought. *Eat dessert…be happy…and get fat?…Or stick with the ole' diet?*

"Maybe split something?" she offered, trying to take the middle road.

"You like blueberry pie? They bake an incredible blueberry pie here," Samael said.

"Sure. I love pie," Claire replied, but before they could get the waitress' attention, a steady, loud beeping sound suddenly filled the restaurant. Fear swept through the restaurant like a brush fire as everyone immediately recognized what it was.

A fire alarm.

The problem was…What to do about it?

For what seemed like entirely too long, everyone sat where they were, looking around as though they didn't see the clearly marked fire exits and were expecting a waiter or the host to make an announcement—probably that it was a false alarm, and that nobody should panic.

But the fire alarm continued its high, piercing beep-beep-beep. In the hubbub, Claire couldn't make out anything anyone around her was saying. She looked at Samael, desperate to take a cue from him. He remained seated and appeared to be unfazed by the sudden commotion around them. In fact, he seemed to be all but unaware of it.

"What do we do?" Claire asked, barely hearing herself above the din of the alarm. She didn't want to panic…not in front of Samael, but she was worried because no one "official" seemed to be responding to the alarm. She leaned forward in her chair, waiting for him to say or do something.

"I doubt it's anything to worry about," Samael replied. She as much read his lips as heard him. "It's probably a false alarm…faulty wiring, I'd guess."

Claire bit down on her lower lip and nodded. It made sense not to panic even when several patrons arose from their tables and started for the door. When the first ones to get there opened it, a funnel of dense, black smoke was sucked into the restaurant. People staggered back, coughing as they scrambled away from the exit.

"Jesus!" Claire shouted.

She wasn't positive she heard correctly, but she thought Samael mumbled, "He's not going to help you now."

They made intense eye contact as the uproar continued and intensified. Smoke was filling the room fast, now, and people were knocking over tables and chairs, spilling dishes and silverware onto the floor as they scrambled for another exit, away from the smoke and—possibly—flames. A doorway at the far end of the room was marked EXIT, but it was on the opposite side of the restaurant. Already it was clogged with a long line of people, trying to flee.

"The problem is," Samael said calmly, "no one is sure yet where or how bad the fire is."

Claire flashed on scenes of the sinking of the Titanic and was concerned that people might be running straight into danger, not away from it, but she and Samael remained where they were, watching the mayhem swirl all around them as if they weren't the least bit involved. The expression on Samael's face confused as much as reassured her. He looked both upset and...pleased, for some reason.

Like he's enjoying the chaos, Claire thought.

"Well," he finally said, pushing his chair back and standing up. He brushed his hands together, "I'd say lunch is on the house today, wouldn't you?"

Forgetting her panic for a moment, she looked into his eyes and couldn't help but smile. His eyes were an island of sanity in a sea of madness as smoke rapidly filled the room with a wide, dark pall.

"What are we going to—"

But that was all she got out, because all she could do was watch as Samael grasped the chair he'd been sitting in by the back and then approached the window that had offered such a nice view of the harbor. Without any hesitation, he heaved his body around to one side and then flung the chair toward the window.

The glass exploded into hundreds of shards that glinted in the sunlight as they spilled onto the carpeted floor and the restaurant's boat deck outside. The absolute glee on Samael's face made him look like a little boy setting off firecrackers on the Fourth of July. His teeth gleamed wickedly in the sun when he turned to her and, in a voice as steady and calm as if he were asking her to dance, said, "Shall we?"

The chaos in the restaurant faded away to nothing as he took Claire's extended hand and led her toward the broken window. Her injured foot ached with a dull throb. By this point, someone had stopped the fire alarm, but Claire could hear the high, warbling wail of approaching sirens.

So this fire is really serious, she thought, but she was amazed that she wasn't panicking like everyone else—everyone, that was, except Samael. He stood calmly by the broken window, holding her hand and smiling at her.

Heavy, black smoke filled into the restaurant now, and a sudden surge of panic made Claire hurriedly step through the broken window. The glass and pieces of the window frame snapped and cracked underfoot. Her enthusiasm dimmed when she saw the narrow walkway running the length of the floating restaurant. Between them and the parking lot...on dry land...there was a heavy curtain of smoke and the flicker of orange flames, like tongues. A crowd had gathered in the parking lot, and the early responders in black firefighters' coats were coming down the gangway to the restaurant with firefighting equipment.

"Look!" Claire said, indicating the flames, shooting out from the restaurant between them and safety. "It's blocked. We can't go that way."

Samael looked from her to the burning boat and then back to her again. His expression remained impassive, as if he were in complete control of the situation.

"Maybe coming this way wasn't such a good idea," she said.

"We may have to jump into the water and swim for it," he said, smiling. "You don't mind getting wet again, do you?"

She didn't appreciate the dig about how she had looked last night walking a half mile or so in a downpour, but the good-humored gleam in his eyes reassured her, and she laughed along with him.

She couldn't stop wondering why she wasn't freaking out and how Samael was so calm...happy, even.

The fire was serious business. More fire trucks, their sirens wailing and emergency lights flashing, pulled into the parking lot. The crowd grew larger as more and more rubberneckers showed up. Tourists and residents alike were using their cameras and cell phones to snap pictures and film the event.

The walkway around the edge of the boat was narrow, and Claire was concerned that, with her injured foot, she might lose her footing and fall into the harbor. She looked down at the water, surprised to see—up close—how murky and dark and full of pollution it was. An iridescent rainbow pattern of oil swirled along the surface. When she noticed a partially submerged beer bottle bobbing up and down on the swells, all she could think about was the other horrible, yucky stuff—both natural and man-made—that had to be down there.

She'd need shots if she ever fell into that water.

A deep trembling fear filled her gut. But when she looked at Samael, those feelings—well, if they didn't go away exactly, they certainly subsided.

Samael had that way about him.

"What do you think?" he asked, still smiling like this was just another normal part of his day.

When Claire took a step away from him, pain shot up her leg from the wound on her foot. Tears filmed her eyes as she realized exactly how dangerous this situation truly was. She wondered about the other people in the restaurant...had they all gotten out safely? Or were they trapped inside as the smoke filled the room and flames swept toward them? They'd die of asphyxiation before the flames got them.

This wasn't a casual adventure...a harmless lark.

This was some serious shit.

"Come on, then," Samael said. He lunged forward and grabbed her by the wrist. His grip was surprisingly strong and actually burned her skin as he jerked her forward so hard she almost lost balance.

Is he purposely trying to make me to fall? She wondered, but she felt remarkably light, like a silk scarf, as he pulled her along with him. By this time, flames were licking out of one of the portholes. As they approached it, Claire could all too easily imagine that both she and Samael would be incinerated, but she had to trust him.

Didn't she?

She realized—again—that she was putting an awful lot of faith into someone she barely knew.

Her feet kept slipping and sliding on the deck. The soles of her shoes made loud squeaking noises, like sneakers on a basketball court. She felt as though she were balancing on a tightrope.

Don't look down!

They were about halfway to the front of the boat when the porthole in front of them suddenly blew open with a flash. Flames and broken glass exploded like shrapnel in front of them, sizzling as it splashed into the harbor. Claire screamed and shied away, but Samael kept moving ahead, getting closer to the tongue of flame that was now licking up the side of the boat. It was almost invisible against the bright blue sky.

Do not look down!

Claire tried to shut out the commotion all around her. She had to focus on taking one step at a time and holding on to Samael. Every other step was like stepping onto a nail. But she had to trust him.

As he approached the virtual wall of flame, Claire looked up, thinking they may have to climb onto the roof of the boat in order to get away, but who was to say the fire wasn't worse up on the roof. Paint on the side of the boat began to bubble up and peel away as the heat inside the restaurant rose higher and higher.

The whole thing's gonna blow up...We're all gonna die, Claire thought.

Tears now filled her eyes when she wondered how all of her friends and family and coworkers were going to react when they heard how she had died. The thought passed through her head that it was at least better than dying a slow, painful death with cancer...or Alzheimer's.

But dying by fire?

She had heard or read somewhere that burning was one of, if not the most painful way to die because you inhaled the flames, and they incinerated your lungs before you died, so you couldn't scream or cry for help. You couldn't even breathe. Of course Samael, being a demon, could have told her a lot about it, but she didn't know that yet.

She looked down at the water again, thinking it might be better to take her chances by jumping in, but Samael kept pulling her forward relentlessly, closer...and closer to the flames that were blasting from the broken porthole and ripping up the side of the restaurant.

When they got there, the fire didn't seem as bad and, as Samael passed by the window first, amazingly, the fire seemed to abate for a second or two in order for him to pass.

"Hurry up," he called back over his shoulder, still holding her hand.

Claire's heart was racing now, and waves of dizziness swept over her, but she focused on where to place her feet—step by careful, painful step. She crouched low when she went past the open window, fully expecting a blast of heat flame to turn her into a charcoal briquette.

When she was beside the window, she looked inside for a split-second glimpse into hell. What had been a beautiful upscale restaurant mere minutes ago was now a raging inferno. The walls and floor were engulfed with flame. Fire had stripped the walls down to the frame. Chairs and tables that had been shoved out of place and overturned as the patrons had fled were blazing like torches. She thought she saw a slumped human shape sprawled on the floor, its clothes burning, but she couldn't be sure. Samael kept a firm hold on her hand and guided her forward.

When they got to the front of the boat, they mingled with the last few stragglers who were lurching out of the restaurant, waving their hands in front of their faces as they made their way up the gangplank. Only when she was a reasonably safe distance away from the fire did Claire let her guard down. She looked at Samael, who still appeared unfazed by what they had just gone through.

Hell, his hair was barely mussed, and no sweat or soot smudged his face the way it did all the other survivors. The firefighters were quickly knocking down the blaze before it spread to the wharf or other buildings, but a good-sized portion of the floating restaurant was severely damaged. A column of black smoke rose like a pillar into the blue sky. People were being treated onsite for smoke inhalation, and ambulances were speeding from the parking lot with the most seriously affected people.

With Samael at her side, Claire sat down on the asphalt and watched it all, trying to take it in. She was swept up by a powerful sensation that none of this was really happening.

How could it be?

She had to be dreaming…or imagining this.

News and camera crews were already on the scene—

How did they get here so fast?

—and were busy interviewing survivors while filming the blaze.

"Do you want to go to the hospital?" Samael asked after a long, silent moment.

"Not again," she said, lowering her head.

It struck Claire as rather odd the way he was surveying the situation. With his arms folded across his chest, he was smiling faintly—a look of what Claire could only describe as contentment or, perhaps, thinly veiled amusement. The firelight flickered wickedly in his eyes, making them appear golden.

"Amazing…absolutely amazing," he said, shaking his head slowly from side to side.

Claire still couldn't get over the simple fact of what had happened and the crazy…yes, crazy…and dangerous way they had escaped. Her stomach ached with a cold, hollow dread whenever she thought about how they might have died in there.

Finally, Samael looked at her earnestly and extended his hand to help her stand up. Claire was certain her legs—especially her wounded foot—weren't going to support her, but somehow—with Samael's help—she stood up.

There was a sudden roar as flames tore through the restaurant where the kitchen, apparently, had been. Moments later, a large portion of the outside wall collapsed inward, sending up a spiraling shower of sparks. They looked like fireflies dancing in the daytime. The restaurant barge lurched to one side and then suddenly began to sink in the shallow water. It went down fast and came to rest with the upper deck lying at the water line. Blackened debris and a wide oil slick rose and fell on the gentle swell of the water.

Claire looked at Samael and was about to say something about how unbelievably lucky they were to make it out of there alive when her stomach suddenly lurched. A cold, sour taste filled the back of her throat, and then—without any more warning—she dropped to her knees, hitting the pavement hard, and began to vomit.

Chapter

4

————Trapped

"I think I've had enough excitement for one day," Claire said as they stood outside the door to her apartment.

Before leaving the scene, they had to give statements and leave their names, addresses, and phone numbers with the authorities. Obviously, the Fire Marshal would have to investigate to find out what caused the fire. After that, Samael drove Claire home. It was time for her medication, anyway, and she knew she should lie down and rest. The thought crossed her mind—several dozen times, in fact—that she should invite Samael upstairs, but there was no way she felt like entertaining…much less consider jumping into bed together.

Besides, he had ditched her twice already, so if he felt a bit of rejection, let him. If he thought taking her to a fancy restaurant and then saving her life—literally—when a fire broke out was his ticket into the sack, then—as her mother used to say—he had "another think coming."

Still, Claire lingered in the entryway of her apartment because she didn't want to say goodbye to him just yet.

The truth was, she did feel safer and more secure when he was with her. She couldn't begin to identify what, exactly, she was feeling, but it both frightened and intrigued her.

Attraction?

Hell, yes. Just look at him. Who wouldn't be attracted to him?

Love?

Don't be ridiculous.

She may say—even now, after everything that happened—that she believes in love at first sight; but over the last few years, her experience had been that it was more like lust at first sight.

Let love develop slowly...always a good—and nearly impossible—thing.

Horny?

Again—Sure...look at him. He had a fantastic body—slim and well-toned, and she tingled with anticipation at the mere prospect of making love to...with him and seeing if he could deliver as good as he looks.

So what was it that made her not want to let him go...not yet, anyway?

Maybe never.

He seemed reluctant to leave, too, but she felt an inner sting when she remembered how crushed she had been last night when, even though he saved her from her attacker, he had not been there—twice—when she had expected and needed him to be.

What were the chances he was already married...or in a serious relationship...or—is it possible?—that he was gay and interested in her for nonsexual reasons?

It hurt her head trying to figure it all out, but before she keyed the door lock, she turned to him and slid her arms around his waist, pulling him close. She could feel the hardness of his body against her, the heat of his breath on her face, and the sensations took her breath away. When she looked up into his eyes—as dark as coals in the shadowed alcove...no golden glint now—all she could think was how amazing it would be to be lying in bed naked with him.

Not right now...not today.

But soon.

Fighting an urge to do more to him, she brought her mouth up close to his and, closing her eyes, kissed him long and strong.

At first, the kiss was chaste, but then she parted her lips and playfully darted her tongue between his teeth.

He responded in kind, and his tongue slid into her mouth, wiggling back and forth...probing...teasing...tasting.

She felt suddenly flushed, but even though she was lost in the embrace and the passion of the moment, she couldn't help but notice something...strange.

Samael wasn't like anyone else she had French-kissed before—even Frankie Sheldon, her sweetie back in elementary school when she had first kissed a boy.

It was his tongue.

It wasn't just big. That would have been unsettling enough. It also seemed—

This is impossible!

—like it had a life of its own.

It slid between her lips and teeth like a snake, nestling into the ground.

It writhed...It twisted...It undulated...It throbbed as it moved in and out of her mouth, almost gagging her with deeper and deeper thrusts but, at the same time, it created a violently sexual rush like she had never experienced before. Every nerve in her mouth was, for the first time in her life, truly alive. Warm, tingling rushes mixed with sharp, jabbing chills that spread up and down her body, centering in her lower belly. The feeling was so intense she actually imagined that his tongue was forked, and each moist, pointed tip was exploring depths of her mouth she hadn't reached even when she had gone down on a man.

This is absolutely insane, she thought as she clung to him greedily and ground her hips against his hips.

She was dimly aware that they were in a public area. Anyone passing by on Congress Street would see them. Any moment now, she expected to hear someone yell: "Hey! Get a room!"

And that's all she could think about.

She wanted him now—his body, mind, heart, and soul—more than she had ever wanted a man. Of course, he had no soul to give her. He had forfeited it eons ago when he had shed his angelic nature and embraced his demonic side.

But Claire knew nothing of that at this moment.

All she knew was that as insane as it was, she had to have him.

Now.

She was relieved to see that Sally wasn't home when they got upstairs. It was only then, when they entered Claire's bedroom and he began to undress that she saw his tail.

Her first thought was that it was a trick of the light or...or something...a shadow cast by the gloom in her bedroom because all the shades were drawn. Then, when he pressed her naked body down onto the mattress, she got a better look over his shoulder at the fleshy appendage as it flicked back and forth.

She had never heard a scream like the one she let out.

It—like his tail—was not human.

It all but took the paint off the walls, and she couldn't help but wonder what her neighbors would think. They probably thought she was being raped and murdered, and as she struggled to free herself of his weight pressing down on her, she thought that's exactly what was happening here.

She kept making strange squealing, grunting, impassioned sounds as she tried to break free of him.

Samael, for his part, wasn't expending much energy to pin her down on the bed and hold her. Even though his grip was firm, it also had a gentleness that made her think how safe she had felt when she was a little girl, and her father had hugged her when she was frightened by lightning and thunder or had had a bad dream.

This is a bad dream!

It can't be real!

The heat of Samael's body was...amazing. Even through her outright panic, she was amazed how holding him—she was hugging him even as she was trying to wriggle away—filled her with a feeling of contentment and excitement...as if he was both the source and the relief of her panic.

"What's...What...How can you...?"

"Shhh..." Samael said, holding his forefinger to his lips and gazing deeply into her eyes.

She was trembling. Her skin was slick and sticky with sweat. Exhaustion wrung her out as if they had already been making love for hours. When he shifted to one side, rolling off of her, the relief from the pressure of his body was almost terrifying.

She wanted...she needed to have him as close to her as possible.

In every possible way, she wanted nothing but to have him inside her.

Now!

"Who are you?" she finally managed to say, no more than a strangled gasp. Her voice was ragged and raw, her throat on fire.

As she waited in the silence for his reply, she was relieved to realize that she didn't hear the sound of approaching police sirens because someone in the building had heard her cry out and had called the cops.

Her body was tingling all over. The pleasurable rushes rippling through her made her drowsy. She had a feeling of imminent danger but, ironically, both the danger and her safety from it were in his embrace.

"You mean what am I, don't you?"

His tone of voice was soothing...mellow, calming, but nevertheless, Claire was jolted by his comment. A chill worked its way deep into her belly. She licked her lips, aware of how dry they were...like they were on fire.

Is that from his tongue? She wondered.

Her neck made faint snapping sounds, like a string of firecrackers going off in the distance as she nodded.

"Yeah," she said, hearing the dry croak of her voice. "What are you?"

Samael's smile widened, and in the preternatural light, his teeth gleamed wickedly.

"Oh..." Samael sighed as he lay on his side, propping himself and resting his cheek on his hand. "I think you have a pretty good idea."

Claire did have a pretty good idea, but there was no way she could articulate it. She was wondering when this had tipped from "normal" to "impossible," and why hadn't she noticed?

"For real? Yes," she finally said.

Gazing into his eyes was hypnotic, and looking at him—his smooth, flawless skin all but gleaming a dusky red in the semidarkness of her room—she realized it had started the instant she had laid eyes on him last night at the bar.

Was it really just last night?

She had been through so much since then—the attack and near rape, the trip to the emergency room, the walk home, lunch at Dominick's, and then the fire.

How could so much have happened in less than twenty-four hours?

It was too much, too fast.

Samael nodded slowly while maintaining steady eye contact with her. It was creepy, but when his head was tipped down, she looked in vain for evidence of horns on his forehead or on the top of his head.

Does he have horns?

Does every demon—because that's what he is…a demon!—have horns?

He certainly has a tail…and a forked tongue.

Claire kept staring into his eyes, telling herself this was totally impossible while, at the same time, trying to accept the impossible.

It had gone on far too long to be a mere dream. Plus, there was a certain logic to everything she had done—things she had said and thought last night and today—that weren't at all dreamlike. She glanced down at her hand to be sure because, long ago, someone told her that you can't look at your hands in a dream.

But she could see her hands as she flexed her fingers.

"You're not dreaming," he said, as if reading her mind.

Still, as she looked back at Samael, trying to figure out exactly what she was feeling and wondering why she wasn't totally repulsed, a terrifying sense of unreality washed over her. She shifted so there was a bit of distance between them. Lying there naked in front of him, she felt vulnerable and open in ways she never had before, but when she glanced down the length of his body, she was in for another, even greater surprise.

He didn't have any genitals.

"What the—?" she squealed as she tried to twist away from him. Yet when they broke contact, she didn't leap off the bed and run, screaming from the room. Still, she put a safe distance between them and stared at him, panting hard.

"You don't have any...? How can you...? What's happening?"

Samael smiled at her, obviously understanding perfectly what had surprised her. He looked at her and then gave her an almost shy shrug and said, "Why do you think they call it Hell?"

"You mean you can't...? But I felt...when we were lying down...there was something...you know, hard pressing against my leg."

"A tail can do more than wag," he said, and he followed this with the most temptingly evil laugh she had ever heard. Memories of his tongue sliding around inside her mouth like a live snake again both repulsed and attracted her.

As if in demonstration, Samael lay on his back and hooked his hands behind his head as Claire stared at his sculpted body. His abs and pecs stood out in sharp relief. Her mouth actually watered.

What happened next absolutely floored her.

His tail slid up between his legs, glowing and glistening wetly in the semidarkness of the bedroom. It kept extending until it was more than three feet long. The shaft of the tail was thick and smooth, and the fleshy tip was pointed, shaped like an inverted heart. She watched in rapt fascination as it began to wave gracefully from side to side like a cobra being charmed.

The impulse to reach out and touch it was overpowering. The tail curled and swayed so sensuously Claire didn't realize she was licking her lips hungrily. Her breath was coming faster and faster, whistling in her throat as a hot rush of blood flushed her face and breasts.

"Go ahead," Samael said with a soft, kindly voice. "Touch it."

Shocked that he seemed to be reading her mind again, Claire gaped at him. Her mouth dropped open, and her vision blurred as her pulse started racing even faster.

"It doesn't bite."

With that, he thrust his hips up off the mattress and watched with her as his tail wagged back and forth as if it had a life of its own.

Ever so slowly, Claire reached out until her fingertips brushed across the fleshy member. Its heat all but seared her fingers as an electric shock traveled down her spine to her crotch. A slow, throbbing ache filled her groin, and all she could think was: *I really am going to go to Hell for this.*

"Go on," Samael urged.

Claire glanced up at him and saw his face, flushed with pleasure and anticipation. He smiled at her wickedly, the sensuous, shimmering glow in his eyes as intense as an acetylene torch. It flared when she finally found the courage to wrap her fingers around it and squeeze it ever so lightly. She shuddered with pleasure when the tail twitched and swelled up like a pressurized hose.

"Oh my God!" she whispered. "It's so...responsive..."

Samael snorted and said, "It's best if you not use that name."

"What name?"

"That name...the one you used just now. It kinda spoils the mood."

"Oh, you mean Go—...Sorry."

"'S okay. I can take it."

His tail was still quivering in her hand, swelling so much she feared she'd lose her grip on it. The skin was oily, and she could feel the rigid muscles beneath. A heavy throbbing deep inside it was keeping time with her rapidly increasing pulse. She tightened her grip all the more and then, without thinking, started running her hand up and down the length of it. She felt compelled to put it into her mouth but resisted that...at first.

Samael was making the most peculiar moaning sound she'd ever heard as he lay back on the bed, rolling his head from side to side. His eyes were narrowed to slits, and he licked his lips with his forked tongue. In a deep, resonant voice, he said, "Please…use it…any way you want to."

She knew exactly what he meant by that, and she also knew that she should stop this right now.

The truth was, she should never have let things go this far, but she was too far gone to care now. She kept running her hand up and down the tail until she stopped with her fist clenching to the top of the shaft just below where it flared out into a fleshy point. It felt like it was about to burst. Flushed with heat and moaning softly, Claire parted her legs and lowered the tip carefully until it was probing inside her.

It was as if his tail had a life of its own. As soon as the tip entered her, the entire length stiffened and thrust forward so hard and fast it surprised her and brought tears to her eyes. She let out a strangled shriek and began to cry, but they were tears of pleasure as well as pain as he thrust deep inside her. It touched places inside her she didn't even know she had.

Before long, the pleasure became so intense she could feel herself slipping away…drifting into—not unconsciousness, but a state of mind that was trippy and terrifying and amazingly satisfying in ways she never could have imagined. Samael's tail kept thrusting in and out…in and out…full…hard…and deep. Claire had no idea how long she remained in that frenzied, dreamy ecstasy. Her mind was filled with exquisite pleasure.

What mattered…the only thing that mattered was that she and Samael were connected and moving as if they were a single being.

~ * ~

"That was…" Claire was panting hard, her body slick and glistening with sweat and other bodily fluids. She licked her lips as she lay on her back on the bed, her hands laced behind her head. She stared up at the ceiling until her eyes went unfocused. "I…I can't tell you what…what that…" She heaved a sigh. "That was unbelievable."

"I know," Samael said with a light, lilting laugh.

Claire wasn't sure if he meant that the same indescribable thing had just happened to him or that he had done the same thing to uncounted numbers of women before today.

She lay there and listened to their synchronized breathing for what could have been minutes…hours…or even days, for all she knew. After a while, she became vaguely aware of life going on around her. As usual, the sound of traffic and pedestrians passing by on Congress Street came through the window and at some point—she had no idea when—she was sure she heard someone…Sally, no doubt…enter the apartment. She started banging around a bit, but then she left shortly after that. The diffused light that bled through the window shades was lemony—the way it got late in the afternoon. She could have turned her head and looked at her alarm clock, but that would have taken too much effort. Besides, it would bring an element of reality into the situation, and that was the last thing she wanted.

It was much better simply to lie here in bed and dreamily run the palm of her hand all over Samael's chest and stomach. The muscles below the skin, cushioned by his flesh, were like curved, metal plates. As sensual and erotic as all of this was, she still felt strange about touching him…down there…where the junction of his thighs and abdomen was as flat and smooth and hard as the rest of him. On some level, the idea of a man not having any external genitalia freaked her out whenever she thought about it, but she kept reminding herself that Samael was no man…

He was so much more than a man.

They lay in bed side by side, listening to the silence and breathing in unison. Claire kept dozing off and then awakening with a start. From time to time, Samael would raise his hand and touch her, stroking her long red hair, brushing his fingers through her curls and petting her, rubbing her hips, her belly, her thighs, her breasts as if she were something rare and precious.

"We have a lot to talk about," she whispered after a long while.

His breathing continued unabated, and she wondered if he had drifted off to sleep, or if he was faking being asleep so he wouldn't have to talk.

Does he ever need to sleep...He is, after all, a supernatural being...so what are the rules? They say Evil never sleeps.

She had no idea where to begin with her questions, but then her hand drifted a bit lower, running along the ridges of his ribs and then lower...and lower until her fingers ran lightly across the shaft of his tail again. It was lying across his thigh like a large snake. She tightened her grip on it, marveling at its smooth, soft power...its magic.

His tail responded immediately to her touch.

"Ah-hah, so you are awake," she whispered with a laugh as she increased the pressure of her touch and then wrapped her hand around his tail, pulling it up like running a length of rope through her hands until she reached the fleshy, pointed tip. He moaned softly as, once again, she was filled by an overwhelming compulsion to bring it up to her mouth.

Which she did.

~ * ~

"So?" Claire said sleepily. "What do we do with the rest of the day...or should I say 'night?'"

Claire kicked aside the tangle of sheets and sat on the edge of the bed, staring at the drawn window shade. She couldn't begin to describe how she felt except that she had never felt like this before.

Ever.

She was completely, thoroughly pleasured in ways she had never even imagined or considered possible. Every other sexual relationship she'd had before now paled to absolute insignificance...even the ones she thought at the time had been incredible, like when she dated Robbie Campbell. She felt both exhausted and exhilarated, as if she had just run a marathon and emerged from a hot tub after a full-body massage. When she stood up, her legs trembled underneath her, and she had to sit back down on the edge of the bed to gather her resources. Her injured foot throbbed with dull pain.

Mentally, she was sharp, her mind amazingly clear. Even when she thought about what had happened last night—that she had almost been raped—there was a peculiar clarity about the incident that gave her a feeling of acceptance and yes, even forgiveness and pity for the man who very well may have intended to kill her after raping her. Claire had been brought up a Catholic, but had drifted away from the Church as she got older. Kindness, charity and forgiveness were deeply ingrained in her, nonetheless.

She got up from the bed again, feeling a bit more stable on her feet, and began dressing. All the while, she looked at Samael, who certainly appeared to be asleep. His eyes were closed, and he was breathing with deep, regular breaths that had the appearance of being asleep, but the thought crossed her mind that he was not only not asleep, he could see though his closed eyelids and was watching her even now as she got dressed.

Feeling suddenly exposed and vulnerable, she turned away from him while she hitched the clasp on her bra and adjusted it, pulled on her panties and jeans, and then buttoned up her blouse.

"You want something? Coffee, maybe?"

"I'm good," he replied without the slightest trace of sleepiness in his voice.

"I'll be back in a sec, then," Claire said.

She walked out barefoot into the kitchen, automatically looking for Mittens, who would demand to be fed. She didn't give it much thought when she didn't see Mittens, and she set about brewing some coffee as if it was early morning. While the coffee was brewing, she grabbed a bowl, spoon, and box of granola. She decided to forego thawing a cupful of blueberries she usually added to the cereal. She poured a bowlful of granola, drenched it with milk, and then sat down to eat.

Moments later, Samael strolled into the kitchen, stark naked. She couldn't help but stare at his unusual physiology. As casual as can be, he sat down at the opposite end of the small table. He had a perfectly neutral expression on his face as he propped his clenched fist under his chin, rested his elbow on the tabletop, and stared—unblinking—at her.

"So," he said, drawing out the "S."

"So, what?" Claire replied, not sure where he might be taking this. She was still wondering if she would ever get used to him not having genitals.

I will if he keeps using his tail the way he did last night, she thought and couldn't suppress a small chuckle.

"What's so funny?" Samael asked, looking at her, his eyes glistening in the dim light like wet marble. His skin looked brick red.

"No...Nothing," Claire said even as she wondered if he could really read her mind and was asking simply to test her or to amuse himself.

"Well, it's gotta be something," he said.

Claire tried to avoid his steady stare because she knew—especially now—just how hypnotic it could be. She felt as though she would do, say, or think anything to please him, until she reminded herself that he was a genuine demon...as in one of the meanest, baddest of the bad guys.

"No," she said, "I was just thinking...there's so much we have to learn, to get to know about each other."

Samael smiled in a way that made Claire wonder if he already knew all about her...no doubt, too much. But before she could say more, her cell phone chirped. Irritated, she grabbed her purse from the counter, fished around inside it until she found her phone, and glanced at the Caller ID.

"Oh, shit," she muttered when she saw her parents' number.

Samael smiled at her. The two tips of his tongue flickered out between his impossibly white teeth.

"Let it go to message if you don't want to talk to her," he said.

That did it. With that comment, Claire knew he had ways of knowing things about her that were not ordinary. Even if he didn't know it was her mother, how did he know the caller was female?

Claire was tempted to answer the phone simply to avoid talking to Samael for the time being, but the phone chirped two more times and then went silent. It was still in her hand, her palm so slick with sweat it made the plastic housing of the phone feel greasy, when it beeped to signal that her mother—or father—had left a message, something they usually avoided.

Maybe something's wrong? Claire thought.

Maybe something had happened to one of them...or her brother, who still lived in Houlton and worked as a mechanic at a local garage.

Her hand was trembling as she placed the phone down on the counter. Then she took a deep breath, held it, and turned, determined to confront Samael, at least on this one minor detail.

"How'd you know the person calling me was a woman?" she asked in a shaky voice.

Samael looked at her, his expression all innocence.

How easy it must be for him to lie, she thought.

"What's that?"

"You said to let it go to message if I didn't want to talk to her. How'd you know it was a woman...my mother?"

Samael laughed and shook his head.

"I didn't," he said without missing a beat. "I was guessing it was your roommate. I know she snuck in when you—when we were asleep, and I know she doesn't like me."

"Really?"

"Yeah...Really." He was still smiling...but the smile didn't look quite so friendly now. His tongue was no longer visible, but his teeth were exposed, making small indentations on his bottom lip. "Yeah...because she wanted me to pick her instead of you."

Pick me?... That sounds ominous...What did you pick me for?

A shiver ran up both of her arms to the nape of her neck. She was about to confront him on this whole "picking me" thing when her phone started ringing again.

"If that's your mother, she's persistent. I've got to give her that," Samael said, but Claire experienced a cold hollowness in the pit of her stomach when she saw on the Caller ID that it wasn't her mother.

It was a number she didn't recognize. If it was the student loan company calling again...

"Hello," she said after snapping the phone up off the counter.

"Yes, hello. This is Boyd Harris at the District Attorney's Office. Is this Claire McMullen?"

Claire's eyes widened and she flashed a look at Samael. For some reason, she was suddenly convinced something had gone wrong, and she was in trouble with the police.

"Yes, this...this is she," she replied, irritated by the tremor in her voice.

"Ms. McMullen," Harris continued. "I've got a...a rather unusual situation here, regarding your case."

He paused, and in the pause, Claire had time to say, "What is it?" while her nerves tightened.

"The man we arrested last night, Ron LaPierre, the person who allegedly assaulted you—"

Allegedly?

"—has asked if you'd be willing to come down to the police station and talk to him."

"Me? Talk to him? Are you—?" She gulped dry air that felt like a hot coal lodged in her throat. "Why would I want to talk to him? Isn't it, like, illegal or something?"

"It's not typical, for sure," Mr. Harris said, "but it's not unprecedented."

Claire considered for a few pulsebeats and then asked, "Well, do you think I should?"

"Your call, but I wouldn't advise it. No point to it. He says he's innocent, so anything you say to him could hurt the case against him. At this point, the evidence against him doesn't look good...for him."

Claire noticed that, as she spoke into the phone, Samael kept shifting in his chair. Maybe he was sitting on his tail and couldn't get comfortable. She wondered if his hearing was sharp enough so he could hear both sides of the conversation.

"You want to speak with him, you can do it. You might want to have your lawyer with you, if you got one. 'Course I or someone from the DA's office would have to be there, too." Harris paused, took a breath, and then said, "But—again, I wouldn't advise it."

"No," Claire said quickly. "I don't think it's a good idea, either...not a good idea at all."

The conversation was bringing back last night's events so fast they rushed over her like a dark tide, filling her with unfathomable dread. Her breathing was hitching hard now, and her body was shaking as if she were facing an Arctic blast. The sound of her pulse was heavy in her ears; her neck and wrists ached with dull pain. When she looked at Samael, he was hiding his smile behind his hand.

Is he enjoying this...what this is doing to me? She wondered.

"It's just," Harris continued, unaware of Claire's reaction, "he insisted that you speak to him. He says he didn't do it."

"Didn't do..." She couldn't finish the thought.

"He says it wasn't him...that he was there, but he has no memory of attacking or trying to hurt you."

"But you—you caught him doing it."

"He says he wants to apologize."

"Which implies that he did do it."

"Look. I'm just doing what he asked...throwing it out there so you'd know. That's all."

"Yes. I...Thank you."

Claire had no idea what to make of it. Why would she want to speak to or even see the man who had tried to rape her?

She wanted to ask Harris more questions, to find out exactly what her assailant had said and why he thought speaking with her would do any good. Maybe get her sympathy and try to get her to drop the charges. She watched as Samael got up from the table and, without a backward glance at her, sauntered down the hallway, back to the bedroom.

Is he recharged and ready to go at it again? She wondered. In spite of what she was dealing with here, a deep warmth throbbed in her lower belly, and she smiled.

Am I ready to go again?

She suddenly had grave doubts about what she was doing—not about the rape charges, but with Samael. As impossible as it seemed...as impossible as it was, she knew in her soul that she should have absolutely nothing more to do with a demon, no matter how charming and attractive he might appear...That was the operant word here:

Appear.

And it certainly didn't matter how good he was with his tail!

"I—I appreciate your call, Mr.—"

"Harris."

"Mr. Harris."

She ended the call, noticing the emptiness inside her without Samael in the same room where she could see him. She considered for a moment—

Why would Mr. Harris from the DA's office be calling in the first place if it wasn't advisable for her to talk to LaPierre?

This was just weird!

Why stir things up like this?

Why not just let things take their course?

She had no doubt that she would experience psychic echoes from last night's events for a long time to come, and she wondered—and worried—that over time, things would get worse instead of better.

It certainly didn't help to have someone from the DA's office suggest something as foolish as going to visit her "alleged" assailant in prison.

She hadn't even known his name until just now—Ron LaPierre.

She told herself that she honestly didn't care to see or hear from him or even think about him ever again. The trial—if it came to that, and she had to testify—would be ordeal enough to sit through. Some women may want to face their attacker and ask him, simply, why?

But not her.

Mr. Ron LaPierre could rot in jail from now until the end of time, for all she cared.

She walked down the hallway to her bedroom. All she wanted to think about was how incredible it felt to be wrapped up in Samael's embrace and experience the thrills that coursed through her body when he penetrated her with his tail.

After this call, she was more than ready to start in again.

"Are you...?" she started to say, but her question died on her lips when she saw that Samael wasn't in the bedroom.

"Samael?"

The lighting in the room was dim. No wonder. Samael liked it that way even on a bright, sunny March day. She looked carefully at the bed to make sure he wasn't under the covers, but the rumpled bed sheets couldn't have hidden him. After looking all around to make sure she wasn't missing him in the dim light, she assumed that he was in the bathroom.

But then a thought hit her—

He doesn't have to urinate...How could he...without a penis?

And then another thought struck her.

Does he also not have an anus?...Does he ever have to excrete?

"This is getting too weird," she mumbled to herself as she walked out of the bedroom and down the far end of the hall to the closed bathroom door. She rapped on the door with her knuckles, a few quick taps.

"You in there?" she called out.

No answer.

"Samael?"

Again, she knocked, and again...

No answer.

Bracing herself, she reached down and clasped the doorknob. The brass knob was slick in her hand. She turned it slowly until the latch clicked; then she pushed the door open a crack and peered inside. When she saw that he wasn't sitting on the toilet, she swung the door all the way open.

The bathroom was empty.

But the shower curtain was drawn.

Is he in there?...Getting ready to take a shower?...Or maybe hiding...planning to jump out and give me a scare?

She entered the bathroom cautiously, approaching the closed shower curtain. The linoleum floor was damp, and her bare feet squeaked on it. Her body was tense, and she told herself she was ready for anything as she got ready to slide the shower curtain open. Her hand wavered only slightly as she gripped the plastic edge, balling it up in her fist.

Holding her breath, she mentally counted to three and then ran the shower curtain open.

The sound of the plastic rings sliding along the metal bar set her teeth on edge, but when she saw what was inside, she realized that she wasn't ready for anything…

Because there…in the tub…was…something.

"What the…" she muttered, so shocked at first that she didn't realize that the thing—whatever it was—was moving.

Only then did she hear the faint buzzing sounds coming from it. At least she assumed the sounds were coming from it. Once she keyed into the sound, it rose steadily in volume…a loud buzzing sound of…

Bees…or flies.

The lighting in the bathroom was never that good, even at noon with the ceiling light on, so she leaned forward and stared at the thing on the floor of the shower.

That's when she realized it really was moving…a writhing ball of…something…something that was so rotten it was swarming with flies. She leaned closer, and the pungent stench of decaying meat hit her like a body blow to the stomach.

"What in the name of…"

At first she thought someone might have dropped a piece of steak or hamburger or something in the shower where it had rotted and drawn flies.

But that didn't make sense.

And where did all these flies come from?

It was March. The apartment windows were closed tight. They might have been wintering in the attic or maybe in one of the other tenants' apartments, but how did they get in here?

Her initial panic began to subside only to be replaced with a wave of nausea as she watched the houseflies crawling over the rotting thing. It was the size of a meatloaf, and tufts of slimy fur poked through the red and black flesh. She knew it couldn't have been, but it looked like it had been here for days…maybe weeks. Her stomach lurched, and the joints of her jaw started to ache.

She knew what was coming next.

Holding her breath and trying not to inhale that rancid smell, she let go of the shower curtain and backed away from the tub. After a few steps back, she pivoted on her heel and dropped to her knees. Clasping both sides of the toilet bowl, she leaned her head down just in time before her stomach heaved.

The first hot blast of vomit hit the water in the toilet bowl so hard it splashed back into her face. But she ignored that as her stomach convulsed several times, and more streams of vomit shot from her mouth. The joints of her jaw were throbbing now, and the sick stench of vomit made her want to heave all the more until there was nothing left in her stomach to throw up.

Behind her, she was aware of activity. Her first thought was that Samael—wherever he had been—had heard her getting sick and come to help her. She wanted to look up to see if he was standing there behind her, but she couldn't stop vomiting.

Through her sickness, though, she realized that it might not be Samael behind her. The buzzing sound of the flies grew unbearably loud, and when her stomach finally settled enough for her to turn and look, she was amazed to see a cloud of houseflies flying in a swirling tornado-like formation, moving behind the shower stall and banging into it hard enough to make the plastic jump.

Her throat was burning as she covered her mouth with the flat of her hand to block the scream that threatened to burst from her. She watched in mute horror as the cloud of flies—there had to be hundreds...or thousands of them—rose to the bathroom ceiling in a dark, whirling mass.

Claire wanted to cry out for help, but she knew she was alone in the apartment. She could feel it, and a cold fist tightened in her gut.

Samael had deserted her.

Again.

Whimpering softly, she lunged for the door and yanked it open. By now, the buzzing sound was as loud as the crackling burr of a chainsaw, and as she staggered out into the hallway, she fully expected the flies to swarm over her like a heavy cloud. All too clearly, she could imagine flies crawling into her mouth and nose and ears, buzzing and chewing her like she was already dead flesh. Nearly blind with panic, she yanked the bathroom door closed behind her and took a few unsteady steps down the hallway until she stumbled over her own feet and fell.

Her knees hit the carpeted floor first, and then she flopped forward like a puppet whose strings had been cut. Her chin hit the floor hard enough to send a bright splash of stars across her vision. Somehow…miraculously…the buzzing sound cut off when she closed the bathroom door, and it took several seconds of lying on the floor, panting hard before she realized she'd trapped them. The flies hadn't escaped from the bathroom.

With tears welling up in her eyes, she somehow found the strength to sit up and take stock of what had just happened. Her gaze fixed on the closed bathroom door.

It was silent in the bathroom. Eerily so…

"Hey, what's up? You okay?"

Samael's voice, coming so suddenly from behind her, made Claire squeal and spin around to face him. Her fists were clenched, her heart racing. He was dressed, and she couldn't help but notice how neat and slick he looked.

Maybe too slick?

The sight of him made her flash with anger.

"What the fuck? Where were you?"

She struggled to hold back the tears that threatened to spill as they stared at each other. The buzzing sound of the flies behind the door gradually faded away. For the first time since she had found out the truth about him, all Claire could see was the demon he truly was.

He was enjoying this…He relished her fear and confusion. It amused him.

"I'd like you to leave," she said, her voice low and broken. "Right now!"

Samael stared at her but didn't say a word, but he took a few steps forward, his arms raised, his hands extended as though to help her to her feet.

"No! Leave me alone! I mean it!" she shouted, glaring at him. And then she gasped.

She knew exactly what it was in the tub.

"I'm serious." She was breathing so fast it hurt. "I want you to leave now."

"But Claire...I thought we—"

"Now!" she said, her voice finding strength even though she was hyperventilating. She raised her hands to her face as though to protect herself from him. She was terrified because right now she could see him for exactly who and what he was.

"You did that...didn't you?"

"Did what?"

"In the bathroom—" She gagged at the thought and had to inhale deeply. "That's Mittens, isn't it?"

"Mittens? Who's Mittens?"

"Sally's cat. You did it, didn't you?"

He started to reply, but his expression suddenly collapsed and, for the first time ever, Claire saw—or convinced herself that she saw—a spark of genuine emotion...of real feeling.

"Did...what?"

"You know exactly what I mean," Claire said. "You killed Mittens."

Even as she said it, she heaved herself forward so she could stand. Samael made a motion forward as if to help her, but she fended him off with a vicious slap to his outstretched hand. The smacking sound was as loud as a gunshot in the narrow hallway.

"I don't know what you think you're doing, but you're not going to get away with it. You're not going to terrorize me like this."

"Like what?" Samael said, his voice now as smooth as ever.

Unsure if her legs would support her, Claire hiked her thumb over her shoulder at the closed bathroom door, but the perplexed look on Samael's face almost convinced her that he genuinely didn't know what she was talking about.

Oh, he's good at dissembling, all right, she thought. *World class.*

"Where were you just now?" she finally asked, telling herself to calm down and reason this through. She had to stay in control and not let him intimidate her.

"What are you talking about? I was in the bedroom getting dressed."

"Bullshit!"

Claire kept reminding herself to see him for what he really is—pure, unadulterated evil. She chided herself for having even the slightest interest in him. She was in mortal danger.

"No you weren't. I checked in the bedroom. You weren't there. You weren't anywhere except—Christ, you were probably...in here."

He winced at that, and she realized her use of the word "Christ" bothered him.

Again, she indicated the closed bathroom door. The lack of the buzzing sounds from behind the door created a dense silence in the hallway that was broken only by the heavy thump of her pulse in her ears and her short, panting breaths. She hadn't realized until this moment just how dangerous Samael was and how vulnerable she was. All she wanted was for him to leave her alone, hopefully without hurting or killing her...much less claiming her soul.

But that didn't excuse what he had done to Mittens. As much as Claire didn't like her roommate's cat, that didn't mean he had to kill her.

"I didn't mean to...or want to, but...Cats are—" He paused and looked at the ceiling as though searching for the perfect word. "Cats can be problems for my kind."

"Demons, you mean," she said with just enough edge to let him know she left enough room to doubt that's what he really was.

"I honestly didn't want to do it. It—the cat forced me to."

"Why, so you could possess its soul? Like you want to possess mine?"

"I can't do that, you know," he said. His eyes held a flat, dead gleam, and his expression was perfectly neutral.

"Do what?" Claire asked, fearing—again—that he was reading her mind.

"Take possession of your soul," he replied.

"You can't, huh?"

Samael lowered his gaze and shook his head.

"That's right. I can't. You have to give it to me…willingly."

"Well I won't give it to you. You can count on that. I don't want to have anything to do with you…not if you're going to lie to me and tease and torment me and…and kill innocent creatures."

"It wasn't my fault, I swear."

Claire laughed at that. How could he expect her to believe little old Mittens was any kind of threat?

"I swear to you. I'm not lying. I was in the bed, sleeping," Samael said. His face softened with what might have passed for sympathy…if he had been human.

But he isn't human.

He's a demon—with a capital D, and she had to do everything and anything she could to get him out of her life.

Now!

"You said you were getting dressed."

"I did?"

"Yes, you did."

"I'm pretty sure I was still in bed. I remember you coming in and then leaving. I assumed to go to the bathroom."

"How can I trust anything you say?" By now, Claire was making no attempt to mask her disgust and doubt. "You're a demon, for Christ's sake!"

"Oww…I wish you'd stop using that name," Samael said. The pained expression on his face did look genuine.

"What, 'demon?'" Claire said, knowing full well what he really meant but wanting to see if she could get him to say the name Jesus.

But Samael lowered his gaze and shook his head, no.

"You know…the other one," he said, sounding wounded.

"Oh, you mean 'Christ?' Does that name bother you?"

Samael winced, hunching his shoulders as though preparing himself for a violent blow. Against every shred of common sense, Claire couldn't help but feel sorry for him. The title of an old Rolling Stones song popped into her mind—

"Sympathy for the Devil."

—and that made her smile.

"What's wrong with 'Christ?'"

Once again, she took pleasure in seeing him wince. So she did have some power over him after all. Maybe things weren't so bad…unless this, too, was an act.

He stepped back, raising his hands.

"Does it really bother you when I say that name?" She stepped closer, watching him retreat. "Or are you faking it, now, because you're trying to get me to lower my guard?"

Samael's eyes were glazed like an ice-covered pond as he nodded his head slowly.

"It honestly does bother me," he said, his voice no longer strong and confident. He sounded to her like a little boy who was lost and frightened. "And—yes, it…it's not like me to tell the truth. It goes against my nature."

"Is it because—?"

"It's more complicated—a lot more complicated than you think, believe me," Samael said, squaring his shoulders. Like switching a TV station, his old confidence and slickness were instantly back. "So…do you really want me to leave?"

Claire stood there, her mouth gaping open. She had no idea what to say. She was trapped with Samael blocking one end of the hallway and, behind her, nothing but the bathroom and those horrible flies and what had once been Mittens. All too easily, she could imagine that the bathroom was now overflowing with flies. If she opened the door, a huge, dark mass of them would spill out on top of her like a tsunami, burying her in a crawling, buzzing, suffocating pile.

I'm trapped, she thought with a rush of panic.

But she was also trapped by her emotions because, when she thought about what was going on here, she couldn't help but feel sorry for him. She was genuinely attracted to him…in ways she couldn't begin to comprehend. He made her feel things she never even suspected she could feel. And it wasn't just because of what he did to and with her in bed. Besides the physical attraction — more than the physical attractions, she felt a genuine emotional connection to him…a deep, overpowering need to hold him and soothe him and be with him and love him forever.

"So?" he said, his voice deep and resonant in the hallway. "If you want me to leave, say so. I will if you command me to."

No, I don't think you will, Claire thought, but she nodded slowly.

When he looked at her, her resolve weakened and almost melted, and when she heard herself speak again, it was like listening to someone else speak.

"I do…" she whispered in a voice so weak and strangled she wondered if he heard her at all. "But only for now. I need time…time to think."

"I understand."

And with that, he was gone.

No puff of smoke, like she might have expected.

Without another word, he turned and walked to the apartment door. And without looking back, he opened the door and stepped out into the hallway. Then the door swung shut behind him, the latch clicking loudly, even though it looked as if he hadn't touched it. Claire was left feeling more alone than she had ever felt before in her life.

Already, she wanted her demon lover back.

Chapter

5

————Two-way Mirrors

The next day—Monday morning—Claire was at work. She was thinking about Samael—as she had been since he left the apartment yesterday afternoon—and nothing else.

She'd had a late-night talk with Sally, who told her she should take a day or two off to relax and readjust, but she refused. She didn't have the heart to tell her roomie about what had happened to Mittens. She cleaned up the mess, putting what was left of poor old Mittens into the Dumpster. After she scrubbed the tub with bleach, the flies didn't return.

She hoped Sally would assume her cat had gotten out of the apartment somehow and would eventually find her way back home. Claire didn't want to take time off because her work would just pile up, and Marty, her boss, would give her a ration of shit about getting orders and bids done and sent out correctly and on time.

She was sitting at her desk in her windowless office that was the size of a broom closet and staring unfocused at her computer screen when her cell phone in her purse rang. She jumped, grabbing the phone from her purse, her heart leaping as she thought…hoped…prayed—

How can you pray for a demon?

—that it would be Samael.

A quick glance at the Caller ID showed her that it wasn't from the phone number he had given her at the restaurant. She had that number memorized.

"Hello?"

She didn't like hearing the tightness in her voice.

"Yes," said a man's voice. "This is Detective Trudeau, Portland PD. I'm trying to reach a—" Claire heard a shuffling of papers and then, "—a Ms. Claire McMullen."

Crushed with disappointment that it wasn't Samael, she wished now that she had taken the day off.

"This is she."

"Ms. McMullen. I'm hoping you can come downtown to the station later today, maybe this afternoon."

"If this is about—"

She began to mention the call yesterday from what's-his-name in the DA's office, telling her that the suspect wanted to talk to her personally, but Trudeau talked over her.

"We need you to check out a lineup to see if you can positively ID the suspect."

"A lineup," Claire echoed, amazed to hear herself talking about doing something she had only seen on TV and in the movies.

But this was real, and the reality of what had happened—

And what had almost happened!

—hit her like a sucker punch.

Nausea swept through her, and she was sure—if anyone was watching her—they would notice how her face had gone several shades paler.

"Why do I need to do that? You arrested the guy there…We have eyewitnesses."

Another twinge when she thought that Samael was one of the witnesses…and her rescuer. Who knows what might have happened if he hadn't shown up?

"It's just a formality," Trudeau said. "We have to make a positive ID before we can bring him up on charges."

Claire didn't want to hear what those charges might be. She so much wanted to put all of this behind her, if only so there wouldn't be such a distraction from her and Samael getting to know each other.

But you kicked him out, she told herself, *and there's no guarantee he'll be back.*

She recognized the absurdity of her situation.

This is beyond crazy!

The more she thought about it, the more she realized the chances Samael was a genuine flesh and blood demon were slim to none...until she remembered the tail and what he had done with it.

Then?

All bets were off.

How could she explain that away?

"Ms. McMullen? You there?" Detective Trudeau said.

Claire shook herself, realizing that he must have said something she had missed.

"Oh—Sorry."

She smiled to herself, wondering what he would think if she told him the truth about Samael.

What would anyone think, other than that she was nutso?

"I said Mr. Harris from the DA's office is available around three o'clock. Would that work for you?"

"I—I'd have to get off work early."

"If you'd prefer, we can schedule some other time."

Claire shook her head vigorously as if he were in the room with her and could see her reaction. She glanced at her wristwatch and said, "No. I can make it. Three o'clock, you said?"

"Yes ma'am."

"And where do I go?"

"You know the station downtown. Just come in through the front entrance. I'll be waiting for you."

"Should I bring a lawyer?"

"You can have a lawyer with you if you'd feel better, but it's not necessary. There won't be any questions, and absolutely no interaction between you and the suspect."

Suspect?...Not rapist?

"I—ah—I'll see you there."

~ * ~

The tightness in Claire's stomach and chest was bad as she mounted the wide, granite steps leading up to the front entrance of the Portland Police Department. A man wearing a straw-colored jacket and blue pants—a lousy combination, especially in March—was standing in the shelter of the doorway. Claire smiled to herself when she saw that he wasn't puffing on a cigarette with a fedora pulled down low over his eyes like a movie detective.

"Ms. McMullen," he said—a statement, not a question, Claire noticed as he stepped forward and extended his hand.

Of course he knows who I am…He's a freaking detective, for crying out loud.

Claire smiled tightly and shook his hand. She noticed that his grip was warm and dry…even on a chilly afternoon like this. For some reason, she found that reassuring, but she instantly thought how much warmer Samael's handshake would be…

Detective Trudeau stepped back and opened the door for her, and she followed him inside. The walls throughout the building were painted a shade of green that Claire was fairly certain didn't occur in nature. They made their way down a hallway, past uncountable offices, and then down a flight of stairs. Their footsteps echoed in the stairwell.

Detective Trudeau introduced her to several people as they went. Standing outside a closed door was one of the officers who had arrested her assailant last Friday night. She couldn't remember his name now, but she smiled and nodded. Trudeau led her into a small room with a folding table and several metal chairs. On one wall was a counter, its white surface marred and smudged from years of use and abuse. On it was a coffee maker as well as creamer and sugar, and numerous used mugs. The carafe was half full of something that looked more like recycled motor oil than coffee.

Trudeau grabbed a clean Styrofoam cup and filled it. Then he poured in three heaping spoonfuls of sugar and four artificial creamers. He glanced at Claire.

"Want some?"

Staring at the grimy coffee carafe, Claire shook her head. All she could think was: *Let's get this over with so I can go home.*

"No, thanks."

"How 'bout a bottle of water?" He walked over to the refrigerator in the corner, but when he opened it and Claire saw several moldy containers that looked like science experiments gone wrong, she said, "I'm fine."

After keeping Claire waiting for ten minutes or so while he talked to the other cops in the room, Detective Trudeau glanced at the wall clock and said, "Well, then, let's get this show on the road."

Trudeau led Claire back out into the corridor. Before closing the waiting room door, he dropped his half-finished cup of coffee into the trash can. It hit with a splash. He and two other policemen led her a short way down the corridor to another closed door. Before they went inside, Claire noticed that down the hall, the corridor was blocked by iron bars.

Trudeau opened the door for her to enter the small room. One wall, she noticed right away, was dominated by a large pane of glass. It was obviously a one-way mirror, but the lights weren't on in the adjacent room, so it looked like a huge slab of polished, black marble. A narrow shelf ran the length of the mirror, and there was a microphone with a silver base on the shelf. Several chairs were arranged around the small circular table so anyone who might be seated would have a good view of the one-way mirror.

"Please. Take a seat, Ms. McMullen," Trudeau said, indicating the chairs at the table. "Make yourself comfortable. We'll bring the suspects in soon. But first, I want to reassure you that you're under no pressure here."

"Okay," Claire said with some hesitation. "I still don't see why, if you arrested this guy at the scene of the crime, I even have to do this."

"Strictly a formality."

Claire nodded, still not liking this, and then swallowed hard.

"And what if I can't identify him?" she asked, suddenly fearful that, in the panic of the night and because of everything else that had happened since—especially with Samael—she might not be able to point out the man who had attacked her.

"It was dark, and it all happened so...so fast...that I...I don't want to screw this up."

"Don't worry. Please. Have a seat. You won't screw it up," Trudeau said, and then he gave a quick nod to the police officer standing in the doorway, who left, closing the door behind him.

Claire was about to say she was fine standing up, but the thought of sitting down was suddenly quite attractive, so she seated herself in the chair furthest from the mirror. After a few minutes waiting in silence, the lights went on in the other room, and the lights in the observation room dimmed. A chill slithered up Claire's back as she waited for whatever would happen next. She took a moment to study the empty room.

The walls were dull white, and the furthest one had several black lines running the length of it with increments of height marked with black tape or paint. There was also a thick black line painted on the concrete floor, obviously to mark where the lineup suspects were supposed to stand when they came in.

She chuckled—out of nervousness—when the song "Toe the Line," popped into her head.

"Love isn't always on time."

"Just be a few minutes, now," Trudeau said, and Claire nodded. She shifted in her chair, hoping to get comfortable, but she found it impossible to relax.

"Will they be able to see or hear me?" she asked.

"Don't worry." Trudeau's voice came from behind. A faint reflection of his face drifted across the glass like a pale, floating balloon. "It's always a little intimidating, but they can't see through the one-way mirror, and this room's perfectly soundproofed. They can only hear us if we turn on the microphone." He indicated the microphone near the mirror.

Claire nodded and cleared her throat, which by now was desert dry. She wished now that she had accepted Trudeau's offer of some water.

This is fucking serious...I have to get this right, she reminded herself. It wasn't a lark, and it wasn't a TV show. This was real life, and a man's future depended on what she said and did in the next few minutes.

The door in the lineup room suddenly opened, and three policemen ushered in a line of five men. They were all dressed casually, and they all walked with the same shuffling gait with their heads bowed as though even the innocent ones were ashamed to be here.

Claire reacted the instant she recognized the man who had attacked her, and almost shouted, "That's him! Right there! He's the one who—"

But that was all she got out because her gaze shifted to the last man in the lineup when he raised his head.

She was barely able to choke back a cry of surprise.

"What the—?"

It was Samael!

His hair was scruffy, his face bristled with dark beard stubble, and his skin was sallow, not the healthy bronze glow she remembered so well. His clothes were rumpled, and hung loosely from his body. He looked thinner and much frailer, certainly not the well-dressed, well-chiseled man she knew and was sure she loved.

It can't be him! She thought, but she looked closely, and there was no mistake.

Samael was definitely staring at the one-way mirror, and a faint smile crossed his face as he stared at the glass as if he could clearly see her through the reflective surface.

Claire still couldn't believe it was him. She looked at his baggy trousers, trying to see some indication of his tail. But even when she didn't, she was positive it was him.

Claire's heart started pounding so hard her wrists started throbbing.

What the hell is he doing there? She wondered, but before she could come up with any rational answers, she questioned if this really was Samael.

It couldn't be.

Samael was a successful businessman who took pride—

Which goeth before the fall.

—in his appearance and his social standing. He would never allow himself to be paraded in front of a lineup like a homeless person.

That has to be someone else…someone who looks like Samael.

But the man standing at the end of the line kept gazing straight into the one-way mirror. Claire squirmed in her chair, knowing that—if anyone could—he could peer through the reflective glass and see her. As he stared directly at her, his lips slowly parted, and he smiled at her with the most mischievous grin imaginable.

He's having fun, doing this...He's teasing me...

For just an instant, his twin-tipped tongue flicked out of his mouth, licked his upper lip, and then disappeared.

Claire couldn't help herself. Her body relaxed, and she started chuckling softly to herself, but not so softly that Trudeau didn't hear. He looked at her, a curious expression on his face.

"Is something the matter?" he asked.

Obviously, a witness had never had this kind of reaction to a lineup before.

He must think I'm being hysterical, Claire thought.

Claire was still smiling, and she wanted to burst out laughing, but she managed to get a grip on herself and nodded.

"Yes...yes," she said. "I'm fine, it's just...I...This is so...so ...." She let the thought drift away, incomplete.

"So what?" Trudeau asked, but Claire could only nod, thinking this was a unique way for Samael to leverage himself back into her life. Shaking off the initial shock of seeing Samael in the lineup, she focused her attention on another man in the room.

"This is nerve-wracking."

"I understand."

After casting a questioning look at her, Trudeau pressed the button on the microphone's base and said, "Everyone turn to your right."

The men in the room did as they were told. Claire saw that one of the policemen was talking to them, but she couldn't hear a word he said, much less read his lips.

"That's him...That's definitely him," she said, her voice low and firm.

Seeing Ron LaPierre again, the man who had attacked her Friday night, brought back every bit of the horror. Her neck and breasts where he had grabbed and mauled her began to ache, and the memory of the emotions that swept through her that night when she was convinced she was going to die all but overwhelmed her.

But then she looked at Samael again, and a genuine sense of peace and warmth spread through her. His gaze grounded her in a most peculiar way.

"Which one?" Detective Trudeau asked.

"The second one from the left…The man wearing the red T-shirt and faded jeans."

"You're sure?"

"Absolutely."

Trudeau exchanged glances with the other cops in the room and then nodded. Leaning forward, he pressed the button on the base of the microphone again and, leaning forward, said, "Thank you. That'll be all."

Claire watched in silence as the cops in the lineup room led the men away. There was a look of stark terror and total confusion on LaPierre's face. He reminded her of a little child who had gotten lost and was confused by the adult world rushing by around him.

Before the officers and men left the room, though, LaPierre turned and suddenly rushed toward the large one-way mirror. His mouth was open. He was yelling something, but Claire couldn't hear what—just a muffled buzzing sound. He clenched both fists and, lunging forward, started pounding frantically on the glass. The thumping sound was distant, like a rapid, muffled heartbeat.

The man was still shouting, and the panic of his face was riveting. Claire felt a flicker of genuine sympathy for him in spite of what he had done—and tried to do—to her.

One of the cops who had been leading the men away came up behind him and, using a billy club, struck him on the backs of the knees. Before LaPierre fell, the cop grabbed him and tried to turn him around to lead him away.

But LaPierre wasn't finished yet.

He shook the officer off and, still facing the mirror, kept shouting. Spittle flew from his lips and flecked the glass. His eyes were wide and bloodshot, filled with terror.

Another cop approached LaPierre from behind. This one grabbed him by the left arm and bent it behind his back until his fingertips touched his shoulder blade. Claire could imagine the pain. In a flash, the cop snapped a pair of handcuffs around the frantic man's wrist. Spinning him to one side, he grabbed LaPierre's other arm and quickly cuffed his other wrist.

Even then, as they led him away, LaPierre turned to the mirror, all the while yelling.

Claire didn't need to hear. She knew what he was saying.

"It wasn't me!...I didn't do it!...I swear to God!...I don't know what happened, but it wasn't me!...You have to believe me!"

As he was led away, out into the corridor and off to the secure holding area, Claire caught a glimpse of Samael as he exited the door into the corridor.

It lasted only for a split second, but she was chilled by his expression. He was grinning like he had been watching a hilarious comedy routine in a nightclub.

~ * ~

Claire moved furtively down the granite steps to the sidewalk. The cold March air bit her nose and throat. Her wounded foot was still aching, making her limp. Otherwise, she would have run away from the police station. The back of her neck was burning hot in spite of the cold March wind blowing off the ocean, and her skin prickled. She was convinced that Detective Trudeau was standing in the doorway, watching her go.

And why wouldn't he?...Who laughs while looking at a police lineup?

And LaPierre's reaction?...And the brutal way they subdued him? It was distressing.

And Samael?...

Smiled at her?

"Hey, Claire!...Wait up!"

Oh, Jesus!

Claire recognized Samael's voice instantly and cringed, drawing herself deeper into her coat collar. She kept walking purposefully down the sidewalk away from him as if she hadn't heard him, wishing she had zero interest in seeing him.

You have got yourself into one helluva mess, girl!

She wished she'd never met Samael, and she wished she didn't want to stop and turn around. The last thing she wanted was to see him...especially after pulling a stunt like that in the police station, making her feel like such an idiot in front of everyone.

"Hey! Come on!" he called out.

The sound of his voice made her tingle as she remembered hearing him speak to her in the semidarkness of her bedroom. She didn't want to think about what it was like to hold—and be held by—him.

Knowing she couldn't ignore or outrun him, she drew to a sudden stop a few blocks down the street from the police station and turned to face him. He was trotting easily down the street toward her, his body moved with such smooth, elegant grace that Claire wondered why everyone in the street didn't stop to watch him. She cast a nervous glance up the street toward the police station, relieved to see that she was out of sight from the front door...in case Trudeau was watching.

"So...how you doing?" Samael asked, not in the least breathless even though he had just run quite a distance at a fast pace. He was smiling, and his dark eyes gleamed in the daylight like chips of black marble. She noticed that he was wearing a three-piece business suit, not the shabby clothes he'd had on during the lineup. She wondered how he could have changed clothes so fast but decided not to ask. He had his ways. She was beginning to think there were a lot of things about him it would be better not to ask.

"I—I'm okay," Claire said, casting her eyes back and forth so she wouldn't have to look directly at him. If she did that, she knew exactly what her reaction would be.

Her first instinct was to yell at him and tell him to go away...to leave her alone, but just seeing his face again—

God, it seems like ages ago.

—was enough to melt the toughest resolve.

He smiled as he gripped both of her arms above the elbows and drew her to him. She was expecting a chaste kiss on the cheek, but he enfolded her in a passionate embrace and kissed her full on the mouth. Claire tensed, waiting to feel his twin-tipped tongue wiggle like a snake into her mouth. She was filled equally with revulsion at the idea and a passionate wish that they were already back at her place in bed.

When they finally broke off the kiss and eased away from each other, Samael was looking into her eyes and smiling a warm, full, genuine smile.

"What the Hell do you think you're doing?" she said.

Samael smiled slyly and cocked his head to one side.

"Now, don't you start bad-mouthing my home," he said, his smile widening enough to show his teeth.

Claire didn't know if she should laugh or scream. Taken one way, he looked positively the embodiment of Evil. Taken another way, he was the most attractive man she had ever seen. She wanted to push him away and scream at him that she never wanted to see or hear from him again while, at the same time, she felt compelled to embrace him and beg him to take her home now so she could be with him forever.

Claire finally got a grip and sniffed with laughter as she shook her head.

"You are a piece of work," she said.

"You thought it was funny, too, huh?" Samael said.

"What you did in the police station? It was insane!"

Samael nodded, still smiling, and taking her by the hand, steered her around so they were walking down the sidewalk side by side. Their bodies were so close she could feel his body radiating heat like a burning coal. And as they walked, Claire kept shaking her head, torn between feeling like the luckiest and the unluckiest woman in the world.

Their footsteps clicked in unison on the cold sidewalk. Their breath—hers, anyway—came out as a white plume of mist that wrapped around her shoulder like a scarf. No mist appeared when he exhaled, and she wondered if he breathed at all.

"So tell me—how'd you pull it off?" she asked.

"You don't think I have friends in the police department?"

Samael laughed derisively, and for an instant, his expression looked truly sinister. His smile hardened into a thin, cruel line, and his eyes held a hint—just a hint, mind you—of dancing red flames.

"I've got connections," he said in a tone of voice that let Claire know there was so much more, but that he didn't want her to ask him...

At least not right now, anyway.

"So why'd you do it?" she asked, still walking. She didn't like walking and talking at the same time. She wished they could stop somewhere...maybe sit down, have a coffee, and talk face-to-face.

Then, she could gaze into his eyes all she wanted and not have to worry about tripping.

"I wanted to see you again," Samael said, "and I figured doing it this way would be fun, too. I like seeing you laugh."

"Laugh?" she echoed, narrowing her eyes and shaking her head.

"Yeah. You know. Make a memorable, if not dramatic entrance."

Claire chuckled and said, "I'm surprised you didn't opt for a blinding flash of lightning and a puff of sulfurous smoke."

"Oh, I save that for special occasions," he said, and there was something in his voice that made her think he truly meant it.

"Like when you come to claim someone's soul or something?"

"Yeah. That'd be one of the times."

Claire drew to a sudden halt and looked directly at him.

"You mean it, don't you?" she asked as gnawing worry filled her gut.

Samael appeared to be taken aback by her vehemence. He regarded her as if he was sizing her up as he shook his head up and down.

"No," he finally said. "I was kidding."

Claire stared at him for a long, tense moment, studying him carefully. Seeing him in blinding bright daylight, she found it impossible to believe he was a genuine demon, and not a person. At the same time, though, she couldn't stop thinking that there were so many things about him that made it impossible to think he wasn't a demon.

"So how'd you change your clothes so fast?" she finally asked. "I was barely out of there, and you show up in a three-piece suit, now."

A sudden blast of cold wind off the ocean grabbed her by the neck and blew her red hair forward so she was looking at him down a long, flickering red tunnel of flames. The view made her shiver. Before he could answer her, though, she noticed the Starbucks across the street and said, "Come on. You want a coffee or something?"

Samael nodded and, still holding her hand, waited for the traffic to pass and then guided her across the street.

When he opened the coffee shop's door for her, a tiny bell jingled. Claire noticed that Samael winced when the bell rang, and she was about to say, "What, did another angel get his wings?" but she didn't as they walked up to the counter to order.

She did file that little fact away, though…that tinkling bells seemed to bother him. She might be able to use that if he ever got out of hand. The first chance she had, she would get a small bell and place it on the table next to her bed…just in case.

~ * ~

"So," Claire said, "as Ricky Ricardo used to say to Lucy, 'You got some '"splainin'" to do.'"

Samael looked at her from across the table and shrugged.

"*I Love Lucy.* I loved that show," he said. "But that was a bit before your time, wasn't it?"

"Whenever I was home sick from school, I'd watch reruns of it on cable," Claire said. "But you're avoiding the subject." She leaned close, her hands folded in front of her.

"What?" He looked around the café as he shrugged. "There's nothing to 'splain.' I wanted to see you again, to make up for—you know, for what happened, and I thought it'd be an interesting and memorable way to go about it."

Claire lowered her gaze and, sighing, shook her head. She sipped her coffee. It was good.

"Why?" she finally asked, and when he looked at her blankly, she went on, "I mean—how did you even know I was going to be there? And how in the name of—" She caught herself before she said either God or Christ. "How did you get into the lineup?"

"You want the truth?" Samael asked.

Claire nodded even as she wondered if he was ever capable of telling the truth.

"I went down to the police station to finish giving my statement. I was talking to Detective Trudeau. He's an old friend of mine. Anyway, we were talking before your appointment, and when he said you were coming in for the lineup, I told him that I'd been trying to get in touch with you, but you didn't want to have anything to do with me after Sunday night."

You got that wrong! Claire thought, but as she considered what he'd said, she began to see there were truck-sized holes in his story. Maybe he wasn't such a good liar, after all.

It would be irresponsible for Detective Trudeau to put a civilian at random into the lineup? And he wasn't just any "civilian." He was a witness to the very crime they were having the lineup for. If the case ever went to trial, Samael would—no doubt—be called upon to testify. If he said or did anything in the lineup room to Ron LaPierre—or had any contact with him at all before the trial—it would ruin the state's case against LaPierre.

So then what?

Was he trying to get him off?

A suspected rapist would go free…to rape again.

What was a city detective doing playing Cupid so Samael could see her again, anyway?

This was all complete and utter bullshit, and she was tempted to tell him that to his face.

For one thing, how could he have seen her through the one-way mirror? He couldn't…unless he was able to see through the reflective glass.

But even if he could, when would he have an opportunity to speak with her? She and the suspects were separated by thick walls and bars and glass because he would have been in the secure holding area along with the others, LaPierre included.

"Bullshit," she said, keeping her voice low so the people sitting around them talking or wanting people to see them writing their screenplays wouldn't hear her.

"What's that?" Samael said, raising one eyebrow.

Claire was positive he had heard her the first time, but she leaned forward and, folding her hands together, said, "I said 'bullshit.'" She hissed the last word.

Samael's smile didn't fade, but he eased back in his seat and stared steadily at her for the longest time without blinking. Maybe it was the lighting in the coffee shop, but for the first time Claire noticed something weird about his eyes. The pupils weren't round, like a normal person's. His were dark, oval slits with flecks of gold in the irises, like cats' eyes.

Is this how he appears to everyone, she wondered, *or—like the tail and the tongue—is he only allowing me to see him like he really is?*

How much can he change or alter his appearance to…anyone? And what is his real appearance?

When she found out the answer to that last one, she was well past being shocked or terrified.

Now, a stirring of disquiet filled her as she wondered how much he could control things—even the way he appeared to humans. She wasn't sure where she found the courage or fortitude—it wasn't like her—but she stared right back at him and never once blinked. She could see her reflection in his eyes, but even now, she had the impression he was looking at her from behind a reflective one-way mirror.

She would never be able to see behind it to glimpse the real him because—

Well, you have to admit it, she told herself, *no matter how much you don't want to*

—he has no soul.

Chapter

6

————Two Kinds of Hell

Two hours later, they were bathed with sweat—at least Claire was—and naked in her bed with Samael on top, bracing himself with his hands on either side of her. If she had thought the first time with him had been mind-blowing, it paled to insignificance compared to what she had just experienced. She had held open the possibility that she might have exaggerated that first experience, but—no. This one had rocked her world even more...and much better—more fulfilling and satisfying, if that was possible. It was like nothing she had experienced or even imagined before with a man.

Then again, she had to remind herself, *he's not a man.*

Under any other circumstances, she might have used the word "heavenly."

Samael's skin was flushed, and in the dimming light of a late winter afternoon seeping through the curtains, tinged with a deep reddish glow that seemed to come from inside him.

Like he's on fire on the inside.

Whenever she touched him, no matter what part of his body, an intense heat radiated from him that was almost to the point of being uncomfortable. But he never seemed to sweat. Even now, after an hour-long bout of lovemaking, his flesh was dry and warm.

"Wow," she said, smiling at him as she gazed up into his eyes. As it turned out, she hadn't needed to ring a little bell to slow down or stop him. There had been no time to get one, anyway.

"Um-hmm...I'll say," Samael replied, not even a bit breathless.

"Yeah."

He rolled off of her and flopped down on the mattress, making the bedspring squeak.

As satiated as she was, Claire decided they needed to talk. It bothered her that she could never figure out if he was lying to her...Maybe he didn't say the exact opposite of what he meant, and maybe he didn't really lie to her, but he twisted his words, giving them nuance and shades of meaning that hinted at things below the surface, sometimes sinister. It was something she was going to have to get used to if they were going to spend any more time together.

And she did want to spend more time with him.

She cleared her throat, determined there wouldn't be any "elephants in the living room," as they say; but she also didn't want to risk saying the wrong thing and pushing—or driving—him away again.

She chuckled to herself and, sighing, shook her head.

"What is it?" Samael asked.

Claire almost said, Come on. You can read my mind...so you already know, but she wasn't absolutely convinced he could read minds. Maybe it was a simple case of him having a much deeper understanding of human nature, having been among humanity for...

How long?...She had no idea. Maybe thousands of years?

He easily could be centuries...even millennia old. She wanted to ask him, but not yet...not now...

Why ruin the afterglow?

"I was thinking...about what you did today...about getting into the lineup."

There you go, she thought, having—like him—successfully avoided what she really wanted or needed to talk about. Now you're getting the hang of it.

She was privately amused and pleased with herself.

Let's see if I can lie to or at least try to deceive a demon and get away with it.

"What were you thinking, pulling a stunt like that?"

Samael rolled over onto his back and laced his hands behind his head, smiling as he stared up at the ceiling. His profile was stunning...statuesque, even. Greeks and Romans should have—may have—sculpted him. Claire looked at his thick, dark hair and reminded herself to check for any horns when she got a chance.

Maybe when he's sleeping...if he ever sleeps.

When he sighed, she could have sworn a faint puff of smoke drifted from his mouth and nostrils like if he was exhaling the smoke of a postcoital cigarette. She chuckled again—louder this time—wondering if that constituted smoking after having sex.

"I wanted to see you again," Samael said almost dreamily. "It's that simple. So I did what I had to do."

"Seriously?" She wanted to believe him, but after all, he was a being who existed to screw around with people...create mayhem and get them to damn themselves.

Well he's certainly created enough mayhem in my life!

"Yeah. Seriously." He shifted on the bed as though trying to get comfortable. Maybe he was lying on his tail.

"And you don't think you could have come up with something a little less...dramatic?"

"What do you mean?"

"I mean, I was there to identify the man who tried to rape me. He could have killed me. You didn't think that might—you know, upset me at least a little that you're just...playing around?"

"I didn't think I was playing around...I guess I didn't think that all the way through." He turned away for a moment, his eyes blinking rapidly, and then looked at her with an intensity that was palpable. His gold-flecked eyes glistened. "I'm not sure what's happening here." His fingers lazily twirled through her red curls.

"But I—I find myself genuinely attracted to you, and I think maybe…maybe for all the wrong reasons."

His words stunned her. A comment like that—"for all the wrong reasons"—was not what she wanted to hear…especially when she was lying in her own bed next to the man who had just pleasured her so intensely.

Samael looked away again, his eyes focused on some far-off point in the distance.

Uh-oh, she thought…*Here it comes. He's gonna use this to leave and never come back, now that he's had his conquest.*

"Well, right or wrong," Claire said, not sure where the words were coming from, "I'm glad we met and…did this."

"You have no idea how much I do, too."

Again, Claire had to wonder how much—if anything—he said was true and how much he was still toying with her, trying to manipulate her. For the first—but not the last—time, she considered that it might be a simple fact of their relationship that she would always be left wondering.

That is, if this even is a relationship…

"I guess your little ploy worked, then," she said, brushing her hand across his chest and marveling at the smooth hardness of his flesh and the rock-solid muscles beneath. As much as the simple act of touching him turned her on, she checked herself because she was filled with a sudden urge to ask him point-blank if he really meant it. She didn't say a word, though, because she still believed she couldn't trust his word on anything.

Rule Number One when dealing with demons, she decided, was: Never take what a demon says at face value.

"So what happens next?" she asked, after a long silence where he just lay there on his back looking up at the ceiling, and she caressed him. She resisted the temptation to take his tail in hand and maybe—she smiled at the terrifying and beautiful attraction of the thought—starting in again.

"What, you mean with LaPierre?"

No! I mean about us, you dummy! She wanted to say but didn't.

"Uh—yeah…What's gonna happen to him?"

She looked directly into his eyes to see if he gave any indication that he knew she had just...well, maybe not lied to him again, but certainly "diverted" him again.

"The police have statements from you and me, and now that you've positively identified him, the DA's office will move ahead and prosecute him. He'll be arraigned in District Court—if he hasn't been already, and they'll determine if he can post bail before he stands trial."

"Post bail?" Claire was stunned. "Are you kidding me? He might get out?"

A faint smile touched the corners of Samael's mouth, but he looked at her, his gold-flecked eyes flat, his expression impossible to read.

"All part of the Great American Legal System, don't yah know."

The way he said that reminded Claire of a movie she'd seen years ago called *The Devil's Advocate*. She wondered if Samael hadn't told the truth about what he did for work and was, himself, a lawyer. It would make sense. He had told her he was in business of buying and selling and maybe trading...but he easily could have lied to her.

"But he—you're telling me a man who...who attacks and...and molests a woman in alleyways may walk free?"

She couldn't accept that her attacker wasn't facing mandatory life in prison or even the death penalty for what he had done. It's what he deserved.

"It all depends," Samael said, and the way he spoke so casually sent a ripple of chills racing through her. She had the distinct impression he was hinting or implying—without coming right out and saying as much—that he could easily take care of things for her if she wished...or maybe even if she didn't wish.

"What do you think should happen to him?" he asked.

His question drew her up short because the first thing that popped into her mind wasn't the terror she had felt that night when she was convinced she was not only going to be raped, she was going to die. That memory was still sharp and clear inside her, and she had no doubts that it would remain inside her for the rest of her life, a kind of PTSD, which—she knew—was very real for many victims of rape and attempted rape.

No, the first image that came to mind was the expression on Ron LaPierre's face when he ran toward the one-way mirror and started screaming at her because he knew she was behind the glass. There was no way he could have seen her, so he must have been looking at the reflection of his own terror-stricken face. She hadn't heard anything he said because of the soundproofing, but she had no doubt what it was.

He had been screaming that he was innocent...that he'd been framed...that he could never have done such a horrible thing to her...that he didn't deserve to be in jail.

That's what they all say, once they're caught, she thought, but as much as she wanted to hate him, her first and strongest reaction was to pity the man.

She couldn't imagine the fear and terror he must be going through even now, while she was comfortably in bed with a man. He was an accused rapist. If he ended up convicted and doing any time in the state prison, a man so weak and frightened wouldn't last a month unless he was in solitary.

He had protested his innocence, and the crazy thing was—even not hearing his voice, part of her believed him.

"What do I think should happen to him?" she said, shaking herself, suddenly aware that she had drifted off and hadn't spoken for some time. Samael had waited patiently for her response. "I have no idea, and I'm glad it's not up to me. I guess I thought he should get, like, life in prison or something, but...I dunno."

"Too bad Maine doesn't have the death penalty—even for first-degree murder," Samael said sounding almost sad about that fact, and—once again—she had the disturbing feeling that, if she asked, he would be more than willing to do something about it.

And then she had a sudden thought.

"You were in the room with him."

"The lineup. Yeah."

"What was he yelling when they dragged him off?"

Samael took a deep breath and was quiet for a long time. Claire thought he might have drifted off to sleep. In the lengthening silence, she convinced herself that if he wasn't asleep, and again she wondered: *Do demons ever sleep?*

No. He was trying to concoct a plausible lie.

But she knew...and he knew that she knew...he would be lying if he said something like that Ron LaPierre had been cursing her and vowing to hunt her down and do unimaginable things to her when he got out of jail.

"Garbled nonsense, mostly," Samael finally said.

"Nonsense?"

"Yeah. He was raving like a lunatic, not making any sense at all. I think—" Samael drew one hand out from under his head and circled the side of his head with his forefinger. "—being in prison has broken down whatever shreds of sanity he had."

"That's so sad," was all Claire had to say.

"Sad? He tried to rape you! And he would have, if I hadn't been there."

"I know," Claire said, but her mind was already squirming with the unsettled idea that maybe...just maybe she had identified the wrong man.

No!...That's not true!...I saw him!

But what if he is innocent?

"Do you think he's the type of person who really could—"

"He'll get what he deserves," Samael said simply, cutting her off. His voice was still flat...perfectly emotionless. "Either in this world...or the next."

His words sent a biting chill through Claire. She rolled over onto her side and, propping her head on the palm of her hand, gazed at him. In the dwindling daylight, his body looked magnificent. The mere sight of it filled her with desperate, sudden lust, but she commanded herself to ignore it while, at the same time, she tried not to feel even a shred of pity for the man who had so threatened and terrified her.

"What he deserves," she repeated softly. "Who was it who said something about if we all got what we deserved we'd all get a good whipping?"

"Shakespeare," Samael said, and he shook his head as though the name evoked a sad, disappointing memory for him. "Now Marlowe," he said softly as if to himself. "He was something else."

Claire wasn't sure what he was talking about, so she let it pass without comment. Besides, her mind was filled with thoughts about Ron LaPierre. The DA's assistant had said he was desperate to speak with her, and today she had seen the abject fear bordering on terror in his eyes.

The thought wouldn't go away.

What if he's innocent?

It unnerved her more than she could say.

And she had to ask herself if she could live with the guilt of knowing she had sent the wrong man...an innocent person to jail and ruined his life by falsely identifying him.

No, she thought, gritting her teeth with sudden determination. *It was him! I was right!...I'm positive!...And he deserves everything bad that's coming to him for what he did...or tried to do!*

As much as she tried to convince herself of this, though, she was left with the nagging thought that maybe...just maybe...there was a slight possibility she was wrong. She wanted to talk about this with Samael...to see what he thought, but she acknowledged that she couldn't believe a word he said. Even if she thought or said the exact opposite of what he suggested, that, too, might all be part of his plan to deceive her.

For what?

To get possession of my soul...Isn't that what demons do?

"Plots within plots," she said softly to herself, and Samael, lying there beside her, didn't even bother to ask what she meant by that.

Hell, he probably already knew...but damned if Claire could tell.

~ * ~

It was night by the time they roused themselves from bed. At some point, they heard Sally come home. Claire glanced at the clock radio by her bedside and saw that it was well past nine o'clock. Sally knocked around in the kitchen for a while, probably rustling up something to eat, and then she went into her bedroom and closed and locked the door. Claire couldn't tell if she had anyone with her, but she doubted it. She would have heard muffled conversation and—no doubt—Sally's giggles. The sad truth was, Sally wasn't very lucky with men.

"I should be going," Samael said, his voice husky in the darkened room.

The mere sound of his voice made Claire want to tell him no and pin him down on the bed. Tie him down if she had to, but then—what would that make her? She knew, of course, especially since he was a demon, that there was no way she could command or control him. Still...it'd be fun to try.

"You sure?" She hoped she masked her disappointment.

Samael grunted as he swung his legs from the bed to the floor. Claire couldn't help but look down at the perfectly smooth junction between his legs. She could almost convince herself that he did have something there, and that it was only the dim lighting in the room—ambient light from the city outside—that only made it look like he had no genitals.

Besides, what did it matter when he could do what he did with his tail?

She'd been to bed with enough men who had the usual equipment and had no idea what to do with it. One thing she could say for Samael—he sure knew how to pleasure a woman.

Claire smiled to herself, wondering how different her life would have been if she'd adopted such a forgiving attitude with the other men in her life.

"You have to work in the morning," he said, "and I have some unfinished business to take care of tonight."

"This late?"

He nodded.

"What kind of business?" Claire said, imagining all sorts of unspeakable horrors—claiming souls, corrupting people, sending them screaming to Hell.

Samael smiled, his eyes sparkling, and his wide, white teeth glowing eerily in the semidarkness.

"I left the office to come down to the police station to see you today. There's still a mountain of paperwork sitting on my desk."

Claire couldn't help but snicker. A demon, she assumed, had one and only one job, and that was to collect damned souls. She had trouble imagining him as an overworked, stressed-out corporate bureaucrat, but in a funny way, it made sense. Any bureaucracy—even the stupid little one she dealt with five days a week at Montressor Chemicals—was her definition of Hell.

He started to stand up to get dressed, but she stopped him with a gentle touch on the arm. He sat back down on the bed and looked at her with unmitigated tenderness.

"The answer is no," he said gently.

"What makes you so sure you know what I was going to ask?"

Samael's smile widened as he said, "Because it's the question any woman would ask at this precise moment."

"Oh? And what is that?" Claire asked, offended by being lumped in with "any" other woman.

"You were going to ask if I'm married," Samael said simply. The toneless quality of his voice was as irritating as the fact that he was absolutely right—that had been the question at the tip of her tongue, and she realized at that moment that she would never get away with it if she tried to lie or deceive him.

Good, she thought. *A relationship can't be built on lies.*

She took a breath, held it, and then asked another question that was on her mind.

"Can you read minds…my mind?"

It just burst out of her. She wasn't sure why. She tensed because she knew—and was fairly certain he already knew—that she wouldn't trust his answer, anyway…no matter what it was.

Samael smiled at her with genuine affection in his eyes.

"I can't," he said. He raised his right hand. "Honest. It's just that I...I have a vast amount of experience with humans."

The way he said the word humans drove home the point that, other than his form, he wasn't the least bit "human." Never had been...Never would be. Again, Claire thought that no matter how she felt when she was with him and no matter how he made her feel in bed, she should end this now.

What if it's already too late? She wondered.

What if I'm already doomed?

What if I'm already damned?

A flood of questions filled her, but she pushed them all aside and tried to revel in the mere sight of him. She watched silently as he got finished dressing and then turned to her. Extending his arms for a hug, he approached her. Still naked, and a bit self-conscious, Claire moved toward him as if in a dream. When they met and embraced, his body heat and the faint spicy smell of his skin made her dizzy. She vaguely wondered if this was one of the ways he had of getting to her and controlling her, but for the moment, she didn't care.

They separated enough so they could kiss, which went on so long Claire's knees began to weaken, and she literally thought she was going to lose her breath. His twin-tipped tongue darted playfully across her lips, sliding gently into her mouth and then out again.

Stop this!...Right now! She told herself. Before it's too late!

And—somehow—she found strength enough to break off the kiss and embrace, and push him away. She knew she couldn't have done that if he had really wanted to keep holding on to her.

Gotta get me a little bell and see what that does, she thought.

Samael looked at her with an amused grin.

"I guess you've had enough of me, huh?" he said.

Claire was speechless. All she could do was shake her head no and stare at him. Then, just like the last time he had been here, he turned suddenly and walked away without another word.

Well, then...if I'm damned, I'm damned, she thought, *so that's how it's going to be.*

She wasn't sure if she should laugh or cry.

~ * ~

This is what happened that night, but Claire didn't find out about it right away. Her first hint came two days later—on Wednesday—when she was preparing breakfast, and the TV was on. The news reported that a man who had been arraigned recently in a criminal case and was out on bail had jumped off the balcony of his condo in the West End. Even before the Channel Six newscaster said the name, Claire knew what was coming.

After the newscaster said the name "Ron LaPierre," she didn't hear anything else.

She didn't need to.

She could put the pieces together herself, even if the news team or even the cops didn't have all the facts.

It turns out she was dead wrong, but she didn't find out about that until later, too.

Samael did, indeed, have some loose ends to tie up when he left her place on Monday night. He hadn't lied about that. True to his intentions, he had driven straight to Ron LaPierre's condo in the West End, where he lived alone following the death of his elderly mother three years ago last January. LaPierre had put the condo up as a guarantee for his bail, which was posted for two – hundred and fifty thousand dollars.

"You from the DA's office?" was the first thing LaPierre said when he opened the door and saw Samael standing on his doorstep.

With the light full on his face, Samael looked like he'd just returned from a vacation in the Caribbean, and that immediately put LaPierre on edge. He didn't like people who could afford to take vacations when he had to struggle so hard to make ends meet. He was lucky the condo was paid off and his expenses were relatively low, but even so, in this economy, only a handful of people were getting ahead.

Who was getting ahead?

For LaPierre, the answer was simple enough: assholes like the guy standing on his front doorstep.

"You a cop? You guys work late."

"I'm not a cop or from the DA's office," Samael said simply with a smile. "But I would like to have a word with you, if you don't mind."

"My lawyer says not to talk about it to anyone."

"I'm not just anyone," Samael said.

LaPierre considered for a few heartbeats. He was close to slamming the door in this asshole's face, but there was something about him—a smoothness and a certain confidence and—

Admit it, he told himself.

—charm that was…well, interesting.

"If you're a reporter or something," LaPierre said, "you might as well leave right now, too. I ain't making any statements to anyone."

He craned his neck to see past Samael in the doorway to see if there was a fleet of news trucks with cameramen and soundmen streaming into the parking lot, swarming like hornets on the front lawn.

"I'm not a reporter, either," Samael said simply.

He cast a glance over his shoulder to see what LaPierre was looking at, but he saw no one there—just the quarter moon over his left shoulder. A good omen, he thought as he turned back to the man.

"It does, however, concern your recent legal troubles—"

LaPierre's shoulders dropped as if he were bearing the weight of the world. Shaking his head, he started to close the door in Samael's face, but Samael placed a foot in the doorjamb, blocking him. Of course, he had the physical strength to force his way into the condo and do whatever the Hell he wanted to, but that wasn't the way he operated.

This was a game much more complicated than chess.

The first rule was: The victim—and, yes, that's how Samael thought of them all, even Claire, as victims—had to damn himself or herself by their own word. The first step toward accomplishing that was that the victim had to invite him into his or her house. Claire had done that, but for reasons he still wasn't entirely ready to admit to, he had delayed her invitation to damnation too long. She was special to him in ways no other human had ever been.

He still wasn't precisely sure why or how.

It certainly wasn't—He cringed, just thinking the word—*love*.

LaPierre, on the other hand, was easy. He could be persuaded to damn himself eternally within an hour, tops…Hell, in the state he was in right now, it might take no more than five or ten minutes.

Yes, Samael was that good, and he knew it. How else had he been promoted through the demonic ranks so fast?

"Mr. LaPierre," he said. "I'll only take a few minutes of your time. I promise."

They made sudden and intense eye contact, and at that moment, Samael realized one slight miscalculation he had made when he manipulated LaPierre last Friday night. There was no way he could have even wanted to attack—much less rape—Claire, because LaPierre was gay.

No wonder today in the lineup room he had been screaming and carrying on so.

"I didn't do it!…There's no way I did it!"

Sure, he might feel inclined from time to time to get a little rough when he was with someone…and maybe, especially when he'd been drinking…he might force himself on a less than willing partner, but that partner most definitely would have been a man. His type was a middle-aged, tall, dark, and chiseled man…

Much like the one standing outside his front door at this very moment.

Tonight, though, LaPierre was so distraught with his pending legal problems that he didn't delude himself. There was no way a man this good-looking would be willing to offer LaPierre anything he really wanted…

Then again, wouldn't it be nice to allow him into his home and play out the fantasy, if only in his mind?

Why the Hell not?

"Sure," LaPierre said. "Sure…Come on in."

Ah, good, Samael thought.

LaPierre let his shoulder slouch and his head drop as though he'd already suffered defeat and rejection as he swung the door wide open so Samael could enter. As Samael walked past him, LaPierre caught a faint whiff of his scent. It was a curious blend that, unfortunately, reminded him of Alex, his most serious lover of several years ago.

"I'm sorry," LaPierre said, pausing for a moment, "but I didn't get your name."

"Samael," was the reply, and LaPierre was left hanging, wondering if that was his first or last name.

Regardless, "Mr. Samael" followed LaPierre down a short hallway into a compact living room. A small fire blazed away in the fireplace, lighting the walls with a friendly orange glow.

"Cold nights," LaPierre said, as if he needed to explain. "Drives the chill away."

"Reminds me of home," Samael said pleasantly. He was positive LaPierre missed the irony.

The room was tastefully decorated with old—not antique, but old—furniture that looked like it belonged more to an old grandmother than a middle-aged gay man. How embarrassing. Samael could see that LaPierre appreciated the finer things in life but, frugal Yankee that he was, he hadn't seen the need to get rid of his mother's perfectly functional and very ugly furniture after she died. One wall of the living room had a floor-to-ceiling bookcase filled with all the right books, mostly history, fiction, and—surprisingly—numerous books about dogs.

That struck Samael as odd.

Why so many books about dogs but not own a dog?

Just as well, he decided. He didn't like dogs any more than he liked cats, and dogs certainly didn't like him, since they all, indeed, went to heaven.

Also on the walls were several paintings and drawings of amateur but quite good quality. They were tastefully arranged and appeared to have all been done by the same artist.

"Please," LaPierre said, motioning toward a comfortable chair that was angled toward the fireplace. "Have a seat."

As Samael sat, LaPierre took the chair's twin, which was also angled toward the fireplace, and sat down.

Samael noticed that LaPierre's hands were trembling slightly. For several seconds, they both sat staring silently into the flickering blaze. It really did remind Samael of home...

"So...would you care for a drink? Scotch, perhaps...or rum? A cup of coffee or tea?"

"I'm fine," Samael said, waving his hand, but even as he spoke, he experienced something—

An emotion!

—he hadn't experienced for...for millennia...

If ever.

As he looked at LaPierre and tried to assess how best to broach the topic of getting him to consign his soul to Samael, Samael experienced...

Pity.

"What in the name of home?" he muttered softly as he shifted uncomfortably in his chair.

"What was that?" LaPierre asked.

Samael could all but smell the desperate loneliness of the man. With the threat of jail hanging over him if he was convicted, he would be much too easy to manipulate. This almost wasn't fun. It certainly had lost its zest. Samael was already running through his mind several tactics he could try.

Should he go the sexual route?

That was the most obvious ploy.

Samael could easily sense LaPierre's interest in him. He didn't need to be able to read minds to know that. From the moment he opened his door and saw Samael standing outside, he'd had...nasty thoughts. Even if the man didn't end up in Hell tonight, he could give him something he would never forget before he was carted off to ten or twenty years in state prison.

Naw...Samael decided. *Too easy...No fun there.*

Okay, then...What?

Maybe he should work on the poor sod's guilt. Make it clear to him that, if his dead, departed mother was still alive, how utterly disappointed she would be in him. That tactic—guilt—often worked quite well with guys like LaPierre, gay or straight.

But, once again, it struck Samael as much too easy.

Where was the fun...the thrill of seducing a despicable human soul to its destruction?

Am I losing my edge? Samael wondered. *Am I so jaded after all these centuries that the game has lost its thrill?*

He cautioned himself to stay focused. If the sexual and the guilt ploys were out, then so were loneliness and desperation. They also would be too easy, too...and much too predictable.

Samael needed some spark to the proceedings. He was quiet for a moment as he mentally ran through his options. He noticed LaPierre's increasing discomfort at Samael's silence. He should begin...say something...get this party started. It should be—as usual—delectable, but something was putting Samael off his game.

What the Hell's the matter with me? He wondered, amazed at the unfamiliar sensations filling him.

Pity?...Uncertainty?...Me?...Impossible!

Fear?...No way...I'm never afraid!...I make people afraid!... That's what I do!

Samael was getting desperate to begin.

I never get desperate, either!

He tried to believe he'd come up with a fun and effective tactic once things got rolling, but he couldn't stop staring at the fire, his mind a roaring blank. The blaze reminded him so much of home he felt nostalgic even as he hoped the flames would inspire him to get this man's soul wrapped up and get out of here.

For his part, LaPierre kept shifting uncomfortably in his chair, too, wondering why he had allowed this handsome strange man into his home.

Where is he from?

What does he want?

Why did I even let him in?

Who does he represent...the prosecution or the defense...?

Is he a friend of the woman I'm accused of attacking and trying to rape?

Is he from the mental hospital, sent here to do another evaluation, this time in my home setting where I'll be more comfortable...more myself?

Such questions were endless, and the longer Mr. Samael sat there, saying absolutely nothing while staring into the flames, the worse LaPierre's agitation became.

He wanted a drink himself, but he stayed where he was, staring at the man—his handsome face lit to a warm copper color by the fire in the fireplace—and trying not to think anything...especially that he desperately wished he could seduce this man.

He simply didn't have the courage or confidence or the Evil to start.

Finally, Samael shifted in his chair and said, "We need to discuss what happened to you."

That got a vacant look from LaPierre.

"Have you ever thought about the only possible way out of your situation?"

LaPierre let out an audible gasp.

"What do you mean?" he asked, unable to believe this man—a total stranger—would come to his home and even hint at such a thing.

Of course he had considered suicide, if that's what this man was implying. Almost every waking moment, the single most thought in his head was that he should end it all as soon as possible. He would be infinitely better off dead.

And why not?

His mother was dead. Alex, the only lover who had ever really meant anything to him, had deserted him. He had no other family or friends he was close to. Every day, his pointless job sorting mail sucked out any remaining shreds of his soul. And now he stood accused of a heinous crime he did not commit. He wouldn't have wanted to commit...unless something inside him had snapped.

His memories of last Friday night were fragmentary, at best, but one thing he was absolutely convinced of was that he had not, and could not have attacked that woman. That was the only thing that prevented him from ending it all. He was determined to establish his innocence, but not at the risk of outing himself.

"I...I didn't do anything...to her," LaPierre said in a voice so low and fragile it actually touched Samael's heart—with pity?—even as he thought, *I can't feel pity...I don't have a heart.*

"I know you didn't do it," Samael said. "That's why I'm here. To console you."

The words were out before he could consider or weigh them. He raised his clenched fist to his mouth and bit down hard on the forefinger knuckle as though wishing he could somehow bring the words back or unsay them.

"You do?...But...how?"

This was the moment, Samael knew, and for the first time ever in his existence, he was...

Conflicted...Yes...Conflicted...That was the current pop-psych term for what he was feeling....

This wasn't going at all the way Samael had expected it would. He'd come over here with the sole intent of manipulating this loser, Ron LaPierre, and driving him—one way or another—into damning himself.

It should have been easy.

Samael had lost count centuries ago of the souls he had collected. LaPierre's soul was nothing more than a solitary drop of rain in all the vast oceans of the world.

Don't tell me at long last I'm losing my touch, Samael thought.

It was beyond human conception how long ago it had been, but at some point in time since the creation of the Universe, Samael had been an angel. In the mythic battle between Heaven and Hell, when Lucifer—the Lord of Light—had been cast down in the fiery depths, Samael—along with a host of other angels—had denied their angelic nature as well and been cast down with Lucifer or, as many people called him now, Satan.

Is that what's happening now? He wondered.

I'm being cast down...again?

No!...It can't be!

The truth was, Samael did not want to get Ron LaPierre to sell or bargain his soul away. He didn't even want him to step on a bug to kill it. He felt sorry for the poor man.

"My word," Samael muttered, wondering what was happening to him as he covered his mouth with both hands.

LaPierre stared at him, wide-eyed and pale.

"You know something?" he said, his voice twisting up an octave or two.

Samael looked directly at him and saw his frail, frightened humanity, and for the first time since...forever...he felt nothing but pity and...

Compassion?

No!...Impossible!

Pity, maybe.

But never compassion!

He didn't plan to do it, and afterwards, he deeply regretted doing it, but he told himself he had to do something dramatic to show that he still had some level of control over the situation. So Samael stood up and, raising his arms above his head, he disappeared in a flash of light and a puff of sulfurous smoke.

Humiliated by his weakness, he was determined not to see or talk with Claire the next day; and throughout the day, he avoided her calls, e-mails, and texts because he needed time to collect his wits and figure out exactly what had happened that night at LaPierre's condo and why he had let the man's soul slip away from his grasp.

If he didn't claim it soon, he'd have some more 'splainin' to do.

Chapter

7

The next day—Thursday—Claire couldn't stop questioning why she was even trying to get in touch with Samael when he so obviously was avoiding her.

Ditched again…That makes three times. You're out.

She had the TV news on as she ate breakfast, and when she heard that a man named Ron LaPierre had apparently committed suicide—they didn't reveal how he had done it. She had absolutely no doubts that Samael was behind it.

He had to be.

That's what he did.

The sole meaning, the entire purpose of his existence was to drive people to damn themselves, or put pressure on them to persuade them or cajole them, or do whatever it took to get them to deliver their souls to him and his minions.

With a bitter laugh, she thought about how he had told her he was a businessman, involved in buying and selling and maybe a little bit of trading. She realized now—

Oh, the irony was deliciously thick.

—that he meant the buying, selling, and trading of human souls.

She wondered how he was going to try to get hers…or if he had already tried…and maybe succeeded…without her even knowing it.

But he had said that she must willingly give it to him, and Claire was certain she hadn't done that.

She thought about when and how they had first met.

Six days ago she thought.

Later that morning, sitting at her desk at work and staring at her computer screen while reflecting on her and Samael's time together, it felt disturbingly strange to think it had been only six days. So much had happened in that time. She felt as though she had known Samael much longer than that, and she realized now that a lot of what he had said to her—maybe most…or all of it—had been layered with irony.

End it now, she kept telling herself, *before it's too late…Call him…Leave him a voice message…Send him an e-mail…Hell, Facebook dump him if necessary…*

If she valued her soul, she had to do anything and everything she could do to get away from him.

But every time she took her cell from her purse and got ready to call, her resolve wavered…and dissolved when she remembered what it was like to be with him…how he had made her feel.

And not just in bed.

Hanging around with him in the apartment or taking walks in the city at night or going to a restaurant—even when it burned—or a coffee shop with him…everything was so much better with him. She couldn't contemplate the terrible emptiness she would feel if she had never met or saw him again…if he was no longer a part of her life.

Thoughts continued to whirl in her head so much it affected her performance at work. Finally, after lunch, even her boss, Marty, who was oblivious to pretty much everything except the mistakes she made, noticed she was off her game.

"Something bothering you?" he asked her when, for the umpteenth time that day, she had gotten up from her desk and started pacing. Her foot still ached, and she limped as she walked.

"I'm fine," she said. Even she heard the whip-snap in her voice.

"Come on. What is it?"

Marty looked at her the way he would a rattlesnake he'd stumbled upon, lying across a trail.

"Seriously…I'm fine."

Tears suddenly welled up in her eyes. She blinked rapidly, knowing if she cried now, it would be all over. She lowered her head and sat back down at her desk, staring at the watery swirl that was her computer screen.

"You need the afternoon off or something, just say so," Marty said. He sounded surprisingly sympathetic. That caught her off guard. She hadn't told him or anyone else at the office about what had happened over the weekend, but someone might have found out somehow…maybe from reading the local crime reports.

So far, her name had been kept out of the reports but she still might be the subject of office gossip. Someone could have found out. She almost laughed when she remembered her mother's term for gossip: "The Devil's Radio."

"I'm telling you, I'm fine," she repeated as she ran the tips of her fingers across her cheeks to swipe away any tears that might have already fallen.

"Well, then," Marty said, moving away from her warily. He was still treating her like she was a snake about to start rattling before striking. "Just lemme know if you need some time off. If not…you know you're overdue with the Winthrop bid, right?"

Fuck you! was on the tip of her tongue, but she was relieved that he was back to his old snarly self…

Filled with frustration and rage and more, Claire glared at Marty's back as he strode out of her office, leaving the door open behind him. Once he was gone, she got up from her desk and shut the door, being careful not to slam it.

~ * ~

Finally, Samael texted Claire. She agreed to get together with Samael, but she insisted that it be on neutral ground…a restaurant or someplace public. She wondered why he hadn't yet invited her over to his place, and she intended to force the issue. She wanted to see how a demon lived in the 21st Century, but she was waiting for the opportune moment…and had no idea when that would be.

So at seven o'clock, she walked into Chang Shao, a new Chinese restaurant on Exchange Street. Samael said he'd already eaten there and didn't like the place, but she insisted. Sally had told her the spring rolls were to die for.

Claire scanned the patrons seated at the tables, and even in the dimly lit main dining room, she could see that Samael wasn't there. She wondered if he was running late or if he was messing with her—maybe even standing her up—because she had been so insistent about meeting here.

"Table for one?" the host—a young Chinese man with a bright smile asked. His eyes had a peculiar gleam that gave Claire pause. She noticed that he spoke perfect English.

"No, I'm waiting for a friend," she said. She turned and looked expectantly at the door when it opened behind her, but it was a middle-aged married couple, not Samael as she had hoped.

"You can wait in the bar, or I can seat you now," the host said.

Claire glanced at the bench against the wall next to a huge aquarium and then, nodding, said, "I'll wait here." She didn't want to take a table, and then have him not show up.

The host smiled and then led the middle-aged couple to a table.

Claire sat down, but as the minutes passed, she became increasingly convinced Samael was going to disappoint her…again.

And that will be the end of it, she told herself.

She wished and prayed she would finally have the resolve to end it now. She'd had enough of disappointment and didn't need any more. Besides, she didn't need to keep putting up with this kind of treatment. It was almost as if he did things deliberately to piss her off…probably because he enjoyed it when she expressed negative thoughts and emotions.

She took her cell phone from her purse and glanced at the time.

Almost seven fifteen.

Okay, she thought. *Ten more minutes, and then I'm out of here.*

She tried to occupy herself by watching the tropical fish glide around in the large fish tank, but her mind—like a terrier with a rat—wouldn't stop chewing on the things she planned to say to him when—

If?

—he finally showed up.

If he didn't come here or call, then it would be easy. She would never call him again, and she sure as Hell would never take his calls…if he ever bothered.

But if he showed up now, there were so many ways she could see the conversation going. She might express anger…or hurt…or disappointment…or she could make it clear to him that he meant absolutely nothing to her…even though he did, and she was fairly certain he knew he did.

Every time the door opened, her heart leapt, and she looked up hoping to see him.

And every time she was disappointed.

She hadn't eaten since lunch, and she hadn't had much then, so the aromas that filled the restaurant were driving her insane. Her mouth was watering, and her stomach was growling so much she was tempted to take a table alone and order something—even if it was only an appetizer of spring rolls.

But the churning in her stomach was more than hunger, and after one final glance at the time on her cell phone—

It was 7:30

—she got up and left.

The walk back to the apartment was far enough to be irksome, especially since the wound on her foot was still throbbing, and she was tossed between rage and tears the whole way. By the time she got to the building, the Canal Bank time and temperature display showed that it was 7:43.

No show…No call…No nothing.

"Thanks for nothing," she muttered as she stepped into the darkness under the archway.

That's when a hand reached out of the blackness and clamped down onto her shoulder. Before she could scream for help, a voice she recognized all too well whispered, "We have to talk."

~ * ~

Five minutes later, they were sitting on the couch in Claire's living room. The flash of traffic lights, passing cars, and store and restaurant fronts filtered through the thin curtains; but other than a small candle which she had lit and placed on the coffee table, there were no other lights on in the room. Samael said he liked it like that and, quite honestly, she didn't want to see him clearly because of what it might make her think and do. She was careful to keep as much distance as she could between them, because now, more than ever, she was determined to end it with Samael.

Tonight.

First, though, she agreed to talk because she had dozens if not hundreds of unanswered questions. Claire wanted them answered before she declared their relationship officially over.

"Okay," Claire said after clearing her throat. "The first thing I want to know is, why did you stand me up?"

For the first time in a long time, she was craving a cigarette. Even as simple an urge as that made her wonder if Samael was trying to corrupt her.

"I didn't 'stand you up.'" He glanced at her briefly, his eyes glowing in the dimly lit room. Then he broke eye contact and shifted his gaze to the floor. "I met you here, didn't I?"

"I was waiting at the fucking restaurant we were supposed to meet at."

"I know. I...I couldn't make it."

"You ever hear of a cell phone?" she asked, unable to hide the bitterness in her voice.

"I tried to call. My cell was dead."

As if, Claire thought, not believing him for a second, but she let it slide. There were other, bigger issues to tackle.

"So instead of walking down to the restaurant, you came and waited here instead?"

Samael shrugged and looked for all the world like he didn't know what to do with himself—where to look and how to sit or even if he should stand and pace or stay seated on the couch.

"There's something..." When he swallowed, his throat made a loud gulping sound like he was really nervous, but Claire couldn't help but think, *Oh, he's good. I gotta give him that.*

"...There's something about that restaurant."

"What, you don't like Chinese? Or are you like a vampire who can't stand the smell of garlic or...or five spices?"

Claire thought what she'd said was funny, and she chuckled, but Samael looked pained as he stared at her. His twin-tipped tongue flicked out and licked his upper lip, which was glistening with sweat. Then, he bit down on his lower lip and shook his head.

"It's not like that. It's...Did you notice the statue in the entryway?"

"You mean the wooden Buddha? Yeah. The one by the door with the fat belly?"

Samael nodded.

"There are two of them, but one is on a shelf in the corner."

"Yeah?...So what?"

"There's an altar next to that Buddha, and there are...offerings on it."

"I barely noticed, but—okay. So there's a Buddha and some offerings. So what? It's Buddhist stuff for, like, good luck and all."

"Did you notice a little piece of yellow paper on the altar?"

It was Claire's turn to bite her lower lip and shake her head.

"Well, it's there. I saw it when I went there when it first opened. There's some writing on it."

"In Chinese, I assume."

"Yeah."

"And...?"

"And...It's a spell."

"A spell."

"The first time I saw it," Samael said, "it made me feel uncomfortable, so I asked the host there what it meant, and he said it's a protective spell against evil. The calligraphy literally says, 'block evil spirit."

"So what are you telling me, you're afraid of it?"

"Not 'afraid.' It just makes me feel...uncomfortable, so rather than deal with that again, I came back here to wait for you. Honestly, I thought you would have been back by the time I got here. You must have waited a long time."

"Half an hour."

"I figured if I walked down to meet you, I might miss you on the street. I wasn't sure which way you'd come."

Yeah, right, Claire thought, not caring if Samael could read her mind or not. Let him pry all he wants, he's got to know he's not going to get to me.

Claire swung her legs up onto the couch and draped her arm over the back of the couch. The candle was guttering in melted wax, the flame growing dimmer. She wanted to look casual and unconcerned because there was no way he was going to get the upper hand on her, no matter how reasonable his explanation.

"So," she said, "we have to get everything straight between us. I mean everything."

Samael smiled faintly and looked down at his hands folded in his lap. His feet were planted firmly on the floor. Claire still couldn't decide how genuine this sudden humility or whatever he was doing was, but she told herself it didn't matter.

Genuine or faking it, she was determined to end it all here and now.

"Everything?" He chuckled, but it was a humorless chuckle, and his expression was dour. "That would take a very long time." He raised his gaze and pierced her with an intense look. His gold-flecked eyes glowed in the darkness.

"For starters, then," Claire said, "how about you tell me if…no, not if…how you got that poor man to kill himself."

The expression on Samael's face instantly froze, and suddenly it looked like a grimace so intense Claire thought for a moment that he might be in actual physical pain.

Is that even possible?

Could he—or any demon—suffer physical, much less emotional pain?

"Ahh, Ron LaPierre, you mean."

"No, I mean the Pope."

For some reason, that joke didn't fly, and Claire wondered if sometime during his existence Samael had in fact corrupted a Pope.

"The honest truth?" Samael cast his gaze downward again, and Claire wondered if he was looking down to Hell—his home—for strength and comfort. "I didn't do it."

"As if," she said with a snort.

Claire sat perfectly still, waiting for him to respond. Then she let her breath out slowly, like she was exhaling a cigarette. Her insides were jumping when she said, "Seriously, Samael. I don't believe a word you say."

The look that passed over Samael's face stunned her.

There was no way he could be acting.

Is there?

The hurt…the abject misery…the depth of sadness that lined his face and dulled his eyes was palpable. He looked like he was aging even as they spoke. Twisting his hands together like he was wringing out a washcloth, he shuddered. His body appeared to be shrinking…like he was growing smaller inside his clothes even as she watched.

"You have to believe me, Claire. I…You have no idea how difficult this is for me to say."

"You mean the truth?"

"Yes. The truth."

There was none of the usual strength and resonance in his voice. His confidence appeared to be gone…obliterated. He looked and sounded like a broken old man. With his shoulders slumped forward, he stared blankly at the floor, shaking his head slowly from side to side.

For her part, Claire knew she shouldn't, but she wanted to reach out and touch him…maybe take his hand…to reassure him, but she still had colossal doubts that anything he said or did was genuine…She still wondered if this might all be part of an elaborate plan to get her to sell or sign away her soul to him.

Because that's what demons do.

She knew what she had to say next, and the thought of it bothered her.

How could she deal with any of this?

It was totally uncharted territory for her and, she guessed, for most people.

Or maybe not.

Maybe people dealt with literal demons all the time, and this was just her first exposure to what was a common, everyday occurrence.

That idea sent a tingling rush of fear dancing up her spine.

Maybe people were tempted like this and gave in all the time. How else could you explain politicians? Maybe this was why the world is the way it is. She had never really considered that evil might be concrete and literal; but here it was, sitting on her couch and looking like it wanted to jump out of its skin and take its true demonic form.

She inhaled deeply, ran her fingers through her hair, and braced herself before saying, "Do I have to say it again, Samael?" He looked at her with a most forlorn look. "I don't believe a word you say."

She could see that her words crushed him. If he had appeared diminished before, he looked positively devastated now. Blasted. The healthy flush on his face was gone. His hands were chalky white in the dimming candlelight. Every bit of his confidence and power was drained...or maybe they had never been there in the first place. Maybe all of his arrogance had been a ruse...or an illusion.

Maybe he couldn't stand up to someone who resisted him like this.

"I...I understand," Samael said, his voice so soft and shattered she could barely hear him.

They looked at each other, and against her will, Claire could feel her heart going out to him.

Again...

How can you do this to him? She asked herself, but the immediate answer was, *I didn't do it...He brought it all on himself.*

"Do you...want me to...to leave?" he asked.

Claire sat there, stunned, her mind a roaring blank. She knew she should say: Yes...Get out of here right now and never come back, but she couldn't bring herself to say the words. Looking at him, all she could do was remember what and who he used to be, and see how much smaller he was now.

I've destroyed him, she thought, and then, surprised to hear the word issue from her mouth: "No."

Her breath caught like a fishhook in her throat, and her armpits were suddenly damp. Little streams of sweat trickled down her sides.

"No?"

He looked at her. A thin trace of hope lighting his eyes.

"At least not before we get a few more things straight between us."

Samael nodded very slowly.

"And you promise that you'll be perfectly honest with me?"

Again, he nodded.

"You'll tell me the absolute truth?"

"Yes...if I can," he replied.

Claire wanted to ask him what he meant by that. Was he already qualifying things? She had a pretty good idea he was incapable of telling the truth about anything because he would do and say anything in order to possess her soul. That was her biggest fear.

"How about we go for a walk?" she said, easing herself off the couch. She was determined not to jump into bed with him, but she could feel her resolve wavering, and she knew if they went outside…in public…she'd be less tempted to yield to temptation if he managed to break down her defenses.

She didn't admit to herself—much less him—that he already had.

~ * ~

The night air was cold, as sharp as teeth. Even with several layers of clothes and a scarf and hat, Claire was shivering as they made their way up Congress Street toward Longfellow Square. Samael was wearing a coat, but it looked too thin for such weather. But the cold seemed not to bother him. Claire laughed to herself, thinking that he had his own source of internal heat.

"'S cold as Hell," she said to herself.

Without looking at her and scowling as he looked down at the snow-crusted sidewalk, Samael muttered, "Hardly."

The streets were mostly deserted, even this early. No one was heading out into the cold without a purpose. Cars and taxis and a city bus or two roared by. A few people—some young and walking quickly; others, shabbily dressed and obviously homeless—went by with shuffling gaits. Claire couldn't explain it, but she felt as though she and Samael moved in their own little protective bubble.

Is that something he can do? She wondered…*Create some invisible thingie to separate us from the rest of the world?*

She wasn't going to worry about something like that when there were so many other pressing issues.

"So you really didn't do it? Make that man kill himself?"

Her breath came out as white puffs that were quickly whipped away by the wind. She looked to see if the same thing happened to Samael's breath, but she couldn't be sure.

"I told you…honestly…I'll admit I wanted to. I went to his condo with every intention of tripping him up so I could…You know…"

"Whoa. Wait a second. What do you mean by 'tripping him up'?"

She stopped short and held him by grabbing him by the crook of his elbow. His body heat was throbbing beneath his coat and shirt.

"Claire...it's what I do," he said. "It's my job—I guess you could call it my job. I never thought of it like that before, but it wasn't until recently. When I—"

His voice faltered, and he had to look away, blinking his eyes. After a long, awkward silence, Claire started walking again, and he quickly caught up and kept pace with her.

"I never considered it a job until recently. Before I met you, it was..." He let out a faint gasp and shook his head as though contemplating something he simply couldn't believe. "It was all I cared about. I gladly, willfully, and willingly collected souls for my master...my boss."

"Your boss...Who is—?"

Samael cast a sidelong glance at her and said, "If you don't mind, I'd rather not say his name out loud."

Claire nodded, thinking, *"Speak of the Devil, and he'll always appear."*

"So you swear—you promise me you had nothing to do with LaPierre killing himself."

"I can't say I had nothing to do with it, but when I left him, I didn't want him to do it. I—" He gulped and swallowed hard. "I pitied him. Do you have any idea what that did to me?"

Then he told her, in great detail, what had happened that night at LaPierre's condo, and against her better judgment, Claire believed—or began to believe—him.

"I'll have to take your word for it, then," she said. Yet even as she said the words, she knew there was still too much distance between them. She wondered if they could ever bridge the gap between human and demon.

They walked for a while in perfect silence, past restaurants and closed stores and the occasional person. Claire wondered if they might also have passed the occasional demon. Two men were having an argument in front of Joe's Smoke Shop, so Claire crossed the street with Samael at her side. It wasn't much better there because a man wearing a dark coat was huddled in the darkened doorway of the porn shop. Claire was confident she was safe with Samael, but she didn't want to interact with anyone else if she didn't have to.

When they rounded the corner of High Street, heading down toward Commercial Street and the docks, the wind whipped at them so hard it took Claire's breath away. She pulled her hat low and snuggled down deep into her scarf, wishing she trusted her impulses enough so they could be back in her apartment. If they were warm and comfortable, though, she was afraid she'd lose her resolve to end it tonight with Samael.

Get out now, while you still have your soul.

"But do I?" she said out loud.

Without missing a beat, Samael asked, "Do you what?"

Claire was taken aback. She didn't realize she had spoken out loud. When she saw Samael looking directly at her, his gold-flecked eyes glowing in the darkness, she never felt more vulnerable and alone in her life.

He was smiling, and she was suddenly convinced that she had been right all along—that this had all been an act so he could seduce her and claim her eternal soul.

"My soul," she said, painfully aware of the tremor in her voice.

"What about it?"

"Do I still have it?"

"Of course you do."

"But it's what you want, right? You don't really care about me. You don't love me…maybe you don't even like me. You're just using me and my…my weaknesses to get to me, aren't you?"

Samael remained perfectly silent for the longest time. The panic rising inside her was gathering strength. Claire listened to the loud crunching sounds their footsteps made on the icy sidewalk. The wind whistled in the wires on the telephone poles overhead like unseen hands, strumming a guitar.

"Do you really want the truth?"

Claire bit down on her lower lip to keep it from trembling and nodded.

"I do."

"All right, then." Samael cleared his throat. "At first—yes. All I was interested in was getting you to damn yourself."

"To damn myself," Claire echoed.

"Come on," Samael said with a brief wave of his hand. "I mean—It's not that bad. Fact is, you'll hardly know you're damned."

"What?"

"If you were damned…you'd barely notice. The soul's not such a big thing."

"That's easy for you to say. You don't have one."

Samael looked skyward and shook his head. Something—a smile or a sneer…Claire couldn't tell exactly what—twitched both corners of his mouth. When he looked at her, his gold-flecked eyes held a faraway gaze, like he was focused on something far off in the distance.

"That's just it," he said at last. "I do."

They hadn't slacked their pace even though the wound on her foot was aching in the cold. They walked past the Mercy Hospital parking lot when Claire paused in the bus stop enclosure, hoping to relieve the pain and get out of the wind for a few minutes. She glanced up at the warm, yellow glow of lights spilling from many of the hospital windows. On a cold night like this, it looked so warm and inviting, but all she could think about was all of the suffering and death and despair that was taking place—right now—inside that building.

"You're telling me—You want me to believe you have a soul?"

Somehow, she had regained a grip on herself because, as afraid as she was, she had to know the answers to the questions that were tormenting her.

And then another thought hit her.

What if this is all part of his plan, too?

What if his goal is to tease me and torment me with all of these questions?

Samael nodded.

"I do or, at least, I did. But you see, that's what's wrong."

Samael's voice was so faint and strangled it sounded as though he was much further away than he appeared to be. Claire wondered if this, too, was another trick of his to get her to lower her defenses.

"But," he said in a low, gravelly voice, "ever since I—"

His voice broke, and he turned and grabbed her by both arms and pulling her so she was facing him directly. Claire winced and shied away, bracing herself because she was convinced he was going to either kiss or kill her right there on the spot. The wind hissed loudly as it blew up the street, but his voice was pitched with frantic desperation that was mirrored in his gold-flecked eyes when he said, "I had a soul, and ever since I met you, I want it back."

Claire was speechless. She put her hand out and touched his arm. He folded her gloved hand into his bare, warm ones.

"At first, I thought you were just another score—a single chick on the make. An easy mark for someone like me. But as I got to know you—that night. When I saw how you handled yourself when you were attacked, I realized that you'd be a unique challenge."

Claire frowned, not sure she liked what she was hearing.

"You're strong, Claire, in ways I don't think even you fully understand. And you're...you're kind and gentle and caring. I like being around you."

"Well, thanks...I guess."

She eyed him warily, but Samael's eyes were blazing with a shifting golden glow.

"And the more time I spent with you, the more I wanted you."

"My soul, you mean."

"No. Not your soul. Your—"

He paused, unable to say the word.

"My what?"

Samael tilted his head back and, looking skyward, cleared his throat.

"When you sent me away last Sunday, I actually felt pain."

"Demons can feel pain?"

"Not usually like this. For the first time in...in a long time, I felt like my heart was breaking."

Tears welled up in Claire's eyes as she looked at him. He was still staring upward.

"Somehow...I have no idea how...you're bringing me back to my better nature...my angelic nature." He heaved a heavy sigh that was whisked away on the breeze and then lowered his head to look at her.

"But why me?" Claire asked as tears carved warm lines down her face. "I'm nothing special. I'm not pretty or even interesting. I'm just a girl from the County. I don't get it."

Samael shrugged, and a sly smile lit his face.

"Maybe it's your hair," he said.

"My hair?"

She couldn't tell if he was putting her on now or not, but hearing him say that, in that tone of voice, somehow made up for all those years of being called "Carrot Top" and "Ginger."

"I've always had a thing for redheads."

"Oh for Chr—for Pete's sake," she said, swatting his arm.

"That doesn't help, either," Samael said, his smile widening.

"What?" Claire asked, confused.

"Saying 'for Pete's sake.' It's a reference to Saint Peter, you know?"

"Yeah...I guess so."

"Well, he and I had a bit of a falling out a few...well, millennia ago. But the truth is, Claire." He turned and stared straight into her eyes. "I love you."

"Was that the word you weren't able to say earlier?"

Samael nodded and said, "But I can now."

Chapter

8

————Samael and the Detective

The next morning, Claire woke up early—an hour or so before sunrise. She didn't have to get up and start getting ready for work for another hour or so, but she was already thinking about calling in, asking for a "mental health" day.

Mental health…There sure as Hell is some irony in that!

Smacking her lips and wincing at the sour taste of "morning mouth," she sighed, rubbed her eyes, and took a deep breath. She didn't need to reach out or roll over to know that Samael was still lying in the bed next to her. The mattress sagged from his weight.

Rolling over onto her back, she laced her hands behind her head on the pillow and gazed up at the ceiling. It was a gray blur in the predawn light. Thin, hazy floaters drifted across her vision every time she blinked.

You'll hardly know you're damned.

Those words echoed in her memory, and she couldn't stop wondering if she was damned already and simply didn't know it.

It certainly seemed possible.

Most people didn't fall in love with a demon without losing at least a little piece of their soul.

She let her gaze shift over to Samael. He was still asleep—

Or is he faking it?

—with one leg lying outside the covers. The smooth, dark skin of his thigh and calf, nearly hairless, looked like hammered copper in the early morning light.

They had covered a lot of ground last night, but Claire still felt unsettled. She kept telling herself she had to accept things as they were—that she would never really know if anything Samael said or did was true...or a wide open door to Hell.

But she also couldn't tell him to get out of her life. He did so many things that—right or wrong, good or evil—made her feel good.

And how can that be wrong?

She rolled over onto her side and was staring at him, his head cradled in the soft well of the pillow. Her thoughts drifted back to the things they had done last night after they had gotten back to her apartment. A warm glow radiated from her stomach and into her chest, arms, and legs. Her forehead was warm, too, as if she were running a slight fever. The word "content" came to mind, and that seemed apt enough; but she wasn't sure any word could come close to describing the levels of pleasure she—no, they—had experienced last night. Even a demon like Samael couldn't have faked or masked the physical and emotional release he, too, received from their encounter.

She recoiled when Samael's eyes suddenly snapped open, and he was staring at her, fully alert without the slightest hint of sleepiness in his gold-flecked eyes.

"Jesus!" she said, and then she immediately covered her mouth with her hand when she saw his reaction. "Sorry."

"It's all right," Samael said. "I guess I...I'll have to get used to hearing things that used to cause me considerable pain in the past."

When Claire nodded, her head made the pillow stuffing crackle like a string of firecrackers going off inside her head.

"I don't have to get up for work for a while yet," she said.

She wasn't sure if she wanted to go another round before she got out of bed. She certainly didn't want to walk into work bowlegged.

"So you're going to work today?"

"Of course. I've got bills to pay."

Samael's face twitched into a funny expression. He looked like he'd just bitten into a lemon. He passed his hand over her head and wound his fingers into the flame-red curls.

"I was thinking you didn't have to have a job anymore," he said.

Claire looked at him, not sure she had heard him correctly.

"I thought...I was hoping that from now on I could...take care of you."

Whoa, hold on there, Charlie, Claire thought.

"That's—umm." She shook her head and heard more faint crackling sounds from the pillow. "You're being a touch hasty, there, don't you think?"

Samael gripped the top of the bedcovers and tossed them aside, exposing the entirety of his naked body. Claire couldn't help but try to take it all in and was surprised to see that she no longer reacted at the sight of his lack of genitals. Her mouth actually began to salivate when she looked at his long, sinuous tail curling and twitching on the edge of the bed.

"I thought after everything we talked about last night you would...you know, be okay with that."

Claire sniffed and said, "Don't get me wrong, Samael. I can't stand my job—especially my fucking boss—but there's no way I..." She shook her head, determined. "I'm not ready to quit just yet. I can't afford to be...you know..."

Her voice drifted away because of the utter disappointment that washed across Samael's face.

"I was hoping I could take care of you from now on," he repeated, a little wistfully.

His words sent an electric jolt through her, but it was equal amounts of fear and thrill.

"What do you mean, 'take care'?"

Samael smiled sweetly, the most irresistible smile Claire had ever seen.

"I think you know exactly what I mean. I mean we should—I want to live with you, and since I already have a house and more than enough money, and no roommate, I don't see why you can't quit your job and move in."

"Today?"

"Yes, today."

"That's a pretty big step, don't you think?"

"Imagine the satisfaction you'll get when you call your boss and tell him you won't be in today...or ever!" He paused, and the smile on his face now was positively devilish. "Unless you want to do it in person, so you can see and savor the expression on his face."

Claire rolled away from him and, self-conscious, now, of her nakedness, clutched the bedcovers to her body.

"I'm sorry," Samael said. "Did I say something wrong? I didn't mean to rush things."

He eased himself out of bed and, entirely unselfconscious, walked around to her side of the bed and, bending down, took her into his arms. His embrace was tight...and hot. For a moment, she resisted, but then she caught a whiff of his scent—musky and strong—and yielded to the steel bands of his arm muscles crushing her against his chest. How could she resist?

"I know I'm jumping the gun here," he whispered into the cup of her ear. The heat of his breath on her neck sent tingles rippling through her. "But I thought...after last night...that you understood."

There he goes again, Claire thought, back to his same old self, but the moment was tinged with as much sympathy and love as bitterness and doubt.

Maybe more sympathy.

Her heart went out to him, and she recalled how vehemently last night he had vowed to her not only that he loved her, but that he was going to do everything in his power to redeem himself, to reclaim his soul.

"Oh, I do understand. Believe me," Claire said. Her voice was muffled against his chest. The mere touch of him nearly took her breath away. "But I...Shouldn't we be, you know, like, cautious?"

"Cautious? Whatever for? Life's for the living...and the taking."

She knew she was on the edge of a precipice, and that what she said or did next would have tremendous consequences. She was painfully aware that she could end up involved in something that was way beyond her. It would be difficult—if not impossible—to control or get out of.

But he was an irresistible force.

And she was hardly an immovable object.

Slowly, she peeled herself from his embrace and looked at him, her eyes blinking rapidly to force away the tears that were gathering there.

"What are you saying, really?" she asked.

She searched his gold-flecked eyes...eyes that looked so inhuman...trying to see beneath the surface to the being—not the person...the spiritual being inside him. He held her gaze steadily, unblinking as he nodded ever so slowly.

"Yes, Claire McMullen." He took a breath as though this was extraordinarily difficult for him, but he finished with, "I want to marry you."

~ * ~

The greasy-haired jeweler slid the ring onto Claire's hand, his touch lingering perhaps a bit too long. Samael shifted uncomfortably and stared at the man.

"Now this is our very best. Practically flawless. Just look at the fire." His smile was more of a smirk, and he seemed to be aware that Samael was watching him closely. "It's almost as bright as your hair."

"You like it?" Samael asked.

"Are you kidding? I love it!"

Claire extended her hand and turned it from side to side, admiring the diamond on her left ring finger. One and a half carats, and blazing with light. The platinum band had delicate scrollwork along the edges. It was perfect. She had never dared dream that she would ever wear...much less own...a ring like this.

The clerk behind the counter seemed pleased, but it was obvious he was only pleased that he had up-sold them. The ring cost more than half of Claire's annual salary… before taxes.

"Plus, we guarantee that none of our diamonds are blood diamonds—"

"Too bad," Samael said, and then he glanced at Claire to make sure she got that he was joking.

"This particular stone is from—"

"Please," Samael said with a casual wave of the hand. "Spare me the sales pitch."

Claire glanced at him again, catching the edge in his voice that she didn't appreciate. Was he baiting this guy? Please, not here. Not now. She wanted to treasure this moment, unsullied. But it seemed as soon as they started dealing with this jeweler—His nametag read: Jeremy—Samael had slipped back into his old ways. The mockery, the taunting tone in his voice was obvious—to her, anyway—and the icy gleam in his gold-flecked eyes made it all too clear that, under any other circumstance, Samael would have done something absolutely horrible to this poor man who was, after all, simply trying to make a living.

"Can we—can you afford it?" Claire asked, turning to Samael so her back was to the clerk. She put her fingers to her lips, and he got the message to ease off the guy.

"Of course I can…Whatever you want, dear."

She deliberated with herself, but only for a moment. She couldn't believe this was actually happening, and she didn't want to say or do anything that might burst the bubble only to wake up and discover she had been dreaming all along.

"I love it," she said.

"Then it's yours."

Samael turned to the clerk and, in a totally different tone of voice—this one icy with command—said, "When can you have it ready?"

"We can size and fit it, and have it ready for you in…three days, if that's satisfactory."

Before Samael could say anything, Claire said, "That will be perfect."

"Excellent," the clerk said. "So when's the happy day?"

Claire froze where she stood.

"We haven't set a date yet," Samael said, his voice as smooth as oil. "But soon." He and Claire exchanged glances, but there was no way she could read his mind.

"Well, you two seem very happy together," Jeremy said. "Now, if you'll step over here, we can execute the paperwork."

Fifteen minutes later, Claire and Samael walked out of the jewelry store holding hands. Claire noticed that Samael's hand was hotter than normal, and as they crossed the parking lot to his car, she couldn't help but comment on it.

"Why's your hand so hot?"

"Is it?"

"Very."

"I don't think it is."

It was a sunny day, but the wind was still coming in off the ocean. It had a damp coldness that bit through her coat, making her shiver.

"It most definitely is," she said as much to herself as to him.

She knew by his reaction that something was up. And he obviously didn't want to talk about it, but it was clear he was holding something back from her.

"So tell me."

"Tell you what?"

"What's the matter?"

"Nothing's the matter."

"Honest?"

The final proof that something was, indeed, the matter came when he kept walking, looking straight ahead and studiously avoiding eye contact with her instead of stopping and talking to her. She drew to a sudden stop in the middle of the parking lot.

"Tell me right now. What is it?"

Samael tried to avert his gaze, shifting his gold-flecked eyes back and forth, but he was unable to make or maintain eye contact for long. He looked like a guilty schoolchild.

"Samael..." She took hold of both his arms, grabbing his thin coat above the elbows, and shook him. "Come on. Out with it."

At last, he looked at her, and the cold, hard gleam in his eyes returned. The pupils of his gold-flecked eyes widened and darkened. They looked like melted chocolate. His mouth drooped down at both corners.

"If you really must know," he said, still acting like a scolded schoolboy, "I did something...wrong."

"Wrong?"

"Okay, something evil."

"What?" She looked at him with shocked surprise, but he didn't speak. When she gasped in frustration, her breath came out as a huge, white ball of steam.

"Back there—" He twitched his head in the direction of the jewelry store. "In the jeweler's. I did something I shouldn't have."

"What did you do?"

A chill wrapped its fingers around Claire's heart, and her first thought was: *If this is how it's always going to be with him, then maybe I'm not sure I can take it.*

But she didn't say anything, and she didn't turn away. When he tried to break her hold on his arms, she tightened it. Then, with one hand, she took him by the chin and turned his head so he had to face her.

"Tell me…right now."

"I—"

He stopped and, instead of using words, he shoved his left hand into his coat pocket and then withdrew it. His fist was clenched, but when he opened it ever so slowly, she saw that he was holding several diamond rings and some other unmounted precious stones.

Claire's eyes bugged out in surprise. A sudden rush of heat drove the cold away as her face flushed. She swallowed, and her throat made a loud gulping sound.

"What did you—? Are you crazy?"

Samael sighed, the most heart-wrenching sigh Claire had ever heard in her life. He looked genuinely pained, but that didn't negate Claire's anger.

"Why did you do that?" She was struggling to keep her voice down. There were a few people passing by, and she didn't want to draw any attention.

Before he could answer her, she took him by the hand as if he were a small boy and guided him toward the car. Her boot heels clicked on the frozen pavement, sounding like a metronome. He fumbled to put the jewelry back into his coat pocket, and then he took out his key ring and pressed the button for the remote keyless entry. The car chirped twice as the doors unlocked, and he walked with her to the passenger's side and opened the door. She shot him a withering glance before she sat down in the passenger's seat and yanked the door closed. He was grimacing as he walked around the front of the car to the driver's side and got in.

"So," she said, crossing her arms and turning to face him.

"So," he said.

"Explain yourself," she said, "because as far as I can see, there's no good explanation for what you did."

Samael licked his lips as though there was something tasty on them, and he wanted to get every last bit before he spoke. He sat with both hands on the steering wheel while staring straight ahead.

"I slipped up," he finally said.

"I'll say you did," Claire said, sniffing with sarcastic laughter.

"I know…This is tough, you know? I mean, giving up a way of life that I've followed for…well, longer than you can imagine."

Still, Claire said nothing. She couldn't stop thinking about how she didn't want anything he had to offer her…not if it was stolen.

Was everything he owned—his house, this car, his fancy clothes, everything he owned—stolen property?

What did he intend to do with those rings and stones?

Give them to her?

Or someone else?

Maybe he had a whole stable of girlfriends he was working to corrupt. Regardless, she certainly wasn't going to accept anything that was stolen.

"Tell me why you did it."

Samael shifted his gaze back and forth, and then he looked at her. He swallowed hard and then took a deep breath.

"I wanted to get that clerk into trouble," he finally said.

"Oh? And why is that? And don't give me any of this 'it's what I do' bullshit."

Samael's eyes blinked rapidly, and Claire couldn't help but wonder if he was madly concocting another lie to try to float past her.

"Well, it is what I do…or what I used to do…what I don't want to do anymore, but that guy—" Samael let out a watery snort that sounded remarkably horselike in the close confines of the car. "That guy was getting on my nerves."

"He was just doing his job," Claire said mildly even as she thought how she hadn't really liked the man, either. He had struck her as pretentious and a bit full of himself, faking an elegance and sophistication that were little more than skin deep—just to make a big sale. But then, she and Samael were only there to get an engagement ring. It wasn't like they wanted to be lifelong friends with him.

"Yeah, but there was…" Samael sighed deeply, his eyes silently pleading with Claire for understanding. "You have to admit, he was irritating. I decided to take this stuff because I knew—I know that he'll be held responsible, and that he'll end up losing his job because of it. I...I've met him before, and I've been working to...to—"

"Get him to damn himself," Claire finished for him.

Samael nodded slowly and said in a feeble voice, "It is what I do, dear."

"Not anymore, you don't," Claire said emphatically.

Samael studied her, his gold-flecked eyes dark and glistening. She wondered if he was trying to hypnotize her, to get her to accept that he was what he was, and maybe he could never change.

"So what do you want me to do?" he asked, sounding like a schoolboy who'd been caught being naughty.

"I want you to take them back," she said simply.

"Right now?"

"Of course right now."

"I can't do that. I'd get arrested."

"Maybe that would do you some good."

Samael shook his head and said, "You sound like you really mean that."

"Maybe I do."

Samael laughed, and his laugh was loud and booming in the close confines of the car.

"You do realize that no jail can hold me, right? I could get away or get out anytime I want to."

"Oh, yeah? Then why are you so afraid about going back to the store and returning what you stole."

"I'm not afraid."

"You seem it to me."

"I'm not, it's just that it's...complicated." His demeanor softened.

"It isn't yours, and I sure as Hell don't want it."

"It isn't his, either." Samael grit his teeth and shook his head in frustration. "Like I said, I know that guy. He's been lifting merchandise from that store on a regular basis. He's got a system worked out that he thinks is foolproof, that he'll never get caught, but with this much going missing all at once, the owner's bound to pin it on him. It's not really any of your concern."

Claire didn't like the way he was trying so hard to justify what he had done. He was wrong, plain and simple, and it frustrated her that he couldn't see or admit it.

"It kind of is, if I want to walk in there in a couple of days and pick up that ring for you," Claire said, fuming.

Samael reached out and took both of her hands into his, squeezing them so hard it almost hurt. Even through her gloves, Claire could feel the heat radiating from him. His brow was slick with sweat.

"I'll tell you what I'll do," he finally said, breaking the tense silence that made the air in the car seem too thick to breathe. "In a couple of days—maybe when we go to pick up the ring, I'll put this stuff into a bag and mail it—or maybe just bring it into the store and leave it on the counter where that clerk will find it. That will get him off the hook."

Still less than one hundred percent convinced, Claire nailed him with a level, steady gaze and waited for a long time before she finally nodded her agreement.

"Can I trust you on this?"

"I swear to—"

His voice cut off so abruptly, and his eyes bulged so much Claire thought he might be having a heart attack or stroke.

Can a demon have a heart attack?

Does a demon even have a heart?

"What is it?" she asked anxiously.

"I almost said…"

He snorted and then started to laugh so hard it seemed he was going to lose his breath. His laughter rose so loud Claire was concerned someone passing by might stop to see what was going on.

"I was…Without even thinking, I almost…"

For a while longer, he still couldn't get a good enough grip on himself to catch his breath and say what he wanted to say. Claire's initial concern that he was suffering a stroke or something soon passed, but she still couldn't see what had struck him as so damned funny.

"Are you sure you're all right?"

His eyes were glistening, and tears sliced oily tracks down his red-flushed face as Samael nodded.

"I am...just lemme...catch my breath."

Finally, once he had control of himself, he looked at her and said, "I can't believe I almost said that I swear to...you know who..."

Claire was confused, but only for a moment.

"You mean, 'God'?"

Samael visibly winced when she said the name, but he maintained his smile and nodded.

"Yeah. I haven't said His name in so long, it caught me by surprise. But you see?"

Claire shrugged. She wasn't quite sure she did see.

"I'm changing, and before you know it, I may even be able to say that name out loud and not feel like there are ants crawling around under my skin...at least I hope so."

Claire grunted and, easing her hands out from his tight grip, said, "Yeah...I hope so, too."

~ * ~

"So, what do you think?"

Claire's eyes were wide as she leaned forward, her hands on the dashboard and stared up the driveway toward the house...

No...This wasn't a house...It's a mansion.

The first thing she thought of was the palatial homes on the Cliff Walk, in Newport, Rhode Island. When she had been looking for colleges after high school, she had checked out Salve Regina University but had decided against both that school and Roger Williams University because she was concerned that there were too many distractions in the area. The schools were wicked expensive, too, but then again, so was Ithaca where she ended up.

But Samael's home was amazing...like something out of a picture book.

"And you live here...alone?"

"Until now," he said, and there was an unusual tone in his voice that made her shift her gaze to him for a second or two before she looked back at the house. "But not really alone. I have a staff that keeps the place going."

"I can imagine," Claire said, and she was about to ask if his staff was human or demonic but remained silent on that point as they drove closer to the house. Samael drove up the gentle curving sweep of the driveway toward a huge portico made of granite blocks and a wooden overhang. Snow and debris had been swept clear, and even on a cold, March morning, the entryway to the house—as big as it was—looked warm and inviting. Claire could imagine rows of fancy, expensive cars lined up, and hordes of elegant guests arriving for summer parties and formal dinners.

"It's...absolutely...amazing," she whispered, and Samael smiled proudly.

But then—unexpectedly—a thought hit her like a dash of ice water in her face.

But he got all of this from doing evil.

Not just bad things...from doing Evil—with a capital "E."

A sudden wave of discomfort swept through her, and she involuntarily looked over her shoulder out the rear window at the receding driveway. The entrance from the road was lost behind a screen of pine trees. She could imagine a huge iron gate swinging shut behind her...and armed guards—or a host of demons—making sure she never escaped.

What she did see behind them was even worse.

Following them up the driveway was a police cruiser and an unmarked car. Samael and she seemed to notice the cars at the same time. His expression flinched, but only for an instant. Then the features of his face hardened. His jaw muscle flexed and unflexed, making it look like he had large walnuts packed between his teeth and lips.

"Do you—?"

"Just don't say anything," he said, his voice sharp with command. "I'll handle it."

Claire nodded and, sitting with shoulders hunched, she clasped her hands tightly together. Samael pulled to a stop at the foot of the granite stairs, killed the engine, and opened the car door. Before he got out, he glanced back at Claire and said, "It's nothing serious. You can get out of the car, too."

She fumbled for the door handle and opened the door. The cold air slapped her in the face, invigorating her. She got out of the car and watched as the cruiser and unmarked vehicle pulled in behind them.

Samael shut the driver's door and, folding his arms across his chest, leaned back against the car, watching and waiting as two patrolmen got out of the cruiser and Detective Trudeau climbed out of the unmarked car. The patrolmen waited for Trudeau to join them before they approached Samael.

"Good morning,'" Samael said, touching his forefinger to his forehead.

Claire couldn't hear the slightest bit of strain in his voice, but she shoved her hands into her coat pockets to hide their trembling.

"'Morning," Trudeau said with a sharp nod. His eyes flicked in Claire's direction, and he added, "Ms. McMullen."

Claire nodded, not trusting her voice to be steady.

"And to what do we owe the pleasure of a visit from you today?" Samael said.

Sounds like dialogue straight out of a movie, Claire thought.

"I'd like to ask you a few questions, if you don't mind," Trudeau said.

"Would you like to come inside? Perhaps have some coffee or tea to warm yourselves up?"

Trudeau eyed Samael for a second or two.

"Actually, I was hoping you'd come down to the station with us," Trudeau said.

Samael eyed the two patrolmen as if taking their measure. Were they here to help if Samael refused...or got violent?

"Are you sure we can't handle this matter inside?" Samael asked, nodding toward the front door. He glanced at Claire.

How does he keep his cool like that? She wondered.

Trudeau seemed to consider for a moment. Then he lowered his gaze and shook his head.

"I'd rather do this at the station, if you don't mind," he said.

Claire was really worried now. This sounded like they were going to arrest Samael. She was relieved in one sense, at least—it wasn't her. If they'd come here to arrest or interrogate her, Trudeau would have spoken to her directly by now. She was suddenly irritated that he was dealing with Samael as if she wasn't even there.

"Could I ask what this is all about?" she said, surprising even herself with the strength of her voice as she stepped forward. Samael let a faint smile crease his upper lip as he glanced at her, but Trudeau looked genuinely surprised.

"This doesn't really concern you, Ms. McMullen," Trudeau said.

"If it concerns Samael, it concerns me," she snapped back.

Where is this coming from…This isn't at all like me…

Trudeau appeared to be caught flat-footed. He looked at her with what Claire took to be a mixture of irritation and bemusement, as if she didn't have a right to speak. That irritated her all the more.

"If you have something to say to Samael, you can say it in front of me."

More lines from a movie.

She still had no idea where this sudden courage was coming from. The brief thought flittered through her mind that this might be a result of being with Samael…that his brash confidence was rubbing off on her.

Trudeau considered for a moment, and then his shoulders relaxed, and he said, "Sure. Fine. Let's go on inside, then, shall we?"

~ * ~

By the time they were inside the house, Claire was genuinely pissed off.

A hell of a way to see the house for the first time, she thought, simmering as she walked next to Samael from the foyer down a long oak-floored hallway to what she assumed was either a well-appointed den or Samael's office. The hallway had some stunning artwork and sculptures along the walls, but the room she entered with Samael and the detective a step behind was so stunning she stopped in her tracks.

Two walls, to the left and right, were covered with floor-to-ceiling bookshelves with a railing running the length of each side with rolling ladders so someone could get a book from the highest shelves. At the far end of the room was a huge picture window that looked out over a wide expanse of lawn that ran down a gentle slope to the shore. The view was a bit dreary today, but Claire could imagine how magnificent it would be in the summertime. Today, traces of snow looking like jagged teeth streaked the lawn, especially under the trees and shrubbery. The ocean was gray and flecked with whitecaps. A solitary lobster boat tossed about on the waves.

Claire looked around the room. The desk alone surely cost more than all of the furniture in her and Sally's apartment combined. It positively glowed with a smooth, mahogany finish that was so bright Claire could see herself and the two men reflected in it. The desktop had a brass lamp with a green glass shade and a leather-bound ink blotter with a set of expensive fountain pens and a bottle of India ink. It all looked so formal and old-fashioned, but the laptop to one side of the desk indicated that Samael had made concessions to the 21st Century.

"Please. Have a seat," Samael said, indicating the plush leather chairs and couch in the center of the room. The Oriental rug in the middle of the floor had an intricate pattern with predominantly red and black designs. "Would you care for a drink?"

"Not this early," Trudeau said with a wave of his hand.

Samael nodded and took a seat on the couch, slouching down and placing his feet on the edge of the coffee table.

"I could get us some coffee," Samael said, and again Trudeau graciously declined while Claire shook her head. Draping his right arm over the back of the couch and looking relaxed enough almost to drift off to sleep, Samael cleared his throat and said, "So, Detective Trudeau. What's this all about?"

"We have a problem…with the LaPierre case." Trudeau's voice was low and gruff.

Claire instantly wanted to ask him directly what the problem was, but she said nothing, letting Samael handle this. Trudeau had told her it didn't concern her, but if there was any kind of "problem," as he put it, with the death of the man who had attacked and tried to rape her, then it sure as hell involved her.

"And what's this problem?" Samael's voice was low and casual, but Claire was sure she heard a catch in his throat. She was sure Detective Trudeau heard it, too.

"Well, you see…We have video from the surveillance camera outside his condo building. According to the time stamp, it appears as though you visited him the night he died."

"Committed suicide," Samael said, correcting him.

Trudeau nodded but didn't appear to be totally convinced.

"That's still to be determined," Trudeau said. When he leaned back in the chair he was sitting in, the leather creaked like an old saddle. "Now that I think about it, I wouldn't mind a cup of coffee."

Samael nodded and, turning to Claire, asked, "And you?"

Biting her lower lip, Claire shook her head no. She was overwhelmed by the opulence of the house and couldn't believe she was sitting in such luxury. And she was still irritated that her first visit—as Samael's future wife—had been interrupted by this unexpected police visit.

Where do they get off?

But her anger masked that she felt very much out of her element. She still couldn't understand how a poor, underemployed girl from the County could possibly spark the interest of a man—

Not a man...a demon!

—as handsome and wealthy, as obviously successful and powerful as he was.

And he couldn't have gotten any of his apparent wealth from doing anything but pure, unadulterated Evil.

Samael picked up a tiny silver bell from the end table beside him and gave it a quick jingle.

There goes the bell idea, Claire thought.

Seconds later, the door to the office/den opened. Claire was sitting with her back to the door, and she didn't think it would be proper—besides, she was too nervous—to turn and look to see the servant or maid who had responded to his summons. She tried not to imagine another demon or, if it was a woman, a temptress in a sleazy, kinky French maid's outfit.

"Michelle," Samael said. "My guests and I would like coffee."

"Right away, sir," the unseen maid replied, and the door shut with a faint click as Michelle left.

"So..." Samael said, drawing out the word as he eased back onto the couch and rubbed his hands together. "You were saying...?"

"Yes. I was saying that we have security footage showing you entering and exiting Mr. LaPierre's condo on the night of his death. Can I ask what you were doing there?"

Samael cast a quick glance at Claire, but she wasn't sure if he wanted her to jump in at any time or if he was trying to warn her to remain silent, no matter what he said. She gazed back at him blankly, hoping that if he could read minds, he would see that she was absolutely lost.

Before anyone could say more, the door behind Claire opened again, and footsteps approached from behind her. Claire's eyes widened when she saw that the maid was an elderly woman—she had to be in her seventies, at the very least—wearing a bright red dress that somehow didn't look out of place in spite of its formality. She walked over to the marble-topped coffee table and carefully placed a silver tray down. It bore a silver carafe, delicate china cups on saucers, a bowl with sugar cubes and tweezers, and a silver pitcher filled with cream. She had also included a small plate loaded with fancy cookies.

"Thank you, Michelle. That'll be all for now."

Claire noticed the commanding tone in Samael's voice, like he was used to ordering people around, but she also caught a note of kindness in his voice that made her think he was good to the old woman.

As Michelle turned to walk away, Claire couldn't help but look to see if she had horns on her head or the bulge of a tail beneath the folds of her dress. She caught Samael looking at her and caught the twinkle in his eyes. She gave him a rueful, quick smile.

"Cream and sugar?" Samael asked Trudeau as he poured coffee into a cup.

"Black, thanks," Trudeau said, watching Samael intently. Claire was grateful that Samael's hand didn't shake in the least as he handed the cup to Trudeau.

"You sure you don't want any?" Samael asked Claire and, again, she shook her head, no. She was too nervous to drink without spilling it all over herself. So Samael poured a cup for himself, added cream and a single cube of sugar, stirred, and then sat back, balancing the cup on his knee.

"You were saying…"

This was the second time Samael had said that, and Claire wondered if it was one—of probably millions—of ways Samael used to control a conversation.

"I'd like you to explain what you were doing there that night," Trudeau said.

Samael appeared to be perfectly relaxed as he leaned back. After staring up at the ceiling for a moment or two, he let out his breath in a slow, controlled exhalation. Then he looked at Detective Trudeau and said simply, "I went over there because I wanted to kill him."

His confession struck Claire like a thunderclap, and she didn't think—not right away, anyway—to make a distinction between wanting to kill Ron LaPierre and actually killing him. She looked at him, aghast. For his part, Detective Trudeau appeared to take it quite well. He rubbed his left cheek with the flat of his hand, regarding Samael for quite some time before saying, "'S' that a fact?"

Samael nodded.

"Who wouldn't want to kill him?" he said. "Look at the circumstances. A man attacks and apparently tries to rape a beautiful young woman. It doesn't matter who she is—"

It doesn't, huh? thought Claire.

"He violently attacks a person who is less able to defend herself. Ignore for the moment that after the incident I..." He glanced at Claire and shot her an enigmatic smile. "How do I say this without seeming a bit too forward? Following the incident, I came to realize that I was—let's say 'attracted' to the victim...to Claire."

Thanks for finally using my name so I don't feel like you're talking about me as if I'm not here, she thought.

"And as I got to know her over the next few days—a handful, really, but enough for me to know that my interest in her—in you—" He looked directly at her now, his gold-flecked eyes glowing. "—was so strong that I wanted to hurt...I wanted to kill the person who tried to violate you like that."

Claire was flummoxed. When she looked at Trudeau, who was leaning forward slightly in his chair as though ready to spring on Samael if he had to, she felt a stirring of anger at him. His presence here this morning had ruined everything. It was a crass invasion of their privacy.

"But while you're willing to admit that you intended to kill him, you're going to tell me you didn't, right?"

"That's correct."

"And you can prove you didn't kill him...how?"

Samael let loose a low, rumbling laugh that sounded to Claire like distant thunder.

"You already know I didn't do it," he said.

The casualness in his voice astounded Claire. She hoped Samael knew what he was doing. He was one cool customer, that's for sure...He'd already said enough to get himself arrested.

Then again, he was a demon.

Even a detective as slick as Trudeau probably wasn't going to trip up a demon.

Probably...

"How's that again?" Trudeau asked. He was still leaning forward in his chair, the cup of coffee untouched.

"You already checked the time stamp on the security camera, and you know that I left more than an hour before Mr. LaPierre jumped from his balcony. The time of that event is well-established because more than a few neighbors heard his scream and the thump he made when he hit that pavement."

Trudeau looked at him for a long time and then—finally—picked up the coffee cup and took a sip.

"Mmm, it's good," he said, savoring the taste after he swallowed.

"Jamaican Blue Mountain. Nothing but the best," Samael replied.

But of course, Claire thought wryly.

Samael and Trudeau talked a while longer, the detective asking, probing from several directions, trying to get Samael to reveal what he and LaPierre had talked about, but Samael was too wary to fall into his trap, and he evaded every question about that night with aplomb. For her part, Claire was concerned that Samael would trip up on something—a tiny detail that only a detective would notice—and that would be that. Eventually she relaxed and, the visit ended with pleasant but pointless conversation. After an hour or so, Trudeau thanked Samael and left.

Samael and Claire saw him to the door.

Then...finally...they had the house to themselves.

Chapter

9

The tour of the rest of the house took the better part of three hours and left Claire absolutely breathless. There was no denying the beauty and grandeur of Samael's estate. Each spacious room looked to Claire like it came from the pages of a magazine. The living room ran the entire length of the house on the west side. It looked out on the vast lawn and bordering woods and the ocean beyond. The furniture was antique but comfortable...inviting. The kitchen was state-of-the-art with granite counters, stainless steel appliances, even a ten-burner chef's stove with three ovens. And everywhere she looked, there were paintings on the wall—gorgeous paintings, some of which she recognized, including a Pontbriand and two Weigles. She didn't have to ask if any of them were originals.

Upstairs, the master bedroom and bath were beyond her wildest imaginings. The bed alone was close to the size of her entire bedroom back at the apartment. The bathroom had a shower with twelve independent shower heads. Next to the shower was a Jacuzzi that could hold at least half a dozen people.

"Do you swim laps in that to stay fit?" she asked, smiling.

"Cannibal soup," he said, but when he laughed, there was something in his laugh that unsettled her. As they continued their tour of the house, she couldn't help but wonder how many women over the years—over the centuries—he might have entertained here.

She certainly wasn't the first...of anything...for him.

And what was she doing in a ritzy house like this with a man—
No, a demon.

—like him?

She thought about the amazing diamond ring he had bought for her and that they planned to pick up tomorrow.

She wondered if she could pull off being the lady of the manor.

Could she ever order servants around with Samael's cool assurance without feeling guilty and apologetic?

The idea that a "County" girl shouldn't aspire to such riches nagged at her. She thought she knew her place in the world, and it certainly never involved living in a house like this...not one where the living room had more square footage than her entire apartment.

But who says I don't deserve this? She asked herself. *Who makes the rules, anyway?*

"So..." Samael said once they had finished their inspection of the upstairs and were on their way back down the wide flight of stairs to the foyer. "There's still the finished-off attic and the basement."

"I'm exhausted. Let's at least take a break."

"Sure thing."

"But it...it's gorgeous beyond words." She was dazzled in spite of the doubts still plaguing her. "It'll take a while for all of it to sink in."

"I understand," Samael said. He grinned as he said this and appeared satisfied that she was suitably impressed.

"You want to go home now, don't you?"

Claire looked down at her feet and said nothing. She didn't dare look at him because she was still embarrassed about how inadequate she felt. This was going to take some time getting used to.

"I can tell," he said. "You're tense. You've been tense ever since we got here because—"

"Because maybe a detective and two cops showed up, for starters?"

"Ahh—" Samael waved his hand dismissively. "Screw them. I was thinking more because of all of...this." He indicated his house with a wide sweep of his hand. "It'll probably take a bit, but you'll adapt."

Claire looked at the daylight spilling in through the windows to her right. There weren't even any dust motes, spinning in the beam of sunlight, and she realized that throughout the tour, she had never once seen or heard even a hint of any of the staff, however many there were.

"Where are the people?" she asked.

Samael appeared to be confused by her question, but then he smiled and said, "Oh, you mean the help?"

"Yes. The...help," Claire said.

The words sounded so pretentious to her...as if she was some high-class woman or something, not the daughter of an oil delivery man and a kindergarten teacher from Fort Kent, Maine.

Is "people" the right word to use?...What do you call maids and servants these days?...Probably still maids and servants...

So far, she had only seen Michelle, and she hadn't been introduced or spoken to the woman. She hadn't noticed anything obviously demonic about her, but Claire wondered if she would ever be able to tell human from demon.

"They're quite good at staying out of sight unless they're needed," Samael said...as if that explained it all. Claire couldn't help but think it might be easy for them to "disappear" because they were probably lesser demons who could become invisible. She shivered, wondering if any of them were invisible now, in the foyer, watching and listening unseen to them now.

She wasn't sure she could ever get used to always wondering who or what might be close by, invisible to her, if no one else in the house.

"So?" Samael said. "Would you like to go back to your place now?"

"I..." She shook her head. "I'm not sure."

"I was thinking, now that that bothersome detective is out of the way, we might relax and enjoy ourselves. You saw the home theater. Are there any movies you've been wanting to see?"

"I dunno," Claire said, shifting her gaze away and wishing she could sound even the tiniest bit decisive. She wasn't used to feeling like this, but the truth was, Samael was right. This house and all it represented was intimidating, not least because of how she assumed he had gotten it by doing Evil—with a capital E—things.

Get over yourself, she thought. *Relax and enjoy yourself for as long as this—whatever it is—lasts…Enjoy his company and sharing a bed with him…Take it for all it's worth…Just don't give anything away…Especially not your soul.*

"Yeah. Okay. Let's watch a movie…what have you got?"

"How about the new DiCaprio?"

"That's still in the theaters," Claire said, not surprised that he knew she was a fan of Leo's. She didn't recall ever mentioning it to him…but she might have.

"No, I have the next one," Samael said.

"How did you—?" But she knew it was futile to ask.

Just go with it…

"Come on, then," Samael said, hooking her arm with his. They turned in unison and headed down the hallway, past the dining room and den, and down into the basement to the home theater.

~ * ~

Claire thought the movie, what she saw of it, anyway, was excellent, but she was going to have to ask Samael to play it again for her…or maybe—like old times—she and Sally would go to the theater to see it when it came out because also, like old times, Claire and Samael got very comfortable on the couch.

And that tail of his…!

~ * ~

Claire spent the rest of the day and night at Samael's. Sometime around eleven o'clock that night, she called Sally to let her know that she wouldn't be home and not to worry.

"What makes you think I'm worried?" Sally asked.

"Because I know you do. You pretend not to, but you do."

"Well I don't. Oh, and by the way, have you seen Mittens?"

Claire's stomach tightened as she remembered that ball of fur and flesh in the shower.

"No, I…I haven't been home."

"I'm starting to get worried she might not come back."

"Don't worry," Claire said, almost choking on the lie. "I'm sure she's all right."

Sally harrumphed, but then, when she pressed Claire to tell her where she was, what she was doing, and why she wouldn't be back that night, Claire became evasive. Sally was no fool, and she guessed correctly that she was with "that dickhead we met last weekend." Claire lost her temper and told her to mind her own damned business—a bit harsh, perhaps. After Claire hung up, she felt terrible, and she wondered if spending so much time with Samael was making her act uncharacteristically less caring...more callous toward her friend.

She wondered if this could be the slippery slope of evil.

"You'll hardly know you're damned."

She shivered as Samael's words echoed in her memory.

Claire's mother had drilled it into her head that evil never announced itself. It had a way of sneaking up on you when you least expected it and, once you finally realized what was happening, it was too late to turn back.

But thinking about Sally, she knew they had been drifting apart as friends long before she met Samael. Of course they were still friends, and they certainly cared about each other, but Claire was beginning to see Sally as being stuck in a certain mindset...wallowing in immaturity. Especially since she met Samael, she realized that life wasn't about working to support your weekends of partying and trying to meet Mr. Right.

There was much more to it than that.

With such thoughts tumbling around in her head, at the end of a long day, she and Samael made their way up to the bedroom.

~ * ~

As usual, Claire awoke shortly before dawn and leaped out of bed, thinking she had to get back to her place to get ready for work.

"Are you sure you want to go today?" Samael asked sleepily.

Claire wasn't convinced he really slept but decided not to ask.

"Either I do or I get fired."

"Uh-huh. And would that be such a bad thing?"

"Getting fired? You bet your ass."

"There are worse things," Samael said.

That drew Claire up short. Not because she didn't want to quit her job. Far from it. For years, she had fantasized she would win the lottery, walk into Marty's office, tell him to stuff it, and maybe spill hot coffee into his lap for emphasis. But she would never do something like that. It simply wasn't her style.

That didn't mean she didn't think about it...or wish she could muster the courage to do it.

"I have to...I need the money."

Samael grunted and rolled over onto his side. The cotton bed sheets rustled as they shifted, exposing the bright red tip of his tail. Claire experienced a rush of warmth in her lower belly.

"I said it before, and I'll say it again—" He sat up, reclining on his elbow so the sheets draped loosely around him, contoured to his body. "I'm absolutely, totally serious. I'm rich, Claire...richer than you can ever imagine. I can take care of all your expenses with my pocket change."

"But what if I want to pay my own way...a pride thing."

He sat up in bed and looked earnestly at her.

"I can...I want to take care of you."

Claire cast her gaze to the floor and couldn't help but notice that she was standing barefoot in a carpet so plush and luxurious it was probably worth more than she earned in a year. She sighed and shook her head, thinking how insane she'd be to say yes or no to him.

"For how long?" she asked, her voice a rasping whisper.

"What do you mean?"

"I mean...how long will you take care of me? Until you get tired of me? Until I get old and fat and ugly? Or only until you find another woman...someone...more interesting?"

Or only as long as it takes for you to claim my soul for your Master.

"I'll tell you what," he said, throwing the bed sheets aside, exposing the full length of his naked body. The sheets fluttered to the floor like a silk parachute, and Claire had a brief impression of a magician waving his cape to distract and bewilder the audience.

Seeing him standing there—naked—Claire couldn't help but feel a powerful urge to go to him and embrace him and let him possess her body, if not her soul. When her vision cleared, he was down on one knee with his hands extended to her like a sinner, imploring to a saint.

"Claire...I swear I will love you and care for you until death does us part."

"You...you really mean it, don't you?" she said. Tears filled her eyes.

Samael stared at her, his gold-flecked eyes gleaming brightly.

"I do," he said, his voice twisted with barely contained emotion. "I—"

His voice caught, and the surprised expression that crossed his face looked genuinely painful, as if he had the worst case of heartburn in history.

"I swear to God, I love you."

When he said the word "God," any doubts Claire had instantly evaporated. The Devil...or any demon...could say whatever he, she, or it wanted to in order to seduce someone to Evil, but there was no way...no way a demon could say God's name if he were lying and trying to corrupt someone.

Claire was trembling as she approached him, no longer caring that she was naked in front of him. She reached down and took his hands and raised him to his feet. He towered over her, and she let herself be engulfed by the strength and warmth of his embrace. Moving slowly and in perfect harmony, they went back to the bed and collapsed onto it in a writhing mass. It wasn't long before they were making love, and Claire could no longer distinguish when she ended and he began.

They were one.

~ * ~

Sometime later—time became meaningless, Claire thought, whenever they were together—they were lying side by side, their bodies slick with sweat and limp with exhaustion.

"You never said it," Samael said, his voice soothing in the semidarkness.

"Said what?"

"That you love me."

Claire didn't respond immediately. She lay on her back, staring up at the ceiling, trying to catch her breath along with her thoughts.

"I meant it, you know," Samael said. "For I don't know how long, I've dedicated myself to Evil. But now I...I have no idea what's happened to me. I feel pity and compassion for a man I wanted to damn to Hell, and I find myself wanting...wanting to get back something I willingly gave up millennia ago."

"And that is...?" Claire asked. She was positive she already knew the answer, but she was determined to hear him say it out loud.

"I want my soul back," Samael said.

The first time he said it, his voice was low and hesitant, but when he said it again—

"I want my soul back."

—there was iron determination and strength in his voice.

The third time he said it—

"I want my soul back."

—he clenched hands into fists and punched the mattress hard enough to frighten Claire.

She was amazed that this was happening, but any lingering doubts vanished. She took a tiny sip of breath and held it until her head started to spin. Then, in absolute disbelief, she listened to her own voice like it was someone else's when she said, "Yes, Samael. I love you, too...and want to marry you."

Marry a demon, a voice inside her head cried out. *Are you fucking crazy?...Are you genuinely in love...or has he cast a spell on you?*

Either way, you're probably going straight to Hell.

In the end, none of it mattered because this was her life, and come Hell or high water, she was going to do whatever she wanted to do...whatever she felt compelled to do. If it was done for love, then it couldn't be bad. And one thing she was absolutely certain of— she couldn't and she wouldn't even consider living a day without Samael in her life.

If she had just sold her soul, he'd been right: She hardly knew it.

All she felt was contentment like she had never known it before.

~ * ~

"So what do you say we get dressed and go out for breakfast?"

"It's not lunch time? It seems like we've been in bed forever."

Claire's stomach was grumbling. One thing she knew for sure: it was already too late to get to work on time or to call in sick. She debated calling the office now and making some lame excuse about her alarm clock not going off, but she decided—to Hell with that.

"There's this great diner out on Route One," Samael said. "Called Ma Parker's. Good, down-home food. Let's grab lunch there, and then I'll drive you over to the office, and you can go in and quit."

"You really think I should?"

"Believe me. You will never have to work another day in your life," Samael said.

The temptation to do something dramatic to end her employment—something memorable and, ultimately, personally satisfying—was strong. She took pleasure imagining Marty's reaction when she walked up to him and told him she quit. She grinned inwardly, picturing herself telling him what she really thought of him.

Hell, that place will fall apart without me around, she thought. *And—Good God-a-mighty, it would be worth anything...maybe even...*

She thought to finish the sentence *my soul* to do it, but she caught herself.

She was determined not to let Samael influence what she said or did. She was her own person, and from now on, anything she said or did was going to be because it was her decision, not Samael's or her parents' or Sally's, or anyone else's.

"I'll even come into the office with you, if you want moral support," Samael offered.

Claire clutched her arms against her chest and shook her head.

"No," she said, moving close to him and embracing him. The heat radiating from him was intense. "I can handle it."

"I know you can," he said.

With that, they collapsed back onto the bed. By the time they were through, it was definitely time for lunch instead of breakfast.

~ * ~

The sky was overcast, a gunmetal gray that was spitting snow as Samael's car pulled into the parking lot of Montressor Chemical Company, and he killed the engine. Across the parking lot, which was filled with eighteen-wheelers, was a chainlink fence. Beyond the fence were the Downeaster railroad tracks. A long string of boxcars was moving by slowly, their wheels squealing and clanking. The ground shook with their ponderous passing.

Claire bit her lower lip.

"I can do this...I know I can."

She kissed him on the cheek, feeling the warmth of his skin beneath her cold lips.

"I'll be waiting right here."

She felt remarkable calm as she walked up the cement steps, entered her pass code numbers, and opened the door when the lock buzzed.

She walked past Edna's desk and nodded a silent greeting to the receptionist.

"I didn't expect to see you today," Edna said.

Claire smiled and shrugged. She'd always liked Edna well enough, but it wasn't like they were friends or anything. They never hung out at work or after hours, mostly because all Edna did was complain about her physical problems and her family life.

"Marty in?" she asked.

Edna nodded and started to say something, but Claire was around the corner and only heard, "But he..."

The door to Marty's office was closed, so Claire gave it a quick rap and then twisted the doorknob and pushed it open. Marty—the little Napoleon—was sitting at his desk with his feet up and leaning back in his chair. He had a sandwich in one hand and was chewing as he stared blankly up at the ceiling.

"Claire," he said. His eyes widened with surprise, and he dropped his feet to the floor and leaned forward. He placed the sandwich on its wrapping paper and brushed crumbs from his chest. "Where have you been? I've been call—"

"I could have phoned it in, but I came to tell you in person."

His eyes widened. He knew.

"I quit. Right now."

The words were out of her—fast and strong—before she had time to reconsider.

And she had been right. The expression on Marty's face was priceless. He looked for all the world like a fish that had been landed with the hook still impaled in its mouth. His eyes bugged from his head, and his face went ghostly pale.

"You...quit?" he echoed.

"Yup."

"I...I, ahh, I see."

He kept brushing crumbs from his chest as though that would restore his dignity. His mouth was making little twitchy motions as if his mind was flooded with thoughts but he couldn't get a single word out.

Finally, he managed to say, "You mean you're giving your two-week notice?"

Claire folded her arms across her chest and pursed her lips.

"No. I mean now. I quit. Today. This instant."

She knew this was the point where she should turn on her heel and leave, allowing him to deal with it any way he wanted to, but she didn't. She wanted to stay long enough to hear what he had to say even though she didn't expect any surprises.

But there was a surprise.

Instead of the anger and vitriol she was expecting, tears filmed his eyes. His lower lip was quivering. His face looked like it was made of pasty, white dough that hadn't yet risen.

"Is it...? Can we talk about this? Is there anything I can do about it?"

Claire hadn't been ready for him to take this so personally, and she experienced a genuine bolt of pity. His shock touched her heart, and she immediately regretted saying what she had said.

But from somewhere that didn't feel like it was coming from her, exactly, she heard herself say, "There's nothing to discuss. I have to move on." And then, as a token, she added, "I'm sorry I have to do it this way."

"Me, too. I mean...is it about pay? Did you find another job? We really—I really need you here. I depend on you in ways I...I...I'm not sure I can do my job without you."

"I'm sorry, Marty," Claire said again, and suddenly she saw him in a completely different light. He wasn't at all the martinet she had thought he was. He was nothing more than a frightened, insecure little man who, she had to admit, was simply doing the best he could under very trying situations. He made her life miserable only because he was an incompetent manager, not because he was a prick. It wasn't as if his job was any more exciting or productive than hers. And the home office sure didn't make it any easier for either one of them. Given different personalities, they could have been a helluva team.

She was tempted to say something...to apologize...to try to take it all back. Marty wasn't such a bad guy after all, she decided. But as she was phrasing her reasonable apology in her mind, the office floor suddenly started to shake. It shook several times a day as trains went by, but this time, the rumbling was more intense than usual.

"What the bloody Hell?" Marty said, shouting to be heard about the thunderous sound.

He lurched from his chair and took three quick steps to the window overlooking the parking lot. Claire started over to see what was going on outside, too, but she checked herself when a sudden flash of bright light flared across her view. A split second later, a heart-thumping boom shook the building. The windows rattled in their frames. Items on Marty's desk vibrated like they were dancing, and the pictures on the wall went crazily askew. The light framing Marty's face got rapidly brighter and began to flicker with a wicked red glow.

"What's happening?" Claire asked, her voice edged with panic. Her first thought was that Samael was waiting outside in his car and that the explosion must have hit him harder than it had the office building.

She clasped the doorframe for support, expecting the office building to blow apart with her in it.

Some fucking irony that would be, she thought.

If something had exploded and was burning out there on the tracks or in the rail yard, she sure as Hell didn't want to be anywhere near a window in case another, stronger explosion sent glass and steel flying.

"Looks like a train derailed," Marty said. "Must have been carrying something explosive."

The brief flash of light had faded, but it left an afterimage. Something outside was on fire, flickered wildly. Claire could clearly see Marty's reflection in the glass.

A stronger jolt of panic hit her in the chest when the fire alarm began to blare.

Is Samael all right outside in the parking lot?

Without another word, she turned and ran down the corridor, past Edna's desk. Edna was already on the phone, talking frantically to someone—no doubt the fire or police department. Hell, these days, it was probably Homeland Security. Without a word, Claire shouldered open the door and rushed outside.

It had started to snow, but Samael was standing at the far end of the parking lot, leaning against his car, his arms folded across his chest as he watched what was going on. Sharp shrieks of twisting, tortured metal filled the air as more railcars derailed. The flames erupted with a whooshing roar, and a thick column of black smoke that looked like an approaching tornado spiraled into the sky. It contrasted starkly with the falling snow. Dozens of men—railroad and factory workers alike—were scrambling about. From far off in the distance, there came the rising and falling wail of sirens.

Numbed by what was going on, Claire walked down the steps and started over toward Samael. She couldn't tear her gaze away from the destruction. In the seven years she had worked here, she had always feared something like this would happen.

And now it had.

She stepped up beside Samael, who was watching the flames rise higher with a look of pure, childlike delight on his face. And at that moment, remembering the scene last weekend at the floating restaurant, a thought too horrible to frame into words came to mind. She was trembling as she placed her hand on Samael's chin and twisted his head around so he was facing her.

"Tell me you didn't slip again," she said.

"Honest. I had nothing to do with it."

"Hand to God?"

He winced when she said the name, but then he fixed his gaze on her and said, "Yes. Hand to...God." It took effort to get that last word out, and she was proud of him.

"So how'd it go in there?" Samael asked, nodding toward the building.

"Fine...until the train blew up," Claire said. She took a deep breath and took in a lungful of the smoky, chemical odor billowing into the sky. It made her throat burn. "It went about as well as you could expect."

It was Samael's turn now to take her by the chin and force her to look at him.

"You are an amazing woman," he said, and he leaned forward and kissed her full on the mouth. His twin-tipped tongue slid out like tiny snakes that worked their way between her lips and teeth. She was upset about everything that was going on, but she melted into his embrace and let him kiss her long and hard.

As they kissed, the sound of approaching sirens got louder, and the first fire truck came screaming onto the scene. She and Samael stopped kissing and, like everyone else who had come to see what was going on, stood and watched as the fire fighters started to knock down the flames. They worked hard to make sure the nearby trees and fields didn't catch fire from the sparks that roared into the sky.

The fire was, indeed, spectacular, the flames mesmerizing; but as she watched, Claire couldn't help but think how convenient this explosion and fire had been. They had occurred at the exact instant she had begun to feel sorry for Marty and was considering taking back what she had said. She might have offered to work a two-week notice or maybe even said she regretted quitting.

Even though he had sworn he hadn't, she had to wonder if Samael had caused the train wreck simply to distract her and everyone else so she wouldn't back down. It was certainly of a piece with his previous behavior. She loved and trusted Samael, but still...

That's the thing about Evil, she thought. *You start mistrusting everything and everyone.*

~ * ~

"I have to get clear on one thing, all right?" Claire said.

Samael was driving as they crossed the South Portland Bridge into Portland. The snow had stopped, and the sides of the road were covered with a glazed coating of white that was quickly melting as the sun burned through the clouds. Casco Bay was gray, the wind-ruffled water looking like beaten metal.

"What's that?" Samael asked casually without taking his eyes off the road ahead.

"You're telling me the truth, right?...About not starting that accident or starting that fire?"

"I already told you. I didn't start...or even cause it."

Claire saw the difference and appreciated that he would point it out.

"Yeah, but still—it strikes me that...and I don't mean to sound critical or anything, but it seems it might be...you know, that you might find it kinda tough to give up your old ways just like that."

She snapped her fingers on the last word and saw him flinch...just a little.

He glanced at her and then focused on the road, correcting his steering when it began to drift.

"The road's getting slick," he said, but it sounded to Claire more like he was trying to avoid the topic.

"Samael...We have to be honest with each other...all the time."

"I know. I never said we didn't...or weren't."

"So?"

"So, what?"

"So...is that what you're feeling?"

"What do you mean?"

Is he being obtuse on purpose?

"Is it tough giving up Evil?"

"Well," Samael sniffed with laughter and gripped the steering wheel tightly as they slowed for the traffic light up ahead, "when you say it like that, it sounds like you're trivializing it. Like quitting smoking or something."

"I don't mean to. Honest."

"I didn't say you were. I said it sounds like it."

Jesus, why so defensive? Claire thought, but she wasn't going to call him on it...not now, anyway. Let him concentrate on his driving.

"We're not arguing," he said, but as he spoke, the muscles in his jaw kept flexing and unflexing like he was chewing a particularly tough piece of meat. He was clearly agitated about something.

"I know we're not, but I know how you like to stir things up...cause a little mayhem—"

"Not this time!"

He shouted this time, but it was more than a shout. It struck her like a firecracker going off close to her head. Her ears were ringing like Chinese gongs as she looked at him and saw the fiery glow in his gold-flecked eyes.

"What did you just do?" she asked, holding her hands to her ears. She wasn't sure she'd be able to hear him when he answered.

Samael drove straight through the intersection of Congress Street, running the red light.

"Do what?"

"When you shouted just then." Claire wiggled both of her forefingers in her ears and then tilted her head and hit her temple as if she had water in her ears. "Your voice just now...It did something...weird."

"Oh, that. Yeah."

Samael smiled easily at her, but only for a second or two. His mouth tightened, and he drove with more concentration than seemed necessary. There wasn't much traffic downtown.

"What do you mean, that?"

"The Voice," Samael said simply.

"It's a thing you do? A...a trick or something?"

"Not a trick. More of a technique. It's a way I can get people to do something I want them to do."

"A control thing, then," Claire said as chills rippled up the back of her neck.

"You might say that. It's helpful when you...you know, do what I do."

Claire didn't want to know any of the details, but his use of the present tense struck her, and she couldn't let it pass.

"What you used to do what you did, you mean. Right? You don't do it anymore, right?"

He shot her another quick glance, and he certainly looked sincere when he said, "Yes...Of course." He slid his right hand from the steering wheel and cupped it over Claire's thigh, giving her leg a gentle but firm squeeze. "I'm surprised by how you reacted to it."

"What do you mean?"

"It's just...usually people—humans—have a much stronger reaction to it. It has the power to pretty much eliminate any human resistance."

"Well maybe I'm tougher than the rest," Claire said, quoting from one of her favorite Springsteen songs.

"That's one of the many reasons I love you so much." Samael gave her a sidelong glance as though he expected to see something she wasn't aware of.

"Don't you ever use that Voice thingie on me ever again. Understand?"

Looking thoroughly chastised, Samael nodded and said, "I promise," without a hint of any secondary meaning in his voice or expression.

They drove past Deering Oaks and took a right turn onto Route 295, heading north. The snow flurry had already stopped, and the Back Bay shimmered blue and bright white now in the slanting afternoon sunlight. Claire thought it a miracle, how the day changed so fast from gloomy and snowing to sunny and bright.

"So...what do you want to do with the rest of the day?" Samael asked as he sped up the road, sticking to 295 instead of veering off onto Route One to his house in Falmouth.

"Actually, I'm kinda hungry," Claire said.

"Again?"

"I didn't eat much for lunch, remember? I was so worried about dealing with Marty."

"Oh, right," Samael said. The steering wheel played loosely in his hands, and he was smiling as he stared ahead at the open road. "You'll have to tell me more about how that went. Then, maybe, we should talk about when you're going to introduce me to your parents."

"My parents?"

Claire was dumbfounded. A cold knot twisted like a snake in the pit of her stomach.

"Yeah," Samael said, smiling as he drove. "I've dealt with them a little bit before in the past, but we've never been formally introduced."

"You what?"

"Don't worry...I never did anything to either one of them. Not that I didn't try."

"I can't believe you—"

That was all Claire could say, but then Samael laughed out loud and said, "I never met them. I'm just teasing you."

Claire glared at him and said, "You'd better be," but even so, she didn't like the way that sounded.

Chapter

10

It didn't take long for Claire to get used to not getting up early to get ready for work, and while it was relatively satisfying—if not outright enjoyable—to tell Marty to shove it up his ass, it was quite a different story when she told Sally she was moving out of the apartment.

"Are you fucking kidding me?" was her response when Claire told her a few days after she had quit Montressor Chemicals. They were in Claire's bedroom, and Claire was filling a box with her books. Every time she ripped off a piece of packing tape from the roll to seal a box, the sound set her teeth on edge.

Or maybe something else was galling her.

"You can't be fucking serious." Sally was pacing back and forth at the foot of Claire's bed.

"For fuck's sake, you don't even know this fucking guy! For all you fucking know, he could be, like, a...a fucking mass murderer or something."

"Or something," Claire muttered to herself, smiling at how Sally would shit her pants if she knew the truth.

Claire could see, of course, that Sally was equally upset about how all this would impact her financially along with the hassle of finding another roommate. She felt guilty for letting Sally down on such short notice, but, hey—it was her life, and the future was wide open.

"What about next month's fucking rent? I don't have the—the fucking time to get a new roommate. And I sure as shit am not very fucking keen about advertising on fucking Craigslist. Jesus!"

"Relax," Claire said. "It'll be all right."

"For you, maybe."

It was a selfish thought, Claire knew, but it irked her that Sally couldn't express even the tiniest bit of happiness for her. Of course, when she thought about it—that she was moving in with a man she had met less than two weeks ago—it didn't make a lick of sense, but she knew she was doing the right thing.

"Well I think you're insane!" Sally said.

Ignoring the snarkiness, Claire sighed and, smiling, shook her head and went back to packing up her books. There were a few— especially the science fiction and fantasy Howie Brandenburg had given her when they were dating—that she would just as soon leave behind. She had tried to read them, and she pretended to like them with Howie, but other than a few books by Michael Swanwick, she didn't think they were even worth burying in a landfill.

"I'm in love, Sal," she said. "Don't you get that? I really am."

"You may think you are, but is he?"

"Is he what?"

"In love…with you? Or are you just another toy?"

"Cut it out. We love each other."

"Guys like that are just looking for the next toy. He'll buy you a flashy ring and promise you the world, but you wait and see. He'll kick you to the curb when he's through with you."

"Nope. This is really real, Sally. It's funny how you don't know until it comes along."

"Aww, Jesus. Now you're going all cheesy on me."

Sally huffed as she sat down on the edge of the bed, bouncing the box of books Claire was packing.

"Come on, girl," Sally said. "Think what he's doing."

"What's he doing?"

"He's using you, is what he's doing. And you don't even see it. He's gonna hurt you. Mark my words."

Claire wanted to yell at her to stop but found it not worth the energy.

"You don't think a guy who looks that good and has the money he has doesn't have a goddamned harem?"

"Maybe he did...in the past...but this is different."

"How do you know he's not a mass murderer or a criminal or something?"

The sour smirk on Sally's face was almost enough to set Claire off, but she fought back the sudden and powerful urge to tell her roommate exactly what she thought of her and her sniveling jealousy.

God, why am I letting this get to me? She wondered. There's no need to be spiteful or hurtful with a friend.

She wondered briefly if Samael was having a bad influence on her, but she dismissed it and turned back to what she was doing, concentrating on filling up the box of books and winnowing out the ones she didn't want to keep.

As for Samael possibly being a mass murderer...she didn't know whether to laugh or cry when she thought about how Sally would react if she had any idea what he really did.

Of course, she doubted Sally would believe her, anyway.

"You can keep any of my stuff you want—the furniture and stuff," Claire said, hoping this would mollify her roomie.

"You mean the couch...and the TV?"

Claire thought about the TV, but only for a moment. It had been a gift from her folks a couple of Christmases ago, and she had a strong sentimental attachment to it. Hell, it's was just a stupid TV. She rarely watched TV as it was, preferring, instead, to read in the evenings when she wasn't going out. But her parents weren't exactly rich, and it had been a generous gift. She knew her father had been joking when he said they were giving it to her so he'd have a nice TV to watch football and baseball on when they came down south to visit.

"Sure. Why not? I don't need it."

Sally looked at her skeptically.

"It's a whole new life for me, Sal. I wish you could be happy for me."

"I am…I am, but—"

She paused and looked at Claire for a long time.

"But what?"

Claire didn't like this feeling that Sally was envious of her. Envy was a bad emotion, and she tried to avoid it whenever possible. She surely didn't want Sally to think she was rubbing it in her face, leaving her in the lurch like this. Sally had, after all, also expressed some interest in Samael that night they met, no matter how much she denied it now. Maybe she wished she had hooked up with him then…if that man—that asshole, Ron LaPierre—hadn't tried to rape her behind the restaurant.

It was a good thing Samael had seen what was going on and reacted.

He probably saved her life.

Claire chuckled to herself, thinking, *maybe he saved my life so I could save his soul.*

"What's so funny?" Sally asked. Claire didn't miss the defensiveness in her voice.

"Nothing…I just…"

She fell quiet.

"Just what?" Sally asked, pressing.

"No. Nothing."

She hoped that would be the end of it, but Sally obviously wasn't going to let it drop. Claire hoped they weren't going to start arguing again. Thankfully, a few seconds later, Sally made an excuse about having to be somewhere and left the apartment.

Just as well, Claire thought. A twinge of sadness almost overwhelmed her when she thought about how she and Sally used to be such good friends and how far they had drifted apart.

Used to be…but that was long ago and far away.

Here she was, opening the door to a brand-new life, and it was sad that her friend couldn't be happy for her.

She glanced at her wristwatch. It was almost three o'clock. Samael had said he would send some people over to her place tomorrow to load up her things and bring them to his house, and here she was, feeling sorry for herself because of Sally.

"Her loss," she whispered.

She still had all her clothes, her tchotchkes, and some pictures and posters to pack. She jumped when the apartment door slammed shut as Sally left. Claire thought about taking the goddamned TV anyway, just for spite. Besides, whether she needed it or not, her parents had given it to her, so she had every right to take it; but in the end, she decided to leave it. It was the least she could do for her ex-best friend.

~ * ~

The next morning, the phone rang…early. Claire startled awake. Her first thought was that it was Marty, calling from work about one of the assignments she'd left behind on her desk. Maybe he was going to ask her—beg her to reconsider. She felt a twinge of guilt for dumping everything on him without notice, but then her next clearest thought was: Screw him!

"H'lo?" she said, squinting to see the caller ID. It registered "Private Number." She wished she'd checked before she answered, but then—

"Good morning, sweetheart."

It was Samael.

What the?

"You ready for a road trip?"

Claire made a piglike grunting sound and wiped her face as she tried to focus. The alarm clock by her bedside read 6:45.

"Road trip? What road trip?" The fog took its time dissipating. "It's too early. I was enjoying my—"

"To visit your parents."

"My parents?"

"Yeah."

"Did we talk about this?"

"Not really," Samael said. His voice sounded hollow over the phone. "I thought we could surprise them…and you."

"Oh, did you now." Claire rubbed her face, wiping away the sleep crust. "My parents don't really enjoy surprises."

"I'll bet they'd like to see you, though. Wouldn't they?"

Claire wasn't sure how to respond to that, but the real question was—did she want to see them?

Today?

"I'm not sure," she said. "'Sides, shouldn't I be here when the movers come?"

"Not necessary. You'd just be under their feet, anyway," Samael said. Even though she was more—but still not fully—awake, she still heard a funny note in Samael's voice.

"So come on," he said. "Get showered and dressed. I'll be by to pick you up in—say half an hour?"

"I can't—"

"Sure you can."

Claire was still trying to clear her mind. She was starting to think it might be a good thing to surprise her folks like this. It would save her the anticipation of a planned meeting…and it might be fun.

"Give me forty-five. I need my coffee," she said, gazing at her ring and chuckling, thinking about how her folks, especially her mother, would react when they saw it…not to mention her handsome—and rich—fiancé.

"All rightie, then," Samael said. "I'll be there at seven thirty."

"Yeah," Claire said, still wondering if she could pull it together that fast. She was used to hurrying out the door to get to work. Now that she didn't need to do that…would never need to do that, she wanted to take her time…luxuriate a little.

"Love you," she said.

Samael muttered something unintelligible and hung up.

Weird, she thought as she swung her legs out from under the bedcovers. Samael was usually so full of sweet nothings on the phone. She decided the signal must have dropped and never gave it a second thought.

Later, she would wish she had, but for now, she trudged from her bedroom to the kitchen to make coffee, vaguely thinking that this was the last morning she would wake up in her apartment.

Starting today—right now—was a whole new life for her.

~ * ~

The drive north on Interstate 95 to Houlton was—as always—achingly boring.

Pine trees…pine trees…and—oh yeah, more pine trees.

Every time Claire drove it, she vowed it was for the last time, but as long as her folks were still alive, she knew she'd be making the trip at least two or three times a year. For the first time in memory, though, the time went by fast. Too fast. She had brought her iPod along, and they played music nonstop. Claire played some of her favorites: The Dodos, Beach House, Raul Malo, and—her guilty pleasure—the oldie band, INXS; while Samael's favorites, not surprisingly, ran more to 60s and 70s hard rock and heavy-metal bands like Black Sabbath, AC/DC, and Alice Cooper. This struck Claire as amusing because she didn't think Samael would fall into such a cliché.

The music was incidental, though—a soundtrack to the day as she and Samael talked about anything and everything. In the first flush of "getting to know you," Claire revealed things about herself to Samael that she had never admitted before to anyone.

Claire told him that in grammar school she had been a "paste eater" and been tormented for it. She couldn't tell if Samael's comment that "paste tastes good" was meant seriously or ironically, but she let it slide. After all, Annie Murchin ate her own boogers, even though she thought nobody knew it. Claire also confessed other, darker secrets—like how she had "experimented" with a brief lesbian fling in college—and a few times in college…and after…when she shoplifted things, mostly food and toiletries she couldn't afford at the time.

At least that was her justification back then. She regretted it now, but she didn't think she'd go to Hell for it.

Samael's comment was something like that was perfectly understandable, but what did she expect, coming from a demon?

When they slowed for the Houlton exit off I-95, her heart began to race a little faster, and she steeled herself mentally for the onslaught she expected—no, she knew was coming when her folks—especially her father—met Samael. She was confident that Samael could hold his own with them, but still—she was nervous.

Hell, she thought, all he has to do is use The Voice, and it'll be done and over with.

But she was looking forward to presenting Samael as her future husband. She prayed they'd be happy she was—finally— getting married and to see that she had caught a good one...who even had money.

"You think your parents will like me?" Samael asked as he took a left-hand turn off the exit ramp.

"How'd you know to turn left here?" Claire asked, suddenly suspicious.

Samael smiled and said, "What, you don't think I Googled Callaghan Road before we left? Besides—"

With a nod of the head, he indicated the on-board GPS that displayed their position and destination even though the sound had been turned off for much of the drive.

"You know, Claire, if this is going to work, you really do have to start trusting me."

Claire choked back any protestation and nodded.

"I do," she said. "I really do. It's just that...sometimes I—"

She wanted to tell him that he seemed distant and aloof today...more than usual. It was probably because he, too, might be nervous about meeting her parents, but what did he have to worry about?

"I know," Samael said with a mild laugh. "I don't blame you in the least. To be quite honest, it's taking me some time getting used to this new way of looking at life."

Satisfied, Claire settled into her seat and decided that worrying about this visit with her parents was worry enough for now. She was sure Samael would impress the Hell out of them, and she chuckled at the thought.

~ * ~

"Nice to meet yah, young fella'," Gus McMullen said, extending his hand and shaking with Samael after giving Claire a quick kiss on the forehead. Claire thought he was putting on the "Old Man Act" a little too thick. He was, after all, only sixty-two, but he still had a fine crop of hair, and his green eyes sparkled like sunlight on a stream.

But as welcoming as he was, Claire thought the tone in her father's voice subtly communicated the exact opposite. And she caught her father staring intently at Samael as if challenging him for possession of his daughter. Regardless, she was determined to make this encounter slide by as easily as possible. No upsets. No arguments. They planned to be on the Interstate heading back to Portland within a few hours.

"Nice to meet you, too, sir," Samael said, his voice as oily smooth as a late-night FM disk jockey...or a used- car salesman, as he shook her father's hand and did a quick bow.

Putting it on a bit thick, there, don't you think? Claire thought, grinning.

When her mother joined them on the front porch, she gave Claire a bear hug that almost stopped her breath. She'd always gotten along much better with her mother than her dad, but he had always been protective of her. She knew it had been for her own good, but still—she had rebelled.

"Oh, my Heavens—what a pleasant surprise," Anne McMullen said, wiping her hands on her tattered and faded apron. Her long gray hair was tied back in a loose bun on the back of her head. Her eyes, unlike her husband's, looked dim and tired behind round glasses that gave her face an owlish look.

Claire had noticed Samael's slight wince when she said the word "Heavens" and wondered—briefly—why that would bother him when he was getting comfortable saying the names God and Jesus.

"You should have called and told us you were on your way," her mother said.

"We wanted to surprise you. Besides, we can't stay very long."

"Nonsense. You're not going to drive all this way and not stay for supper," her father said.

"You should have let me know," her mother said. "I'm a frightful mess. I wasn't expecting company today." She tucked a loose strand of hair behind her ear and adjusted her glasses.

"It was kind of a spur-of-the-moment thing," Claire said, glancing over at Samael and smiling.

"A five hour road trip is 'spur-of-the-moment'?" her father said.

As usual, he had a cigar going and, as usual, the smell both repelled Claire and filled her with nostalgia, reminding her she was truly home. He held the door open for them, and they all entered the foyer.

"I don't see any luggage," her mother said. "Surely you're going to stay the night."

Claire and Samael exchanged glances. They had already agreed what they would say when this subject came up.

"Sorry, but we can't," Claire said simply. "Samael has to get back to the office first thing in the morning for an important meeting."

"Oh?" her father said, turning to Samael. "And what is your line of work?"

Samael smiled but said nothing.

"He's a businessman," Claire said, realizing that she still wasn't sure exactly what he did. How could she explain that he gathered—or used to gather—souls? She didn't see how getting people to sell their souls could be profitable, but she wasn't about to bring it up now.

Clair's father squinted around a wreath of cigar smoke and said, "What exactly might that business be?"

"Shipping and receiving...business equipment."

"Your business ever bring you up here? You look kinda familiar, like maybe I've seen you 'round town."

"My territory covers all of Northern New England," Samael said smoothly, "but I don't come up this way often...Not enough customers to make it worthwhile."

"And what—exactly—is it that you sell?"

"Buy and sell...Business equipment. Photocopiers, computers, office furniture. The whole gamut." He waved his hand as if displaying his inventory.

"Sounds fascinating," Claire's mother said before turning and heading back into the kitchen. "Let me put on some coffee. And I'll get you a little something to eat. Sandwiches? You must be famished after such a long drive."

"We're all right for now. We stopped along the way," Claire said.

Laughing a little too loudly, her father said, "Still have to stop every twenty miles or so to hit the restroom?" And then to Samael, "She has the smallest bladder I ever heard of."

"Da-ad," Claire said. Someday she'd tell him that he embarrasses himself more than he embarrasses her with comments like that. She wished he would stop teasing her like she was still twelve years old.

Today, though, wasn't the day for that conversation. She wanted to get through this visit as smoothly as possible, and then get back to Portland. She was looking forward to sleeping in her new bed—Samael's bed—tonight...if you could call it "sleeping."

It didn't take long for her mother to get a pot of coffee brewed. Since her father had such a sweet tooth—and it showed both in his girth and his blood sugar levels—she had cookies and half a blueberry pie to serve. They gathered around the kitchen table and talked as they ate snacks and drank coffee.

While they were chatting, Claire picked what she thought was the right moment and held out her hand to show the ring. Her mother started crying and then gave her a hug and a kiss. When she kissed Samael, his discomfort was far too obvious. Her father, on the other hand, examined the ring carefully...as if he could tell whether or not it was a fake. When he shook Samael's hand and said, "You'd better take good care of my little girl," his eyes were cold and distant.

"Oh, Dad," Claire said, swatting him on the arm.

After about an hour of being alternately fawned over and interrogated, Samael eased back in his chair and gave Claire a look of desperation that all but screamed: Get me out of here!

"Weren't you going to show me around, Claire?" he asked, scanning the kitchen with a faint air of disdain.

Feeling protective of her childhood home, Claire took slight offense, but she got up and conducted him on a quick tour of the house. She told herself not to be embarrassed in any way by the home she grew up in. A lot more people lived in modest homes like this than in mansions like Samael's. Still, she was bothered by his patronizing attitude. It hurt, and she meant to talk to him about that later. It wasn't like him to be so openly snarky.

They spent quite a bit of time in her bedroom, going through the childhood things her mother had kept as though—someday— the little girl she had been before college would miraculously return and pick up her life right where she had left off. She was never going to want any of the clothes or other mementos—dolls and posters and such; and she doubted she'd ever have children who would be interested in them. Maybe her grandchildren would like them for nostalgia's sake. She wondered who was having the harder time letting go—her or her parents, and she decided she should clean out the rest of this junk sometime soon.

Not today, though.

"It's...modest, I know," she said, "but it was a nice place to grow up. Certainly better than a lot of my friends."

"I'm sure," was all Samael said. He sounded a bit bored by the whole adventure, and that bothered Claire, too. He barely glanced at her childhood mementos, and she couldn't help but wonder if something was wrong.

This had been his idea, so where was the charm and elegance that swept me off my feet?

Claire suddenly had an idea. Brightening and casting a look out her bedroom window at an all too familiar landscape, she said, "There's something else I need to show you."

She caught Samael looking at her like he was studying her. His expression was flat, impossible to read.

"This was a mistake, coming here, wasn't it?" she said.

Samael's expression didn't change as he shook his head and said, "No. I'm having fun."

You're sure as Hell not showing it, Claire thought but didn't say.

She took his hand, noticing but not commenting on how uncharacteristically cold it was, and they went downstairs together. Claire's mother was still in the kitchen, tidying things up. She turned to them as Claire led Samael toward the back door. They grabbed their coats, hats, and gloves. Claire wrapped a scarf around her neck and pulled it tight.

"Where are you off to?" she asked.

"I want to show Samael 'The Pond.'"

An odd expression crossed her mother's face, but she and Samael left before she could say anything more. They were out onto the back porch, the screen door slamming shut behind them, when Claire's mother yelled, "Your dad's gone to the store to buy steaks for supper. You'll stay for supper, won't you?"

Feeling exactly like she had when she was a child, racing off to meet up with her friends at "The Pond," Claire shouted back, "Don't know yet."

And with that, they walked down the steps and across the field, which was still covered with a good six inches of snow. They were silent as they headed into the woods.

~ * ~

Claire could follow the trail to "The Pond" even if she was blindfolded. Every twist and turn of the path, every change in elevation, every tree, rock, and shrub was burned into her memory. But on this particular March afternoon, with the sun already slanting down in the sky, Claire felt a subtle change in...everything.

The woods seemed smaller than she remembered, and the trail had somehow lost its mystery and magic for her. Trees and underbrush had taken over the land, and places where she had played with her friends and imagined all sorts of mystical fantasy creatures now seemed—somehow—dull...lifeless...as if something—its life force—had been sucked out of everything.

A shiver ran up her back, and not just from the cold air. She squeezed his hand tighter, but the feeling didn't pass. Even his hand felt cold and lifeless instead of the intense warmth she was used to. She might just as well be holding a dead fish. She kept glancing at him as they walked, his profile etched against the deepening blue sky, and the thought of explaining to her parents what he really was sent a stabbing chill through her. She wanted to say something to him, to talk about what she was feeling, but she was afraid, and she had no idea where or how to start.

Instead, she began a running narrative of the paths and the woods and, especially, "The Pond" where she used to play, even though—now—it seemed so far away.

"We'd swim here all the time, me and my friends. And I can show you the exact spot under the tree where I used to sit and read. *Alice in Wonderland* was my favorite. I'd come out here by myself sometimes—a lot of times—and just sit and think. You know?"

"I—I never had an experience like that," Samael said. The cool detachment in his voice bothered her, but she still didn't want to confront him about it. Why ruin what was supposed to be a fun afternoon, even if that wasn't exactly how it was turning out.

"No, I...I guess you wouldn't, being a demon and all," Claire said sullenly.

The snow got deeper as they followed the path further into the woods.

"Right there," Claire said, pointing to a large granite boulder that stuck up out of the snow like a huge tooth, "is where I saw a black bear once."

It pained her to see that someone—probably some high-school punks—had spray-painted the rock with scrolling, illegible initials and logos.

"Did it attack you? The bear, I mean?" Samael asked. For once there was a spark of interest in her past life.

Claire shook her head.

"Nope. It never even made a move toward me. It was eating blueberries from that bush over there, and he just watched me as I passed on by."

Samael nodded but said nothing more, seemingly totally uninterested in any of her nostalgic stories. They walked for a long time in silence. The angle of sunlight filtering through the trees along the path was more familiar to Claire than her own bedroom. She inhaled the fresh, pine-scented air, letting the woodland smells take her back to a happier, simpler time.

So to Hell with him...Even if he can't appreciate any of this, I certainly can.

But the closer they got to "The Pond," the more unsettled she became.

One obvious thing that bothered her was how everything looked so small and...limited was the only other word that came to mind. In her memory and imagination, this had been a mighty forest, as deep and dense—and dangerous—as the Black Forest in Germany. It could hide countless numbers of mythical, magical creatures and dangerous, supernatural beings.

The closer they got to "The Pond," the more litter and trash she saw strewn around. And not just old, rusting stuff. There were empty beer cans and liquor bottles...food wrappers...and other junk everywhere, blighting the scene and Claire's childhood memories. Several of the larger trees that she remembered had either fallen down or been hacked down for campfire, the rough axe marks obviously not those of experienced woodsmen. Even the ground itself—the snow-covered path—appeared to be worn out.

"Beautiful, isn't it?" she asked, trying as much to convince herself as Samael.

He said nothing but kept walking, his eyes fixed straight ahead as though he wasn't even a part of this world. Claire was confused and frustrated by his detachment. She wished he would talk to her...tell her what the problem was.

If Claire had been feeling disappointment before, though, it crashed down on her when they arrived at "The Pond."

"Oh, my God," she whispered, struck with amazement by what she saw before them.

The instant the word—the name of God was out of her mouth, Samael let out a low, slow moan that sounded as if he were in great pain.

Claire turned to him and saw a wicked fire dancing in his eyes, making them glow with a deep orange light that matched the disk of the setting sun.

His eyes look different, she thought, but the thought flittered away because of her concern for him.

"Are you all right?"

She was convinced that something was seriously wrong with him...something he didn't want to discuss with her.

When Samael looked at her, his face shifted back to the same blank expression he'd worn all day. She had the distinct impression he was wearing a mask, and that she couldn't see and had never seen what was beneath that mask.

"I'm fine...I'm fine," he said, even though his tone of voice was that of someone who absolutely is not fine.

Claire wanted to let it drop, so she looked out across "The Pond," awed by how pitifully small...actually tiny it looked.

"Things sure do change, don't they?" she said.

"How do you mean?"

"I...For years, I've had such powerful memories of this place, and now looking at it, it seems so insignificant."

"Your world—your horizons have expanded," Samael said. "And as they do, we see some things for what they really are."

Claire wondered if there was a veiled message in what he said, but she ignored it and kept staring at "The Pond." The surface was covered with a layer of dirty snow on top of ice that Claire knew would be too thin to support them if they ventured out onto it. There were signs that someone—teenagers—had been partying out here recently. To the left, on the narrow sand beach where Claire and her friends used to sunbathe, there was evidence of a huge fire. Charred logs and crushed beer cans lay all about in the mess of footprints in the snow. Someone had left behind a single boot.

"We used to swim here all the time," she said, trying hard to conjure up her best childhood memories. "My brother and his friends would come out here, too, so we'd stay away when they were around because they were always teasing us, calling us names and—you know, being rude."

"You mean acting like they wanted to fuck you," Samael said.

Claire was shocked.

"What?" she said, her voice scaling up.

"I'm just saying the truth. That's what they wanted, right? Only I'll bet the little assholes were so insecure not one of them would have known what to do if you or any of your friends showed any interest. Probably the lot of them had tiny dicks, too, that would have shriveled up to nothing if a woman or even a girl ever saw them."

Claire was astounded to hear him speak like this. It wasn't at all like him to express himself so crudely...unless, she thought, this was another side...maybe a side of him he had kept hidden from her...

Until now.

"Are you—" she started to say, but she let it drop.

Samael was beginning to frighten her. It was all but impossible to believe that such a small, sad-looking pond like this had meant so much to her. And seeing it through his eyes, the loss of innocence stung deeply. Like the small house she had grown up in and the small town that had defined her horizons until she went off to college, seeing "The Pond" now all but overwhelmed her with melancholy. Fighting back tears, she turned away from Samael and let the sadness sweep through her.

Finally, unable to hold it back any longer, she began to cry. Warm tears carved tracks down her cheeks as sobs wrenched her body, making her shiver.

She waited, for Samael to reach out and touch her gently on the shoulder and then take her into his arms and hold and caress and kiss her. She wanted to feel safe and secure with him...

But he didn't, and he remained aloof as wave after wave of emotion washed over her until she felt like she was sinking down into the slimy, murky depths of "The Pond."

She wasn't even sure what she was crying about.

Her childhood?

The sadness of times past?

Her hopes and worries for the future?

Her desire and need for Samael's love?

She wiped her eyes with the flats of her hands as she cried, wishing she didn't feel so utterly alone.

"You know," she said, her voice halting as she stared at the woods on the far side of "The Pond." "Sometimes I feel like..."

When she turned to him to seek comfort in his arms, she was stunned to see that he wasn't there.

~ * ~

"Samael?" she called, her voice echoing hollowly from the opposite shore.

She looked around, wondering where he could have gone so fast. He was nowhere to be seen, not even on the path leading back to the house,

An icy blade of panic slid between her ribs.

She looked at the ground, but in the confusion of tracks made by the teenage partiers, she couldn't distinguish her and Samael's from the mass. She started moving toward the woods, scanning the snow for his tracks. She thought he might be playing a trick on her and had hidden so he could jump out and scare her.

But as she continued to look around and study the ground carefully, she still couldn't see any signs she could positively identify as Samael's.

"All right!...You got me!...Come on out!" she called.

She wondered if he had the ability to make himself invisible and was using it now to tease her or freak her out, for whatever reason.

But if he truly loved her like he said he did, why would he do something like this—even if he was only teasing her? It wasn't very nice, considering how vulnerable she was feeling at the moment.

"Samael!" she shouted, louder. Her voice echoing from the woods on the opposite shore redoubled.

"...ael..."

Her eyes widened, and she viciously wiped away the gathering tears, trying to see. Frustrated, she scooped up a handful of snow, made a compact snowball, and sent it flying out onto "The Pond." It hit the slushy snow with a dull thud.

"This isn't funny anymore!" she shouted, anger now mixing with hurt. "It wasn't funny to begin with!"

"...to begin with..."

He's hiding somewhere...trying to scare me, she thought, wanting to believe it.

Or maybe he's really gone?

Is he so bored being here...with me...that he's decided to ditch me? Again!

She didn't like these thoughts, but the only other thing she could think of was that he had never been here with her in the first place...She had imagined him being here all along...and now the reality of being back home had proven him to be the illusion he was.

A sudden mistrust of reality swept over her, and she began to tremble.

Her legs were numb and as stiff as sticks as she started back the way they had come. Keeping a careful watch for his footprints on the ground, she finally arrived at the point where they had exited the woods.

There they were—two sets of tracks, side by side heading toward "The Pond."

But there were no third, fresher tracks leading away from "The Pond," so she knew he hadn't come this way.

So where did he go, and how did he disappear so fast? She had just been standing there talking to him, and...poof!

She looked back at "The Pond," half-expecting—and desperately hoping—to see him standing there in the gloomy afternoon light, but he was nowhere to be seen.

"I'm heading back now," she called out, feeling a lot less courageous than she sounded.

"...back now... "

"You wanna screw around? Fine!"

"...Fine..."

The echo of her voice faded away. There were no other sounds, not even the song of birds—chickadees or sparrows—tweeting in the pine trees.

Foolish childhood fears reared their heads as they began to untangle inside her. Too many memories of being out here—either with friends or alone—and getting spooked only served to fuel her rising panic. When she was a kid, she had never come out here alone after twilight.

During the day? Sure.

But not when it was getting dark. She and her friends had told themselves too many horror stories about the evil things that lurk in the darkening woods and would gladly eat you.

Goblins...ghosts...and demons...

But if Samael was here, he'd protect me, she thought.

But that was just the problem.

He wasn't here, and he was exactly one of those things she had been afraid of when she was little.

She realized that she had to face these fears now all on her own.

Like life...

Samael wouldn't be doing this to her...not if he loved her.

No one who loved someone would put them in a situation like this without warning.

"For the last time!"

"...time..."

She looked to the west, at the streaks of purple clouds in the rapidly darkening sky.

"Come on out!"

"...on out..."

She tried not to think about how she had never...never been out here after dark, even as a teenager.

"I know you're hiding."

"...hiding..."

She heard the nervous quaver in her voice and told herself that, if she didn't start back for the house soon, it would be pitch dark by the time she got halfway home.

It's already too late, a voice whispered in her head as those old fears rose up like phantoms all around her. She half-expected to see ghostly shapes, drifting in the gathering gloom.

Trembling with fear, she started back along the path. The snow glowed with an eerie blue light. The footsteps she and Samael had made on their way out here were as dark as inkwells punched in the crust of snow. Claire's boots made loud crunching sounds as she walked...sounds that, when she was a kid, she always imagined were the grinding teeth of something—

A demon!

—coming up behind her, wanting to catch her...and eat her.

She followed the winding path, tension winding up steadily inside her; but then an idea struck her. Reaching into her pocket, she took out her cell phone and hit the speed-dial number for Samael's phone. She'd tell him a thing or two if he answered.

The phone rang once...twice...and on the third ring, he picked up.

"Hello?" he said, sounding his usual chipper self.

"Where in the Hell are you hiding?" Claire said. She didn't want to snap at him, but she wasn't able to stop herself.

"Hiding? What are you talking about?"

Now there was the hint of a frantic edge in his voice, and his question all but knocked her off her feet.

"Where are you?"

"I'm at the office," Samael said. "I've been calling you all day, but every time, your phone goes straight to message."

Her breath was burning in her lungs, and the darkness closing in all around her made it impossible to breathe deeply enough. It took her a moment to realize that the heavy thudding sound she heard was her pulse in her ears, not the sound of rapidly approaching footsteps.

"Hold on...Hold on," Claire said, fighting confusion. "You're telling me you're in Portland?"

"I've been here most of the day, cleaning up some loose ends, but now I'm home. Your things got delivered, by the way. When are you coming home?"

Even through her panic, Claire's heart warmed to hear him say the word "home" to her.

"But we...you and I drove up to Houlton, to visit my parents. We've been on the road all day."

Claire's eyes widened as she looked around at the darkening forest. The cold breeze blowing through the trees froze her face. She looked up at the skeletal branches of trees overhead. They created a vast network like a spider web that was winding tighter and tighter around her.

"What are you talking about?" Samael said, his voice clear and firm. "We talked about it, but we never picked a date. I was surprised when you weren't at your apartment this morning to oversee the movers."

"The movers...but you told me I'd just get in the way."

"I did? When?"

"This morning. Early this morning."

"That's funny. I tried calling—must've called twenty times or more, but your phone went straight to message. We decided to settle for lunch, but—like I said, your phone went straight to message every time I called. I thought maybe your battery died or something."

Claire was stunned. The sense of unreality only got worse as she considered where she was. She was suddenly fearful that none of this was happening...that she was imagining it all, and she had fallen into a trap she might not be able to escape.

"You picked me up at the house at, like, seven thirty." She still didn't believe she hadn't spent the whole day with him. "We drove up to Houlton. You met my mother and father, and I showed you around the house—my bedroom, and then we went out to 'The Pond.'"

"The Pond?"

"Yes! The Pond! Where I went swimming and skating when I was a kid. And then, when my back was turned, you were suddenly...gone."

"Oh, no," Samael said. The fear in his voice cut through Claire like a surgical blade.

"What?...What is it?"

The tremor in her voice all but strangled her as fear bubbled up inside her.

"It's started," Samael said simply.

Claire wasn't sure if she had heard him correctly.

"What has?…What's started?"

She staggered to the side and grabbed on to a tree trunk for support.

"They're coming," Samael said, his voice deep and hollow.

Claire didn't want to believe that she heard fear in his voice. She might be losing her mind, but Samael was always confident and in control of any situation.

"What do you mean? Who's coming?"

"Listen to me, Claire. Listen very carefully."

He paused, and the phone suddenly went so silent Claire was afraid her battery had died or the call had dropped. She held her breath and waited for him to speak again. In the short silence, she was ready to start screaming, but she managed to control herself and say, "Samael? Are you still there?"

"Yes, yes."

Her body flooded with relief. Just hearing his voice made her feel much safer. Tears welled up in her eyes when she thought how far away from each other they really were and wondered who she had driven north with.

"All right, then," Samael said. "This is what you have to do. There's a bus station in downtown Houlton, right?"

"Yeah…Greyhound or maybe Trailways. I used to take—"

"Get to town as fast as you can and take the bus back here."

"Should I—"

"No! Don't go back to your parents' house. It will only place them in danger, too. They're coming after you in order to get to me."

"Who is? What are you talking about?"

"I'll tell you when I see you," Samael said. "What you have to do now is get the Hell out of there as fast as you can. Once you're on the bus…don't talk to anyone, got it? Not even the driver."

"Samael, I'm scared."

"Don't be. It'll all be all right."

She found a measure of reassurance in his voice.

"Yes...but I don't see why—"

"Just do what I say." Samael's voice was strong and encouraging, and that gave Claire another boost of confidence. "Just stay calm. They won't hurt you. They're just messing with you because they want to get to me."

"Who...who's doing this?" Claire shouted into the phone.

Her voice echoed from the darkening woods, and her panic rose even higher when she saw how fast night was falling. It was at least three or four miles to the bus station downtown. No matter how fast she got there, she had no idea when the next bus would leave, heading south.

What if there are no more busses going out today?

Where will I go?

What will I do?

And worst of all was the thought that when she got there, what if this...this thing masquerading as Samael had guessed that's what she would do, and he was waiting for her there.

What will I do then?

"Save your phone battery," Samael said, "but call me as soon as you're on the bus, okay?"

Claire grunted and nodded. It felt like an iron band was steadily tightening around her chest. Her pulse was racing fast, and in spite of the cold evening air, sweat stood out on her forehead beneath her wool hat.

"Okay," she said breathlessly, "But please. Before I hang up. Tell me. Who's doing this to me...to us?"

"Other demons," he said simply. "They don't like what I'm doing."

"What do you mean?"

"They don't like that I've fallen in love with you...that I want to redeem myself."

Chapter

11

————Closing In

Later that night, several things happened that Claire said could only have been miracles. Two weeks later, when she finally told Samael about them when he was in jail, he said that he agreed they were miracles because there was no other explanation. After all, he more than anyone else—even Claire—believed in the supernatural. The good thing is, these miracles were on the side of the angels.

But they didn't feel like miracles at the time.

As night descended, Claire struck out through the woods in a different direction, one that would not have taken her back to the house. She was less familiar with it, but she had taken it enough times when she had gone directly from "The Pond" to either Patty's or Jennifer's or Amber's house for a cookout or sleepover.

But never in the dark. Never in March. Even her winter coat, wool hat, gloves, scarf, jeans, and L.L. Bean low-cut boots weren't enough to keep her comfortably warm.

I could freeze to death out here, she kept thinking, and: *I can't believe this is really happening.*

Her feet made loud crunching sounds in the snow, and the thin, icy crust cut into her shins whenever she lost her balance or stumbled in the dark. She didn't know if the oily feeling running down to her ankles was sweat or blood, and she couldn't stop now to check.

And she had to keep it together as much as she could because she would never escape this situation alive if she didn't.

Knowing Samael was only a phone call away gave her a measure of reassurance, but she began to wonder why he couldn't do something else...something more.

Aren't demons supposed to be able to fly?

Or, why can't he conjure up some spell and instantly transport me back to Portland?

Is he able to do such things?

She had to assume if he could, he would have, so whatever the case, she was on her own for now.

Other thoughts plagued her.

Who are they?

Why do they want to get at Samael?

And what will they do to me to get to him?

The sun had long since dropped below the horizon, and the sky was as dark as smoke, pressing down on her. Through the ragged breaks in the clouds and between the leafless branches overhead, a few stars appeared, glinting in the darkness like fireflies seen at a distance.

Claire shivered and drew herself deeper into her coat. She had never felt this lost and lonely in her life, even as a child. Being an adult only made it worse. She constantly had to resist the urge to start running, telling herself that if she hurried, accidents would happen. She wasn't going to make things worse than they already were.

And they were pretty bad as it was.

She kept wanting to call Samael, if only for the reassurance of hearing his voice, but she didn't want to run down her phone's battery. She did pause and call her parents, though. Her mother answered.

"Hello?"

"Hey, Mom."

It took a great effort to control the tremor in her voice. She wasn't sure how successful she was.

"What's the matter, dear?" her mother said.

So much for hiding my nervousness.

"Something's come up, and I—I'm not going to be able to come back to the house before we head back to Portland."

"Oh, dear. I hope it isn't anything serious,"

Oh, no. Not at all, Claire thought ruefully, just some demons out to get me.

"Samael came back alone and took off in the car. I was a little hurt he—and you—didn't come in to say goodbye."

Claire could hear her father, muttering in the background, words like "totally rude" and "so full of himself." All too easily, she could imagine what he and her mother were thinking, but she drew up short when she realized anything they thought was not nearly as irrational and—truth to tell—a lot worse that they could ever imagine.

"No...It's...nothing's happened. I—uh, I wanted to go for a longer walk than...uh, he did, so he went back to get the car and...umm...picked me up downtown."

"Uh-huh. I see," her mother said, making it obvious that she didn't "see" at all. "If you'd like your father to—"

"I'm fine, Mom. I'm really sorry we couldn't stay for supper, but we'll be back soon, I promise."

She wondered—as she had so often when she was a child—if her mother was fooled by her lies and not letting on, or if she really was truly in the dark. Usually, her father had been the one to trip her up when she lied or did something wrong, but she always wondered how much her mother knew but didn't say.

"Well, then...It was a terrific surprise to see you. You'll have to visit again soon and stay longer."

"Sure thing, Mom."

"I think your young man seems very nice."

"He liked you, too, Mom. Both of you. Tell Dad buh-bye for me. I'll be in touch."

"Call when you get to Portland."

I will, Claire thought, *that's if I get back to Portland.*

A bone-penetrating chill wrapped around her. All she needed now, she thought, was to hear the fluttery hooting of an owl or the mournful wail of a coyote in the distance to make this the perfect cliché of being lost in the woods.

I'm not lost...I know exactly where I am.

Squaring her shoulders, she pushed on into the darkness.

She had no idea what kind of progress she was making. She felt like she was wandering in a black void, and from time to time, she wondered if she was lost. Houlton wasn't much of a town, and the surrounding wilderness went on for hundreds of miles in all directions. It would be easy for her to get turned around and head in the wrong direction. She might never find her way out.

Of course, the easy thing—and what she had been told repeatedly to do if she was ever lost in the woods—was to stay put. Don't move. If she was still lost when dawn came, she could always trace her footprints in the snow back to "The Pond" and home. She'd have a hell of a time explaining to her parents what had happened then, but it sure beat dying alone in the woods.

She kept wishing she had never quit smoking because, if she still smoked, she would have a cigarette lighter in her pocket, and she could start a fire for warmth and as a signal fire to let someone know where she was.

Unless that "someone" was whoever or whatever had pretended to be Samael.

"I'm not gonna make it to downtown if I stop walking," she said, speaking out loud to bolster her courage. She had to admit the truth. The longer she hiked in the night-soaked forest, the further she went, the worse it would be if she decided to backtrack.

With every step, fear bordering on outright panic wound up inside her. The tiniest sounds were magnified in the dark. The snap of a branch underfoot sounded like a gunshot. The swishing sound her coat made as she walked, swinging her arms, sounded like the hushed tread of someone creeping up behind her. Even the wind, winding through the thin branches overhead, sounded like voices whispering in a language she didn't quite understand. And when she looked up at the sky, she didn't recognize the usual patterns of stars. There were new and strange constellations, unrecognizable...as if she had been transported magically to another hemisphere.

"You're gonna be all right...You're gonna be all right," she kept whispering to herself.

She resisted the temptation to call Samael again. Apparently there was nothing he could do from Portland, and he didn't have the means to get to her quickly.

What's the use of being a demon if you can't fly? She thought bitterly.

But she recalled how Samael had told her that different demons had different abilities and powers. So maybe he didn't or couldn't fly, and he didn't know any other demons he could trust who did.

Never in her life had she felt so isolated…so afraid. This was worse than her amazement when she realized for the first time she was sleeping with an actual demon.

Much worse.

As these and other unsettling thoughts ran through her head, she kept walking…trudging through the snow. It was much deeper under the trees, halfway up to her knees. Often she'd stumble and almost fall when she tripped over something—a rock…a fallen tree branch…even her own feet.

She patted herself on the back, though, congratulating herself for even attempting this. When she was growing up in Houlton, she would never ever have dared to hike from "The Pond" to downtown—alone or with friends—at night. She had heard—and told—too many scary stories about things lurking in these woods, waiting to pounce when you least expected.

Only now, she knew all too well that there were things in the forest to fear. There was a good chance the demon who had masqueraded as Samael might be chasing after her in the darkness…coming for her.

Does he know I'm heading to the bus station?

Will he be waiting for me there?

Or will he grab me and whisk me away before anyone else sees or can intervene?

She took little consolation in what Samael had said—that a demon can't destroy her unless she'd already signed her soul away.

"But they sure as Hell can make your life miserable," she said out loud.

So on she went, shivering and stumbling. Her tears froze on her face before she wiped them away with the flats of her gloved hands. And all the while, she was thinking that the woods and this night were never going to end. Her legs felt increasingly leaden, and she staggered more and more, like she'd been drinking. Whenever she stopped and leaned against a tree for support, her breath came out in a silver mist that rapidly dissolved into the icy darkness.

"I can make it," she whispered. "I know I can."

So on she went...into the darkness...

~ * ~

Until finally...amazingly...a glimmer of light shone through the trees.

At first, Claire didn't believe her own eyes. She wondered if this might be another trick the demon who was after her was playing on her...like a will-o'-the-wisp. She hadn't crossed B Road—or any road—yet, and she knew she couldn't have missed it, even in the dark and snow.

But where am I?

She made her way toward the light, if only to see if it was an illusion or real. She wondered how far away the light—and maybe B Road—was, and if she could walk that far, much less all the way to the bus station. The light appeared to be shifting away from her, no matter how slow or fast she walked toward it.

This has to be a trick, she thought, *a demonic trick.*

Her eyes kept dancing back and forth as she looked around the dark woods, trying to get a fix on what was ahead of her. She was tensed, poised and waiting for a shadow—or shadows—to separate from the darkness and close in on her.

The forest closed down around her like a dark, heavy blanket.

Every footstep became increasingly labored, and the thought that she would die before she ever saw civilization again filled her with a deep, gnawing fear that fueled her efforts. She tried to block out any images of her corpse, rotting away in the woods, being picked apart by crows and the turkey vultures who hovered over the potato fields in the summer and fall.

"Just...keep...moving," she said. She couldn't help but think about the Jack London story, "To Build a Fire," which she had read in high school.

"Don't go, but if you do go, don't go alone."

Good advice, but who could she trust to go with her?

Certainly not the demon who'd been impersonating Samael all day.

Whoever...or whatever was trying to deceive her was good. He had her fooled most of the day. But now that she thought about it, throughout the drive north, he had been acting uncharacteristically distant and curt. She had taken it as an indication he'd been more nervous than he had let on about the prospect of meeting her parents.

But he was a demon...At least in her experience, demons didn't get nervous.

She was filled with a sudden, desperate need to hear Samael's voice.

For the last time?

Don't think it!...You'll make it...You'll get through this...

Iron cold clenched her chest. Her hands were shaking as she peeled off her gloves and hit the speed dial for Samael's number.

He answered after the first ring, and Claire knew he'd been waiting, anxiously, to hear from her. Her spirits lifted...a little.

"Where are you?" he said, his voice snapping like the crack of a whip through the phone. "Are you all right?"

"I'm lost...in the woods," she said as tears filled her eyes, blurring her vision and choking her voice.

"What do you mean?" His voice was calmer now, and she felt closer to him than she ever had before. It was almost as if he were standing right here next to her in the dark.

"I'm not sure where I am or which way to go."

There was a long pause at the other end of the line. Claire could hear him breathing into the phone, and she thought—wished— hoped he was thinking of something he could do to help.

But how could he help when he was hundreds of miles away?

"You have to keep on going," Samael finally said, his voice firm and tinged with concern. "You can't give up now. You can't let them get to us."

I'm the one who might die, Claire thought but didn't say.

"Does your cell phone have a GPS or Google maps…something that will point out where you are?"

Claire shook her head bitterly and said, "Mine just makes phone calls. It's not a smart phone. Besides, I'm probably too far north to even have that service."

"We'll have to get you one when you get back," Samael said, and she liked the way he assumed there would be a future time when they could get her one.

"So you'll have to figure out where you are," he said. "Just stay calm."

She used her glove to wipe the tears from her eyes and took a calming breath as she looked around. She focused once again on the single light, glimmering like an illusion through the trees.

Speaking as much to herself as to Samael, she said, "I will."

"I love you," he said, his voice as soft now as when he whispered to her in the darkness of the bedroom.

"And I love you," she said, fighting hard to contain the emotions that were welling up inside her. "I really do."

"Call me as soon as you're safe and on your way home, 'kay?"

"I will," Claire said.

And then she ended the call and started walking toward the pinpoint of light.

~ * ~

Claire had no idea how she eventually made it to the bus station, but sometime before dawn, at the end of a night she had been convinced would never end, she found herself sitting in the waiting area of the bus terminal. The heater was going full blast and was making her sweat.

The light she had seen through the trees had, in fact, turned out to be a house—the Crosby house, as it turned out. She had known the Crosby family since she was a kid growing up here. Their children— a son, Andrew, and a daughter, Alice—had been a few years ahead of

Claire in school. They were old enough so she had never been friends with either of them, but she knew them well enough to smile and say "hi." As far as she knew, the old folks were still living in the old family home. At least her parents had never mentioned to her that they had died, and her mother was good at keeping her posted on who had died in town.

She had approached the house, thinking she'd wake them up and ask for help, but as she got close to the house, their dog started barking. He sounded mean enough to avoid, and she decided that if she showed up at this ungodly hour, word would definitely get back to her parents. Then she'd have some explaining to do.

But at least it was a familiar landmark. She knew where she was.

So she had kept on walking until she made it to the bus station about an hour later.

She sat on a bench in the far corner of the room where she could keep an eye on anyone and everyone who came or went. Not that there were many people around at this hour. Houlton wasn't exactly a bustling town, and she didn't want to be seen by anyone who might report back to her parents. And she certainly didn't trust any strangers she might see because he—or she—might be the demon who was trying to trick her.

The front desk didn't open for another hour, so she bought a Pepsi and some Ritz crackers with peanut butter from the vending machines, and sat as far away from everyone as she could.

When dawn broke, the sun shining a bright orange beam across the floor, Claire was wrung out with exhaustion, she didn't dare to nap now because she still didn't feel safe.

When will I feel safe? She wondered.

She doubted she'd feel much better even once she was on board a bus heading south. Even then, if she didn't recognize anyone on the bus, she wouldn't dare let her guard down. The strain was getting to her.

The office finally opened at six A.M. She recognized the man behind the desk selling tickets. He was Mr. Henry, a friend of her father's. He'd been working here since before she'd left home for college, and this morning, he was as efficient as a machine, going through the routine of selling and verifying tickets. A young woman with two children—one in a stroller—were in front of Claire. Once they were set, she stepped forward. When Mr. Henry recognized her, he smiled and greeted her warmly.

"Well, now, good mornin' to yah, Claire," he said, but then his expression darkened and he added, "What in the blazes, if you don't mind me askin,' are you doin' here this time o'day?" Mr. Henry had a thick Maine accent and pronounced the word "here" as two syllables—"He-ahh."

"I'm heading south," Claire said, hoping to keep her voice friendly and firm.

She knew she must look a wreck after spending the whole night thrashing around in the woods, but there wasn't much she could do about that now. First thing when she got to the bus station, she had gone into the ladies room and fixed herself up as best she could, but her hair was still a tangled mess, and her makeup was gone.

"Just like old times, huh?" Mr. Henry smiled. "I 'member when you was in college, you comin' in and takin' the bus back to university after holidays and such."

"That was a long time ago, Mr. Henry," she said with a tight smile. Truth to tell, Mr. Henry didn't look to have aged much in the intervening years.

"I didn't know you was in town. Your father never mentioned it."

"We—I just came up for the day yesterday." She hoped that would satisfy him, but this was small-town Maine, and word of mouth would get around about her being at the station at the crack of dawn, buying a ticket south.

"I had a bit of—ah, car trouble, and I have to get back to Portland for work."

"Bus won't get to Portland 'till after two o'clock this afternoon," he said as he handed her the ticket. She fumbled in her purse—glad she had hung on to it—and paid with a credit card.

"I'll have to do my best," she said.

"Ay-yuh. Wouldn't want to lose a job in this economy."

Claire nodded and started to leave so the person behind her—an elderly man wearing a tattered and faded suit coat—could buy his ticket. She didn't recognize him and scanned him surreptitiously, wondering if he was the demon who was after her. How easily could he assume a new disguise?

Before she left the ticket desk, though, Claire turned back to Mr. Henry.

"Somethin' the matter?" he asked.

She realized he must be reacting to the expression on her face, but her voice was steady as she lowered it to a whisper and said, "I'd appreciate if you didn't mention me being here to my folks. They think I left yesterday evening, and they'd just be worried if they knew…"

Her voice faded away because she didn't know what else to say. She had no doubt that, before the morning was over, Mr. Henry would make a call to her father and tell him the whole story.

Since there was nothing more she could do about it, she took her ticket and went back to the furthest corner to wait. An hour and a half later she was sitting in a Greyhound bus, heading south on I-95.

~ * ~

Claire sat at the back of the bus, hoping her position clearly communicated to everyone: *Leave me the fuck alone.* Fortunately, the young woman with the two kids sat up front behind the driver. They started whining as soon as the bus, belching a huge plume of dense, sooty exhaust, pulled out of the station. There were only a few other passengers. The old man she had noticed earlier was seated about halfway to the back of the bus. He smiled and nodded to Claire as she passed, but after that, he appeared to studiously ignore her.

Appeared…Claire thought, wondering if that was exactly how he would behave…until he managed to get her alone.

There were other passengers—the usual mix of bus riders— people who for whatever reason didn't have or use private transportation. A couple of kids who looked like 60s hippies sat closer to Claire. They had, obviously, gotten baked first thing in the morning before their bus trip. They kept looking around and giggling like harmless morons.

Or are they harmless? Claire wondered. What if the demon is one of them? It's perfect cover for the unsuspecting.

Claire shook her head, telling herself to stop being so damned paranoid, but another voice in her head told her she had to stay alert for any and all possible dangers. Still, she didn't have to get paranoid and jump or cringe at every sound or anything that moved. No matter what she told herself, her hands were shaking as she drew her cell phone from her purse and hit the speed dial for Samael's number.

The phone rang once...twice...and by the third ring, a vague sense of uneasiness stirred within her.

"Come on."

The phone rang a fourth time.

"Answer the phone..."

Or will it kick over to voicemail?

"Pick up...Pick up," she whispered.

Beads of sweat formed on her forehead and ran, tickling, down the sides of her face and back of her neck. The hot air vent was blowing directly into her face, but try as she might, she couldn't get it to shut off. She considered switching seats but didn't want to draw attention to herself.

Remember, they're really after Samael, not you...but they'll use you to get to him...

A fifth ring, and then the phone clicked.

What if they got to him already?

For what seemed a terribly long moment that, in reality, must have been only a second or two, tops, there was utter silence. Her breath caught like a hot coal in her throat. Her heart was racing so fast her vision jumped in time with it.

And then—

"Hey."

It was almost impossible to hear him over the roaring sound the bus was making, but relief instantly flooded Claire.

"Hey, yourself," she said breathlessly, leaning forward and cupping the phone with her hand so the stoners or anyone else wouldn't hear her.

"So where are you?" he asked. He sounded nervous...edgy, and Claire thought that was a good sign. "Are you safe?"

Claire scanned the passengers in the bus. Except for the young mother, who was trying to breastfeed the infant, everyone else was either dozing or reading a morning newspaper. The hippies were chatting and texting on their phones. The steady loud rumble of the bus was far from soothing, but in her relief, Claire realized just how exhausted she was.

"I think so. I'm on the bus, heading south," she said. "I won't get into Portland until—" She fished her ticket from her pocket and checked the ETA to be sure. "Looks like two forty-five this afternoon."

"I'll be there. Greyhound, right?"

"Yup."

"I'll be there. Don't worry."

A little late for that advice, Claire thought but didn't say.

"So how are you?" she asked. "Did you have any...trouble last night?"

There was an uncomfortably long pause at the other end of the line. Claire sensed he was debating what or how much to tell her.

"Nothing I couldn't handle. Bush-league stuff," he said finally. It was vague and threatening enough so she did, in fact, begin to worry.

But a cell phone—easily compromised—was not the way to discuss it.

"So you must not have had any trouble finding your way out of the woods."

Like Samael, she decided not to tell everything so he wouldn't worry. At least that was over!

"I was so worried about you last night. I couldn't sleep."

DO you ever sleep? Claire wanted to ask but didn't. She smiled at the note of genuine concern—worry, even—in his voice. Closing her eyes, she imagined they were already back together.

"I'm beat after hiking all night. It's weird because...it's like it was all a bad dream or something."

She sighed and shook her head.

"Well, don't fall asleep yet," Samael said. "You have to keep your eyes open. Know who it is."

"Who?" Claire asked as an icy jolt speared her gut.

His comment removed any doubt. This was all real. As crazy as the events of last night seemed, Samael had just validated all the danger and fear she had been through—and still had to go.

The threat was real.

"Can you tell me?"

"Not over the phone."

"Okay," she said, not satisfied but accepting it.

She started to chuckle, amused to realize how they were talking in clipped sentences like they were spies on a secret mission or something, but then she realized the seriousness of what was going on here.

Samael's life and hers—maybe even their souls—were in jeopardy.

"So..." Her throat caught, and she had to clear it before she could continue. "So what do I do? How much danger am I really in?"

"Hard to tell, but I think you'll be fine. Just don't talk to anyone...and certainly don't go off alone with anyone."

"Don't worry about that, but am I...?"

She didn't dare finish the sentence, but she knew that Samael knew what she had been about to ask.

Is there a chance I could get hurt or killed?

"You'll be fine. None of them can do anything to you except maybe frighten you. But they can't harm you, per se."

"Per se, huh?"

"I'm absolutely positive. There are...certain guidelines and restrictions. It's too complicated to get into right now."

Claire was about to say something when she happened to look up and see the old man, staring down the length of the bus aisle, looking directly at her. Her breath caught as if she'd been sucker punched. When she met the old man's steady stare, he didn't blink or turn away. He kept staring at her, his eyes shining with a pale light.

"I think I see him," she whispered into the phone.

The old man leaned further out into the aisle all the while keeping his gaze fixed on Claire. She sank further into the corner of the seat, wishing she could disappear, but he didn't look away.

Don't get up...Don't start coming toward me...I'll scream...I swear to God I will.

"See who?"

"There's an old man on the bus," she whispered. "And he's—watching me. It's really creepy."

"Has he said anything to you?"

"No...not unless he said something in the bus terminal this morning when I first noticed him then, but I was...I don't remember if we spoke or not. I don't think so."

"Don't say a word to him. No matter what he says. Even if it's to tell him to leave you alone. If you feel at all threatened, say something to the bus driver—"

"How do I know I can trust him?"

There was a slight pause, then Samael continued: "Then start yelling for help or something crazy to draw attention. He—we can't bear the scrutiny of large groups of people. We mostly have to keep it on the D.L."

Claire chuckled to hear him use the slang for "down low."

But her amusement rapidly faded when she realized that the old man—if he was the demon—was between her and the bus driver...and the exits. If he came back here...if he forced a confrontation, she would be trapped.

"You got that?" Samael said. "Don't talk to him." His voice sounded faint with distance, and Claire was all too aware of the miles and miles that separated them.

Even once she was back with Samael, how could she know for sure she was safe?

"He's freaking me out."

"What's he doing?"

Claire shifted up so she could see over the empty seat in front of her. Sure enough, the old man was still turned around in his seat and staring back at her. He never blinked. Claire couldn't see his eyes clearly, but she was positive they didn't have ordinary pupils. She was sure she could see golden, catlike ovals. She wondered if someone like, say, the stoners, noticed what he was doing. Would they react, or was this an illusion designed specifically to creep her out?

"He just...keeps staring at me," she said. The tightness in her throat made her voice sound funny.

"Then ignore him. He can't do anything to you."

"Are you sure?"

"Yes! I'm sure," Samael said, sounding like he was getting a little bit impatient with her.

"Well he sure as fuck is getting on my nerves."

"Just look out the window. Ignore him. Read. Enjoy the trip as much as you can. It'll be over before you know it."

You could say that about life, she thought, and she chuckled grimly.

She wanted to convince herself that—demon or not—the old man was a harmless old coot. She snuggled down in her seat and stared at the back of the seat in front of her.

Samael said, "Call me if you have to."

"I will...for sure."

In the short pause when neither of them spoke, Claire could feel her heart being stretched a couple of hundred miles down Interstate 95.

"I love you," she said as tears filmed her eyes.

"I love you, too, Claire, and I'll see you this afternoon."

"Bye-bye."

Before Samael said anything else, her phone beeped three times. The battery was almost drained.

"I gotta hang up," she said. "My battery's gonna die. I'll call you when I get to Portland."

"Or if there's any trouble."

"Right. If there's any trouble," she said, but then realized that if there was any trouble, she was on her own here.

"Love you."

The phone beeped again, three times.

"Gotta go."

"Love you, too," he said before she quickly killed the call.

As she slid her phone back into her purse, the feeling of abandonment was absolute.

I am on my own!

The old man's gaze was still boring through the bus seat in front of her, still fixed on her. She was tempted to make a scene and go up to the front of the bus to complain to the driver. Maybe she could have the old man removed from the bus as a potential danger or something, but she decided just to let things be.

Like Samael said—stay low…don't speak with anybody…and try to enjoy the long bus ride.

"As if…"

~ * ~

Claire awoke with a start.

Sunlight was flickering through a stand of pine trees on a hillside, creating a weird, old-time movie effect. For a panicked second or two, she was disoriented and didn't know where she was.

Then it all came back: the cold night, her panicked hike through the woods, the wandering and the nervousness—no, the outright panic she experienced even after she got onto the bus. She had been at a crisis level for more than twelve straight hours, now, and no amount of dozing was going to replenish her strength.

She sighed, rubbed her eyes, and then sat straight up, looking to see if the old man was still turned around and looking at her.

To her shock, he was not there.

A quick glance around the bus confirmed that he hadn't changed seats so, unless he was in the restroom, he must have gotten off—

Or disappeared, she thought with a shiver. *The way the demon I thought was Samael had.*

What if he's sitting right there beside me—invisible—and watching me, relishing my fear and paranoia?

Had the bus stopped while she was asleep, and he had gotten off?

She couldn't have slept through that, could she?

She looked around at the passengers but couldn't be sure if anyone else was now gone or if there were any new passengers. Her mind was slow and hazy with sleep, but it worried her that she might have slept through a stopover. With a sudden surge of panic, she clutched her purse and then opened it, making sure her wallet, cell phone, and other valuables were still there.

They were, so she relaxed a bit.

When she cleared her throat, it felt like it was plugged up with dried mucous.

Had she slept with her mouth hanging open and drooling…like some idiot?

She tried to find the strength to get up and move to the front of the bus. For some reason, she thought she might be safer up there.

Where the Hell are we, anyway? She wondered?

When she looked out at the highway, all she saw was the gray asphalt strip slipping by and the seemingly endless stretch of pine forest. That's all there ever was to see on this godforsaken part of the Interstate. Years ago, she had heard that a famous travel magazine had designated I-95 in Maine as one of the ten most scenic highways in the US.

As if, she thought. They must not have driven this far north.

And like she had so many times before, she wished these tedious miles could somehow magically melt away.

She was still wondering about the old man and where he had gone to. It was entirely possible that while she was asleep, the bus had stopped—maybe even in Bangor, if they were already that far south—and he had gotten off. She was working to accept that was what had happened when the door on the bathroom beside her clicked. The sound hit her ears like a gunshot. She looked up and saw the old man exiting.

A lance of ice ran through her, and she couldn't help but gape at him.

Instead of returning to his seat, he braced himself with one hand on the wall, the other on the back of a seat, and stared down at her. Up close, Claire was positive she saw a golden glint in his catlike eyes, but she turned away quickly and stared out the side window.

The muffled thumping of her pulse in her neck was painful.

Claire watched his pale reflection in the window—

At least he has a reflection.

She wanted to turn to him and challenge him, but she remembered Samael's warning not to speak to or even look at him. Still, she couldn't ignore his reflection that loomed in the bus window with the pine trees flickering by.

"You seem lonely and frightened," the old man said. His voice had a mellifluous tone—soothing, trusting…"Where are you headed, child?"

Claire continued to ignore him and kept her gaze fixed on the scenery. She was running through her options. She could get up, push past him without saying a word, and sit up front directly behind the driver. If her cell phone hadn't been dead, she could call someone—who? The police?…Samael?…the bus company?—and report that he was harassing her.

Maybe she should reach into her purse and pretend to grab something—a gun or a can of pepper spray—and hope the old man recognized the threat and backed off.

But if she did that, she'd be the one who ended up in trouble and probably get arrested at the next stop for terrorist activities or whatever. Maybe they'd even have a squad of police cruisers pull the bus over and arrest her on the highway like they did to a guy a few years ago in Portsmouth, New Hampshire.

"If yah want, we could talk about whatever's bothering yah."

His voice was still laced with honey smoothness, but she detected a wicked edge lurking like a hidden serpent underneath it. She kept staring straight out the bus window until her eyes hurt. The bus was in the passing lane, and she jolted with surprise when she saw a car, speeding up on the right side until it was beside the bus, directly outside her window, keeping pace.

"No way," she said. Her breath steamed the bus window, obscuring her view.

It was Samael's black Mercedes!

And Samael was driving! In spite of the cold day, the windows were rolled down, and she could see him clearly.

A surge of desperate hope filled her.

She stared down at him, but he was staring at the road ahead as if he didn't know she was there. Claire had no idea where they were. She hadn't seen a road sign for the longest time, and she wondered how he could have gotten this far north so fast, turned around, and found her bus, heading south.

"Samael," she whispered, tapping furiously on the window with her forefinger. For a moment, she forgot all about the old man in the aisle beside her. She clenched her right hand into a fist and started banging harder on the window.

As if he can hear me...

"Samael!"

She kept knocking, harder, until a passenger—not the old man—shouted, "Hey! Yah wanna keep it down back there? I'm trying to sleep here!"

Claire felt defeated as she watched Samael, wishing—praying he would glance up and see her.

He has to know I'm on this bus...

But he sure as Hell wasn't acting like it. She gazed down at him, admiring his handsome profile with the morning sun beaming through the windshield, lighting up his face. As she stared at him, he slowly rotated his head much further than was possible for a normal human, like a mechanical toy, until he was looking straight at her. His eyes were huge, black pits—like holes punched into an icy pond. A wicked smile spread across his face, exposing long, pointed teeth that dimpled his lower lip as he looked at her and clearly mouthed the words: "Fuck you!"

Claire's heart froze.

Still not looking at the road ahead, Samael—

No!...That's not Samael!

—started to speed up, pulling away from the bus.

Leaning forward in her seat, Claire pressed her face against the window as she watched him go. His head had now rotated a full hundred and eighty degrees, and he was staring at her over his back, not looking at the road ahead. Before he pulled out of sight, he raised his left hand from the steering wheel and slowly extended his middle finger until he jabbed it in her direction. Then, still not looking ahead but watching her with a cold, pitiless expression, he sped away.

Claire was crushed, but at least she knew now that the demon that was tormenting her was not on the bus. Blinking back tears, she turned away from the window. Already what she had seen outside seemed unreal—like a fragment from a nightmare. She slumped forward, face in her hands, and sobbed low, dry sobs that wrenched her hard.

"I see," the old man said, his voice still dripping with so much kindness and understanding it was sickening. "Problems with your boyfriend...maybe your husband, huh?"

He paused as if expecting Claire to answer or at least acknowledge him, but as she stared down at her lap, all she could wonder was: *Why the Hell does he think I want to talk to him about anything?*

In a sudden rush of anger and hurt and fear—yes, genuine fear that the danger was far from over—she raised her head and looked at the old man.

Only he wasn't a man.

Standing in the aisle was a large misshapen mass that had only the vaguest indication of a human shape. Claire's eyes widened with shock which jacked up even higher when she realized the old man was in reality made up of a swarming mass of wasps. They buzzed and crawled, vibrating their wings and making loud, clicking and crackling sounds that vibrated madly in her ears. The old man's figure shifted and shuddered as the mass of wasps seethed, their buzzing sounds getting steadily louder, as if they were irritated.

Claire was frantic to get away from him. Without thinking it through, she lurched out of her seat and pushed past the old man. Her knees started to fold up under her, and she bumped into him. Immediately, her hand and wrist got stung in at least a dozen places. Her winter coat protected her arm, but her hand and wrist felt like it had been peppered by numerous tiny heated pinpricks.

When she looked up at the old man's face—the wasp demon— what appeared to be his mouth opened wide, and a swarm of wasps shot out like darts. Claire squealed and ducked down just in time to avoid them. One caught her on the side of the face and stung her under the eye. Whimpering, she made her way to the front of the bus where the seat directly behind the driver was now available. The mother and two kids were sitting a few seats back. The older child was asleep, and the baby was nursing.

Claire sat down, her hand covering the sting on her face. A prickling sensation washed over the back of her neck, and she imagined dozens if not hundreds of wasps, crawling all over her skin. When she swatted herself, the loud smacking sound drew the attention of the young mother, but Claire didn't dare make eye contact.

Who's to say she isn't a demon, too...that the whole bus isn't filled with demons, determined to torment me and wait until I slip up and damn my soul?

The thought was like a wedge of ice slicing through her gut—

They're following me...tracking me...watching me all the time...maybe so I'll lead them to Samael.

Hands shaking, she took her compact from her purse and looked at the sting under her eyes. It pained her with a fiery jab, but in reflection, she couldn't see even the tiniest mark.

What the Hell is going on here?

She wished she had the courage to look behind her at the old man—the wasp demon—but she knew she'd scream in terror if she still saw the buzzing mass of wasps that she knew was his true form. Instead, she sat there, frozen with fear and leaning forward with her elbows on her knees.

She took her cell phone from her purse and stared at it. She wanted desperately to call him. It would be so reassuring to hear the quiet, measured calm of his voice again.

But she also had to save her cell's battery for emergencies. As the bus rumbled along, all she could think was—as much as she had suffered from the cold in the forest last night, her problems—and Samael's problems—were far from over.

In fact, they were just beginning.

Chapter

12

————Ding Dong

The thought crossed Claire's mind that she might already be damned and in Hell, forced to ride on this bus forever.

It seemed as though the bus took every exit off the Interstate to pick up or drop off passengers. More often than not, though, there was no one waiting or getting off at the station. Still, they had to keep to their routine and schedule, just in case. It was looking like all of the passengers—even the wasp man at the back of the bus—were heading to Portland or points south.

She didn't know what she would do if the wasp man approached her, either on the bus or when they arrived in Portland...

Would she be safe in the bus terminal?

Terminal...Now there's a good word!

Well, she figured she'd have to make sure she didn't get into a situation where he could corner her and get her alone.

But what if she had to use the restroom, and he barged in?

Would he be that bold?

What if he manipulated her somehow and got her alone?

And when they finally arrived in Portland, what if Samael, or whoever appeared to be Samael, was waiting there in his black Mercedes. She had no way of knowing if it was really Samael or an imposter.

She moaned softly and pressed her head against the headrest of the seat, wishing to God that none of this had ever happened, but that didn't extend to not meeting Samael.

That she would never change!

Demon or not, he was the love of her life…"for better or worse"…and being trapped on a bus with a wasp demon was right up there with "worst."

There were so many infinitesimally small things that could have gone differently, and she would never have met Samael…or he might have noticed Sally first…or if she, not Sally, had gone to the restroom in the restaurant, then Ron LaPierre might have attacked Sally, not her.

Infinite possibilities…especially when you're dealing with a demon, but it all came down to this —

It doesn't matter because this is what's happening now, and come Hell or high water, she had to deal with it…or else.

"Right," she whispered, squeezing her eyes tightly. "Or else…what?"

Feeling somewhat secure sitting directly behind the driver, she settled. The monotonous hum of the bus's wheels on pavement soon lulled her, and she drifted into a hazy half-sleep. Before she settled down, she found the courage to look into the driver's huge rearview mirror and check on the old man—the wasp demon. He was sitting straight up in his seat, not hunched over, as she had expected. His hands were folded in his lap as he stared forward, straight at her. He looked perfectly normal…except for that creepy stare. The mask of wasps—or had she seen his true form and was looking at the mask now?—was gone.

Claire didn't like him staring at her, but what could she do?

Telling herself she was safe, at least right now, she cuddled up as best she could and drowsed. One thing that kept coming back to her mind…buzzing like a bothersome wasp…was wondering what Samael's true shape was.

Is what I see…what I love…a mask, too?

At least with her head below the top of the seatback, the wasp demon couldn't see her although she sensed that still—somehow—he could see her through the cushioned seats.

Fuck him, she thought. Fuck him and all of them!

She opened her eyes in time to see the sign for Waterville flash by her window, and she smiled, thinking, I may make it after all.

~ * ~

And make it back she did. At some point in the trip, she fell asleep again. She was amazed that she had, considering how wound up she was, but she was also wrung out from being awake more than twenty-four hours straight.

She awoke with a start when the bus's air brakes made a loud gasping sound that hit her ears like the blast of a foghorn. The sudden deceleration ripped her from her sleep, and she let out a little squeak of surprise as she shook her head, blinked her eyes, amazed to see that the bus was on the exit ramp for Congress Street, heading to downtown Portland.

Home sweet home, she thought as the bus roared past the old, familiar landmarks—streets and buildings that told her she had made it. The bus driver clicked on the intercom and said, "Ladies and gentlemen, we're arriving in Portland. The time is two fifteen, so we're a little ahead of schedule. If you had friends or family members meeting you here, you might want to give them a call and let 'em know you're a bit early."

He clicked off the microphone before taking a wide, sweeping turn off the ramp.

The relief Claire experienced was indescribable even though she knew the danger was far from over.

If anything, it was only going to get worse, but she was sure she could face it as long as she was with Samael. She was almost frantic to see him, wondering—hoping—that he had gotten to the bus terminal early. She dug out her phone and dialed his number, relieved when he answered it on the second ring.

"Hello, darlin'," he said.

"We're almost at the terminal," she said, pushing aside any paranoid thoughts that this might not be him. Hearing his voice and knowing this had to be the real Samael made her feel as though everything she had gone through over the past twenty-four plus hours would all be worth it when she was finally safe in his arms, feeling his body pressing against hers.

Before she could say anything more, her Call Waiting beeped. She scowled when she saw it was her parents—probably her mother, worried as usual—calling. The bus heaved and swayed as it navigated the narrow streets of the city, making its ponderous way to the Greyhound station on outer Congress Street.

"Hold on a sec. It's my folks."

"I'm on my way. See you in a few," he said and then hung up.

Claire clicked to take the incoming call from her parents.

"Hi Mom," she said, trying to sound more chipper and bright than she felt.

"Well, finally," her mother said. She sounded like she had just run up a flight of stairs and was winded. "Are you all right?"

"Yeah. Sure. I'm fine," Claire said. She almost added 'Why do you ask?' but decided not to encourage any more probing than necessary.

Her phone beeped three times, and she said, "My battery's almost dead, so can you make it quick?"

"Yes. Your dad was talking to Wilfred Henry today. He said something about you taking a bus out of town first thing this morning. Is that true?"

Busted!

But she had known it would happen.

Claire took a breath, trying to collect her thoughts, but there wasn't much she could come up with...unless she told the absolute truth.

But if she told the truth, her mother would worry all the more and probably have her committed. Nobody would believe the truth...unless they had seen what she had seen.

"I—ah. Yeah, we had some car trouble, and rather than wait around to get the car fixed, I decided to take the bus back home while—" She almost choked, saying the name because she knew her folks hadn't met the real Samael after all. "Samael decided to have it fixed."

"He's still here in town?"

"No. We were down the road a ways."

"Where?"

"It doesn't matter," she said, hoping to end the interrogation.

Her phone beeped three times again.

"We're fine, Mom. Look, my phone's gonna die soon. I'll call you once I get back—home." She hesitated on the word home because she wasn't exactly sure what "home" was.

"You mean to tell me you thought it was easier—it made sense to sit in a bus station all night—rather than come home?"

"I didn't want to bother you—"

The phone finally died as the bus heaved heavily to the right as it took a corner onto Congress Street. The lurching motion almost threw Claire out of her seat. She grabbed the seat in front of her to hold on. Up ahead was the bus station with another huge bus, waiting out front as people milled around, getting ready to board.

"Look. Ma. Everything's okay. I swear," she said into the dead phone. Then she closed it and slid it into her purse.

Yeah, right, she thought.

~ * ~

The relief of Samael holding her tightly in his embrace was almost too much for Claire to handle. She burst into tears and pressed her face against his chest, nuzzling into his neck and deeply inhaling his scent—smoky and musky. Tears carved warm traces down her cheeks, and she couldn't stop shuddering.

"Don't worry," he whispered as he stroked her hair, cupping the back of her head. "You're safe now."

The steel-tight muscles of his arms crushed her against his chest, making it difficult for her to catch her breath. Tiny white dots of light sizzled as they zigzagged across her vision. She was afraid she might pass out, so she pushed him away and leaned back, looking up into his eyes.

How do I know it's really you? She wanted to ask, but the light in his gold-flecked eyes and the smile on his face was proof enough that this was the real Samael.

She wondered how she could have been deceived so easily.

"You have any more trouble along the way?"

Biting her lower lip, Claire shook her head no, but then she told him about the wasp demon. Samael said he knew who that was but wouldn't elaborate. She also told him about seeing "him" out the bus window, the imposter who had driven by in his Mercedes and flipped her off, but other than that—no, no problems.

"You didn't touch him, did you?" he asked.

"Who?"

Samael hesitated, and then said, "The wasp demon" as if he didn't want—or dare—say his...or its...real name.

"I brushed against him when I was trying to get away from him. I felt a few stings, but other than that...No."

Samael nodded as though deep in thought.

"So what do we do now?" she asked. Her voice trembled as she exhaled.

They walked across the parking lot to Samael's car, their arms wrapped around each other so tightly they staggered a little. Anyone seeing them would have guessed they were madly in love—which they were—and being reunited after a long separation.

"We go to my place," Samael said.

"Is it safe there?"

Claire stopped him on the sidewalk and turned to face him.

"It will be," he said.

She stared into his gold-flecked eyes, feeling like she had truly come home.

"They're after you, not me," she said, her heart filled with worry.

Samael was silent for a moment.

"So," she continued, "the only real danger I'm in is if I get in their way, right?"

Samael looked to one side and then shrugged. Finally, he said, "Well, not entirely."

"What do you mean by that?"

"I mean it's a lot more complicated than that."

"How so?"

"He's taken a little part of you, and you probably have a part of him still on you."

"Then I'll take a shower and wash it off...with you," she added with a flirty wink.

"This is serious, Claire. If they find an opening...if they see a chance to claim your soul, they'll do it. And now that you touched...him— They can get inside your head. They'll try to convince you that giving them your soul will save me."

Not gonna happen, Claire thought as a shiver ran up her spine. She felt like she could start crying and never stop, but she had cried enough over the last twenty-four hours when they had been apart. Now that they were together again, she wanted him to see just how tough a "County Girl" could be.

"So we have to be extra careful, then," she said. "Are you sure we're safe at your place?"

Samael gave his tight smile as he nodded and said, "I have help."

Claire was bursting to ask him what he meant by that, but they had arrived at his car. He opened the passenger's door for her. An amazing flood of relief swept over her as she slid onto the car seat, and he closed the door firmly. As she watched him walk around the car to get in on the driver's side, she noticed her iPod, right where she had left it yesterday, on their drive up to Houlton.

She nearly threw the car door open, got out, and ran as far away from him as she could.

How could her iPod be here in his car unless it had been him in this same car yesterday?

What the Hell is going on?

"Samael!" she exclaimed.

"What?" He looked at her, shock and surprise on his face. "Did you see someone?"

It took effort, but Claire shook her head and then looked at him with a cold, steady gaze. She was so close to screaming in terror, but she kept hold of herself, knowing if there was ever a time to be strong and deal with things upfront, this was it.

"Do you swear it wasn't you?" she asked.

She had no idea how she kept her voice from shattering.

"Was me? Where? What are you talking about?"

"Yesterday...on the drive north...and again this morning."

Samael's brow furrowed with concern. There was deep hurt in his gold-flecked eyes.

"I...I don't get what you're talking about," he said softly. He started to reach in to touch her, but she swept his hand away. They locked eyes, and she could see emotions struggling inside him.

"When we—when I and you or whoever was driving this car started out yesterday, I plugged my iPod into your system," she said.

"Yeah...and...?" He looked confused.

"*And*—"

She indicated the iPod with a curt nod.

"It's still connected to your sound system," she said evenly, trying hard to mask her nervousness. "If that wasn't you driving with me yesterday, how did my iPod get here?"

Samael's expression suddenly went slack. He shook his head and was silent for a long time as he stared straight out the window.

Please, please, please let there be a rational explanation for this, she thought.

"Well...?" she said, drawing out the word.

Samael shook his head as though bewildered and said, "Claire, you have to believe me. No matter how it looks. Your iPod wasn't here yesterday, when I drove home from work."

"You specifically noticed that?"

Samael nodded and said, "I'm very observant."

I'll bet you are, she thought but didn't say. Instead, she said, "So...What? It magically appeared here out of nowhere now that I'm back in town?"

Again, Samael shrugged and shook his head.

"I don't know what to say." And then his eyes brightened, and he snapped his fingers. "Wait a second. You saw him—the imposter—pass you on the highway?"

Claire nodded thoughtfully, seeing it coming.

"So what's to say he didn't come by my place and put it there...knowing that when you saw it, you would immediately doubt me?"

Samael shifted in the seat and turned to face her. The loving earnestness in his eyes was too much to take. Claire had to look away in order to hold her ground.

"Sounds reasonable enough," she said, "but is it the truth?"

"You have to believe me," he said. He took her hand and squeezed it. Her hand was sweaty in his grip. "You have no idea...no idea what they're capable of doing. If you don't believe me, then I...You have no idea what I'm risking here."

"And I'm not?"

"I told you. You're not the one they're after. They can't stand it when one of us decides to renounce our Evil ways. And they'll do anything and everything they can to stop it and make sure I pay for it.

"My torments would never end, and it's only you...your love that—"

His voice hitched, and tears brimmed in his gold-flecked eyes.

Holy crap! Claire thought. *He's crying!...Can a demon do that?*

"You have to trust me, Claire. Please," he said, squeezing her hand tightly. "And you have to promise me you'll never let me go." He swallowed hard, his gold-flecked eyes moist. "And you have to remember..."

"Remember what?" she asked.

"You're my salvation...my only salvation."

"Samael—" she started to say, but her voice choked off when she saw the earnest determination in his face.

"You're the whole reason I'm doing this," he continued, "and to be honest, I don't think I can do it alone. Without you, I'm not even willing to try. I can only do this as long as you're with me."

Claire was stunned. Speechless. She pulled a glove from her coat pocket and used it to gently wipe away the tears that were now streaming down his cheeks.

His tears were warm—hot, and they tingled like weak acid on her fingertips, an almost pleasing sensation.

"I am," she said, her eyes tearing up as well. "I'm with you all the way, and...and I always will be."

~ * ~

"Something's wrong?" Claire said as they pulled into Samael's driveway. Above the pines in the direction of the house, a thin column of black smoke was tumbling up into the slate -gray sky.

Samael squinted and leaned forward over the steering wheel as he navigated the gently winding curve of the driveway. Claire tensed in her seat, staring intently at the pillar of smoke. When they rounded the corner and could see the portico of Samael's house, they realized it wasn't the house that was on fire.

"Looks like it's out behind the house," Samael said as the car skidded to a stop. They hurriedly got out.

"Thank God," Claire said, and he shot her a quick smile. He dashed around the car to her and put his arm around her shoulder.

"Doesn't look too bad now," Samael said. And, indeed, the thick smoke was all but gone.

She shot him an "are you sure" glance, and he nodded as they started up the steps to the front door, holding her protectively to his side.

When they entered the house, Michelle was striding down the hallway toward them. The heels of her shoes clicked on the Italian tile floor and echoed in the vastness of the room. She looked perfectly calm, but Claire thought she detected a level of agitation lurking below the surface.

"Is everything all right, Michelle?" Samael asked. He, too, seemed to be trying to mask his concern.

Michelle nodded and said, "Michael's out back. He has everything under control."

Who the Hell is Michael?

Hand in hand, Claire and Samael walked down the long hall. They finally arrived in the breakfast room, which had a screen door leading out onto the back porch, which ran the length of the house. A man was standing on the lawn at the foot of the steps, looking out across the lawn at the smoke drifting up into the sky. It was coming from a small, black mound in the middle of the lawn.

Claire gasped when the man—obviously "Michael"—turned and regarded her with a long, steady stare. She had noticed, without too much amazement, his long, perfectly snow-white hair that cascaded to his shoulders. But when he turned, she was stunned to see his eyes. They had no pupils and were pure silver. Even in the dim daylight, they flashed like white fire.

Samael, still holding her hand, sensed her reaction and gave her a reassuring squeeze as he leaned close and whispered, "I understand…It's always surprising at first."

You could say that again, Claire thought as they moved closer to the man.

No…This most definitely was not a man.

"Michael. I'd like you to meet Claire," Samael said simply. "Claire. This is Michael."

Claire was dumbstruck. She could only stare at him in amazement. His presence was overwhelming, and she couldn't decide if she should shake his hand, curtsey, or bow down.

"Don't be afraid," Michael said in a sweet voice that was at once soothing and powerful. He held his hand up with the palm facing toward her, like a minister giving a blessing.

Claire sensed great love and understanding…and power. She bowed her head in acknowledgment.

"Michael's here to help," Samael said to Claire, and then to Michael he said, "Tell me what happened."

A faint smile passed across Michael's lips, and his eyes flashed. Claire noticed that his face had an odd translucence that made his skin look waxy and pale, as if an inner light was shining from him.

"One of them tried to get into the house," Michael said. When he nodded in the direction of the still smoldering heap, a cold shock went through Claire's heart.

That burning pile used to be a person…or a demon…or whatever…

"A feeble attempt," Michael continued. "They can and will do much better. We can't lower our guard for an instant. I suspect they made such an inept attempt as their first move perhaps to lull us into a false sense of security."

"Makes sense," Samael said, stroking his chin. He stood for a while, deep in thought as he stared at the pile of ashes. The smoke had diminished now to a thin, black smudge against the sky. Claire couldn't tell if Samael was angry or worried or satisfied or…what? And she sensed that now was not the time to bother him with questions. All she knew for sure was that he—and she—were in grave danger and, possibly, more than she could imagine. But after seeing the wasp demon on the bus, she didn't think anything would surprise her. She moved closer to Samael and tucked her hand into the crook of his elbow.

"Everything else is secure?" Samael finally said.

"As good as I can make it," Michael replied.

"Then it's better than secure."

Finally, a look of pure relief—the first she had seen since they reconnected—came over Samael's face. He smiled when he said, "Well, then, what say we go back into the house and refresh ourselves. It's been a helluva day.

And, I suspect, it's going to be a helluva night."

At that moment, Claire had no idea what an understatement that was.

~ * ~

Claire was feeling way out of her depth as she sat with Samael and Michael in the living room. They talked until the sun had set. Then, the spacious room filled with soft, gray arms of shadows stretched across the plush carpet. Even in the waning light, she couldn't stop herself from looking at Michael's eyes. They shined even more as the room grew dark, and she knew without asking that he could see as clearly in the darkness as he could in the daylight.

She also sensed that whenever he looked at her, even if for only a flashing instant, Michael could see clear into her heart and know what she was thinking and feeling. She knew without being told that he understood her in ways that even she didn't.

How can I not be afraid? She thought.

This spiritual being…this angel—because she knew that's what he was—was frightening in spite of his silver aura. She chuckled to herself, remembering a time when, in confirmation class, she had asked her Sunday School teacher, Mrs. Carmody, about angels. While reading the Bible, she had noticed that in every or nearly every instance, when an angel first appeared to a human being, he—it always seemed to be a male even though most paintings of angels depicted them as female—said, "Be not afraid," or words to that effect. She had asked Mrs. Carmody why an angel would say something like that, and she concluded at a young age that angels must be terrifying beings to behold.

And now she knew.

They were.

But—somehow—not in a bad way.

Here she was, sitting in a darkening living room with a demon who professed to love her and wanted to reclaim his angelic nature, and an honest-to-God (pardon the phrase) angel.

It was surreal, to say the least.

She tried to focus on the conversation Samael and Michael were having, but it seemed as though they spoke in code, at times, or else used an entirely different and incomprehensible language. Maybe she was still exhausted from her ordeal in the woods overnight and the terrors of the bus ride back to Portland. But much of the conversation passed way over her head.

Long after the room was too dark for her to see more than vague shadows—and no one made a move to turn on the lights—she sat on the couch, her hand clasped by Samael's so tightly it grew slick with sweat. But she didn't take it away. She wanted—she needed—the reassurance of physical contact to ground her in a reality that seemed to be slipping away rapidly. She rested her head against Samael's shoulder.

Their voices—especially Michael's—were amazingly soothing. Warm, rich, and mellow. She felt so comfortable she started to doze off. As she floated in and out of hazy half-dreams, she felt a safety and security she had never known before.

He really will take care of me...They both will...

And then—is this still part of the dream?—Samael kissed her lightly on the cheek.

"Claire...Com'on, Claire...It's time to wake up and go to sleep."

She floated back to consciousness slowly...begrudgingly ...hating to leave her warm, safe hiding place.

"Mmnn," she said, licking her lips and tasting something sour in her mouth.

"It's late," Samael said. "Almost midnight."

"What?"

"I don't blame you for falling asleep," Samael said mildly. "You had a Hell of a day, and Michael and I had a lot to catch up on."

"I can imagine," Claire said, thinking vaguely that the two of them had probably known each other for millennia. She wanted to ask him more about Michael, but she sensed that Samael wanted to keep their discussion private.

Which was just as well.

The more she knew, the more she would worry. And in a way, she also knew that much of it was beyond human understanding.

"How about we go to bed?"

She was feeling none too steady on her feet, so Samael helped her keep her balance. She let him take her by the arm and guide her up the stairs to the bedroom. Without bothering to undress, she collapsed face-first onto the bed and was out like a light within seconds.

~ * ~

It was still dark when Claire awoke with a start and realized Samael's tail was wrapped around her protectively. When she opened her eyes and looked at him, she was not surprised to find him looking back at her. The lamp on the bedside table was on, and he had the most gorgeous smile, but his eyes bothered her. They glinted like chips of black ice, the gold flecks barely visible. She couldn't help but wonder if it was the lighting in the bedroom or if his eyes were…changing, for some reason.

"Hey there," she said sleepily.

"Hey there, yourself."

His tail tightened around her, and she considered getting something started to pleasure both herself and him, but it somehow didn't seem appropriate…not now, anyway, considering everything that had gone on over the last twenty-four or so hours.

Plus, there was an angel in the house.

"How'd you sleep?" she asked, only to make conversation. She snuggled up closer to him, relishing his warmth.

"All right, I guess," Samael replied. "Well enough. How about you?"

"Like a rock."

He released his tail and gently played the tip of it over the curves of her body, finally burrowing it in between her legs.

"Are you sure it's okay?" she asked.

"Damn! It's more than okay."

Without any more urging, Claire began to run her hand up and down the length of the shaft. She shifted her other hand to his chest and started running it across the ridges of his stomach muscles. It felt as hard and flat as an old-fashioned washboard.

"Let me make you feel good," he whispered as she shifted onto her side and then lay on her back. She slipped off her jeans and panties and kicked them to the foot of the bed. Samael's tail seemed to take on a life of its own, darting forward like a striking snake and plunging into her without warning.

Claire bucked on the bed and let out a surprised shriek, but then she collapsed back onto the mattress and lost all sense of who was doing what to whom. All she knew was that—once again...as always—Samael was taking her to new levels of physical and emotional pleasure.

Maybe an hour later, as the sky lightened with a predawn glow, after she was absolutely satiated, she collapsed onto the bed. Her head nestled in the well of his armpit like a bird's egg in a nest. An oily sheen of sweat covered her skin, and she was breathing in slow, irregular breaths as mild aftershocks rippled through her.

"Happy?" Samael asked.

He was lying on his side, his head propped up on his left hand as he smiled down at her. His right hand was sliding up and down her sides, pausing with every upward stroke to caress her breasts. Every now and then, he'd lean forward and nuzzle his face into the fiery cascade of her hair.

"Umm...Yes," she said, more gasp than words.

Samael chuckled softly.

"What?" she said, knowing even as she asked that he wouldn't tell her anything he didn't want her to know.

"Oh, nothing."

"It's not nothing," she said. But after spending time with him, she knew Samael didn't yield his secrets easily.

He shifted around and raised himself so he was arched over her, his hands planted onto the mattress on both sides, trapping her where she lay.

"Seriously, what?" she asked again, her voice rising. She felt an element of danger in his position. He was panting, his breath warm and moist on her face.

She looked up at him. His head and shoulders, framed by the blank gauzy gray of the bedroom ceiling, looked immense...like a statue, about to come crashing down on top of her.

Samael smiled as he gazed down at her, his eyes glowing unnaturally.

Even in this light, the gold flecks weren't as apparent. She wondered if she should mention it to him—ask him what was going on—but decided not to. She could still see nothing but love reflected in his eyes, darkening as they were.

"I wanted to ask you something," he said.

"What's that?"

"I was going to ask if you wanted to get married today."

Claire was taken aback, and she wondered if she had heard him correctly. Her mouth dropped open, and Samael chuckled as he put a finger on her chin and to close it.

"Wha—what did you say?"

"I asked if you wanted to get married today. It's a simple enough question."

His smile lit up the bedroom, and hearing him ask twice finally convinced her that she hadn't imagined it the first time.

"Married..."

"Not right away. We can take our time. Take showers and have something to eat," Samael went on. "But I figured since Michael's here, he can stand in as my best man. And you can ask your roommate...Or someone else, if you want. But—yes. I think we should do it. Today. This morning...or afternoon at the latest. I mean, why not?"

"Why not?" Claire echoed, and then she snorted. "You make it all sound so romantic 'Why not?'" Sliding one hand out from under him, she swatted him on the shoulder. "Why not say 'because I love you madly, and I want to marry you?' God. You can make anything sound like a...like a business transaction."

"I don't mean to." He actually looked chastised. "I'm new at this, you know, but I do know that I want you by my side. How's that?"

Samael's face lit up with the most amazing smile, his gold-flecked eyes gleaming. Then he slowly lowered his head until their lips were less than an inch apart. His breath was hot on her face, and she detected a not-unpleasant hint of fruitwood smoke when she inhaled.

"Because I do love you," he said. "And I'm willing to risk everything...and I mean everything—even my own existence—to prove how much I love you."

As much as she tried to stop them, now tears did fill Claire's eyes. She wondered why, ever since she had first met Samael, she had been crying so much more. She had always considered herself a fairly tough woman. Not unemotional—but she certainly thought she had her emotions under control.

But not anymore...Not with this guy...

"I love you with all my heart," she said, her voice hitching as tears streamed down both sides of her face. "And I want you always. Don't ever leave me, Samael."

"Trust me. I won't."

She shifted around so she could reach up and embrace him, and as she drew him down on top of her, his weight pressed her into the mattress so hard it was difficult to breathe deeply.

But it doesn't matter...Let me die right here...

This was the moment...the moment she had dreamt about and wished for all her life and, as she grew older, began to think might never actually come. But here it was. She now knew, beyond any and all doubt, that this man—no, not a man. A demon truly loved her...and she loved him.

Although she hadn't answered him directly—not yet, anyway—she knew that he already knew her answer. They kissed, long and hard, his double-tipped tongue slipping into her mouth like a living thing and whisking around, sending sparkling thrills all through her body. When they finally broke off the kiss, she was still gazing at him. Tears still clouded her sight, but she took a tiny sip of a breath and said, "Yes...Yes...Yes. Let's get married today. As soon as we can."

Samael's mouth split into a wide grin that exposed his wide, flat teeth. No matter what he said or did, he still had a dangerous edge to him, but she figured now that she would simply have to get used to it.

Just part of his charm, I guess...

"Fantastic!" he shouted as he pushed himself up and off the bed. He jumped up and down a few times, looking like a kid on Christmas morning, and then he did a little shuffling dance step as he turned and started for the bathroom. Claire couldn't help but laugh, seeing his tail sketch wild figure eights in the air. Before he closed the door, he shouted joyously, "Married! I'm actually getting married! Who'd a 'thunk it!"

What a piece of work he is, she thought.

For the first time in...she couldn't remember when...she smiled so hard her cheeks ached.

Chapter

13

————To Have and to Hold

The next couple of hours passed by in a blur.

It annoyed Claire that she hadn't had time to plan...well, pretty much anything.

Even when she called Sally to ask her to be her bridesmaid, Sally was at work and said she couldn't just up and leave for the day. It took quite a bit to convince her. Claire insisted, time and again, that she could meet her back at the apartment and help her get ready. Finally, Sally said that wasn't necessary and promised she'd meet them at City Hall at eleven o'clock.

Claire had her doubts, but she had no Plan B.

That barely gave her time to pick out a dress, buy some flowers, fix her hair, and put on her makeup. It didn't seem fair that all Samael had to do after he showered was blow-dry his hair and put on one of the scores of expensive suits he had hanging in his closet. Claire's clothing options were limited because she didn't have any dresses she thought were acceptable for her wedding day, rushed though it was. She certainly didn't have time to go buy something new.

After rummaging around in her closet for over an hour, pulling out and trying on dress after dress, she was about to tell Samael that she wanted to postpone getting married at least a day to give herself time to plan. She hadn't even called her parents to tell them yet and, as it turned out, her parents hadn't met Samael…at least not the real Samael.

"You about ready?" Samael called from somewhere downstairs when Claire was in the bathroom, putting on her makeup.

"Can you give me…I dunno…maybe a week or two?"

She frowned at her reflection in the mirror. She had always imagined she'd wear a white gown with a train and veil to her wedding, not a cream-colored sweater dress and high-heeled suede boots. In a gesture to Samael, she left her hair loose, the way he liked it.

A wave of tangled emotion swept through her—a curious mixture of sadness and frustration…of nervousness and indescribable joy. She wished she had someone—a closer-than-close friend she could talk to about it, but in truth, she didn't have many—any?—close friends.

Of course, she felt close to Samael. She loved him and wanted to spend the rest of her life—

My mortal life.

—with him. And she wanted to do anything and everything she could to help him regain his angelic nature. But that presented situations and problems she couldn't begin to comprehend much less deal with right now.

"What the Hell am I doing?" she asked her reflection as she leaned close enough to the mirror to fog the glass with her breath. She stared into her own eyes, wondering, *And who the Hell are you*?

She jumped when footsteps sounded on the stairs, and she forced herself to smile as she turned to face the bathroom door. She was mildly surprised when she saw Michael, not Samael, in the doorway. He was wearing a white suit. His shirt and tie—even his shoes, were white, but nothing was whiter than his shoulder-length hair. The only color—if you can call black a color—were the silver sunglasses perched on the top of his head. His silver eyes were dazzling, and Claire realized he couldn't go out in public and let everyone see his eyes.

"Have you got a minute?" Michael asked.

His voice was amazingly calm and soothing; it cut through the emotions tangled up inside her.

"Yeah…Sure … What's up?"

"I would like to tell you that you are, in all likelihood, not in any danger, and that I appreciate everything you are doing—the effort you're putting out to help Samael. I admire the love you have for him. It's more important than, I think, even Samael realizes."

Claire had no idea what to say to that.

What can you possibly say to an angel who, essentially, is giving you his blessing to marry a demon?

Too weird!

"I've known Samael for…a very long time."

How long? Claire wanted to ask but didn't. Something told her that even "time" for beings like Samael and Michael wasn't the same as it was for people…mortals like her.

"And in all that time, I have yearned and prayed for him to renounce his evil ways."

"How…how evil is…or was he?"

The corners of Michael's mouth twitched into a tight smile as he shook his head.

"That's not the point," he said softly.

"Oh," Claire said, flummoxed for a moment. "So what is the point?"

She didn't like that she let her impatience show, but heavenly being or not, he had to understand that she was under a lot of stress here, getting ready to get married.

"The point is simple." Michael's smile widened, and Claire could feel the peace and warmth radiating from him. "I am happy for you and him, and I hope this marriage is a blessing to you both."

"Thank you," Claire said with an involuntary bow.

How -DO you talk to an angel?…What are the rules?

She had to avert her gaze because he shone with a light that wasn't just the reflection of the fluorescent light on his clothes and hair. The glow was coming from inside him—a pulsating radiance that filled her with a deep, indescribable peace.

"I realize you have a lot to do to prepare," Michael said, "so I'll leave you alone for now." He turned to leave but then stopped and, looking back at Claire, extended his right hand, palm-out to her, and said, "Blessings unto you," and then he was gone.

He didn't walk out and close the door behind him. He was...gone.

A feeling of serenity—and a new resolve—filled her as she turned back to the mirror to finish with her makeup. Her eyes sparkled, and her long, red curls billowed around her face and flowed down her back like a fire-fall.

Not bad, she thought. *Who really needs a fancy white dress, anyway?*

She gave herself one final, satisfied look in the large mirror in the bedroom, and then went downstairs to join Samael and Michael, who were waiting for her in the sunroom. They had been talking about something quite intensely, but they stopped abruptly when she entered the room.

"Amazing...absolutely amazing," Samael said, his voice tinged with awe as he got up from his chair, walked over to Claire, and gave her a hug. He kissed her on the mouth, but only for a few seconds. She broke it off, feeling funny, making out in front of an angel. He stepped back and, raising his left arm, glanced at his wristwatch.

"We ought to get going," he said.

Claire was suddenly dizzy with anticipation. As she walked out of the house between Samael and Michael, she felt like her feet were hovering a few inches above the ground. Her head felt like a helium balloon tethered to a string, bouncing in the air.

Samael opened the car door for her and waited until she was settled before closing it. As he walked around the front of the car to get to the driver's side, he stopped and looked at her through the windshield. His smile gleamed in the sun, but still, his eyes looked strangely dark. He brought both of his hands up to his mouth and sent her a huge kiss.

Claire laughed and bounced in her seat like a little child, positive she had never been happier in her life.

Michael got into the back seat behind her, and then Samael got into the car and started it up. As they pulled away, the tires chirping on the asphalt, Claire looked longingly out the side window as the house and then the yard slowly slipped past her. It suddenly hit her—This is real! She was about to marry a demon and live in a house suitable for a princess...with servants and everything.

What am I doing? She thought and then said out loud, "What am I doing?"

When Samael said, "Huh?" instead of saying something like, Oh, nothing, she repeated herself.

"What am I doing?"

Samael glanced at her before pulling out of the driveway onto the road. She looked at him and—as always—was entranced by the contours of his gorgeous face. He stepped on the gas, and the car purred with smooth, quiet power. Once they were underway, he answered her.

"I'll tell you what you're doing," he said with a big grin. "You're doing the best thing you've ever done in your life."

She wasn't sure, but she thought she heard Michael in the back seat whisper, "In more ways than one."

~ * ~

The scene at City Hall was about as romantic as a dentist's office. A crowd of people, most of them in jeans and flannels, were waiting to register their cars, renew their licenses, get dump permits, and other mundane tasks. Claire felt conspicuous, carrying the small bouquet they had picked up along the way at Skilling's Greenhouse.

People couldn't help but gawk at her, but more people stared at Michael, who presented quite an image, dressed as he was in white from head to foot and wearing silver sunglasses. Claire chuckled to herself, wondering what anyone there would have said or done if they had known the truth.

After filling out the necessary paperwork, which didn't take as long as Claire had expected it to, she was growing increasingly irritated because Sally still hadn't shown up. She, Samael, and Michael took seats off to one side while they waited for the Justice of the Peace to call them in to perform the ceremony.

Typical Sally, Claire thought. *Never on time for anything!*

Or maybe she was being a no-show on purpose for whatever reason...jealousy or simply to make the point that she didn't approve.

"You think you should call her?" Samael asked when he caught Claire looking around, glancing at the front door for the umpteenth time.

Claire considered and then shook her head.

"No...She said she'd be here, and she'll be here." She took a deep breath. "And if she doesn't make it in time, we...we'll ask someone else...someone here—" She indicated the people waiting in line with a wide sweep of her hand.

"I think you should call," Samael said, "just to be sure."

Claire was determined not to let Sally ruin her big day by being predictably herself, but after a few more minutes of waiting, she pulled her cell phone from her small handbag and hit the speed dial. She tried not to fume as she listened to the phone ringing—

Once...

Twice...

Three...and then four times...

When the phone clicked over to message, Claire cut the call and put the phone back into her purse without a word.

"Maybe she's on her way and when she saw it was you calling, she didn't bother to answer," Samael said, but Claire was suddenly sure that Sally was not on her way. She sighed, a little sad... and hurt...that Sally would be so petty as to not show up for her wedding.

But that wouldn't change a thing.

She glanced at Michael, who was standing a short distance away from them. His arms were crossed, and he was leaning against the wall with his feet planted squarely in front of him. Claire noticed that people were still casting sidelong glances at him, like he was someone famous they should recognize but didn't. They certainly didn't want to approach him.

"This isn't like her," Claire said, more to herself than Samael. "She wouldn't let me down like this."

"I'm really sorry," Samael said.

Claire had no idea what to do next. Her impulse was to get up and leave…go over to the apartment and make sure Sally was all right. She should have been here by now.

Unless something's happened …

Something…but what?

Claire's mind filled with several scenarios.

None of them were good.

"I'm ready for you now," a woman said, speaking so suddenly that Claire let out a surprised cry that drew the attention of people sitting nearby.

An elderly woman, wearing a conservative dark blue skirt and jacket with a white blouse walked over to Claire and Samael. She had a small book in her hand and a folder with the papers they had just signed.

"Sorry," she said. "I didn't mean to startle you."

Claire shook her head as if in denial and said, "No…It's all right…I'm just a—a little keyed up."

"That's perfectly understandable," the woman said before she turned and led them to a closed door that she opened with a pass card. She stepped to one side to allow them to file into the small office. Then she shut the door and, still smiling broadly, walked over to the desk on one side of the room. A different door opened, and another woman—this one much younger and more stylishly dressed—entered.

"Well then," she said. "We're here for a happy occasion." She held her hand out for each of them to shake. "My name's Barbara Moody. This is my assistant, Debbie Powers. And you are—?"

Claire started to answer, but Barbara looked at the sheet of paper she was holding and read aloud, "Ms. Claire McMullen and Samael—" Her mouth twitched like she had a nervous tick. "Pierson…Mr. Samael Pierson."

Claire glanced at Samael when she suddenly realized she didn't know his last name—if demons even have last names— Was this something he had made up for the occasion?

Pierson…Claire Pierson…Yeah, I can get used to that…

"So," Barbara said, "if you have the rings—"

A sudden jolt hit Claire when she realized they had never bought wedding rings. How could she have forgotten such a simple thing? But then Samael reached into his jacket pocket and said, "Got 'em right here." He held out two matching jeweler's boxes and snapped open the tops. The rings glistened brightly as he held them out for her to see.

Would've been nice if you had told me, she thought.

"Where did you get—" she started to say, but then she realized she had to play along with it and ended by saying, "I knew I could count on you, dear."

The ceremony itself was brief and somehow anticlimactic. Throughout her life growing up, Claire had always imagined that her wedding day would be like something out of a fairy tale, with flowers and elegant lace dresses…scores if not hundreds of friends in St. Andrew's, the big Catholic church she had attended back in Houlton.

And here she was, standing in some city bureaucrat's office, exchanging vows with someone whose last name she hadn't even known until a few moments ago.

I am definitely out of my mind, she kept thinking as she repeated what the Justice of the Peace told her to say. The words came out of her mouth as if someone else was speaking them.

"Then with the power vested in me by the State of Maine, I now pronounce you husband and wife," Barbara said. And then, to Samael, she said, "You may kiss the bride."

Claire wasn't ready for it when Samael swept her into his arms and leaned her backwards. She let out a squeal before he planted a firm, passionate kiss on her mouth. Automatically, she slipped her tongue into his mouth, but she caught herself and made the kiss much shorter than she wanted it to be.

Besides, Michael was watching, and who knew where he was looking with those reflective sunglasses.

"Congratulations," Barbara said, extending her hand first to Claire and then to Samael to shake. Claire noticed the sidelong glances the woman kept shooting in Michael's direction, and it was no wonder. He did look stunning dressed all in white and with a beam of sunlight pouring through the office window, lighting him in glorious silhouette.

The assistant, Debbie, cheerfully signed as Claire's witness and then, thanking them for adding something quite unusual and interesting to her day, went back out into the lobby to go to work.

Michael produced a digital camera from his jacket pocket— another surprise for Claire because she hadn't thought of that, either—and began taking snapshots of the bride and groom. After all the handshakes, hugs, and photos, while Claire and Samael waited for the official documents to be signed and sealed, Claire turned to her demon husband.

"First thing we have to do is go to the apartment and check up on Sally."

She and Samael were walking toward the door with Michael trailing a few steps behind. Claire had the distinct impression he was acting more as a bodyguard than best man or friend. The only concern was: How conspicuous is he? Nearly everyone who saw him stopped and stared in amazement.

They walked down the steps of City Hall and over to Samael's car. Although it was in a tow-away zone, it was still there. Not even a parking ticket under the windshield wiper blade. Claire decided to take it as a wedding present.

"The apartment's not far," Claire said. "We can walk if you'd like."

Samael looked up the street and then shot a quick glance at Michael as if to ask, *What do you think?*

Michael raised his shades, his silver eyes glinting in the sun like quicksilver as he scanned the area.

"The trouble is," he said softly as he stepped closer to them, "we don't know what the opposition is going to do next."

His words sent a dash of chills racing up Claire's back. In spite of the warm, sunny day, she shivered.

"You make this sound like...like *The Godfather* or something," she said tightly. "It's like there's a rival mob family that's going to attack us soon, and it's time for us to 'go to the mattresses.'"

It was a poor joke, and even she didn't laugh...not after she saw the hard, neutral expression on both Samael's and Michael's faces.

"How serious is this, really?" she asked, glancing back and forth between the two of them.

Neither Samael nor Michael spoke for an unnervingly long time. In that time, the tension inside Claire wound up to an almost unbearable pitch.

"Samael?" She took hold of his arm above the elbow and shook him. He stared straight back at her, but for the longest time he still didn't say a word.

"Samael!"

"There's no way of knowing," he finally said.

As if they had reached a decision, they started walking up the street toward Congress Street. Claire had the peculiar feeling they were somehow isolated or protected from the mundane reality going on all around them, like they were in a transparent bubble. Cars and trucks and busses whizzed by, belching exhaust fumes into the air. Pedestrians streamed by in all directions, everyone focused on their own immediate goals. No conversation. No human contact. Overhead, seagulls whirled in wide spirals above the city, their harsh cries almost—but not quite—lost in the hubbub below.

Claire took Samael's arm and hugged it. He smiled absently at her, his eyes active...alert and focused on every passerby. Even though she was worried about Sally and the unknown dangers she and her husband still faced, she felt suddenly confident. She chuckled to herself as "Stand by Your Man" began playing in her head.

As they neared the apartment, Michael slowed his pace until he had dropped back more than fifty feet behind them. Then, without a word, he veered off down the alleyway that Claire knew ran behind her old apartment building.

"Oh, God," she said, and Samael snapped his head up and looked at her with an expression of utter panic.

"Where?"

Confused for a moment by his reaction—his overreaction—she looked at him. Then she understood.

"No. No. It's not Him," she said, her voice strained. "It's just… it feels so weird coming back here. Like another life."

They walked up to the front door, and as she looked up the façade of the building, a powerful feeling of nostalgia swept over her like a fog bank. Her mind filled with memories of first moving in here more than six years ago. All of her dreams and hopes, her disappointments and fears welled up inside her. Although she knew it was because she was emotional after the wedding—which already felt like a dream or the memory of a dream—a gnawing worry settled over her heart.

She opened her purse and took out the key ring. She hadn't given her keys to the apartment back to Sally yet, but as she prepared to open the door and go inside, she suddenly felt like an intruder.

"Maybe call first?" Samael suggested.

Claire nodded and took her cell phone from her purse and hit the speed dial for Sally's number.

The phone rang four times until it went to message.

"Still not answering," Claire said, suddenly fearing the worst.

"Well, then…" Samael said.

Before she moved, though, she looked up and down the sidewalk.

"Where'd Michael go?" she asked, but Samael shook his head and didn't answer her. She slipped the key into the front-door lock, turned it, and—holding her breath until her chest hurt—pushed the door open.

~ * ~

The old familiar smell of the entryway—a combination of floor wax, disinfectant, and wet dog—assailed her nostrils as she swung the door open, stepped inside, and then shut it behind them. The tightness in her stomach intensified as they started up the stairway to the third-floor landing. The old wooden stairs creaked underfoot, the only break in the silence that enveloped them. Claire felt like she had somehow slipped into an alternate reality where she was part of—but also frighteningly distant from—what she had taken all her life to be "reality."

It's like I'm dead...and I'm a ghost wandering through what used to be my life, she thought with a shiver. They reached the third-floor landing and started down the long hallway to the door to what was...that is used to be—

In another life.

—her apartment.

She slipped the apartment key into the lock and turned it. The bolt made a rough grinding sound as it turned, but before she twisted the doorknob and pushed the door open, she hesitated.

She couldn't get over the unsettling feeling that something was seriously wrong, and she knew—when she opened that door, she would find out just how wrong it was.

She couldn't say what it was or how she knew—not yet, but the building, even the air seemed...

"Too quiet," she whispered.

"Huh?" Samael asked.

She turned to him again, searching for strength and security in his face.

"This place...It's never been this quiet. Someone is always blasting their TV or music way too loud, or the Andrews' dog is barking." She looked around. "This is...weird."

She sucked in a quick breath, held it, and opened the door.

"Sally?" she called out.

As she waited for a reply, her eyes took in the sight before her.

"Are we in the right place?" she whispered to Samael.

At first glance, it sure seemed they had made a mistake. Claire and Sally had never been the best of housekeepers, but the entryway and kitchen looked like a tornado had ripped through it. It wasn't just a matter of dirty dishes and laundry piled up. Everything—chairs and tables, pots and pans, clothes and household items were strewn everywhere. Broken dishes and uprooted plants were scattered on the upended furniture. The refrigerator door was open, its contents spilled out onto the floor. The milk had long since curdled, and spoiled fruits and vegetables and containers of leftovers were furred with mold and crawling with flies and other insects. The smell of rotting vegetables mixed with a powerful jolt of rotten eggs made Claire gag as she looked down at a wide puddle of some dark liquid that had spilled across the floor, forming a rough letter C.

Is that blood? Claire wondered as her pulse kicked into high gear. Then she noticed the upended bottle of Pepsi lying in the debris at the base of the counter by the sink.

"My God," Claire whispered, awestruck. She took shallow sips of air and waved her hand in front of her face to avoid breathing the stench too deeply.

Even on a cold March day like this, flies were buzzing about and crawling across the garbage strewn on the floor.

"This is bad," Samael said, frowning and looking worried as he took it all in. He appeared to be maintaining his poise, but his shoulders were hunched as if he expected that whoever or whatever had done this might still be here, lurking out of sight...ready to pounce.

"Sally?" Claire called out again, her voice sounding unusually loud in the deserted apartment.

No response except for the buzzing of flies that reminded her of the fur-covered thing that had once been Mittens which she had found in the shower. Claire was convinced that, when they went into the living room or bedroom, they'd find Sally—

Dead!

Still waving her hand in front of her face and gasping for breath, Claire tiptoed through the debris to the living room doorway. A flickering light—several flickering lights, in fact—lit up the living room. A wavering pale, orange glow reached across the floor and painted the doorjamb.

"Sally?" Claire called again, her voice stronger in spite of her twisting nerves.

She stepped on something that sounded like she had crushed a bag of potato chips underfoot. She kept moving forward as she glanced down to see what it was, so when she raised her head and saw Sally in the living room, she let out a squeal of surprise.

She was sitting on the couch, perfectly still and staring down at the floor with a blank, unblinking gaze. Every available flat surface in the room, it seemed, held one or more lit candles. Some were on plates; others were stuck in puddles of melted wax to the surface of the coffee table, chair arms, bookcase shelves, and the floor. Their flickering orange glow filled the room and cast confused, wavering shadows. It took a while for Claire's eyes to adjust.

She's dead, was her first thought upon seeing Sally.

Her roommate's skin looked translucently pale in the glowing light, her cheeks mottled by dark spots that looked like she'd rubbed soot under her eyes. Darker lines that looked like ink streaked her face and hands.

A more rational part of her mind told her that Sally couldn't possibly be sitting up straight like that if she was dead...not unless who-or-whatever had killed her had propped her up.

Holding her breath, Claire stared at her roomie, waiting...praying to see some sign of life. Anything would do—a slight stirring of breath...a quick blink of the eye. So long as she knew Sally was still alive.

"Sal?..."

No reaction.

Claire moved a few steps closer, her hands poised defensively.

"Are you...all right?"

Still nothing.

"What's going on, Sal?" Claire felt like she was approaching a cobra, coiled and ready to strike.

She jumped when Sally slowly raised her head and looked directly at her. Her swollen eyes were blank, empty pits. When she moved, her neck bones made faint crackling sounds.

"What do you want?" Sally asked. Her voice was cracked and dry, as if she hadn't spoken for days. She kept staring at Claire with a blank expression as if she didn't recognize her.

"I...I came to see why you...why you didn't make it today," Claire said.

"Today?...What's today?" Sally asked. She rolled her head back, exposing the bloodshot whites as she rapidly blinked her eyes a few times.

Claire shot a look over at Samael, who was standing in the doorway.

"Call 911," she said, and then, turning back to Sally, "Are you okay?"

No answer other than a lingering blank look.

"What happened here?" Claire asked, struggling to keep down the frantic rush inside her. Still getting no response, she said, "I think you need to go to the hospital."

"The hospital?...Today?" Sally said hollowly. Then she sighed and shook her head slowly from side to side. The sound of the bones in her neck cracking got louder. When she took a breath and exhaled, it sounded like hot, dry wind blowing through the grass.

Claire went to Sally and knelt down in front of her, taking her hands. She noticed her bloody fingernails and the bruises on her wrists—like she'd been tied!

"They're coming for you, you know," Sally said softly...tensely. The slow susurration of her voice made it sound like she was mumbling in her sleep.

Before Claire could respond, Sally suddenly jumped as though she'd be hit by an electric jolt. She jerked her hands out of Clair's grasp and looked at Claire, her face a mask of barely repressed terror. Her eyes cleared, and her face seemed suddenly fuller...more lively.

"What's that, Sal?"

Claire's voice shook as a painful clenching gripped her gut. She thought she might know exactly what Sally meant, but she wanted to believe she hadn't heard her correctly. She cast a quick glance at Samael, who was standing in the living room doorway as if he didn't dare enter the room.

"I saw them...They've been here..." Sally said in a watery rasp.

"Who has?" Claire asked even though she already knew the answer.

Whoever or whatever was trying to stop Samael from abandoning evil was obviously trying to get at Claire and, thus, Samael through Sally. Claire was furious that the forces ranged against them would start by using an innocent bystander like Sally. She didn't deserve to get dragged into any of this, tied up and beaten to a pulp.

Sally's eyelids were flickering rapidly as she looked at Claire. And then, without warning, she threw her head back and started to laugh. It certainly wasn't a joyous laugh. It was low and rumbling, like the sound of distant thunder on a hot summer afternoon.

Sally's laughter gradually built. It set Claire's nerves on edge with its sinister tone.

"Wha—what's so funny?" Claire finally asked, unable to bear the sound any longer and wishing she would stop.

"They did a good job," Sally said in a voice as low as her laughter.

"What? Who did a good job?"

"They did...They did a good job of imitating my roommate."

With that, she leaned forward and, gripping the flesh of Claire's left cheek between her thumb and forefinger, pinched and shook her so roughly it hurt. Claire yelped and pulled away, her face stinging.

"I...I'm not an...an imitation," Claire said.

Her heart was breaking, seeing her roommate like this. Sally had always been so strong...so independent. To see her reduced to...to this was too much to take.

Claire turned to Samael, who still hadn't left the doorway,

"Did you call the ambulance? We have to get her out of here. Now."

Samael stared at her, unblinking for a moment, deep in thought. Then, looking grim, he nodded,

"Not to the hospital, though," he said.

"Are you nuts?" Claire asked. "Look at her! She needs medical attention!"

"I don't need to go to the goddamned hospital," Sally interrupted. Her voice was lighter now, and she sounded perfectly rational. "I'm okay. It's just…Now that they're gone…I can get away from them…for a little while, at least."

Them! Claire thought with a chill. She and Samael exchanged worried glances. She didn't need to ask who Sally meant by "them."

"Sal," Claire said, turning back to her. "I'd like you to come with us—"

As she spoke, she reached out and touched Sally on the shoulder. It was a gentle touch, but it might as well have been a punch to the gut because of the way Sally reacted. She let out an ear-piercing shriek and swatted Claire's hand away with a vicious blow that, Claire knew, would leave a bruise. Caught by surprise, Claire fell back and scrambled out of Sally's reach. She clenched her fists and tensed, expecting Sally to attack her, but her roomie settled on the couch, an utterly blank expression on her face.

"Jesus!" Claire said.

"Language. Please," Samael said with a wry smile.

Claire noticed that he hadn't moved any closer. He would have been of no help if Sally had gone nuts and attacked her. She looked at him, feeling empty inside.

"What are we going to do?" she asked, not even trying to mask the desperation in her voice.

Samael regarded her steadily, his no longer gold-flecked eyes wide as he shook his head.

"We have to get her to the hospital whether she wants to go or not," Claire said.

Samael kept shaking his head, and the longer he did, the grimmer his expression became.

"No," he finally said. "I don't think we can do that."

"What?"

"We can't take her to the hospital."

Suddenly furious, Claire walked over to him and, bunching up the front of his coat with both fists, pulled him so close their noses almost touched. The heat of her breath rebounded from his face. This close, his eyes looked like deep, dark wells with no bottom.

"Why not? We have to do something!"

Samael couldn't maintain eye contact for long, and he shifted his gaze away. Between Sally's condition and Samael's detachment, Claire was suddenly enraged. She took a deep breath, struggling for calm.

"We're married now," she said, her voice low and level. "That means we help each other out."

In the pause she took to catch her breath, Samael said nothing to fill the void.

"I know you don't know Sally very well—and I know you don't like her, but she's the closest friend I have, and there's— something's wrong with her. I'm not—I repeat, I am not going to abandon her."

"I didn't say that," Samael said, surprising her with such a mild tone in his voice. He raised his hands and pried Claire's hands from the front of his coat.

"What did you say?"

"I said we can't take her to the hospital."

"But look at her."

With a flick of her head, Claire indicated Sally, who was still seated on the couch, staring off into space and looking like she had no idea they were there discussing what to do with her. Dried blood crusted her nose and the corners of her mouth.

"She needs to see someone."

"But not at the hospital," Samael said evenly. "Whoever did this to her—and I have a pretty good idea who—could easily gain access to her there and…finish the job."

"What do you mean, 'finish the job'?"

"Well…it's obvious whatever happened to her—whatever she saw—snapped her mind. You don't think, if they wanted her eliminated, they couldn't get to her at the hospital?"

"So what do we do?" Claire looked around. "We can't leave her here. Not like this. And we certainly can't stay—"

She stopped herself and stared at Samael.

"Hold on. Are you saying what I think you're saying?"

"Uh-huh. We take her back to my place."

"But—" Claire glanced over her shoulder at Sally, who remained catatonic on the edge of the couch. Lowering her voice, she said, "—if they come for us, she isn't going to be any safer with us, is she?"

"She'll be safer with Michael and me to protect her. I can guarantee that."

Claire looked back and forth between Samael and Sally. She had no idea what to say or do. It hurt that her love for Samael had caused so much collateral damage to innocent people in her life...her parents, Sally, Marty...When would it end?

But Samael and I...We're in this together...right to the end...whatever that might be...

"We can take care of her," he said mildly. "Trust me."

"I trust you, but..." She punched him on the arm. "Not like I have a choice, right?"

Samael chuckled and kissed her hand where Sally had slapped it. Her skin burned as if she'd been stung by a bee, and that thought brought back the horrifying image of the wasp demon.

"Okay, then," Claire finally said. Taking a deep breath, she turned to face Sally.

"Sal...Hon'," she said as she moved cautiously toward her and bent down so their faces were level with each other. Claire felt like she was standing next to a keg of gunpowder, unsure if the fuse had been lit or not.

Sally shifted her gaze and looked at her. An unnaturally wide smile spread across Sally's face, cracking her swollen lips like she was wearing a mask. Her skin, especially in the orange glow of all these candles, looked livid. Her eyes were vacant.

"Sal, can you hear me?"

Only the slightest of nods indicated that she had.

"I want you to do something for me, Sal. Will you do that?"

"Do what?" Sally asked after a long pause.

"I want you to do me a favor. Do you understand?"

"A...favor?"

Claire noted that she was echoing back whatever she said as if that was all the room she had left in her mind.

"I want you to come with us," Claire said.

"Come with you."

"That's right."

It took great effort for Claire to keep the rising edge of nervousness out of her voice. She was poised...tensed...ready— she thought—to react if Sally suddenly lashed out at her again.

"Where can we go?" Sally asked, focusing a bit more clearly on her.

"I want you to come with me to—"

"They're everywhere, you know." Sally took a deep breath that sounded like a torrent of wind whistling through a small opening. "We can never get away. Not from them. They'll find me. No matter where we go."

"They're not looking for you, Sal." Claire said. She was painfully aware of the tremor in her voice, but she couldn't prevent it.

"They'll find me, no matter where I go. You can't help me."

Claire's throat choked off, and she found it all but impossible to catch her breath.

"You'll be safe if you come with us. Samael and I will take care of you."

Claire slowly reached out and placed her hand on Sally's shoulder. She felt her flinch, but this time—at least not yet—she didn't lash out. Claire increased the pressure on her friend's shoulder and then, with her other hand, took hold of Sally's elbow and, as gently as possible, guided her until she was standing. It was like handling a fragile crystal vase.

"I want to get your coat and help you put it on," Claire said, her voice as soft and cooing as a dove's. "And I want you to come downstairs with me and Samael. His car's parked a ways down the street."

Sally regarded her with the most pathetic expression—a haunting mixture of terror and confusion and mistrust.

"It's not far," Claire said, taking her gently by the arm and urging her to move.

"How do I know I can trust you?" Sally asked. "How do I know you're not one of them?"

"Sal…It's me. Claire."

Sally paused and looked at her intently, like she was studying a specimen. She cocked her head like she was a bird, about to peck some seed…or her eyes.

"I don't…Do I know you? We went to school together, didn't we?"

Claire had no idea if she should play along with any delusion Sally came up with or tell her the truth.

And will it matter? She asked herself, thinking…dreading that her roommate was already too far gone. The blankness in her eyes was frightening, and her expression looked like a wall had already gone up behind her eyes, closing out reality.

She doesn't know the half of it, Claire thought.

"Come along, now," Claire said, gently guiding her.

Surprisingly, Sally allowed herself to be led into the kitchen where, after a quick search amongst the trash, they found Sally's coat. It was in the cupboard under the sink, and was covered with spilled coffee grounds and a couple of rotting banana peels. Claire shook the garbage out onto the floor, telling herself it was going to take a Hazmat team to clean this place, anyway.

"There you go," she said mildly, like she was speaking to a child as she helped her get her arms into the sleeves. Sally seemed to have been reduced to a docile ten-year-old, but when Claire reached to zip the coat up, Sally batted Claire's hand away like she was wielding a knife at her throat.

"You ready to go?" Claire asked.

"Go where?" Sally replied.

"You're going to come with us. We're going to take you to a safe place."

A wicked smile lit up Sally's face, and her eyes widened until they were perfectly round, glistening orbs.

"Don't you try to kid me," Sally said. "I know exactly what's going on, and don't think I don't."

Claire refrained from asking her what was going on because she sure as Hell didn't know. As far as she could see, Sally was completely divorced from reality. If she had any idea what was happening, Claire didn't want to hear anything she might have to say.

With Samael's help, they got Sally down the stairs to the first-floor landing. When Samael opened the front door for them, cold air blasted into their faces with such force it took Claire's breath away. She tucked Sally's arm into her own and gently guided her down the sidewalk. Samael followed a few steps behind, watching for anything unusual.

It wasn't long before they made it to Samael's car. With Sally and Claire huddled in the back seat keeping their heads low, Samael drove. It was only after they had gotten onto I-295 that Claire realized something.

"Where's Michael? Oh my God. We left him back at the apartment."

Samael glanced at her reflection in the rearview mirror and smiled.

"Don't worry. He'll be all right," he said.

"Are you sure?" She twisted around in her seat and looked out the rear window as if she expected to see Michael following after them.

"He's fine," Samael said.

"That's what you think," Sally said with a deep, hollow laugh.

Chapter

14

When they got out of the car at Samael's house, Sally looked up at the entryway with an expression of dazed, childlike wonder. Claire and Samael exchanged worried glances as, each of them holding Sally's arm above the elbow, they led her from the car, up the marble front stairs, and into the house. Michelle met them at the door and said, "The green room is ready for your guest, sir."

Samael nodded and said, "Thanks."

Claire was left wondering how Michelle could have known and gotten a room ready in so short a time. She assumed Samael had snuck in a phone call to her while Claire was distracted, tending to Sally. Still supporting Sally by the arms, Claire and Samael led her up the wide sweeping stairway and down the long hallway to a large bedroom halfway down on the left. Like every other room in Samael's house, this one was gorgeously appointed. A king-sized bed, freshly made and turned down with silk sheets, was placed between two large windows that looked out over the side yard. Vases of fresh-cut flowers—roses and baby's breath—were in expensive vases on the bed stand and bureau.

Where do you get flowers like that in March? Claire wondered.

Michelle had laid out a pink, flannel nightgown on the bed, and Claire asked Samael to leave the room so they could help Sally change into it after washing her and bandaging her face and hands.

Michelle produced ice packs for Sally's eyes and wrists. Fortunately, no bones appeared to be broken.

Sally did everything she was told without complaint or resistance, and Claire was glad for that. She was sure she wouldn't be able to handle it if Sally started freaking out or resisting.

Samael had given Claire a sedative to give to Sally, which she took without complaint. Once Sally was tucked into bed and drifting off to sleep, Claire began to relax for the first since…she wasn't sure when.

As Sally's eyes fluttered and closed, and her breathing became deep and even, Claire walked over to the windows and drew the shades down. The semidarkness in the room was warm and restful. Once she was sure Sally was asleep, Claire realized how utterly exhausted she was, too. She considered going down the hall to the master bedroom and climbing into bed, but she had to go back downstairs first and spend some time with Samael.

This was, after all, their wedding day.

They had a lot to talk about.

~ * ~

"Some honeymoon, huh?"

The humorous edge in Samael's comment made Claire smile…at least a little; but the truth was, she was consumed with anger and worry about Sally, not to mention their own danger. She was also frustrated that her wedding day—a day that was supposed to be so special—had been ruined like this.

What do you expect when you marry a demon?

The sun had dropped behind the horizon long ago, and the sky through the living room curtains was a deep steel blue that was slowly blending to black as storm clouds closed in from the west. It was cold outside. The bare branches of the trees cut the fading sky into lacy black patterns. A strange silence pervaded the house. Samael started a fire in the fireplace. Claire almost said something when he used matches and kindling instead of snapping his fingers or something to start the blaze. Soon, the crackling wood and flickering flames pushed back the encroaching darkness.

Claire pushed her cascade of hair over her shoulders.

"I hear the Caribbean's really nice this time of year," she said with a sigh.

Samael didn't say anything, but he didn't have to. They were safest here, but for how long?

"Where did Michael go? Will he be back soon?" she asked.

"'S hard to say."

His grim expression as he stared into the flames did little to calm her down. Even in the firelight, his eyes looked as shiny and black as polished marble without a single fleck of gold.

"You'd think he'd at least contact us, wouldn't you?" she asked. She felt safer with Michael around even though his presence unnerved her.

Samael offered to get her a drink, and when he returned with it—scotch and soda—she sipped it, relishing the slow burn of the alcohol as it reached deep into her stomach. The carbonation of the soda water tickled her nose, making her feel like she had to sneeze.

"Well…?" she said, as if there had been no interruption in their conversation.

"You mean about Michael? I'm not sure," Samael replied. The hint of worry in his voice bothered Claire.

Has something happened that he doesn't want me to know about? Or is he as in the dark about Michael's whereabouts as I am?

Regardless, she felt less safe without Michael around. His otherworldliness, as intimidating as it was, exuded a level confidence and competence that even Samael didn't give her. She took another sip of her drink and found it so soothing she took another. When she looked out the window again, it was full dark, no stars. White streaks of snow zipped past the window, looking like random laser beams.

"That's the bitch of it," Samael said, not sounding the least bit amused. "If they came right at us, it'd be one thing. But this way…" He sighed and, looking at the floor as if he was utterly exhausted, shook his head. After a long silence, he leaned back in his chair and, staring up at the ceiling, rubbed his eyes.

So apparently even a demon can get tired and stressed, Claire thought. The thought struck her as mildly amusing, and she started to laugh. Before long, tears were streaming down her face as she found release in seeing the humor of it all.

It felt good to laugh, and as she did, she realized just how much tension she'd been carrying around inside her ever since...well, ever since she realized she and Samael were in real danger...since she had driven to Houlton with someone—something that wasn't Samael.

Now, all of that seemed like it had happened so long ago...to another person in another lifetime.

Hell, since then, I've become a married woman, and that's only within the last twelve hours.

As she continued to laugh, the absurdity of her situation hit her even harder. She realized she was laughing hysterically as she doubled over and gasped for breath. Her stomach muscles ached.

Samael sat down next to her on the couch.

"Take it easy, love," he said, looking at her curiously. "You're going to hurt yourself."

Claire struggled to gain control of herself, but the ridiculousness of what she had gotten herself into was stunning. She forced herself to lean back and take another sip of her drink. Then she decided, *to Hell with decorum*, and downed the rest in three quick gulps. She hadn't eaten all day, and the alcohol hit her hard, going straight to her head.

This is exactly what I need, she told herself...something to get me out of my head.

"Can I have another?" she asked, holding her glass out to Samael.

He flashed his old, wicked grin at her as he got up, took the glass, and walked down the long hallway to the kitchen.

Claire heaved a sigh and tried to settle back on the sofa, but her gaze kept shifting over to the dark rectangles of the windows that overlooked the yard.

And as she stared blankly out at the falling snow, she saw something else outside...a shape darker than night had shifted up close to the window. Claire could feel as much as see the presence. She wanted to do something—either call out to Samael or else get up and leave the room, but she was rooted to the sofa.

The longer she stared at it, the more clearly defined it became until she realized that she was looking at a vaguely human shape that seemed to be swelling in size as she looked at it.

It grew to be a lot bigger than any person she knew and now filled the window, blocking out the night.

She wasn't sure when, but Claire realized she was staring into a pair of eyes that glowed dull red in the darkness, like coals in a dying fire. The longer she stared at them, the brighter they glowed.

"Samael…" she called out, her voice little more than a strangled whisper.

It felt as if unseen hands were gripping her throat and squeezing. The air in the room seemed suddenly to be ten or more degrees lower.

Somehow—later…she could not have said how much later—she managed to get off the couch and ease herself slowly into a standing position. Her chest was tight, her heart racing as she focused on the window.

As she did, the figure became more distinct until she was sure she was staring into the face of a demon. Through the glass, she saw a huge face, as blue as solid ice, grinning in at her.

"Samael…" she called out again. She yelled as loud as she could, but the air in the living room seemed suddenly thick. It muffled her call and any other sounds.

Her eyes were wide and as she neared the window, and the face became more distinct. For an instant, she wondered if it was Michael, who had come back and not been able to get into the house for some reason. But Michael's eyes were silver…not red, and she felt safe in his presence, not suffocated. She remembered how the demon had impersonated Samael all through the drive up to Houlton. One of their enemies—maybe more—could assume any form they wanted in order to fool her. Maybe it was something all demons could do. She wished now she'd asked Samael about it. But one thing she did remember was not to speak to them.

Ever!

Through the reflective panes of glass, she watched as the figure resolved more clearly. The wicked red gleam in the creature's eyes grew brighter, and the blue face was smiling at her maliciously.

"…Claire…" a voice whispered faintly.

It sounded as if the speaker was standing close behind her...

Or inside her head.

She froze and stared, unblinking as the face pressed against the glass. Flakes of snow swirled in a tornado around it like it was captured inside a huge snow globe. When its mouth moved, long, pointed teeth slid back and forth behind fleshy black lips.

And then it opened its mouth.

The gaping hole looked suddenly huge, and inside...behind the rows of razor-sharp teeth, she saw...people.

It was like looking into a canyon except, instead of rock walls on each side, there were huge teeth on the top and bottom. And now she could see dozens...scores of people, writhing in pain as they thrashed about inside the gaping maw.

"...Claire..." the voice said again, and this time the mouth moved in unison with the sound of her name.

She wanted desperately to call out to Samael, but she couldn't catch her breath. The icy air in the living room was numbing her.

The demon raised its hands to the window, its claws hooked and vicious-looking as they tapped on the glass like wind-driven ice pellets. Then the blue-faced creature flattened its hands against the glass and began to push.

Claire jumped back but couldn't look away. She was fascinated as the huge blue hands blotted out the night. She stared at the lines on the palms of the demon's hands, positive that the winding, spiral patterns had some supernatural meaning. The claws continued to tap and scratch on the glass with loud squeaking and rasping sounds, but gradually the sounds altered until they took on a slow, drumming cadence...like the steady thumping of a distant marching band.

"...Claire..."

Frozen with terror, she watched as the being outside leaned forward, its blue face contorted into a horrible grimace as it opened its mouth in a silent scream and pressed its full weight against the glass. Faint traces of crackling white light ran up and down the creature's arms, sparking off its fingertips. Spikes of light danced like threads of static electricity. Some penetrated the glass, reaching out as if to grab Claire.

And then—unbelievably—the glass began to bulge inward, as if it was no longer glass but some soft, fluid plastic. Glistening, glassy lumps caught the light and reflected it back in wild, distorted patterns that took on the rounded contours of the claws. Claire was convinced that—any second now—those cruel-looking points of bone would tear through the glass and slash her to ribbons.

"Sam..." she said, no more than a croaking whimper.

Instead of hearing Samael's reassuring voice, though, a low, gravelly growl filled her head.

"You can't resist," the voice said. "You've already lost. Samael is one of us...Always has been. Always will be. And no matter what you do, tonight you will lose your life, and your soul will be cast into eternal damnation."

The fuck it will! Claire thought but couldn't say.

She knew that the being outside—whoever or whatever it was—could read her every thought. She felt exposed...naked...and vulnerable as numbing cold filled her chest and stomach. At first—for only a few seconds—it was reassuring...proof that she was still alive, and her blood was still flowing.

But within the span of a few heartbeats, the cold intensified until it felt as though she were frozen solid inside.

"Come...to...me...now," the voice said. Every word was punctuated by a crackling hiss like a nest of snakes writhing inside her head. Claire's teeth were rattling like someone shaking dice in their hand.

Claire shook her head, resisting with every ounce of energy she had, but the glass sagged further inward, closer...closer. The claws skittered and squealed on the window like someone raking chalk across a chalkboard.

"Your...soul...is...already...mine," the voice said.

Claire drew on her last reserves of strength, opened her mouth, and screamed, "Never!"

The blue face loomed closer, almost touching her but still separated from her by the glass. Normal dimensions of space seemed no longer to make any sense. The face—the being—the blue-faced demon—looked like it was already inside the house. It had nothing to do but snatch her up and drag her off into the night.

As the face in the window pressed against the flexible glass, its features gradually shifted. Whereas first she had seen a horrible demon, she now saw —

No!

—Samael!

He was reflected in the glass, his expression grim and unmoving as he came closer to her.

The he reached out and grabbed her, his hands clamping down hard on her shoulders from behind…hard enough to make her wince and cry out.

"It's all right," Samael said calmly.

At least it sounds like Samael's voice.

Claire wondered how his voice could be coming from behind her when he was clearly standing in front of her, his hands reaching through the window to grab her.

The pressure of his fingers pressing into both of her shoulders was so strong she was sure his fingers would leave bruises on her skin.

A force as powerful as a hurricane wind suddenly yanked her backwards. She was sure her soul was being ripped out of her, but a sudden rush of cool, refreshing air wrapped around her, bringing her back.

She blinked her eyes and discovered that she was sprawled on her back on the couch.

The figure in the living room window withdrew slowly, and after a while, the glass resumed its normal, flat shape.

Claire was breathing hard, her breath burning her throat and lungs.

When she looked up, she was surprised to see Samael standing over her. He was smiling grimly as he looked down at her.

"I told you. The house is protected," he said softly, "but it's not a good idea to test its limits…or our luck."

Claire gaped at him in disbelief. Her eyes shifted from Samael to the pitch-black night outside.

The blue-faced demon figure was gone. The clawed hands had withdrawn, dissolved into the depths of the night.

"What just…Where were you? Why didn't you come when I called?"

"I came as fast as I could once I knew there was trouble," Samael said. He sat down beside her on the couch. The weight of his body pressing down the cushions was reassuring.

Reality!

Claire couldn't help but wonder when she would trust reality again.

What she had just seen and been through defied explanation.

"What was that?" she asked, her voice tight and small.

"You saw the Hell Mouth."

"The Hell Mouth," she echoed.

Samael nodded.

"It's difficult to understand, but—put simply, you don't really go to Hell. You…it swallows you."

"How did it…" she started to say but then fell silent. The sense of relief flooding through her was too intense. She had to absorb it and try to process what she had seen. She wondered briefly if she could ever trust this reality after what she had just witnessed, but when she slid over and pressed her face against Samael's shoulder, inhaling his scent, she knew she could.

"That was a close one," Samael said simply, patting her back. "They're stronger…and more determined than I thought."

"Do you know who they are?" Claire asked, her voice muffled in the comfort of Samael's shirt.

"I know one of them. Yes," Samael replied.

When he didn't offer more, Claire wanted to demand that he tell her everything, but she realized it might be for the better this way. If she knew the full extent of the dangers they faced—

Like the Hell Mouth.

—it might be too much to handle.

She decided—for now, anyway—to let the mystery be.

"We're safe, right? You're sure of it?"

"To be honest, after what just happened, I…I'm not sure."

Claire pulled away from Samael and stared at him, her eyes wide.

Samael said calmly, "They've arrayed some powerful forces against me."

"Against us," Claire said softly to let him know he wasn't alone in this.

"You're right," he said, squeezing her hand tightly. "Us."

He sighed, looking so sad and careworn it all but broke Claire's heart.

"But you have to remember," he said, "they're not after you. They want me. They can't do you any harm, really, except to try to terrify you."

"Huh! They're doing a pretty good job of it so far," she said with a humorless laugh.

"Just keep in mind, they're using you to get to me. At least they're trying to." He took a deep breath and exhaled. "But like I said, Michael has created a strong defense here. I'm positive it'll hold."

"Do you have any idea where Michael is now? Have you heard from him? "

Claire couldn't miss the worry in his eyes when he shook his head, no.

"Don't worry," he said. "I'm sure he's all right."

How can anyone harm an angel? Claire wondered, amazed to be thinking in such terms and accepting it so readily.

"Nothing out there can get inside just like nothing inside can get out. The barrier's strong, and it will stay that way until Michael lifts it."

"And if something does go wrong?"

"I swear to God"—and here he flinched a little—"Nothing will harm you as long as I exist."

She stared into Samael's eyes, comforted by the determination she saw, and remembered why she fell in love with him in the first place. She slipped her arms around his neck and drew him so close their noses were touching.

"I love you, you damned fool," she said in a low, husky voice. "And I will do whatever it takes to save you."

"Yes," he said, "but are you willing to sell your soul to redeem mine?" Samael pulled back and looked at her, his eyebrows raised to devilish points.

Claire regarded him with a long, steady look before saying, "Samael. I'm your wife. I love you. I gave you my heart, but I—" She choked before she said the words: "But I will never give you or anyone else my soul. It belongs to me."

"I know that."

A long, dense silence stretched between them, broken only by the gritty sound of icy pellets slashing against the windows.

Finally, Samael smiled at her and said softly, "Correct answer."

And then their mouths came together in a passionate kiss that made the rest of the world melt away.

~ * ~

It was almost midnight, and Claire and Samael were sitting side by side on one of the couches, their arms wrapped around each other. They hadn't been talking much.

"Look at it snow," she said, gazing contentedly at the white streaks shooting past the living room window. The light from inside the house illuminated them for one brief shining moment, and then they were gone.

Like a mortal life to him, Claire thought.

But more snowflakes followed. It was snowing much harder now. Although she hadn't had time to consider checking the weather forecast, Claire guessed there would be several inches of new snow — if not lots more — on the ground come morning.

Samael's expression didn't vary as he looked from her to the window. She wondered if, since snow and cold were the exact opposite of what he had known for so long and probably thrived on, the thought of snow and ice and cold bothered or even unnerved him.

But then again, the Hell Mouth had been blue, and it had filled the living room — and her — with a bone-snapping chill.

"Great night for a romantic walk in the snow, huh?" she said.

Samael sniffed and looked at her, shaking his head.

"Considering the circumstances," he said, "I'd say that's probably not the best idea."

Leaning forward, she pressed her face against his chest, reveling in the simple joy of listening to his steady heartbeat —

Yes…demons do have hearts.

—and letting her head rise and fall with each breath he took.

"I mean—this is going to end, right? And we'll be able to live like normal people, right?"

Samael was stroking her red hair as he looked at her and nodded.

"Absolutely," he said, and she knew that either he was telling the truth or was absolutely determined to make it so.

"And what do we do in the meantime?"

"We wait here where it's safe."

Her arms tightened around him, squeezing.

"For richer or poorer," she whispered, her face pressed against his chest.

"In sickness and in health," Samael added.

That made a smile twitch the corners of her mouth, but she knew—to the depths of her being—that this...this was where she belonged.

Still, that didn't assuage the fear and nervousness and exhaustion.

"We should go to bed," she said.

"I think I'll stay up a bit more and...see what happens."

The note of resignation in his voice bothered her, but she knew there was little—if anything—she could do.

And she was exhausted.

"Is it all right if I go to bed, then?"

Without saying a word, his gaze fixed on the living room window, Samael nodded.

Claire turned to go, but she hesitated at the door. It felt odd...uncomfortable to leave him alone like this. She felt a strong wave of pity for him and what he obviously had to face for...however long. She also felt a surge of admiration...and gratitude. He wouldn't be in this mess if he hadn't fallen in love with her. Nobody had ever loved her enough to risk death, much less eternal redemption...and she had never loved anyone the way she loved Samael.

"Samael?"

He looked over at her.

"We'll be all right," he said softly. Then he smiled and nodded, his expression gentle. "It may be tough going for a while, but—yeah. I have no doubt we're gonna be all right."

With that, Claire turned and walked down the long hallway to the staircase leading up to the second floor. Even in the hallway, she could hear a soft tearing sound as the wind wrapped its arms around the house. She had a momentary image of the house being lifted off its foundation and flying away into the night like Dorothy's house in *The Wizard of Oz*.

But there'd be a hell of a lot more than the Wicked Witch of the West and Munchkins waiting at the end of this ride.

She was half-amused and half-scared by the thought.

Sliding her hand along the polished mahogany handrail, she climbed the stairs slowly. With each step up, her feet felt heavier. She wondered if the strain of the situation was tiring her so much, or if— somehow—the demons or dark forces ranged against Samael were wearing her down. She believed Samael when he said she wasn't the target, but that didn't mean she was safe. They could—and would— use her to get at him.

Isn't that how evil operates?

Find the weakness and vulnerabilities, and exploit them.

"So...what are my weaknesses?" she asked herself out loud as she scuffed up the stairs.

The sound of her voice reverberated oddly in the wide stairwell, and she had the impression someone else had spoken simultaneously with her. Wide-eyed, she turned and looked down the sweeping stairway, but there was no one...or nothing...in sight.

Still...that didn't mean she was safe, even here...

About halfway up the stairs, with every nerve in her body prickling, she felt a subtle electrical charge running from the stairs up her legs to her chest and throat. Off to one side, there was a wide, double window. She glanced at it, not knowing what—if anything— she expected to see.

All she saw was the dark slab of night. The lights on the stairway reflected off the glass with a harsh glare that made it impossible for her to see the falling snow outside. She let out the breath she hadn't realized she was holding, but then the thought occurred to her that the darkness outside the window appeared to be too dark.

How is that so?

It was like something...outside...was pressed against the glass, blocking out any view outside because whatever was at the window was watching her.

It's nothing, she told herself, but the feeling that there was something out there wouldn't go away.

Gripping the handrail with one hand, she glanced up and down the stairs as if expecting to see...

What?

A hellish, drooling creature, waiting to pounce on her and rend her limb from limb?

A smiling, blue-faced demon, ready to seduce her soul?

Or something—she couldn't image what, but something she wasn't expecting?

She returned her gaze to the window. It was now plain that there was something out there. Her first thought was that the blue face—the Hell Mouth she had seen outside the living room window had gotten up there and was still watching her...gathering strength as it waited to strike again. She didn't know the layout of the house, inside and out, well enough to know how or if anything could get up there. Maybe it had wings and was hovering in the night...or claws that let it cling to the side of the house.

Of course they can go anywhere, she told herself. They're demons. They can do anything they want, can't they?

Well, maybe not anything. As far as she knew, Samael couldn't fly. And after all, Michael had done something to the house to make it so nothing could get inside or out.

As she was staring at the shape in the window, it hit her.

It wasn't just one shape.

It was many shapes...many small, black things.

She realized with a jolt that a swarm of bats was fluttering against the window. Their wings and claws were scratching and skittering across the glass as they tried to pry the window open and get inside.

"Bats?...In a snowstorm?" she said to herself.

But the longer she stared, the clearer she could make out the hundreds of tiny fanged faces staring at her. Their small, yellow eyes glowed like flying cinders in the snow-swept darkness, and then it hit her.

They all had miniature versions of Samael's face.

Claire was so startled she wasn't able to call out to Samael, and finally she decided not to because—she told herself—*This is just another illusion that's supposed to frighten me.* She didn't want to look like a frightened little girl who freaked out about everything. If Samael said the house was safe, the house was safe.

"Fuck you," she whispered as she raised her middle fingers and thrust it toward the bats. The motion—or something—set them off, and they started scrambling and squeaking all the more.

And then she turned her head and continued up the stairs, confident that neither the bats—not anything else—could get inside.

~ * ~

Before she went to the master bedroom, she decided to check in on Sally.

Hopefully, she was sleeping peacefully and recovering her wits, but Claire knew that, whatever had happened, Sally would never again be the same.

Tears welled in her eyes as she approached the guest room door. Her fingers grasped the doorknob lightly and, after taking a breath, she turned the doorknob as softly as she could. She didn't want to disturb Sally if she was asleep. Still holding her breath, she pushed the door open quietly, its bottom edge whispering across the plush carpet.

The room was dimly lit—just as she and Samael had left it—and Sally was lying on her back on the bed, the sheets and blankets covering her body to her chin. Her head was propped up on several pillows, so she looked almost like she was sitting up.

Claire stopped short.

Sally's eyes were wide open, and she was staring at her.

Claire also noticed that Sally's face and hands were completely healed—no swelling, no bruising, no puffiness.

Uh-oh, was Claire's first thought. *There's some major shit going down here.*

The glassy, blank expression on Sally's face chilled Claire. The look in her eyes was far from human. Her eyeballs glistened wetly in the dim light. They seemed to glow with some strange, internal fire. The cold, steady gaze was reptilian. It fixed Claire where she stood.

Claire returned Sally's stare, not wanting to back down. She had no doubt who was the more powerful one here. She knew—without doubt—this wasn't the real Sally as her former roommate stared at her without blinking.

"Are you okay, Sal?"

Even before Claire finished her question, Sally slipped her tongue out between her lips. It extended much further than was possible, flickering back and forth like a snake's tongue, sniffing and testing the air.

Claire was mesmerized, and only gradually she realized she was moving again—without willing it—slowly toward the bed where her friend lay. She looked down at her feet as if they belonged to someone else, watching in amazement as they slid forward, gliding over the carpet like she was sliding on ice.

When Claire looked up at Sally, she was shocked to see her sitting straight up in the bed. She pushed the bed covers aside with a casual sweep of the hand. They floated, moving in slow motion and fell aside, exposing Sally's body.

Only it wasn't Sally.

Her body was seriously altered. It had thickened into two...no, three thick coils. It looked as if the bones in her body had turned into pulp, and she was slowly extending and unflexing until her body was a long, thick, winding tube.

Even as Claire watched, her terror rising, the monster that was no longer Sally began to move. It shifted with a heavy slithering motion, its body growing larger with each passing second until the coils of the body no longer fit onto the bed. A thick looping coil dropped to the floor with a heavy thud that sounded like a distant gunshot.

All the while, Sally's face was changing, too. Her nose and chin extended outward, elongating into a V-shaped snout that pushed her eyes—now wide, yellow slits—back to the sides of her face. The huge slit-like irises—as black as night—expanded to take in more light as a strange, golden glow shifted across her face. Instead of skin, Sally was now covered with small hexagonal scales that glimmered like tiny rainbows in the dim light.

All the while, the creature...the beast that was or had been Sally...was staring directly into Claire's eyes.

Unblinking.

Cold.

Cruel.

Reptilian.

She's trying to hypnotize me.

That thought was oddly distant to Claire…like someone else had spoken the words to her. Her curiosity temporarily overcame her fear, and she tilted her head, listening.

"How do you want it to end, Claire?" the reptile said, speaking with freakishly precise human enunciation.

End what? Claire thought but didn't say.

She opened her mouth to speak, but it wasn't necessary. The steady glow in the snake's eyes indicated that it understood as clearly as if she had spoken.

"I mean," the snake replied, "that you have a choice to make."

Oh, I do?

"Indeed, you do…a very important choice."

And that is…?

Instead of answering, the snake raised its head and began swaying back and forth like a cobra reacting by the motion and music of a snake charmer. Its body continued to enlarge until the thick coils flopped heavily onto the floor on both sides of the bed.

And then, its sides rippling like a stream of water, it rose until its head touched the guest room ceiling. In a subtle, sinuous motion, it shifted slowly from the bed onto the floor.

"Will you willingly give me your soul in order to save him?"

What do you mean?

"Exactly what I said. I want you to give me your soul."

The snake's eyes flashed with cold light that pulsated in time with Claire's rapid heartbeat.

"It's quite simple," the snake said. "Your beloved Samael—" When it hissed the "S" in his name, it sounded like cold water splashing on hot coals—"wants to regain his angelic nature, correct?"

Claire felt oddly calm, facing the snake. Far from hypnotized, she found she was able to collect and focus her thoughts.

"He didn't tell you, but he can't do it without a sacrifice. Otherwise, it would be entirely too easy," the snake continued.

If he asks forgiveness, he'll get it…That's how it works, she thought.

The snake made a loud hissing sound that, Claire realized, was intended to be laughter.

You don't have any power over him or me...You're not the one who decides.

"That's what you think."

If it's possible for a snake to smile, the thing that had once been Claire's roommate suddenly thrust its head forward and, hissing, smiled at Claire.

"Didn't he tell you?"

Tell me what?

"He should have been completely honest with you from the start...especially now that you're married."

The tone of utter scorn in the snake's voice chilled Claire.

"He should have told you that he was grooming you."

Grooming me?

"Yes. To be his replacement...the sacrifice he will have to make in order to make the transition."

Bullshit!

Complete and total bullshit!

Claire opened her mouth to shout for Samael, but she stopped when she realized that's exactly what this thing wanted.

It's using me...as bait...to lure Samael here...playing on my fears...and my doubts.

I have to face it down on my own...

This is my temptation.

Iron resolve filled her.

If I can defeat this demon on my own...if I can expose it for what it is...maybe then I'll be able to end this insanity...

"You actually think you can defeat me? Your beloved Samael has already come to an agreement with us. You give your soul to me, and he'll be free to do whatever he pleases." Again, the long, drawn out hiss on the "S" in pleases.

Claire suddenly thought of Eve in the Garden of Eden.

She was framed, she thought...but not this time. She laughed softly to herself.

"You have no idea of the forces coming down on you," the snake said.

As it spoke, the scaly body kept rippling...coiling and uncoiling in a smooth, flowing motion as it started to move forward...closer to

Claire. Its triangular head was raised and sweeping from side to side, slowly...sinuously.

Neither do you...I know you're lying...and you won't win.

Without warning, the snake darted forward at blinding speed and looped its body around Claire once...twice...three times. She was soon engulfed by the dry, scaly folds that immediately began to squeeze her, pinning her arms to her sides.

"Then die, bitch!"

The snake's body contracted, squeezing Claire so hard her breath burst out of her. Hot, salty pressure started pounding inside her head. Her eyes bulged until they felt like they would pop out of her head.

I don't care what you do to me...You're not going to get me to give up Samael, and you'll never get my soul, asshole!

The snake made more hissing and chuffing sounds that might have been laughter.

Tiny pinpoints of white light zigzagged across Claire's vision. The pounding in her head was so strong it hurt.

This is it...This is how I'm going to die.

"Yes, you are going to die...and your soul will be mine unless you do what I command."

Fuck you!

"Have it your way, then."

The coils tightened even more. Tiny crackling sounds that she knew were her bones breaking echoed inside her head. Her vision swelled as dense blackness deeper than any black she had ever experienced spread out from the edges and reduced what she could see until it was no more than a single pinpoint. And in that pinpoint was the face of the snake staring at her as it opened its mouth wide.

I'm...so...sorry.

"Sorry for what?"

That this is happening...that I have to...die like this...that I won't ever get...to live...my life...with Samael...

"You're pathetic, but if you think you can get me to pity you, you're dreadfully mistaken."

Not as pathetic as you.

The coils tightened until a sudden huge explosion of white light flashed across her vision with a huge concussion of air. Claire had the vague thought that something in her brain had exploded. From a great distance, she heard a huge crashing sound like wood and glass and bricks exploding inward. A sudden gust of icy wind tore at the small part of her face that was still exposed from inside the snake's coils, and then—miraculously—the pressure that had seized her began to relax.

Am I dead...or dying...?

The utter silence that followed made her think for a moment—a moment that seemed to last forever—that she had left the world. An incredible feeling of relief and acceptance that all of her worldly troubles were over filled her like the white light that bathed her.

And then her body took over, and she gasped raggedly for air. Her chest filled with burning pain, and...faintly...she heard voices.

They were far away...lost in the bright white light that had danced all around her. As the light began to fade, she opened her eyes and saw a luminous figure hovering above her. From the center of the blazing light that emanated from this being, there shone two silver eyes as bright as the sun. It hurt to look at them directly, but she couldn't turn away.

What's happening to me?

The thought rang like a bell inside her head.

Still unable to see clearly, she felt something...someone grabbed her arm and started to pull her. Claire found it impossible to take a deep breath. Every one of her ribs seemed to have been shattered...like porcelain, but—somehow—she sucked in enough air to fill her chest. It was like gulping fire.

But with the fresh oxygen, her head began to clear, and she gradually focused more clearly on what was happening around her.

The bedroom was filled with a dazzling light.

And the memories were coming back to her...

She had come in here to check on Sally...to see if she was resting...

One of the bedroom windows had exploded inward. Shards of glass and splintered wood littered the floor everywhere, and standing amidst the ruin was a glowing white figure. The light was dazzling.

Michael!

The angel filled the room, towering so high his head brushed against the ceiling as he faced the monstrous horror that writhed and coiled on the floor beside the wide, queen-sized bed. A high hissing sound filled the room, mixing with the deeper roar of the icy wind that blew in through the broken window. Pinpricks of snow and ice swept across Claire's face, refreshing her and drawing her even more fully back to awareness.

Every joint, every bone, every muscle in her body ached and burned and throbbed. Her head pulsated in time with her rapid heartbeat, and her vision was spinning, but that was mostly because of the snow and the glorious, radiant light that filled the guest bedroom.

The snake—the demon that had been Sally—coiled in upon itself and raised its head so it, too, was pressed against the ceiling. Its blood-red forked tongue kept flickering in and out of its mouth. Its eyes glared with a cold, piercing flare, but was it anger…or fear?

Claire sensed motion behind her and, turning, saw Samael in the doorway. He watched, amazed to see what was going on in the room. His expression looked as awestruck as Claire felt. When he caught her glance, he smiled, and for some reason, that simple act was more reassuring that anything else. He came to her and knelt down on the bed, gathering her into his arms.

"You can't defeat me," the snake said, its voice high and shrill.

"I already have," said Michael as he brandished the sword he was holding. Beams of light reflected off the blade like shining silver splinters, but Claire was convinced the light was coming from inside the sword. Small tongues of silver flame licked up and down the length of the blade.

The snake hissed and spat in frustration, and then it made a sudden dart toward Claire and Samael. But Michael lunged forward quickly and swung the sword around in a whistling arc that sliced its neck. The snake coiled and uncoiled in frustrated rage and pain. Its thrashing body made loud scuffing sounds on the carpet.

"Go back to where you came from," Michael said in a low, resonant voice. "And don't come back. It's over."

The snake's face split into a vicious grin as it weaved its head from side to side like it was trying to hypnotize Michael. Thick, black blood ran down the demon's sides.

"It's never over," the snake said. "You know that as well as I do."

"At least it's over for now," Samael said.

The snake turned its full attention onto Samael, who was standing at the foot of the bed. It lifted its head as if to strike at him, but Michael took a quick, threatening step closer. Hissing wickedly, the snake shrank back until its winding coils were pressed against the furthest bedroom wall.

"You thought you could keep me out by using your powers," the snake said. Its unblinking eyes were fixed on Samael. "But you made one simple miscalculation, like everyone does…eventually."

"Oh?" Samael said. "And what was that?"

It struck Claire as amazing as well as bizarre that Samael, the man—no, the demon she had married—could speak so calmly and reasonably to a demonic creature like this as if things like this happened every day.

"You made a barrier you thought would keep things out, but you don't know what you've already walled inside."

The snake's words sent a chill through Claire, but Samael's grim smile didn't falter. Glancing at Michael, he raised his left hand and held it with his palm up. Michael took hold of the flaming blade and handed the sword hilt-first to Samael. Samael's arm seemed to droop for a moment from its weight, but he braced his feet and brought the blade around, gripping the hilt with both hands like it was a baseball bat.

The snake's head continued swaying from side to side, but Claire was sure, now, that she saw sudden panic in the creature's unblinking eyes. Its scales changed color in rapidly shifting waves as Samael raised the sword above his head and, with three quick steps, approached the snake just as it struck.

Samael quickly sidestepped the strike and then, planting both feet about shoulder-width apart, swung the sword down in a single, swift blow. The blade whistled through the air and caught the snake behind the head, cutting deeply and ending with a loud thunk sound when it was stopped by the snake's spine. The snake hissed as it coiled in upon itself, making as small a ball as possible—which was still considerable. Another furious hiss sprayed a clear liquid across the room. The tiny amount that hit Claire's forearm burned like a wasp sting.

Samael, however, seemed not to notice as he placed his foot on the snake's body and yanked the blade free. Then he swung again…and again…and again until the snake's head was finally severed. It hit the floor and rolled over so the pale-white underside of its throat was exposed. The flesh around the throat was convulsing as thick, black blood spurted onto the floor. The snake's eyes rolled back and stared at the floor. They quickly lost their light.

An unimaginable sense of relief swept through Claire as she watched the creature's body snap and twitch until it finally came to rest. Samael stepped back and, wiping sweat from his face, smiled at Claire. She wanted to rush to him and embrace him, but she was so wrung out she couldn't get to her feet.

Samael handed the sword back to Michael and then moved toward her.

"Are you all right?" he asked. His voice was soft and had an odd resonance. Claire knew it was because her hearing was distorted, not his voice. As the first wave of shock began to subside, and she began to absorb what had just happened, the darkness that had threatened her when she was trapped in the coils of the snake came rushing back.

She looked up at Samael and tried to speak.

She wanted to let him know that every inch of her body throbbed with pain, and that she was worried that whatever was happening still wasn't over…that this had been only the first wave of several more to come.

But the only sound she made was a low, whimpering moan before she pitched forward, and the darkness dragged her down.

~ * ~

She awoke to the sound of voices and a vague sense that someone—

Maybe many someones

—was touching her.

The sensation was so diffused she couldn't be sure it even related to her. She tried to open her eyes but wasn't sure she remembered how to do something as simple as that.

Am I dead? She wondered again but—oddly—that thought didn't frighten her.

"Am...I...dead?"

This time, she was positive she spoke the words, but there was no answer, reassuring or otherwise. The voices kept talking to each other, getting louder and seemingly ignoring her. One of the voices had a sharp, rasping hiss that reminded her of...something...

What?

She knew as she came closer to consciousness, things would only get worse, so she listened to the two voices as they spoke in weird, buzzing tones. She couldn't make any sense of anything, but she didn't care. She actually felt comfortable and warm, floating as though she had risen from the floor...or ground...or bed...or wherever she was lying and drifting along on the warm current of air that was blowing over and around her.

But she wasn't flying.

She was relieved when she realized she was still very much in the real world. No one could feel as rotten and confused as she did and be dead.

So she just lay there, trusting that whoever or whatever was close to her had her best interests at heart. No matter what was going to happen, she wanted to believe that—for right now, at least—everything was fine because...

Samael saved my life...There was a snake...An impossibly huge snake...And he killed it...

It was also the last clear thought she had before the darkness sucked her back down, and she was gone again.

~ * ~

"Feeling better?"

When Claire's eyes snapped open, she found herself lying on her back, looking up into Samael's face. He was smiling reassuringly as he leaned over her. He had a cool washcloth in one hand and was gently wiping her forehead and cheeks.

"Umm...I do now."

She managed a weak smile. When she focused past him, she realized she was in his bedroom...lying on the master bed. Behind him, sunlight poured in through the windows, lighting the gauzy curtains with a nimbus of white light that hurt her eyes. In the distance, she could see that the yard was covered with a fresh coating of snow.

Snow?

It was so bright and clean it reminded her of...

"Michael!"

The name was out of her mouth before she could stop it.

"Don't worry. He's fine," Samael said gently. "He's...taking care of a few things."

Claire caught the hesitation in his voice but wasn't sure she wanted to know what he meant by it. She was confident she would find out...eventually.

As the sleep fog cleared from her mind, hazy memories of what had happened returned.

Had it really happened...had she imagined it...had she dreamed it?

"Last night...Did we really—"

"Ut-ut," Samael whispered, placing his forefinger gently over her lips to silence her.

But Claire wasn't having any of that. She swatted his hand away and then hiked herself up in the bed so she was leaning back on her elbows.

"No!" she said, speaking so sharply it hurt her throat. "You have to tell me everything that happened. I saw what I saw, and you can't pretend I didn't."

"I'm not pretending anything," Samael said mildly. "I just don't want you to get upset."

"Upset? What the Hell are you talking about? Of course I'm upset! Last night I saw my roommate turn into a—"

Claire choked on what she had been about to say and ended up coughing so hard pinpoints of light skittered across her vision. Samael leaned in close to comfort her, but she pushed him away and, still coughing, shifted around so she was sitting cross-legged on the bed.

"You want a glass of water?" Samael asked.

She shook her head no and, covering her mouth with her fist, waited for the coughing to subside. Once she could catch her breath, she asked the most pressing question on her mind.

"So what happened to Sally?"

Samael broke eye contact with her and turned to stare out the window at the early spring winter wonderland.

"Samael..." Claire took hold of his arm and shook it. "Come on. You have to tell me what happened."

She paused, but the only sound he made was a deep sigh.

"Was that really Sally who...transformed? Or was that a demon?"

No answer.

"Tell me! Is Sally dead?" She all but choked on the word.

Samael turned to face her. His expression said it all.

"Oh, my God!" Claire said, staring at him over her clenched fist. "You mean she...she...Last night...Did you really use Michael's sword to...to kill her?"

Samael's shoulders dropped as if he were a car tire that had a sudden leak. He lowered his head and then started shaking it slowly from side to side.

"It's more complicated than that," he finally said, "but that's some of what Michael's taking care of right now."

Chapter

15

————Body Double

The day after I got married...this morning...should have been a lot different.

That was pretty much Claire's only thought as she busied herself about the kitchen, making breakfast for herself and Samael.

There was so much to talk about, but she had no idea where to begin. It was up to him and Michael, who joined them for a while. Before long, Michael excused himself and left by the front door without explanation. So Claire and Samael sat there in the kitchen, eating silently until Claire said what was on her mind.

"You have to tell me everything."

Samael considered and then nodded.

Once they started talking, Claire kept quiet, letting him do the talking while she tried to understand something she was beginning to think she could never fully comprehend.

Samael confirmed her memory of events...to some degree, but parts of his narrative seemed—at least by the way he acted, not by what he said—to diverge from her memories, confused though they were. The ultimate horror and sorrow was his statement that he feared Sally was, indeed, dead, but not by his hand.

"But you...you cut the head off last night. I saw it."

Samael bowed his head and shook it. It bothered Claire that he wouldn't make direct eye contact with her or, when he did, he wouldn't hold it for long.

"Okay, then...who was it...or what was it?"

"I'd say the snake was a...an emissary."

"An emissary?"

Samael nodded.

"From"

"From my..."

A genuine smile lit up his face.

"From my former 'supervisor.'"

"You make it sound like you had a regular job," Claire said, picking up on his amusement.

"You want bureaucracy? Try working for Hell. It's quotas this and deliveries that...The only difference is the usual commodities—"

"People's souls, you mean."

"Yeah."

Samael's expression dropped, but for some reason what they were discussing struck Claire as so ridiculous it bordered on the absurd. She started to chuckle and then had to struggle not to laugh out loud. Maybe laughter was the only sensible relief from the total insanity of what she had been through...what she had witnessed last night.

In the clear light of day, as it were, she couldn't accept that the person she had thought was her roommate was, in fact, a demon. Or had a demon possessed Sally and was masquerading as her? Or did that snake demon have nothing to do with Sally, and she was safely at home or at work?

Her memory had the hazy overcast of a nightmare, now, rapidly dissolving in the daylight, but her aching ribs reminded her that whatever it was, it had been all too real.

"I thought my job at the chemical company was bad," she said, "but your boss sounds like a real dick."

Her remark didn't get the reaction she wanted or expected. Instead of laughing or even smiling, Samael was silent as he looked at her with a pained expression.

"What is it?" Claire asked. "You're not telling me everything, are you?"

Samael remained silent for a considerable time. The only sound was the steady tick-tock of the kitchen wall clock.

"What aren't you telling me?" Claire said, trying without success to keep the edge out of her voice. She shifted forward in her chair and, reaching across the table, took both of his hands in hers. They were burning hot, and they had a slick, oily feeling.

"A lot," he finally said. "Too much."

"What do you mean?" Her hand tightened on his. "You know you can tell me anything…everything!"

He continued to avoid eye contact with her, and she shook his hands roughly, banging her elbows on the table in the process.

"Samael, I'm not some little wallflower you have to protect. I'm your wife, for Chri—for gosh sakes."

Samael didn't say a word. His expression remained flat…unreadable. He stared down at his coffee cup and twirled it around inside the saucer, spinning it by the handle. The china made a high-pitched ringing sound that immediately irritated Claire, but he seemed not to notice…or care.

She tried again to connect with Samael.

"Is it really dead?" she asked. "I mean, how can you kill something that's supernatural like that?"

"It can be destroyed…at least driven away for the time being."

"Does that mean you're also in some ways mortal?"

"As far as you're concerned, it's dead…Leave it at that, okay?"

"I don't want to leave it at that." It was difficult to keep her anger in check. "I have to know…We have to share everything!"

"Even if it causes you pain?"

"Yes!" she said impatiently. "Even then"…although she wondered even as she spoke what she had just agreed to.

Samael looked at her now, his eyes as dark and glistening as black onyx. The wounded expression on his face made her heart swell with love and pity.

"You want to know even if once you know it, you will utterly despise me?"

"I couldn't...I would never despise you, Samael. I love you."

Samael sniffed, making Claire feel as though her concern and care were inconsequential. That hurt. She stood up and began pacing back and forth across the kitchen floor. Her bare feet made faint squeaking sounds every time she turned and continued pacing.

"I don't give a damn about anything else," she said, still struggling to control her anger, "but tell me...What really happened to Sally? I mean really. Is she all right? Or did you...did you really kill her last night with that sword?"

"It wasn't her," he said simply.

Relief flooded Claire like a geyser of cold water.

"Then who was it?"

"He has many names...and many manifestations, but other than a few things I have to do—some loose ends, you could say, that I have to tie up, it looks like it's over for now."

"Are you positive?" she asked.

"Come on, Claire. Be sensible. Do you think Evil is ever defeated or ever goes away?"

Claire was silent.

"Evil is always around—always has been. Always will be. And it takes any form that suits it in order to weasel its way into your life. Try as we might—even someone as kindhearted and forgiving as you are—will eventually be tripped up."

He lowered his gaze and clenched his fists so tightly they looked like ridged rocks on the table. Claire tensed. She had never seen him this angry...or dangerous...before.

"So if you want to know if it's over, I say yes, for now it is. But I have to...to do some things before I can be certain."

"What things, exactly?" she asked.

"You'll find out soon enough, I'm afraid, but first—"

He sighed and reached out to her. She walked quickly over to him and, leaning down, clasped both of his hands. They trembled like captive birds in her grip.

Samael sighed and pressed his face hard against her chest. His breath was hot on her skin through the fabric of her clothes.

"First, then." He heaved a shuddering sigh. "There's something I have to tell you."

An icy blade of anticipation sliced through Claire, and she involuntarily held him all the closer, wishing she could engulf him. After a few moments, he pulled away from her.

"You may want to sit down."

Claire looked at his upturned face, seeing the heavy sadness in his eyes. With a pang of foreboding, she went back to her chair and sat down.

"All right, then," she said. She put her hands over his, took a sharp breath, held it, and then let it out in a long, slow exhalation. "Tell me."

"That night—" he began, and Claire knew instantly that he was talking about the night they met outside Margarita's Grille. It had only been a couple of weeks ago although it seemed a lifetime—if not ages—ago.

"Uh-huh," she said, coaxing him to continue.

"It was me," Samael said simply.

Claire was jolted by what he said, but she was also confused.

"Of course it was you."

On some level, she knew something bad was coming, but she had no idea what.

"We met after that horrible man tried to—"

"No. That's not what I mean." He took a heavy breath. "I was the one who tried to rape you."

Saying that, Samael hung his head. Claire was stunned.

"I...I don't quite get what you mean," she said. "It was that creep...that LaPierre guy who...who did it. And you showed up and saved me."

Samael started shaking his head from side to side and let out the most pitiable groan she had ever heard a man—or a demon—make.

"It wasn't LaPierre." He tilted his head back and sighed, blinking his eyes rapidly as he stared up at the ceiling for a long time. "I possessed him. I made him do it."

With those words, it felt like the bottom fell out of Claire's stomach.

"You...you what?"

"I saw you in the restaurant," Samael said, "and after we talked, I waited for you to come outside. When you did, and you were alone, I did something I know now I shouldn't have done.

What was that? Claire wanted to ask, but she was afraid she already knew.

"I took possession of LaPierre, who was nearby. I entered his body. I used him—used his body to try to attack you—"

"Rape me, you mean."

Samael was staring down at his feet.

"But then I looked at you, and I changed my mind, so before he—or I—did it, I left him and returned to this body so I could rescue you...so I could be your white knight."

Claire was beyond stunned. Her mouth was hanging open, and there may have even been some sounds coming out of her, but they were far from intelligible or even human.

"I did it to...as a way to get to you..." He looked directly at her now, his eyes shimmering with unshed tears. "You have no idea how sorry I am...how humiliating this is—how ashamed I am now that I would even think to do something like that. It sickens me."

His voice took on a high-pitched buzzing quality that made it difficult to understand what he was saying. Claire remembered the wasp demon on the bus and wondered if that had actually been him...his true form.

"But that was before I—"

His voice choked off. Tears ran freely down his cheeks.

She was surprised—again—to realize that demons—at least her demon—could cry.

"Before you what?" she asked, her voice surprisingly strong for the emotions she was feeling.

He regarded her steadily now, his eyes glistening, black. For some reason, seeing him vulnerable like this made it easier to hold back her own tears and rage.

"Before you what?" she said again, even stronger.

"Before I...wanted to...change," he said softly.

The volume of his voice was a fraction of what she knew it could be. She had never seen anyone so crushed...so utterly defeated, but instead of being angry or upset, because love knows no reason, her heart ached for him and what he was going through. He had lost all of his former power and confidence, as if his life force had suddenly drained out of him.

But a hot wave of anger also churned deep inside her.

How can I love a man...or a demon...who would do something like that?

He tricked me!...He used me!...

Why?

"You used me!" she said. It hurt like Hell to say it out loud, but she released his hands and scooted her chair back, away from the table. "How could you?...You didn't need to...and LaPierre. Framing an innocent man...and...and driving him to suicide—"

"I didn't do that," Samael said. "That was his choice, all the way."

"But he might not have done it if you hadn't set him up in the first place."

"Trust me. He would have, but I know you're right." Samael's face had lost its ruddy hue. He looked pale and gaunt. With the ceiling light shining down from above, his cheekbones stood out in stark relief. The shadows under his eyes were infinitely dark and deep. He looked both pathetic—a mere shell of what he once had been—and, at the same time, absolutely evil. His eyes, as black as polished marble, fixed on her.

Where did the gold flecks go?

He opened his mouth to speak, and she saw his double-tipped tongue flickering back and forth like a snake's, tasting the air...smelling her emotions.

"That's the whole fucking problem," Samael finally said. He squared his shoulders and looked as if he was about to stand up to come to her, but when Claire flinched, he sat back down.

"You have to understand," he said in a low, trembling voice. "I've done a lot of evil things...things I'm not proud of—things that will take centuries to be forgiven—if they ever are, but you have to know before I go away that I truly love you, and that you really are the one—"

"The one?"

"I don't know how or why this happened when it did, but— yes, you're the one...the only person...the only mortal I've ever met who made me want to change. That's why I married you...to make an irrevocable commitment to you, not to Evil."

Claire was filled with conflicting emotions. All she could do was look at Samael as she tried to sort her thoughts. He'd given everything up for her, and she believed in him—she truly did. She trusted him...with her life.

"I know you did...and I'm amazed beyond belief that you would do that for me," she said. "But I gave up my life, too. For you. And—look at us! Stuck in this house with these...these creatures that I couldn't even imagine before I met you trying to...to destroy us."

"They're only after—"

"Yeah, yeah. I know they're after you, but you have to face the fact that I'm...it hurts that I didn't get a fine romance and a fancy wedding much less a honeymoon."

"I can make that up to you."

"When? How long is this...this attack going to last?" She chuckled softly to herself. "I don't think we're going to have what anyone would call a normal life, and the way I see it, the future doesn't look so bright, either."

Samael stared at her, his mouth a thin line.

"Does that mean you...you don't—"

"Love you? Of course I love you, Samael. And I think—no, I know I made the right choice. It's just..."

A smile played across Samael's face as he looked at her. Claire could tell he wanted to get up, walk over to her, and give her a tremendous hug and kiss, but she could also see that he was holding back. Then she remembered something he had said…something that had slid right past her.

"Wait a second," she said. "You said…What did you just say about maybe having to go away?"

Samael looked at her without saying a word. The expression on his face was impossible to read, now, but then he slowly nodded.

"I did…I do…have to go away," he whispered.

"You mean you're…leaving me?" Claire was stunned. A cold emptiness opened up in the pit of her stomach. "Are you saying…"

"I'm saying I have to go away…for a while…as part of my redemption."

Claire was dumbfounded by this, and without realizing it, she started shaking her head from side to side as if she still hadn't heard him correctly or as if she didn't believe him.

"Where are you going?" she asked with a desperate edge in her voice. "Why do you have to—? What's this for?"

"You'll know soon enough," Samael replied, and Claire was happy to hear more of the usual iron in his voice once again.

As if on cue, the doorbell rang, the deep-throated gong reverberating through the house.

She cringed when she heard Michelle's slow footsteps echo in the entryway.

And then the door opened. A moment before Michelle entered the kitchen, a draft of chilled air wrapped around Claire's ankles like a sudden flood of water.

"Detective Trudeau is here to speak with you, sir," Michelle said simply.

Claire looked at her, wondering for the first time where Michelle had come from.

Was she here last night?

Does she have any idea what had happened?

There was no way of knowing, and Claire was positive Michelle, for all of her apparent subservience, would never tell her if she asked directly.

Samael's mouth tightened into a thin, pale line. His face was bloodless, as white as chalk as he nodded. When he stood up from the table, placing both hands on the table edge for support, Claire could not believe how the life had drained out of him. They made brief but intense eye contact. His dark eyes were flat...empty, as if he had already died, and his body was animated by something else.

She knew she had to go to him. She had to stand by him. Those wedding day vows, as clichéd as she thought they might be, were real. She had to be there for him no matter what had happened...or was going to happen.

She followed Samael out of the kitchen and down the hall to the foyer. Detective Trudeau was accompanied by two uniformed policemen. He was talking intensely to Samael, but they broke off the conversation before Claire joined them. She didn't miss the look—of what? Sympathy? Pity?—Trudeau gave her before acknowledging her with a nod.

"Mornin' Miss McMullen," he said.

"That's Mrs. Pierson," Claire said. Even before the words were out of her mouth, she had the disquieting thought that this was not Samael's real name. He probably didn't have a real last name and had adopted Pierson for legal reasons...to get him by in the world.

"You're married?" Trudeau said, looking genuinely surprised. "When did that happen?"

"Yesterday afternoon, as a matter of fact," Samael said.

The expression on Trudeau's face hardened like lines scratched in concrete as he turned to Samael and said, "Well, that doesn't change anything. You still have to come with us."

One of the officers snapped a pair of handcuffs off his utility belt and started toward Samael, but Trudeau held out a hand and checked him.

"That won't be necessary," he said. After a moment's hesitation, the officer scowled at Samael and then backed down.

"Would someone please tell me what's going on here?" Claire asked. It was obvious the police were here to arrest Samael...or at least take him downtown to the station, but why?

"We want to ask your husband a few questions," Trudeau said. "He won't be gone long."

There was something in his tone of voice, though, that made it clear—at least to Claire—that it might not be the case. If Trudeau had his way, Samael wouldn't be back...maybe ever. She could see that the detective had it in for Samael. If he couldn't pin LaPierre's suicide on him, he was trying to find something else to hang on him.

"I'll walk you to the car," Claire said, seeing the cruiser parked out front. At least its lights weren't flashing. When she took hold of Samael's arm, she noticed that both police officers changed their stance as if they were expecting her to freak out or start fighting.

"You don't have to," Samael said, smiling at her mildly. For some reason, his smile reminded her of Michael. And when they looked each other in the eyes, she saw—once again—that his directness and control was back. Relief all but overwhelmed her.

They were in this together.

"Come along, then, Mr. Pierson," Trudeau said.

He stepped aside so Samael could grab a coat from the closet, and then they walked outside with the patrolmen a few steps behind.

Claire walked proudly with Samael down the steps to the long, curving driveway. She smiled as Samael got into the back seat of the police cruiser. Before they closed the door on him, he looked at her. She couldn't possibly miss the twinkle in his eyes as he waved to her and whispered, "I love you."

"I love you, too," she said.

She leaned down, kissed him on the cheek, and then stepped back before one of the officers closed the cruiser door. As she watched them drive away, she almost believed that everything was going to be all right.

Almost.

Because something deep inside her told her things weren't even close to all right.

~ * ~

Later that day, about three hours after Samael had driven off with Trudeau and the police, Claire's cell phone rang. Her heart leaped when she thought it would—finally—be Samael calling to tell her what the Hell was going on.

But, now—it was Sally.

"What the—" Claire muttered as she raised her phone to her ear.

"Sally?"

"Now do you believe me?"

Claire was caught completely off guard.

"Sally...How are you? Where are you?"

"I'm in the frigging hospital, is where I am."

"The hospital?"

"Yeah, thanks to that scumbag boyfriend of yours...or is it husband, now?"

"Yeah. Husband. We—ahh. You never showed up yesterday, and when we came by the apartment to—"

"That's because your creep-a-zoid husband of yours got there first."

"What? When was that?"

"Around ten o'clock...I was getting ready to come down to City Hall, and—"

"No. That's not right."

"Bullshit! He came here, and he...he..."

"That's impossible. We were together all morning. He couldn't have been—"

"And now I'm in the hospital...because of...of what he did to me."

A sudden pressure clamped down on Claire's chest, making it difficult to breathe. Her vision shimmered and flickered, like the air was dancing with heat lightning.

"You're in the hospital? When...? How did you—?"

"He beat the crap out of me, Claire!"

Sally's voice choked off, but her words cut through Claire's confusion and rising panic. At first, she didn't believe what she had heard. Then she wanted to say something in Samael's defense, but it felt as though unseen hands were holding her by the throat.

"Did you hear me? That piece of shit came to the apartment...on the day he was going to marry you...He beat me up and he...he trashed my apartment."

"No...Not Samael," Claire said.

Sally was sounding hysterical, now, but Claire couldn't stop wondering: Who the Hell did we pick up at the apartment yesterday and bring home with us?

As far as she knew, they had gone to the apartment and found Sally—the real Sally—looking and acting like she was having some kind of mental or emotional breakdown.

"And after that...after that..." Sally was having trouble catching her breath, and her voice was breaking up over the phone. She was crying and sniffing. "After he did...he did what he did to me, he tied me up and—and put duct tape over my mouth and a pillow case over my head and threw me into the hall closet."

"It wasn't him. Samael wouldn't do something like that," Claire said, finally catching her own breath. She might just as well not have spoken. Sally was on a tear now.

"Can you imagine?...Can you...Can you even begin to understand what I went through?"

"No...I—I can't," Claire said, not sure if Sally was even hearing her.

"I told you that guy was a creep. Didn't I? Didn't I? From the moment I saw him, I knew there was something really wrong about him...something fucking evil."

You don't know the half of it, Claire thought but didn't say. She almost laughed at the thought, but Sally went on, piling on horror after horror.

"I thought I was going to die. He hurt me real bad. I've got a broken nose, three broken ribs, half my hair's pulled out, and my left eye is swollen shut. And before he shoved me into the closet and left me there, he called me all sorts of terrible names, saying how after he married you he was going to come back here at night and do all sorts of terrible things to me."

"Oh, my God, Sally," Claire said, holding her hand against her cheek and staring straight ahead.

"Once I came to—in total darkness—I had no idea where I was. I thought I was dead. But then I started banging my feet against the wall and floor. I kept doing it until—finally—Old Mrs. Hardy, downstairs, called the cops, and they broke in and found me."

Sally started sobbing so loudly she was barely able to speak. Claire's heart went out to her, but as unsettling as this was, she was barely aware she was speaking when she whispered into the phone: "It was the double."

"The what?" Sally asked.

So she has been listening after all, Claire thought, but she was convinced this was something she would have to explain to Sally in person.

"I'm coming to visit. What hospital are you at?"

"Maine Med., I think," Sally said. "I'm not sure." There was an odd shrillness in her voice that set Claire's teeth on edge.

Is this the real Sally?

It sure sounds like her, but this could be another trap.

Samael said they would use me to get to him.

After last night, Claire had a fair estimation of the forces ranged against them. She took some comfort knowing that Michael was on Samael's side, but he had disappeared so fast this morning she wondered now how much help he could possibly be.

But she had stood up to the snake demon—which, she guessed, very well could have been the imposter in a different form. She was confident she could handle Sally now. What worried her was wondering when all of this collateral damage would end.

"I'm so sorry all of this happened," Claire said.

"I know," Sally replied, "but don't you worry. I'm going to make sure that son of a bitch gets what's coming to him, I can guarantee that!"

Wait a second...That's my husband you're talking about, Claire thought but didn't say. She was too stunned to speak.

"I'll sue his ass. That's what I'm gonna do. And trust me—I'm not going to rest until he's thrown into jail and they throw away the key. You should see what he did to me." Her voice choked off with emotion.

"I'm sure it was horrible," Claire said, but her voice trailed off. She was trying to figure out some way she could convince Sally that it hadn't—it couldn't have been Samael.

How much can I tell her...and how much will she believe? She wondered. She could just imagine Sally's acid-tongued comments, questioning her sanity.

"I'll be there in—"

She checked her wristwatch and saw that it had been almost four hours, now, since Samael had been taken downtown to the police station.

Why haven't I heard from him?

"—within half an hour."

Sally sniffed, as if to say don't bother.

"Take care," she said. "See yah soon," and before Sally could come back with something sarcastic or hurtful, she ended the call.

And then immediately dialed Samael's cell phone.

~ * ~

He answered on the second ring.

"Hey," was all he said. He spoke with a low voice—almost a whisper—so Claire knew right away that whatever he was going through wasn't over yet.

They obviously had brought him in to answer Sally's accusations.

"Hey yourself," Claire said. "Tell me. What's going on?"

Samael took a deep breath but didn't say anything for the longest time. And in that time, the tension inside Claire coiled tightly.

"They've charged me with aggravated assault and criminal restraint," he finally said.

"You can't be serious!"

"All too serious," Samael replied.

"But you know and I know you didn't do it. You didn't have time to do it."

"So you know?"

Claire made a grunting sound in the back of her throat and said, "I talked with Sally, and I know it's simply not possible, I know you'd never hurt someone I care about."

"There are some who would doubt the veracity of that."

"Not me," Claire said sharply, and she felt the conviction deep in her soul.

Samael heaved a sigh, and Claire knew he was relieved to know she believed in him.

"They have Sally's charges. This is serious stuff."

"You haven't faced worse?" Claire asked, and she smiled when she heard him chuckle.

Claire was suddenly jolted to silence. Over the phone, she could hear someone rattling and banging something—maybe the drawers of a steel filing cabinet or something. People were talking in the background, but she couldn't make out what they said.

"So what are you going to do?"

"I've already got a call in to my lawyer, Terry Traut. We're waiting for him to come by the station."

"And do what? Can he get you out?"

"We'll see if they let us post bail or if I have to stay here until the trial."

"Trial?"

Claire's insides felt like cold jelly as she looked around for someplace to sit. Instead of sitting down, she backed up against the nearest wall and then slowly slid down into a squat on the floor. The air in the room sparkled with spinning white dots that burned like stars in the bars of sunlight.

"Stay there…" she heard herself say.

Over the phone, it sounded like someone in a nearby room was speaking for her.

"Look, Claire. I know how hard this is—how hard it will be for you. It's hard on me, too. Believe me. But I have to do this. Just knowing you have faith in me is all I need."

"Oh, Samael…"

"Because if you don't love me," Samael went on, "if I didn't have any reason to hope, and if you didn't believe in me…if you didn't trust me, then there's no point in doing what I'm doing."

And what—exactly—are you doing? She wanted to ask.

"I'm coming to see you," she said abruptly.

"I'm not sure that's such a good idea."

"Oh, yeah?…Well I do!"

Samael chuckled and said, "Well, I'm not going anywhere."

And then the phone line went dead.

~ * ~

As Claire drove from Falmouth to Portland, she wished she had a Xanax—or a stiff drink—to quell her anxiety. The storm had passed, leaving the world covered by a thin coating of fresh snow. The sun was shining brightly, and with temperatures soaring into the high forties and low fifties, the snow would melt soon. She tried to enjoy the beauty that surrounded her.

Every day passes entirely too fast.

But try as she might to enjoy the day and forget her worries for the moment, her stomach felt like a nest of writhing snakes. She wondered briefly if she could be pregnant, but then dismissed the idea.

How can I get pregnant from a tail?

But now that she was thinking about snakes, she couldn't ignore the kaleidoscopic images of what had happened last night. The images were too horrible, and the psychic echoes of fear and revulsion and stark terror were still strong and would probably remain that way for the rest of her life.

She had seen it.

She had lived through it.

And she had survived it.

Earlier this morning, she had checked the bedroom where Sally—or the demon masquerading as Sally—had been. Miraculously, the walls were intact, and there was absolutely no evidence of any struggle

So either it had never happened or she had imagined it.

The only other possibility was that the fight had taken place on some different level of reality...some celestial plane that most people in this world never experienced.

One of those explanations had to be right, she decided, or else Samael, Michael, and maybe Michelle were supernaturally good at rebuilding and cleaning things up. The police would have noticed something was wrong if one side of the house had been torn apart, and a huge headless snake lay dead on the floor.

She wished Michael had come back to the house before she left so she could ask him about it. She needed answers...something conclusive...something that would remove all of her fears and doubts.

Could he ever do that?

Or is living life exactly that?

Maybe all it amounts to is naming your fears and doubts, and moving through them.

Ultimately, because she knew this was the only way she could ever handle it, she told herself to accept that she would never know all of the answers.

Because what did it matter?

~ * ~

Claire pulled into a space in the parking lot next to the police station. A small snowplow was moving back and forth, pushing the already slushy snow into thin ridges along the perimeter of the parking lot. The plow's warning beeper started when it backed up for another pass.

Claire got out of the car and locked the door, but before she walked up to the front entrance, she purposely took a moment to enjoy the thrill of being alive.

Take a deep breath.

Look up at the beautiful vault of blue sky.

"Not a cloud in the sky," she whispered to herself, smiling tightly because she was all too well aware of the clouds that darkened her life...and were getting worse.

She took another deep breath, smelling the salty tang of the nearby ocean and the thin pine resin in the air.

"This is life…This is really happening."

People passed by on the sidewalk, and cars drifted by heading in all directions. Life went on in spite of her worries. She looked around at the ordinary activity and felt like she was the still point in the turning world.

The hub.

The axis.

But that feeling soon passed, and she started up the wide granite steps to the front door of the police station. The thought that Samael was in there somewhere…locked up…alone…filled her with pity.

She grasped the door firmly and entered.

~ * ~

The smell of floor wax filled the entryway as she walked up to the front desk. A dispatcher—an elderly white woman—was hunched over her desk, talking to someone on the radio. Without even turning to look at Claire, she raised a forefinger to signal that she'd be with her in a moment.

Claire stepped away from the window, taking a moment to look around. Her eyes were drawn to the assorted postings on a corkboard—leaflets, "Most Wanted" posters, and advertisements for apartments and various other small businesses around town. All the while, she couldn't stop thinking that somewhere in this building—

Probably in the basement.

—Samael was locked up in a prison cell.

She shuddered at the thought and was determined more than ever to get him out of here no matter what.

"How can I help you," the dispatcher asked, startling Claire, who turned back to face her.

"Oh, I—I'm here to see my husband."

Hearing herself say the word husband still sounded strange.

"And he is…?"

"Samael Pierson. He came in earlier today with—"

"Detective Trudeau. Yeah," the dispatcher said. She reached for a phone, picked up the receiver, and held it to her ear. Then she pressed a button on the phone's base. After a short wait, the woman spoke into the mouthpiece, nodded, and then put the phone back in its cradle.

"He'll be up to see you in a few minutes," the dispatcher said.

"Who, my husband?"

"Detective Trudeau. Have a seat, if you'd like."

And that was all. Without another word or any more consideration, the dispatcher turned back to the array of electronic gear that was chattering with faint voices broken by bursts of static.

As she took a seat, Claire felt like a cancer patient waiting in her doctor's office for word as to whether or not she was terminal. While she waited, she watched a variety of people file in and out of the station, going about their business. She wondered what their stories were—what fears and doubts they lived with, but her impatience was steadily mounting, and she was anxious to resolve this situation now and be done with it.

If I ever can be done with it.

She involuntarily jumped to her feet when a loud buzzing sound filled the waiting room. She turned toward the heavy metal door just as it slammed open, and Detective Trudeau appeared in the open wedge of the doorway. His face was set, showing no emotion as he approached Claire. His footsteps echoed in the wide room.

"Mrs. Pierson," Trudeau said, holding out his hand for her to shake. "What can I do for you?"

Claire shook hands with him, noticing that his grip was warm and dry. She wondered why she would be friendly to the man. It wasn't like she was here on a friendly visit.

And Trudeau certainly wasn't a friend. He was the man investigating whether or not her husband had assaulted her roommate.

"I'm here to see my husband," she said, blurting out the words. "Please," she added.

Detective Trudeau regarded her for a moment as if he had something important to say. Then he nodded and, without a word, stepped to one side, indicating that she should approach the door. After another short ear-shattering buzz, the door lock clicked, and Trudeau held the door open for her.

Once they started down the hallway, and the door slammed shut behind them, the atmosphere suddenly shifted. It became oppressive…stifling. Claire and Detective Trudeau walked side by side down a long corridor that echoed with the sound of their footsteps and the faint sound of voices and the clacking of keyboards from offices on either side of the hall.

"He's innocent, you know," Claire said. She felt foolish doing so, but she had to say something to break the awkward silence between them.

Detective Trudeau glanced over at her and said, "That's not for you or me to decide. I just do the investigation."

"I was with him all last night and all day today. There's no way he could have gone to Sal—to my roommate's apartment and done what she says he did."

"Like I said, Mrs. Pierson. That's not for me to decide."

They had reached the top of a flight of stairs, but before they started down, Detective Trudeau said, "Maybe you can tell me what happened last night."

"Last night?"

The image of the demon snake…and the Hellmouth and blue-faced demon outside the living room window…and the flock of bats that all had Samael's face arose in her mind, but she resolutely pushed them aside and focused on the business at hand.

"Do you really want the details?" she asked. A smile tightened the corners of her mouth. "It was, after all, our wedding night."

Detective Trudeau eyed her for a few seconds and then started down the stairs. Claire followed behind him, eager to see Samael again.

~ * ~

Samael was wearing a bright orange prison jumpsuit as he sat in the prison cell, his head bowed. He was leaning forward with his hands clasped together tightly between his knees.

At least he isn't handcuffed, Claire thought when she saw him. She smiled at him and said, "Hey."

He didn't register the least little surprise, and he looked up at her slowly as if he had been expecting her all along. Any expression on his face—whatever it might have been—instantly faded away. He stood up and walked over to the barred door. Claire leaned forward so her face was pressed between the iron bars, and they kissed, long and passionately.

"Jesus," Samael said softly once they separated.

Claire flinched and said. "I thought you were uncomfortable saying names like that."

"I'm getting better at it," Samael replied, a roguish twinkle in his dark eyes. "It doesn't hurt as much as it used to. So..." He stood back, admiring her. "How are you doing?"

"I'm doing okay..." She took a breath. "I'm also lying. Oh, Samael! I'm really wor—"

"Ut-ut. Not now," he said.

She knew it wouldn't do either of them any good to let him see how anxious she was, but the simple act of touching his hands, not to mention kissing him through the bars, both comforted her and made her want to burst into tears.

"So what's going on? Have they charged you with...?" She couldn't finish her question and turned away as her eyes began to sting with tears.

"Of course they believed Sally. I've been charged with aggravated assault and criminal restraint...but—Hey!" He reached out with one hand between the bars and gripped her shoulder tightly. "You have to be strong for me. Got it?"

"I am...It's just...It's not fair. You and I both know you didn't do it. You couldn't have done what she says."

Samael nodded while maintaining steady eye contact with her.

"We'll have to prove it," he said with a slow, measured tone of voice. "Either that, or I'll take the punishment that's coming."

"You can't! You didn't do anything!"

"But there's no way I can prove I'm innocent...not without revealing...you know."

"That you're a de—"

"Don't say it out loud," he said, and his grip on her shoulder tightened painfully. He lowered his gaze until he was staring down at the cracked, linoleum floor. "I mean—all things considered, if I got punished for everything I've ever done wrong, your great-great-great-great-great-grandchildren wouldn't see me get out of prison."

"I don't think you'd want to be in prison that long," Claire said wryly.

He sniffed with laughter and shook his head slowly from side to side at the thought.

"Actually, it's not funny, Samael," Claire paused, bracing herself before saying, "So what are we going to do?"

"We'll have to see what happens."

"You mean you'll just wait around for...whatever?"

"At this point, it's Sally's word against mine. No witnesses, so the police will investigate, but my double's fingerprints are all over the apartment from when I was there."

Samael kept shaking his head and staring down at the floor as he spoke, then he raised his head and looked directly at her, his dark eyes shimmering. "Barring a miracle, they have enough to put me away for up to ten years, according to my lawyer."

"Ten years? Are you—?"

Samael nodded.

"Tony says he can probably plea bargain down to five years."

"Ten years...or maybe five," Claire said, trying to grasp just how long that would be—

Half of eternity.

"It'll be tough, I know." Samael gritted his teeth. "It sounds like a long time to you."

"A day is too long away from you."

Samael nodded and said, "I keep forgetting how—"

He didn't finish, but he didn't have to. Claire knew he meant to say: How short your human lifespan is.

And it was true.

Even if she lived with him as his wife to a ripe old age of, say, ninety, it would be no more than a blink of the eye for someone who was practically immortal. But in the grand scheme of things, that small amount of time was all she would ever have with him, so every day meant everything to her. She wasn't about to let even the tiniest bit of it slip.

"You're going to fight it, right?" she asked.

"Of course. Like I said, I'm going to plead innocent, but if I get convicted, we can argue for the least possible time in jail. It's not like I have a criminal record or anything."

"That they know of," Claire whispered, and they both chuckled at that.

They were still touching through the bars, and she tightened her grip on the sleeves of his orange jumpsuit and shook him as hard as she could. "We're not going to let them get away with this."

Samael cocked his head to one side as though he was listening to something far off…something she couldn't hear.

"Well…? Are we…?"

"There's…" He took a quick breath and held it. Then he let it go. "I'm not entirely sure I can control any of this. There are forces at work here that even I don't fully understand."

"But you're totally innocent!"

"Yes! Absolutely! I'm not lying to you. But there's a lot more I'm being held accountable for by…others."

"Who are they? Who's holding you accountable?"

Samael's only reply was a sad shake of the head as he stared into her eyes so intently she was positive he was reading her mind.

"You keep saying there are things I won't understand…that it's all too complicated. Well, seriously. How stupid do you think I am?" She was speaking so fast, the words pouring out of her, she became breathless. "I'm your wife, Goddamn it! You have to tell me everything that's going on!"

Samael regarded her sympathetically, and in a low, gentle voice, said, "I've told you everything I know."

"Everything you want to, you mean."

"Everything I can, Claire. Some things are beyond words. I'm not trying to duck your question, love. But I really can't explain it all."

"Could you use...you know..."

"Magic?" Samael scowled. "Of course I could...but I won't."

"Why not? If it means—"

"Because if I do—if I use it, I'll...I could slip back into my old ways. Once I gave that all up, I— No." He shook his head. "I can't. So—please. Don't ask me to."

Claire wanted to say something—to insist that he was wrong...that they could still fight this one way or another, but she couldn't find the words. All she could do was stare at him and think that everything she had hoped and prayed for was slipping away inexorably...that it had already slipped away.

The life she had hoped to have with Samael was already dead and gone.

But only now was she noticing that sad, simple fact.

"So...so what do you need me to do?" she finally asked, her voice husky with emotion.

Tears filled Samael's eyes, and she could see that he really was one hundred percent honest and sincere when he said falling in love with her had changed him and made him want to repent. She didn't understand why, but it was a fact.

"Just keep loving me, Claire. Don't leave me."

"Loving you is the easy part," Claire said. She leaned closer and lowered her voice in case Trudeau or someone was monitoring their conversation. "But you still have your powers...your supernatural powers, right?"

Samael's lack of a reaction unnerved her, and they stared at each other for a long time without speaking until the answer occurred to her.

Days, months, and years later, Claire was never sure if it was her own thought or a thought Samael planted inside her head through the power of suggestion or whatever. Maybe he had even spoken it out loud, but finally, she knew or at least had an inkling of what the answer was.

He had given up some…maybe all of his supernatural powers when he decided to repent.

Is that what's happening now?

Is he becoming mortal…like me?

When—not if…when he got out of prison, would he have as short a lifespan as any normal person?

"Will you stay with me?" he asked, looking desperate. His dark eyes gleamed.

"You don't have to ask me that. You know I will." Raw emotion twisted her voice, and a burning sensation took hold of her throat. It was difficult for her to continue without breaking down, but somehow she maintained control. "I don't care how long it takes. Even if you go to prison for something you didn't do, I'll be faithful to you and wait for you no matter what…even if you have to go to Hell."

Samael beamed a smile at her, but then his expression drooped, and he backed away, extending his arms to display his orange prison jumpsuit.

"I'm already in Hell," he said softly, "because I'm not out there with you."

~ * ~

The next few weeks and months certainly were a living Hell for Claire, mostly because she felt totally insignificant and helpless as the wheels of justice—or injustice, as she increasingly came to regard the legal system—ground slowly onward.

There were so many times she wanted to call Sally or go over to the apartment and visit her, but Tony, Samael's lawyer, said it would be illegal for her to have any contact with her husband's accuser. The court might construe that as witness tampering or an attempt to threaten or intimidate the plaintiff.

As it turned out, Michael returned to the house the day after Samael was taken off to jail. Over the next few weeks and months, he came and went seemingly as he pleased. Claire knew enough not to ask him where he was going or what he was up to, but she sensed important things were astir...major issues were being decided. Michael volunteered little to no information.

His simple presence was an amazing emotional support for Claire, giving her comfort and confidence that she could cope with anything that came her way. Still, even with the support of an actual angel and Samael's lawyer, whose origin—demonic or angelic—Claire never could determine, Samael was found guilty on all counts. Because of Claire's earnest testimony in Samael's defense, and because Sally's testimony was inconsistent to the point of irrational, almost like she was relating a bad dream, and because of the smooth sophistry of Samael's lawyer's skill, Samael received the minimum sentence.

With time off for good behavior, he'd be out in less than five years.

That was still too long as far as Claire was concerned. She hated being separated from him for even an hour.

Immediately after the trial, Samael was sent to the state prison in Warren. His lawyer, of course, planned to appeal because Sally's testimony had been so erratic and contradictory, but Claire doubted it would do any good.

Less than five years still seemed like half an eternity to her.

Every day did.

One thing that bothered Claire was she never heard from Sally again, even though she called her several times after the trial. Finally, after three months, she gave up, resigned to the fact that she had lost her best friend.

Over the first few months while Samael was in jail, Claire kept insisting to him that she should sell the house and either buy or rent a place closer to the state prison so she could visit him as long as possible every day. Samael told her not to. He explained—obliquely, as he often did—that there were aspects of the house that would be impossible to hide from or explain to any prospective buyers. Michael confirmed Samael's decision, but when she asked him why, he—like Samael—told her not to worry about it. She was irritated at being given another "It's too complicated for you to understand" explanation, but she still secretly held out the hope that Samael and Michael would use their supernatural powers to help him escape.

During the third week of June, something unusual happened.

It was Wednesday night. The weather was much warmer than usual for Maine with the humidity climbing so high that even at night it felt more like August in Philadelphia than June in Maine. As she did every day, Claire had driven from Falmouth to Warren and visited with Samael, who—as usual—told her that he was holding up just fine, all things considered.

It was so good to see him she let his little white lie pass. She could tell by the expression on his face that being separated from her was hurting him as much as it was hurting her.

Claire matched him lie for lie and told him she was doing fine, too.

The lies became a game between them, but each of them could see through the other's façade. One June day, though, before she left, she turned to him and said, "So tell me—honestly. Did you lose your supernatural powers or are you purposely not using them."

"Things are…changing," he said.

Claire didn't appreciate the evasion.

"All I want to know is, could you get out if you wanted to."

He didn't answer for a long time, and then he finally said, "You wouldn't or couldn't understand the forces I'm at the mercy of."

"You mean inside? They're still trying to get to you inside?"

Samael shook his head.

"You don't have to worry. Honest."

"So what's changed?" she asked.

"You'll find out all in due time," was all he said…rather cryptically, but that wouldn't satisfy her, and they both knew it.

Late that same night after this conversation, exhausted from the drive and the visit, Claire was lying in bed, unable to fall asleep. The house always seemed much too big and empty without him…as did the bed. The night air was sticky with humidity. Claire found it odd, but somehow unsurprising that such an elegant home would not have central air. She was restless, feeling desperately lonely for Samael.

Like tonight's any different from any other.

She still hadn't figured out where their maid Michelle kept herself during the days or nights, but she had the uncanny ability to appear whenever her services were needed and then disappear just as quickly and mysteriously. She did, however, notice that Michelle's attitude had improved. She was almost cheerful and chatty these days. Maybe she'd made an arrangement with Michael.

Thinking and worrying about Samael kept Claire tossing and turning until well past midnight. She was despairing because she was going to have to get up early again tomorrow morning and drive to Warren.

But the harder she tried to fall asleep, the more awake she became. She lay there outside the covers, listening to the leathery rustle of oak leaves, stirred by a few fitful gusts of wind. She hugged the pillow to her chest and inhaled, convinced that faint traces of Samael's scent still lingered on it, even after all this time.

"I'm like a damned dog," she whispered to herself in the dark and smiled.

At some point—she wasn't sure when because she had finally started to drift off—the sound of the leaves fluttering outside in the wind took on a steadier sound that gradually invaded her awareness. After a long while, she thought that it sounded like a mass of buzzing insects—hornets, perhaps...or flies—somewhere in the room...in the window, perhaps.

Claire stirred uneasily in bed, tossing from side to side, her mind coasting along with the sound as it rose and fell in the darkness. It created a white noise that lured her further into a dreamlike state until—finally—she remembered that she had heard that sound before.

On a bus...

Leaving Houlton!

What the hell is that sound?

She jerked awake, sitting bolt upright in bed and looked around.

The bedroom was perfectly silent. A thin trace of moonlight spilled through the south-facing windows, lighting the curtains with a gauzy light. The memory of the sound remained like a faint echo or a buzzing inside her head.

"Is...is someone there?" she called out.

Her eyes shifted back and forth as she tried to pierce the darkness in the room. She could reach across the bed and turn on the bedside light, but she didn't dare move. She didn't want to feel any more exposed in the sudden burst of light. She felt totally vulnerable, like when a bloodthirsty predator has fixed its attention on its prey...only she was the prey.

Is the house still safe?

Are Michael's defenses still up?

Her body stiffened, and she let out a faint whimper when she saw a dark shape filling one of the bedroom windows. A blacker-than-night silhouette was etched against the glowing night sky.

Her first thought was that it was Samael, leaning in through the opened window and watching her. She almost leaped from the bed, but then it hit her.

He couldn't be outside a second-story window, standing like he was on solid ground.

"Is that...you?" she called out in a dry, strangled whisper.

There was no answer, but the silhouette in the window shifted.

And as it did, the steady humming sound of buzzing insects that had awakened her got louder. She also heard faint clicking sounds, like dozens or hundreds of insects were bouncing against the window screen.

Moving slowly, she got up off the bed and, still keeping all of the lights off, approached the window. When she was about halfway there, she stopped and, peering into the darkness, tried to make out the figure.

It was still there. It hadn't moved. Its edges were rough, irregular, and the whole silhouette appeared to be vibrating along with the steadily rising buzzing sound that filled the room, setting her nerves on edge.

Claire wished she had a flashlight she could shine on the figure. There was one in the bathroom for emergencies when the power went out during a storm or whatever, but she didn't dare turn her back on…whatever this was outside her window.

She sucked in another breath and whispered, "Samael?"

The buzzing sound paused for a moment, leaving behind an eerie vacuum that made Claire's ear thump in time with her rapid-fire pulse.

Then—

Is this really happening … or am I dreaming?

—the solid black figure in the window shifted and became more solid.

"…Claire…"

He whispered her name so softly she didn't believe she actually heard it, but it had definitely sounded like Samael's voice.

Is it in my head?

She was convinced now that she was dreaming, but to determine if she was awake, she pinched the back of her hand. It felt like a bee sting, and when she looked down at her hand, she saw a dark insect shape—a large wasp—crawling up the back of her hand to her wrist.

She let out a shrill scream and swatted it at the same time, feeling the hard shell of the insect's body crushed against her flesh.

When she looked at the dark figure in the window again, it was darker than a shadow in the night. The features were impossible to see, but the silhouette certainly looked like Samael.

Her gaze was transfixed as she stared at the dense, black shape.

"Aren't you going to let me in?" Samael said.

His voice was oddly distorted, as if it was being made not by vocal cords, but by the synchronized buzzing of the insects that were massing against the window. The dark shape was pulsating in the darkness. Claire was swept by a feeling of vertigo and felt as if she would suddenly pitch forward and fall into it.

"It's your house," Claire said, deciding to put whoever or whatever it was to the test. "Do you need to be invited inside?"

"Not at all," a voice that sounded incredibly like Samael's said. "Only vampires need an invitation. I just didn't want to frighten you if you saw me in my original form."

Without another word, the dark figure pressed against the screen, making it bulge inwards. The buzzing sound dropped away, and Claire watched, fascinated, as the dark shape oozed through the fine metal mesh and began to take form in front of her.

The human—or demon—shape was darker than ink, but patches of it—especially the eyes and face—were flaking off, and a dull, luminous glow shone through.

When she recognized Samael's face, Claire was filled with joy. She started moving toward it, her feet sliding like in a dream, but then she suddenly halted.

"How can I be sure it's really you?"

The glowing figure standing before her was hazy, difficult to focus on in the dark. It kept jumping around, shifting from side to side.

"This is the only way I can appear to you right now," Samael said. "My true form after I sided with Evil."

The odd distortion in his voice was unnerving, but Claire was convinced this was really Samael, not an imposter. A rush of cool wind surrounded him like a cyclone, and the glow coming from his form grew steadily brighter as the figure consolidated in the darkness of the bedroom.

"It is you, isn't it?" Claire's voice slid up and down the scale.

"It is, my love," Samael said, and he held his arms out to her.

"Say 'Honest to God.'"

Without hesitation, he said the words: "Honest to God."

Claire went to him and wrapped her arms around him. It wasn't arms at all that embraced her, but she was enwrapped by something warm and powerful and loving.

"You have to have faith," Samael said simply.

"I do," Claire said, and then she raised her face to his. The darkness was peeling away, flake by flake, and a warm, glowing blue light emanated from him. It was warm on her face...insubstantial...prickling like pins-'n-needles.

Claire couldn't believe it, but the sensation of pure joy being with Samael once again was almost too much to handle.

"So this is it, huh?"

She shifted closer and wound her arms around his waist, pulling him tighter. His hug was warm...passionate.

"It's the best I can do...for now," Samael said in a warm, honey voice.

He paused, and in that pause, Claire sensed that there was something he still wasn't telling her.

"What is it?" she asked, tightening her hug and pulling him so close the rapidly receding darkness all but engulfed her.

"What's what?" Samael said.

"You're still not telling me everything," she said.

For a long time, Samael said nothing. The only sound in the room was the gentle sighing of the wind, blowing through the leaves outside in the darkness.

"This is who I really am," Samael said finally.

"But you're changing. I can see it happening."

She looked at him and felt an overpowering stirring of love deeper than anything she had ever experienced.

No regrets.

"And in the end, it doesn't matter. I love you for who you are," she replied.

But instead of embracing her tighter, Samael shifted away from her.

"You don't understand," he said, his voice low and flat. "For however long I'm in jail, I can come to you...I can be here with you, but only in my true form."

He extended his arms wide, but then the truth hit her...hard.

He isn't human at all!

What she saw...what she had fallen in love with...was nothing more than an illusion.

This mass of dark emptiness is who or what he really is.

"I can't make love to you in this form," Samael said with a trace of sadness and bitterness distorting his voice. "I can't be with you the way...the way I want to be."

"The way I want you to be, too, but it doesn't matter," Claire replied.

"You're not afraid? You don't think I'm hideous?...Most people are horrified when they see my true form."

Claire was surprised that she didn't feel the tiniest bit of revulsion as she pulled him close, crushing herself against him. Tilting her head back, she placed both hands on his jaw and brought his face down until their mouths met. The warm tingling of his touch intensified until it raced throughout her body like a powerful electrical current. Her knees grew weak, and she wondered again if this might not be real...It couldn't be...It had to be the most intense dream she'd ever had.

But the kiss went on...and on.

She had no idea how long it lasted.

It could have been for less than a minute...It could have lasted for half of eternity...

"I'm your wife," she whispered huskily, "and I love you...no matter what."

She gazed into his eyes, which were shining now with streams of liquid silver light. The tingling sensation of his touch raced all over her body.

"Whatever's going to happen next, we'll deal with it," she said. "We're together right now, and right now is all that matters."

They kissed again...and this kiss may very well have lasted the second half of eternity.

The End

CPSIA information can be obtained at www.ICGtesting.com
Printed in the USA
LVOW13s1707041013

355483LV00003BA/502/P